THE TATTERED LANDS

What Reviewers Say About
Barbara Ann Wright's Work

The Pyradisté Adventures

"…A healthy dose of a very creative, yet believable, world into which the reader will step to find enjoyment and heart-thumping action. It's a fiendishly delightful tale."—*Lambda Literary*

"Barbara Ann Wright is a master when it comes to crafting a solid and entertaining fantasy novel. …The world of lesbian literature has a small handful of high-quality fantasy authors, and Barbara Ann Wright is well on her way to joining the likes of Jane Fletcher, Cate Culpepper, and Andi Marquette. …Lovers of the fantasy and futuristic genre will likely adore this novel, and adventurous romance fans should find plenty to sink their teeth into."—*The Rainbow Reader*

"*The Pyramid Waltz* has had me smiling for three days. …I also haven't actually read…a world that is entirely unfazed by homosexuality or female power before. I think I love it. I'm just delighted this book exists. …If you enjoyed *The Pyramid Waltz*, *For Want of a Fiend* is the perfect next step…you'd be embarking on a joyous, funny, sweet and madcap ride around very dark things lovingly told, with characters who will stay with you for months after."—*The Lesbrary*

"This book will keep you turning the page to find out the answers. …Fans of the fantasy genre will really enjoy this installment of the story. We can't wait for the next book."—*Curve Magazine*

"There is only one other time in my life I have uncontrollably shouted out in cheer while reading a book. [*A Kingdom Lost*] made the second. …Over the course of these three books all the characters have blossomed and developed so eloquently. …I simply just thought this whole novel was brilliant."—*The Lesbian Review*

Thrall: Beyond Gold and Glory

"Once more Barbara has outdone herself in her penmanship. I cannot sing enough praises. A little *Vikings*, a dash of *The Witcher*, peppered with *The Game of Thrones*, and a pinch of *Lord of The Rings*. Mesmerizing. …I was ecstatic to read this book. It did not disappoint. Barbara pours life into her characters with sarcasm, wit and surreal imagery, they leap from the page and stand before you in all their glory. I am left satisfied and starving for more, the clashing of swords, whistling of arrows still ringing in my ears."—*Lunar Rainbow Reviews*

"In their adventures, the women must wrestle with issues of freedom, loyalty, and justice. The characters were likable, the issues complex, and the battles were exciting. I really enjoyed this book and I highly recommend it."—*All Our Worlds: Diverse Fantastic Fiction*

"This was the first Barbara Ann Wright novel I've read, and I doubt it will be the last. Her dialogue was concise and natural, and she built a fantastical world that I easily imagined from one scene to the next. Lovers of Vikings, monsters and magic won't be disappointed by this one."—*Curve Magazine*

Paladins of the Storm Lord

"This was a truly enjoyable read…I would definitely pick up the next book. …The mad dash at the end kept me riveted. I would definitely recommend this book for anyone who has a love of sci-fi. …An intricate…novel one that can be appreciated at many levels, adventurous sci fi or one that is politically motivated with a very astute look at present day human behavior. …There are many levels to this extraordinary and well written book…overall a fascinating and intriguing book."—*Inked Rainbow Reads*

"I loved this. …The world that the Paladins inhabited was fascinating… didn't want to put this down until I knew what happened. I'll be looking for more of Barbara Ann Wright's books."—*Lesbian Romance Reviews*

"*Paladins of the Storm Lord* by Barbara Ann Wright was like an orchestra with all of its pieces creating a symphony. I really truly loved it. I love the intricacy and wide variety of character types…I just loved practically every character! …Of course my fellow adventure lovers should read *Paladins of the Storm Lord*!"—*The Lesbian Review*

Coils

"…Greek myths, gods and monsters and a trip to the Underworld. Sign me up. …This one springs straight into action…a good start, great Greek myth action and a late blooming romance that flowers in the end…"—*Dear Author*

"A unique take on the Greek gods and the afterlife make this a memorable book. The story is fun with just the right amount of camp. Medusa is a hot, if unexpected, love interest. …A truly unexpected ending has us hoping for more stories from this world."—*RT Book Reviews*

"The gods and monsters of ancient Greek mythology are living, breathing entities, something Cressida didn't expect and is amazed as well as terrified to discover. …Cressida soon realizes being in the underworld is no different than being among the living. The heart still feels and love can bloom, even in the world of Myth. …The characters are well developed and their wit will elicit more than a few chuckles. A joy to read."—*Lunar Rainbow Reviewz*

House of Fate

"…Fast, fun…entertaining. …*House of Fate* delivers on adventure." —*Tor.com*

Visit us at www.boldstrokesbooks.com

By the Author

The Pyradisté Adventures

The Pyramid Waltz

For Want of a Fiend

A Kingdom Lost

The Fiend Queen

Thrall: Beyond Gold and Glory

The Godfall Novels

Paladins of the Storm Lord

Widows of the Sun-Moon

Children of the Healer

Coils

House of Fate

The Tattered Lands

THE TATTERED LANDS

by

Barbara Ann Wright

2018

Acknowledgments

A big thank you to my readers, Angela, Deb, Erin, Matt, Natsu, Pattie, Sarah, and Trakena. You've fed my pets and given me a place to stay whenever needed. You're irreplaceable.

A continuing thank you to Bold Strokes Books: Radclyffe, Cindy, Sandy, Ruth, Stacia, and Sheri. You never fail to wow me.

I love you, Mom.

Dedication

For Erin

CHAPTER ONE

Time seemed to slow as Vandra poured grains of sand into a heated crucible. A bead of sweat slid down her temple, and she hissed, moving her head slightly so when the drop landed, it struck the scarred mahogany table rather than the slowly combining mix of components. If one drop landed in the unstable mixture, it would throw off her entire formula.

Students gathered around her, and though they had been cautioned to be still, she heard gasps. Even the other professors who gathered near the edge of the crowd mumbled to themselves and were quickly shushed by their neighbors.

As Vandra set the sand aside, her sister, Fieta, dabbed her brow with a cool cloth and whispered, "Sorry."

Vandra nodded, resisting the urge to glare. Fieta had only volunteered to assist because their brother, Fieta's twin, was busy, and Vandra needed someone she trusted. Fieta wasn't an alchemist, let alone a professional forehead wiper, but Vandra was certain she'd stressed how important it was to keep the mixture untainted.

But Fieta wasn't as good at paying attention as her brother.

Vandra added a few flecks of lead, the last part of her original formula. Then all that was left was to stand back and wait. The whole room exhaled. Fieta gave Vandra another swipe with the towel and winked. Nearly ten years younger than Vandra, she was at least a foot taller, and her athletic build put the academics in the room to shame, though her dark hair and dusky skin blended in with most. She wore her dark gray City Watch uniform, the reason everyone peered at her as if wondering why she was there. Maybe they thought that if the experiment got out of hand, Fieta would beat it into submission.

"Better mind the pot," Fieta said softly.

Vandra sighed and stared at her experimental mixture. It had gone like clockwork this time, just as when she'd first performed it. And the five times afterward. The only difference being: the first time, it had worked.

It would work this time. It had to. The crucible was the same. The candle was from the exact same candle maker, made from the same sort of wax, and even made at the same time of day, if the maker was to be believed. Her measurements were exact. The tools were exact. After five minutes ticked down, she should have a crucible full of syndrium, the most sought after, most unique element in the land, made from a handful of common items. She'd done it once. There was no reason she couldn't do it again.

As before, visions danced in her head. All the machines in the city of Parbeh and in the kingdom of Citran—the last of the five human kingdoms—ran on syndrium. With a surplus, they could create machines to unclog the overworked sewers, to dig more wells for the swollen population, like the thousands of refugees whose lands had been claimed by the slow tide of corruption known as the tattered lands.

Of course, the first time Vandra had done this experiment, she hadn't been thinking such grand thoughts. It was only one formula in the midst of dozens, but she'd hit it right. No one had been more surprised than her when after five minutes, the crucible full of nothing had been transformed into pure syndrium. Since she'd been the only person there, many believed she'd made up the story, yet they couldn't prove where she'd gotten a stray pot of syndrium.

Now they'd all see. Now no one would have to worry that the syndrium-powered pylons that guarded their borders would fail. Humanity would be safe from the tattered lands forever. She crossed her fingers and prayed to every god, large and small, that it be so. Her mama would have reminded her that she didn't want the attention of larger gods anyway, just in case they were of a mind to remember her when they wanted something in return.

Vandra glanced at her hourglass. The five minutes were nearly up. A few people whispered from the back of the room. After her second failure, she'd shooed everyone out, but only after her colleagues had made certain she had no syndrium on hand. But the people didn't matter, couldn't matter. She had to trust the formula.

There were only a few grains of sand left. The smoke from the crucible would take on a bluish hue. There! Right on schedule. And then…

The last of the grains ran out. Vandra leaned forward, brushing away the smoke. It had to have worked this time. She made herself believe, made herself smile.

More gasps from the crowd. Professor Lisander whispered loudly, "I loaned her that crucible, you know."

Beneath the smoke, Vandra spied a glimmer, not the silvery-blue glow of syndrium, but a speck of one of the other metals catching the light. It had failed. Again. Vandra was still smiling, but she no longer had control of her face. What would happen if she yelled that it *had* worked then hustled everyone out of the room?

Her audience was waiting. As she stared at them, her stomach sinking and panic gripping her guts, their smiles faded one by one. At the front, Lisander frowned hard, lending more lines to his pale skin. He was always complaining that Parbeh's laboratories were not as fantastic as his old university in the north, but the tattered lands had taken that. Vandra wanted to snap at him now that if he thought he could do better in the tattered lands, he should go. Then the airborne malice could twist him into something unrecognizable, which would probably be an improvement.

But she had to remain calm, confident, polite. "Perhaps next time—"

The crowd began to disperse. A few professors smirked or tittered, but Fieta glared at them until they fled. Most of the students gave her pitying looks. Lisander glared at the crucible he'd lent her, then stormed from the room, creating a gap in the retreating crowd. It stayed parted when Headmistress Chani appeared.

If Vandra's heart sank any further, it would lodge in her heels.

"No luck?" Chani asked, giving the crucible a quick glance. "Bit of a letdown, eh, Singh?"

Vandra had no choice but to nod. "Yes, Headmistress."

"And after all that hoopla? Ah well, better to know now rather than when someone is really depending on the outcome."

Vandra wanted to say, "Besides me and my career," but she bit her lip.

Fieta turned her threatening stare in the headmistress's direction. She never took shit off anyone unless they were wearing a uniform. Vandra poked her hard in the leg.

"I'm sure, Headmistress," Vandra said, "it must be a miscalculation in the—"

"Course it is, course it is." Chani's eyes held the same false sympathy as when a student's parents insisted that their child really *was* a hard worker and only needed a little *encouragement* to pull themselves up from a failing grade. She wasn't a bad person, but she'd been an administrator far longer than she'd been an alchemist. "Better luck next time, eh?" She turned to go, then swiveled as she got to the door, an old tactic that allowed her to have the last word. "Maybe next time, do a test before you invite everyone, eh?"

Vandra wanted to say she'd conducted *many* tests, but the headmistress was already gone.

Fieta rolled her eyes. "Uppity bunch of bookworms." She clapped Vandra on the shoulder. "Don't worry. You'll figure it out."

Vandra slumped against the table and put her head in her hands. Where had she gone wrong? Maybe one of the metals hadn't been as pure as she'd thought. Maybe she'd been off in her original calculations slightly, and now she stuck to them too rigidly. Maybe it was the sand that she'd gone through grain by gods-cursed grain! She wanted to sweep the whole thing off the table and hope she got lucky enough to burn the building down.

Fieta was still oozing false cheer. "Pietyr's probably done with his rounds by now. Come have lunch with us."

Vandra shook her head. Their brother would also try to cheer Vandra up, and she wasn't in the mood. She loved her family, but they didn't understand.

"You're going to stay here beating yourself up instead?" Fieta asked.

Vandra nodded. "Until I solve this thing or pass out. Whichever comes first."

Fieta kissed her temple then gave her a light shove to even out all the caring and feeling. "I'll be back later."

Vandra nodded again but didn't watch as Fieta left. Without people, her black thoughts poured in to fill the empty room. She'd created syndrium just after graduation, when the world seemed to stretch before her in endless waves of possibility. Her successful experiment had gotten her an appearance before the assembly. The head assemblyperson had told her that the five monarchs were proud. Everyone had been waiting, breathless, to see what she might do next as the pride of Parbeh.

People had laughed off her first failure. It was proof that no one was immune to slipups; it made her relatable, likeable. She hadn't known until then that she needed a colossal screwup to be more likeable, but she'd tried to laugh it off.

Now, six failures later, she was either a laughingstock or a subject of pity. When she introduced herself, people's faces scrunched up as if trying to remember where they'd heard her name, then they'd say things like, "What a shame."

After hearing that so many times, Vandra thought she'd be used to it. To her surprise, it hurt. Every. Single. Time.

"Give up or wake up." She went back to her desk and pulled out her books on syndrium again, one of which she'd written as her dissertation. Many people now used it as the final word on syndrium. If not for her original success with her formula, her dissertation would have been her legacy. Only alchemists would have known about her, but she could have lived with that.

Now she had to start over from the beginning. Again. Maybe she should rewrite her dissertation and disavow any knowledge of her former life. "No, I'm not that Vandra Singh. I'm a different one who wrote a very important book and did absolutely nothing else!"

Someone knocked on the door. "Show's over for today," she called.

"Pity," a familiar voice answered, "I was looking forward to it."

Vandra stood so fast, her chair fell with a thud. Ariadne Bahn, junior assemblyperson, stood watching Vandra and smiling. She had dark circles under her eyes, and her black hair seemed a bit limp. No one seemed to be sleeping well in the government these days.

"I didn't…" Vandra cleared her throat and bowed. "Assemblyperson Bahn. A pleasure, as always."

Ariadne laughed. "You don't have to be so formal." She smiled softly, a look Vandra remembered from their brief time as lovers. Ariadne had held some lower level government job at the time, and Vandra had been a student. Nearly the same age and constantly run off their feet, they'd been happy with a quick exchange of kisses and caresses in whatever space they could eke out. Work eventually took them away from each other, but that was all right. Life had too much to explore for slow, ever-burning love affairs. Better that they should flame out as quickly as they'd kindled.

Vandra cleared her throat. "What brings you by?"

"Right to the point, eh?" She sighed. "There's always more work to do, isn't there?"

She sounded bitter, and Vandra didn't know what to say. There *was* always more work. Unless Ariadne had been hoping for a quick round of sex. After all this time? Vandra's cheeks burned. Not only could she not spare the time, but after her failure, she wasn't in the mood.

But no, Ariadne seemed sad. Maybe her rise in stature had turned out as disappointing as Vandra's had. "What's wrong?" Vandra asked.

Ariadne shut the door and sank onto a stool as if she had the world on her shoulders. Her long tunic and loose trousers were bright yellow, save for a red satin sash that led from her right shoulder down across her chest. It didn't move, sewn to the tunic, and Vandra wondered if all her clothes had the assembly sash sewn in. That would certainly save time.

Ariadne hooked her booted feet under the stool. She'd never gone in for the slippers that many in the ruling class favored. She always had somewhere to go, she'd said, and boots would get her there faster and without blisters.

Vandra smiled at the memory as she righted her own chair and sat. The sting of her failure faded, but she felt it hovering in the back of her mind like a cloud of flies.

Ariadne opened her mouth then shut it again. Vandra tensed. Ariadne never had trouble speaking her mind.

"One of the pylons has gone out," Ariadne said, almost a whisper, as if she feared her words would have more weight when spoken aloud.

Vandra leaned forward; she couldn't have heard right. The one thing that kept the remnants of the five kingdoms from succumbing to the horrors in the tattered lands could not have simply *gone out*. "Failing? Stuttering?" She pawed through her books. "With one pylon malfunctioning, we should be all right, and if it's only a glitch—"

"Gone out. Ceased working. Three days ago. One of my sources who lives near the border sent a message." Her dark gaze seemed to take up the whole world. "We need corroboration before word gets out, and I can't send an entire team or the population might get wind of it."

Vandra waited for more, her heart thundering. A small part of her thought Ariadne might have come to her for comfort, but by the way Ariadne stared, almost as if she was willing Vandra to see her point, Vandra suspected it was something else.

They needed someone to check on the pylon, someone who knew about syndrium. An alchemist. But surely Ariadne wouldn't ask her. There were more senior alchemists who weren't viewed as failures, who…

"Oh." Vandra's heart thundered louder. No one would miss the failure when she'd gone. "Me."

"You're an expert on syndrium."

"Yes, but that's not the whole reason you asked me."

Ariadne simply stared, waiting.

"I'll do it," Vandra said, hoping she sounded less bitter than she felt. "It'll be nice to finally have failure working in my favor."

Ariadne stood and crossed the room to take Vandra's hand. Her fingers were cold. They always had been. "Whatever you can tell me, you'll be rewarded. Someday. For now, no one can know."

Vandra nodded and gave her a squeeze before letting go. The remains of the five kingdoms had been crammed into the last kingdom standing. Every town and village was full to bursting. If people found out a pylon had gone out, even if the other nine pylons still stood, there might be riots, not to mention a massive exodus where people ran farther south to get away from the threat nipping at their heels. Vandra imagined the pressure on the coastal towns as people sought passage on ships that could go nowhere. Some might even try swimming into the ocean, thinking the taint of the tattered lands couldn't follow them there.

They were wrong, at least to a point. The tattered lands corrupted everything they seeped over, flora, fauna, and mineral. It certainly changed the creatures of the sea as well.

Vandra shook the thought away and put her bitterness aside. "Of course. Yes. I won't spread any news, but I'll need someone to come with me. There are bandits near the border."

"I can get your brother and sister released from the Watch for a few days. You can tell everyone you're going north to visit relatives."

Vandra nodded. She hoped no one would ask. She'd never been good at pretending. But Fieta and Pietyr could lie enough for all three of them. They'd probably have an entire extended family invented by dinner.

"You can do this," Ariadne said. "The only way we could find a better expert than you would be if we could resurrect one of the original builders."

Vandra smiled. That was true, even if Ariadne was just saying it to bolster Vandra's ego. "When do we leave?"

"Tomorrow. I took the chance you'd say yes and set the wheels in motion. I'm afraid I couldn't requisition mounts without looking suspicious, so you have a few days of walking in your future."

Vandra nodded. A failure of an alchemist going to visit relatives wouldn't rate a mount. That meant backpacks as well as walking, but Vandra didn't mind a nice long hike. For her research, she'd had to explore the syndrium mines, and she'd even visited a pylon. She enjoyed the outdoors and fresh air…and the lack of people. It was a shame she'd have to hurry back to Parbeh afterward. Maybe she'd send Fieta and Pietyr back with the information and find somewhere lovely and quiet to stay in the countryside.

Where she wouldn't be a failure. But she would be bored to tears.

CHAPTER TWO

Lilani breathed deep and let the scents of the forest surround her. She tried to relax, but the ritual posture consisted of resting on her knees, sitting back on her feet, arms along her legs, with her palms turned upward. It gave her cramps in three different places.

Especially if she had to sit for what felt like an eternity.

She could feel Faelyn watching even though he stood behind her. She'd once asked him how he imbued his gaze with such weight, and he'd said it was the mark of a good teacher. She pitied any offspring he might one day have.

"Forget I'm here," Faelyn said, but that seemed impossible when he insisted on staring.

She shifted, frowning.

"You're not relaxed."

She knew he leaned against a tree; she could picture his crossed arms and irritation. But she'd not even begun to annoy him yet. Her mother once said she could perturb even the eldest seelie, and they didn't move for anyone or anything.

But now wasn't the time to think about that. After a sigh, she tried to relax into the feel of the sunlight coming through the tangle of leaves overhead and become lost in the sweet scent of lavender. The breeze whispered over her skin, ruffling her hair and the edges of her long-sleeved tunic. She heard birdsong and the whine of insects. Not far away, some creature rustled through the underbrush. So perfect.

So boring.

"Your shoulders are tense," Faelyn said.

Lilani groaned. "I can't forget you're there if you keep talking."

"Hush. Focus."

Right. She must become lost in the sounds of nature as she sometimes did when falling asleep, only now she couldn't accidentally nod off. She would become one with her surroundings and let them flow around her, carry her into the background until she became hidden, shrouded from sight. A natural ability of her people, they could fade from the view of other creatures. But not without practice. Masters of the technique could even hide from other seelie. She'd done it once when she'd been scared out of her wits, but seelie were supposed to be able to do it whenever they wished.

Some were better at it than others. Maybe she'd be the first in history who had no natural ability whatsoever. The idea should have upset her, but she would trade any natural ability for the opportunity to skip this lesson, grab some wine, and spend the afternoon with friends.

By the elders, she'd trade the ability for the opportunity to stand up and stretch. She wriggled her toes inside her soft boots, trying to bring life back to her feet.

"I saw that," Faelyn said.

Of course. What made her think he *wouldn't* see her toes through her boots? With a frown, she unfolded and sat, wincing as the blood flowed back into her legs. With a sigh equal to the one she felt inside, Faelyn sat beside her.

He wore the lower half of his blond hair loose; the top half tied in a braid at the back. Like hers, his hair moved on its own, shifting in an invisible breeze, moved by his natural seelie magic, the same magic which allowed them to shroud.

If they could master it.

Faelyn's pale features were as sharp as his crystal blue eyes that stared into the forest, and the slight point of his ears stood in line with his cheekbones. He'd come to this forest long ago when the seelie of the ice-bound northern enclaves fled the tide of humanity and the creep of the tattered lands. But now what was left of humanity crowded against the forest of the Court, the last remaining enclave of the seelie, and there was nowhere to run.

Everyone had to be a master at shrouding now.

"Maybe if I stood up and tried?" she asked hopefully.

He snorted a laugh and took one of her light brown hands in his pale ones. "My dear Princess, you can try standing on your head if you wish, but unless you relax, it won't matter."

She resisted the urge to jerk away, not wanting him to know how easily he annoyed her. "I'm not a princess." He only said it to show her he didn't care that her mother was the empress. Or to let her know he had to report back to her mother whether she had a successful training session or not.

Well, there went any hope of lying to her mother. Not that she ever would. "I was thinking about our mathematics lesson the other day—"

"Stop." He rubbed his forehead. "I know you love mathematics and history and everything but this. I do, too, but you cannot distract me. This lesson is necessary, so says your mother."

She grinned. "I can get around my mother. All you have to say is—"

"No."

"We could go for a run! We could grab the telescope and climb the Highpeak—"

"Forget it."

"I started reading the history of the—"

"No, no, no! No equations, no running, no telescopes, and no history! No books of any kind!" He sighed. "That is a terrible thing for a teacher to say. No books of any kind *right now*. Sit properly and concentrate."

Lilani groaned. She hated sitting still unless she had a book in her hands. Even then, she never read at a table like a proper student. She had to have one leg thrown over the arm of the chair or be lying on the rug with her legs stretched up the wall. Her mother had reprimanded her once for lying across her bed with her head off one side, reading upside down.

"Books, especially ancient ones, have to be treated with respect!" her mother had said.

Lilani didn't see how a book could care one way or another. Besides, she was careful, if not exactly respectful. A book never left her care in worse condition than when it arrived.

Lilani tried to sit on her knees again and fell backward in the grass. "What if I promise never to leave home? Then I won't have to learn how to shroud."

He gave her a wry smile. "You're prepared to make such a promise?"

She thought of how close these woods and the Court would seem if she did. "No."

"Then up! Relaxation pose." He prodded her leg. "We'll stay out here all night if we have to, and won't that be *so much fun*!"

Lilani resisted the urge to roll her eyes. "Master Poet Janlyn says sarcasm is a mask for those with no true wit."

"Master Poet Janlyn can stuff it. Get up."

Lilani laughed as she knelt again. "I'll tell her you said that."

"Do. I love being attacked by poets. Now, focus on the forest, on Master Poet Janlyn, or whatever you need to focus on. Relax."

With another chuckle, Lilani closed her eyes. Her thoughts drifted to Janlyn, Lilani's first crush when she'd been old enough to know what a crush was. As she'd gotten older, she found she still respected the poets and philosophers, but she wanted to have fun with singers and actors, the seelie who appreciated a laugh. Everyone in the Court was older than she was—as their long-lived race didn't often produce children—but many were still young at heart. She recalled fine evenings in this forest, running through the moonlight, laughing and singing. There'd been a few wine-soaked kisses, some heated caresses, bodies intertwined in soft leaves.

Like a lover's sigh, her magic flowed around her, covering her like a warm blanket.

Faelyn's sharp intake of breath interrupted her reverie. She opened her eyes to find him staring.

"What?" she asked.

"You shrouded!"

"I did?" She beamed, but her surge of elation faltered when his shocked expression didn't change to one of pride. "Isn't that what I was supposed to do?"

"Yes, but..." His smile seemed tentative. "I can usually see a shimmer when someone shrouds. Only the elders and the Guard can hide from me, but I couldn't see you at all."

She blinked, trying to process what he was saying and how it could possibly be bad. She grinned. "Well, then! It seems the ability comes naturally for me. Test over." She stood and took a few steps toward home.

Faelyn caught her arm. "Do it again."

She tried not to look worried. She had no idea how she'd done it in the first place. She started to kneel, but he wouldn't let her.

"No, do it standing. Members of the Guard can do it while running or fighting, and the elders, well, some vanish for centuries."

"All right." She closed her eyes. What had she been thinking of? Running? Moonlight? Wine? A few minutes passed, and her magic didn't rise again.

"I can still see you, naturally gifted one," Faelyn said.

"Give me a minute!" So, not wine. Singing and laughing, then. And after that, she'd remembered... Oh, sweet elders. Was it the sex? How embarrassing!

"Still not happening." He moved around her, and she opened her eyes but couldn't meet his gaze. "What were you thinking about to make you so relaxed?"

She told herself to blurt it out, that they were both adults, but he was so much more...adult than her. She tried to say it and couldn't, and now she felt the heat rising in her cheeks. He blinked at her several times, frowning, before his frown turned into a smirk, and she wanted to run for home.

"Something...*personal*," he said. "I see."

Why did he have to say it like that? "I was only thinking of... having fun instead of kneeling here and listening to nothing, and—"

He held up a hand. "Whatever you need to do. I'm not judging your methods." He was; there was no denying his grin. He waved as if telling her to get on with it.

She turned her back and closed her eyes. She couldn't think about lovers with his gaze still pinned on her. She needed something else, like running or exploring, climbing rocks and trees, tracking deer. She remembered the first time she'd climbed the Highpeak: breaking through lines of scraggly trees and crevasses after hours of scrambling upward. She'd turned to see the forest of her people spread below her, but in the distance, she'd spotted the hint of a human city. She'd read about humans, but she'd never seen one or anything they'd constructed. At that moment, the world seemed far wider than she'd imagined, even with all her studies.

Now, she felt her magic gather around her again.

"There," Faelyn whispered. "Hold on to that."

His words broke the spell, and her eyes snapped open.

He crossed in front of her, hands on his narrow hips, and even though he was a little shorter than her, he still managed to radiate authority. "All right. If you have to think of lovers or—"

"I was not thinking about that!"

He shrugged as if to say it didn't matter, but she couldn't help feeling as if it did, imagining what he might tell her mother, of what others might say, of the teasing she'd have to endure. "Lilani has to think about sex in order to shroud," they'd say, tittering. No one cared who she loved or how often, but to have to focus on it while doing a task that should have been as easy as eating or sleeping? Who needed to think of sex in order to eat?

And it wasn't about sex, anyway! "I was thinking of *freedom*," she said. "Running free, exploring. Obviously, that's what relaxes me."

"Among other things."

She put her hands on her hips and tried to summon her mother's regal air, but she couldn't think of a good retort. She raised one eyebrow instead, going for imperial.

He rolled his eyes. "For the elders' sake, Lilani, I'm not going to tell anyone. Your mother only wanted to know if you succeeded, and I will tell her you did."

She fought the urge to fidget and blushed again, elders knew why. "Just so *you* know I was thinking about freedom."

His next eye roll seemed a bit friendlier. "All right. So, thoughts of *freedom* and excitement in its *many* forms…"

She glared.

"…is all you need to relax and focus. Let's try it a few more times until you can recall the feeling, wrap yourself in your magic, and shroud at a moment's notice. The elders know you won't be able to stop and think about climbing rocks or kissing poets when a bear is charging you."

She opened her mouth to argue, but he pointed at the ground. In a huff, she sat, and he waited until she'd calmed. This time, she thought of swimming in a nearby lagoon and diving down through the bright water. With each memory, her magic seemed to cover her more easily, and she began to recognize the feeling. She let it wrap around her and shroud her for several seconds at a time, not daring to move for the first few attempts. When she'd done it ten times, she moved her arm back and forth, keeping the shroud, letting the magic flow, but as soon as she looked to Faelyn in excitement, she lost her focus.

He beamed at her anyway.

After the last attempt, she pressed a hand to her belly, feeling a cramp as if she'd run too far too fast. Her lunch threatened to reappear.

"That's enough for today," Faelyn said as he helped her up.

"At last." Lilani opened the small pack she'd brought and took a drink from her canteen.

"Practice more tonight, but don't exhaust yourself. You've already learned that the harder you reach for it, the more elusive it is, no matter how…*happy* the memory."

She turned to tell him off, but he'd shrouded, and she saw a shimmer in the air as he fled through the trees. At least he had the good sense to hide from her wrath. She picked up her pack and started home, rubbing her belly. It wasn't fair to have the ache from running without actually getting to move anywhere, but the closer she came to the Court, the better she felt. The presence of the seelie and the syndrium under their home had suffused the place with power, and as it mingled with her own magic, she breathed easier.

It was hard to believe that any human entering this forest would be plagued by the sense that they should turn back. Their skin would be crawling before they breached the edge of the trees and entered the valley below the Highpeak. If one managed to get to the actual Court, they'd be a gibbering mess. In theory.

But if the humans knew how much syndrium the Highpeak contained, they'd have all died trying to reach it. She'd read that humans tore their own mountains down searching for the rare metal. They couldn't simply feel it, couldn't let its magic wash over them, so they had to search every stone. After using syndrium to build their pylons and keep the spread of the tattered lands outside their borders, the humans should have stopped questing for it, should have let the land be.

Or that's what the histories said. Lilani didn't see why an entire race should be content when they could explore. And she didn't think *all* humans could be so quick to tear the Highpeak to shreds.

She reached the edge of the valley and paused to look upon the Court, the towers and minarets made from gleaming white stone. Every structure seemed fragile from a distance, like homes made from spider webs, but she could pick out the subtle ways they anchored to the mountain and one another. Some sat upon the mountain itself, surrounded by paths of volcanic rock, dangerous to anyone who didn't know their secrets. The sense of hard and soft only added to the beauty, along with the shining domes of blue, black, or gold. With the underground river that surfaced at the Highpeak's base, the seelie had everything they would ever need in their valley, their forest. It was a paradise fit for eternity.

Or so she'd been told. Again and again. By everyone.

With a sigh, Lilani descended. She waved to those who tended the small fields along the Court's outer edge. She nodded to those who were coming back from getting water and those who were busy creating beautiful works of stone or metal in their workshops and forges. Everyone moved with a hazy slowness, as if they had all the time in the world. If they weren't killed by some disease or accident, they had that time. Their natural magic protected them from the ravages of age, and the eldest seelie sometimes grew so slow and contemplative that they ceased to move altogether, living only through their magic, needing neither sleep nor food. Some vanished, shrouding naturally and staying that way. They sat along the river or up among the mountain stones, with only garlands marking where they were so no one ran into them. It made her sad to think of it, though few shared her sentiment.

She couldn't imagine sitting for eternity. By the elders, she needed to have a little fun soon or she'd go mad.

Lilani headed for the great library at the center of the Court. Maybe one of her friends would seek her there, and if not, she could lose herself among the books. In the brightly lit interior, she stopped, inhaling the smell of wood polish and parchment. Shelves full of books hugged the gently curving walls, parting only for a large window at the library's rear. More shelves followed the winding staircase up to the second and third stories, every available space taken by the knowledge of the seelie.

When Lilani glanced at the large wooden table in the middle of the floor, she started. Her mother sat there, leaning over an oversized book, and Lilani knew what it was without looking: the birth and death records of their people. Empress Dyrana and her daughter might have shared a love of reading, but lately, Lilani's mother always sought out the same book.

Hair a shade bluer than Lilani's own shifted over her mother's shoulders; their eyes were the same bright violet with the same ring of gold around the iris: royal eyes, but she would never get the chance to lead, not with all seelie now living under the Court. There'd be no need; her mother would live forever, and there would never be a separate enclave. Lilani would never have to sort out anyone else's problems, but her mother would order her around forever, too.

Her mother tucked a strand of hair behind one pointed ear and sighed heavily. Lilani cleared her throat. When their eyes met, her mother smiled. "Lilani, how did it go?"

"A success," Lilani said with a wide smile. She hoped proof wouldn't be demanded. As much as Lilani loved the library, she didn't know if she'd feel free enough to tap her magic indoors.

Well, maybe if she were upside down with a book in her hands.

Lilani crossed the floor and glanced at the giant record book: the births and deaths of the seelie. The entries had slowed over the years. The very last birth name was hers, and she was nearing thirty, barely an adult to some seelie but fully grown nonetheless.

If anyone well into their several-hundreds would ever acknowledge that fact.

"You're going to drive yourself crazy," Lilani said, sliding the book away and shutting it.

"There has to be a reason why there haven't been any children in thirty years." She put her head in her hands and didn't seem an empress for the moment, never mind the gauzy purple gown shot with threads of gold and silver that moved like flower petals as she walked.

Lilani shrugged, but she had her own thoughts about why the seelie weren't reproducing. So many had died making their way to the Court, but still, they fit only…comfortably in their forest. There wasn't room for many more.

Still, her mother likely knew that. "Maybe there should be more celebrations," Lilani said. "Drums and dancing, a bonfire, barrels of wine." And soft sighs in the dark. Her magic fluttered just thinking of it.

Her mother gave her a dry look. "Sex is not the problem. I've asked."

Lilani stared, jolted out of her memories. "You've asked?" She conjured up images of her mother sitting down to tea with various people and saying, "So, how often do you have intercourse?" Maybe living long enough cured one of embarrassment.

At least that was something to look forward to.

Her mother raised an eyebrow. "Perhaps I should turn my attention to your friends and inquire there?"

Lilani fought a wince. "No, that's fine. We're fine." She pushed the book farther away. "Brooding over these names won't help. Come on before you turn to stone." She started out of the room, knowing her mother wouldn't be able to resist that bait.

"They are not stone," her mother said as she followed. "The elders are simply communing with…"

Lilani paid no attention, not bothering to hide a grin. Outside, the sun was setting, and people were carrying tables into the street, getting ready to dine together as the seelie did every night. Lilani took her mother's hand. "Let's sit together. Unless you're going to mope all night. Then I'm leaving you on your own."

"Callous child. I should embarrass you in front of your friends just for that." The tone was light, but before Lilani could pull her closer to the tables and lanterns, she stopped. "Lilani, wait."

When they were in shadow, her mother said, "The lack of births is not the only thing troubling me." In the near dark, her eyes seemed to glow, the hints of gold picking up the light. "One of the humans' pylons has gone out."

It took a moment for Lilani to know what that meant, even though she'd been thinking about the pylons not an hour before. But she didn't see why it should cause such dread. Even if the tattered lands broke through the pylons, it couldn't break through seelie magic. "And?"

Her mother sighed and seemed ancient, the flickering light making her features as elderly as a drawing of an old human. Lilani gasped and stepped forward, but as the light struck at a different angle, her mother was as beautiful as ever.

"It is the pylon closest to our border. The humans will be coming to investigate."

Lilani laughed, her worry dissipating. "They'll never find their way in here, and if you're dreading telling me that I have to stay out of the forest a few days, I don't mind. Truly." She winked, but her mother barely smiled.

Instead, she looked out on the gathering of their people, on the laughing faces. "Come." She pulled Lilani back into the darkness of the library. "I have much to show you before we can rest."

Fear threatened to rise in Lilani's heart, but she followed her mother back into the shadows. What was worse, pining for adventure or having it in varieties she'd never imagined?

CHAPTER THREE

Lilani had been reading for hours, and she still couldn't digest everything she'd learned. For all her love of books, she'd barely made a dent in what the library had to offer. With her mother guiding her, she began to see how much she'd missed.

She glossed over some events she knew: the spread of the tattered lands and a brief history of the human retreat. Her mother wanted her to focus on the pylons themselves. Lilani had never taken much interest in them. The ancient history of the seelie was so much more fascinating. And whenever seelie books mentioned humans, they were quick to remind the reader about how barbaric, petty, and small-minded humankind was. With their short lives and shorter memories, they were doomed to keep making the same mistakes.

But with the pylons, it seemed they had learned something, at least enough to create new technology. The author of one history, a seelie scribe named Awith, didn't have the same opinion of humans as the other books. She described daring human battles against the overwhelming denizens of the tattered lands, of noble humans refusing to leave comrades behind to face being torn apart. Awith didn't shy away from human brutality, but she also stressed that when humans were united in a common cause, they were as perfect and inescapable as the seasons. She had fought by their side, helped with their evacuations. She had loved some of them.

Lilani gasped at that. Awith had many human friends and lovers. She seemed fascinated by them, and she'd wanted her people to embrace humanity despite past misunderstandings.

Of course, later scholars had made notations in the margins of Awith's history and had added pages to her work. Some refuted her claims about the sequence of events and cited instances that were supposed to prove her wrong. Since Awith had no response within the pages, Lilani had to conclude she hadn't survived her encounters with humans. Perhaps she'd believed that all of them were as noble as the ones she befriended, and in the end, they'd betrayed her.

Lilani kept reading as her mother stayed silent. What was it she was supposed to learn from this? That she should try to help the humans with their pylon? That she shouldn't? When Awith's history came to the construction of the pylons, Lilani read closer.

They were huge constructs made completely of syndrium. The way Awith described the plans for them, the humans wanted them to be nearly alive, not just delineating the border but actively guarding it. Awith suspected the humans had found some way to tap into the magic in syndrium, though they had no natural magic inside themselves.

As she kept reading, Lilani's mouth dropped open. Awith wrote about how she intended to work *with* the humans, to help the pylons shroud the human lands, but the details were rough and hazy, written hurriedly. More like a journal than a history, these pages were all about what Awith planned to do and not what she'd actually done.

Lilani looked up. Her mother was straightening some books, but when Lilani caught her eye, she said, "Keep reading."

Lilani obeyed, turning the page. The handwriting changed, the notes of another seelie, along with a few passages in what Lilani recognized as one of the human languages. It said the seelie had received notice of Awith's death, that she'd fallen while helping erect the pylons. The humans praised her bravery, saying she'd stayed with the pylons until the denizens of the tattered lands were upon them. She'd succeeded in her mission, giving her life so the humans might live.

The human words radiated emotion: love and grief and gratitude. Lilani wondered if they were written by one of Awith's lovers; the seelie who'd copied them into the book didn't say. Lilani sighed, feeling a spark of their grief. Their words seemed so heartfelt she couldn't help feeling an ounce of what Awith must have felt for them. Compared with a seelie hand, their letters seemed brutish, but the depth of their feeling screamed from the page. No seelie felt so deeply, not after a certain age. Maybe to bear such a long life, they had to sacrifice passion.

A terrifying thought.

"She helped them," Lilani said. "And they loved her for it."

"But didn't hesitate to sacrifice her."

Lilani glanced back down at the book. It read as if Awith had sacrificed herself.

"If the pylons are failing," her mother said, "the humans might seek our help again." She walked around the table. "We could shroud from the tattered lands, but then we'd spend all our energy simply staying out of sight. It's why the seelie fled south in the first place."

"But Awith helped build the pylons for the seelie *and* humanity," Lilani said, caressing the page.

Her mother cocked her head. "Many see the survival of the humans as a mere side effect of Awith's deeds."

The words held no malice, but like the seelie who'd left annotations in this book, she seemed devoid of sympathy for the humans, no doubt thinking of conflicts and seelie deaths that were hundreds or thousands of years in the past.

But Awith had been clear about her intentions, her feelings. "Will we help them?"

"Some have suggested we construct our own pylons at the border while the humans succumb to their fate."

Lilani arched an eyebrow. "So, it's their *fate* to be turned into monsters or torn apart?"

A shrug, and Lilani's belly went cold. She didn't harbor a love for humans like Awith had, but she didn't want them to go extinct. No one who'd written of Awith's sacrifice with such blinding passion could be evil.

She thought back to drawings she'd seen, to the seelie who'd found the beauty in humanity's muscular forms. Many drawings were marred by a sense of violence, as if death was part of humanity's very nature. Some said the influence of the tattered lands simply brought out the core of the humans, twisting their bodies to match their souls.

It couldn't be.

Lilani stood slowly. "I...think we should help." She touched Awith's book again, knowing she'd reread it often. "We can study the pylons, figure out what Awith did, and re-create it. And if we do it before more pylons give out, we shouldn't lose any lives. Awith had to

hurry. If we help the humans now, there won't have to be a sacrifice."
She hoped.

Her mother stared so long, Lilani feared she had become like one of the elders. "No."

Lilani waited for more, but her mother took the book and carried it away. "That's it?" Lilani asked, following, her anger rising. "If you're not even going to discuss it, why show this to me?"

"I had hoped you would see Awith's tale for what it is: evidence for what needs to be done."

"How could a tale of love and grief make me see that humans deserve to be abandoned?"

"They take, Lilani. That is what this tale shows us. Some of them may have loved Awith, but they still took all she had, including her life."

Lilani shook her head, fighting disbelief. "From the way she wrote, she gave those freely."

"I'm sure they *convinced* her that it was all her idea."

"Mother—"

Her mother whirled around, anger in her eyes at last. The tendrils of her hair lifted, buoyed by her power. "It is *seduction*, Lilani. Their youth, their energy, those are their lures. They draw our kind in, and then we are blind to their brutality. They offer with one hand, but the other, the hidden hand, is holding a club waiting to strike." She took a deep breath, and her hair settled. She placed the book on a shelf. "I know of what I speak. My father ruled here for thousands of years, and I took charge of one of the enclaves. He befriended the humans, and eventually, they struck him down, jealous of our longevity."

Lilani had heard the sad story of her grandparents. But she'd also noted that the humans the old emperor had befriended were several generations removed from those who'd killed him. Living with humans required a shift in seelie thinking, one that many didn't seem able to manage.

And by that rare flash of anger, Lilani knew she wasn't going to get her mother to listen that night, especially if there was a chance that the story of her grandparents would be repeated. If anything happened to her mother, Lilani would have to lead her people, a role she wasn't prepared for.

Lilani left the library, her thoughts whirling. Change was coming, that much was clear, and it involved the humans whether the seelie liked it or not. But they had time enough to take a look at the border, maybe spy on a few humans, and see what all the fuss was about.

❖

As Vandra suspected, Fieta and Pietyr were eager to go on an expedition. They didn't care that they had to invent fictitious relations near the border. Vandra stumbled over the lie, but her ineptitude seemed to work in her favor, at least with her colleagues. The piteous looks they gave her said they suspected a lie; they probably thought she was running away after her failure. As much as the thought made her squirm, anything that shielded her true mission was a boon, or so she told herself.

Her parents were harder to convince. As an alchemist at the university, Vandra was entitled to lease a small apartment so she wouldn't have to live with her parents and youngest siblings. That didn't stop her family from dropping by to see how she was doing and bringing the youngest—little five-year-old Sita—to charm her into coming home for dinner. And she knew she'd have to have a meal with them before she left *and* when she returned or she'd never hear the end of it.

They wouldn't accept a story about anonymous relations. At the table that night, Vandra told them the university was sending her to the border on a fact-finding mission. It was true enough.

But Fieta felt the need to add, "They want to count the people living there who have no permanent houses."

Vandra glared. They hadn't discussed this particular lie! How was she supposed to—

"The five monarchs want to make sure no one's living too close to the border," Pietyr said. He didn't even glance at his twin as he lied. Sometimes, Vandra thought they shared a brain. No wonder they'd always been adept at sneaking out of the house.

Like Fieta, Pietyr wore his black hair tied back from his face, but he'd shaved the underside. His dark eyes were as smiling and raucous as Fieta's, but unlike her, he had several tattoos on his face, a star to the side of his left eye, and a small line following the curve of his lower lip, relics of when he'd flirted with becoming a gang member before joining the Watch. Fearing he'd be singled out for the marks, Fieta got a tattoo on each wrist, a hawk and a butterfly, the fierce and the beautiful. Their parents had ceased complaining about the tattoos now that neither of them were gang members.

Though they were still inveterate liars.

"Why does it have to be you, Vandra?" Mama asked as she handed food around. She was short like Vandra, and her curves had begun to soften with age.

"And with only the twins for escort?" Papa said. "They should send more." He sat at the table, letting Mama bustle around. Most of Vandra's childhood memories included him kneeling or sitting on the floor. A tall man, he hated to loom over his children, though the twins were nearly his height.

"They should send the Palace Guard," Mama said. "Since you're doing the city a favor."

"Palace guards are too scared to leave the inner city," Pietyr said.

Fieta grinned at him. "They might stub a toe."

Vandra broke her bread in half and dipped some in her stew, hoping she wouldn't be forced to answer any questions.

"Look at her frown," Papa said, pointing. "She doesn't want to go."

"I'll send the university a letter," Mama said with a nod. She looked around to make sure everyone had food before she sat. "They can find someone else."

"No!" Vandra yelled. When everyone glanced at her, she clutched her napkin. At least only four of her siblings were home, the twins and the two youngest. She wouldn't have to lie to the other four, who were probably doing something much more enjoyable than being interrogated.

"Mama, Papa, please," Vandra said. "I'm happy to go. It'll be good to get out of Parbeh, and going will earn me…favor." With Ariadne, perhaps, but not with the university. Even that small tweak of the truth made her wince.

Her parents knew how bad she was at lying, but they wouldn't be able to figure out the truth from her expression. When they glanced at each other and resumed eating, she relaxed. They began to speak about their days. As a weaver and a banker, her parents kept busy. The twins had once asked how they'd found the time to raise nine children, but Vandra had snorted at the question. They'd raised two, Vandra and her elder brother, then had them raise the rest. Her childhood had been an endless parade of soiled diapers.

The twins spoke about their day, too, covering for her, and they soon had everyone laughing. When Vandra left that night, her parents hugged her and offered to get her out of the trip. She rolled her eyes but hugged them back, reminding them that they didn't need to fight her battles, especially when there was no war.

"You can't fault a parent for worrying," they said, nearly at the same time.

Sometimes, she almost could.

The next day, a courier delivered a packet of money to Vandra's apartment, along with a note from Ariadne to buy whatever food and supplies she needed. Vandra grinned. She hadn't outfitted an expedition in years, and she'd missed it. After rushing through the shopping and pillaging some equipment from the university, they left Parbeh by midmorning.

A tent city had sprung up beyond Parbeh's walls. The locals had taken to calling it Lowtown, as it sat on the bottom of the slope that led to Parbeh. Every settlement across Citran had acquired such a place. There wasn't enough room in the cities to accommodate everyone, even fifty years after the retreat and the construction of the pylons. Tents that were supposed to be temporary had become permanent. Lowtown had some order, a semblance of streets, and some of the structures incorporated wood or tin, giving them a more permanent look. The major avenues were patrolled by the Watch, keeping Lowtown from becoming as lawless as some places near the border of Citran, where the desperate lived within spitting distance of the tattered lands.

The twins walked on either side of Vandra, both a foot taller than her and more imposing, even without their Watch uniforms. Maybe it was the tattoos that made people move out of the way, or it could have been the spear across Fieta's back and the sword at Pietyr's hip. Whichever, Vandra was grateful. The last thing she needed was some silly physical confrontation keeping her from her task.

When they were past Lowtown and into the fields, the twins chatted amiably, but Vandra barely listened, running through scenarios in her head, trying to see every variable even though she didn't know the full scope of the pylon problem. She lost all track of everything else until an ache built in her feet and back.

When Pietyr pulled her to a halt, she blinked at him. "What?"

"Are you trying to walk all the way there in one go? It's time to stop. We're hungry."

They were out of sight of the city, though the fields that supported Parbeh still rolled on each side of them. No wonder her back hurt. "I suppose we should rest. It is recommended from time to time."

Pietyr snorted a laugh. Fieta plonked down on the ground. It wasn't long before she was stretched out, feet propped up on her pack. Vandra sat at her side and took a more careful look around. In the nearest field, a large farming machine chuffed away, moving slowly and tilling the soil as it went. The sun struck its metal carapace and flashed like a signal fire. Several people trailed behind it, casting seeds back and forth. The five monarchs owned this land, and only those who grew crops for Parbeh would be given such a device and the precious syndrium needed to power it.

In another field, Vandra spotted a few shacks. They probably belonged to the farmers who worked the land, but they could have been squatters who'd soon be rousted. Every inch of this land was spoken for by crops, and the demand never went down.

The road through the fields led to Saribelle, the next closest city to Parbeh and the third largest in Citran. After that, there were no large settlements between Saribelle and the Seelie Forest, where the road turned north. No one seemed inclined to live near where those mysterious creatures dwelled.

Vandra remembered the tall trees from her first trip to the pylons. She'd been sorely tempted to explore the forest, maybe catch a glimpse of a seelie. She'd been enchanted with them when she was younger, would have loved to ask some questions. Of course, one could be standing right next to her, and she'd never know it, not with their famed ability to vanish from sight.

The thought made her shiver. "Don't get too comfortable." she said, nudging Fieta. "It's only midday."

"I like to rest to the fullest," Fieta said, her eyes closed.

Pietyr handed out traveling rations: bread baked with nuts and berries, and a roll of soft cheese for them to share. "I suppose you'll say it's too early to break out the beer."

She gave him a look. "If you want to finish our journey today dehydrated and with a headache, be my guest." She held out the water skin and quirked an eyebrow.

He took it with a sigh. "Yes, Mama."

"Since I cared for you as children, and you survived to adulthood, I take that as a compliment."

Fieta snorted. "Shut up and eat your cheese, Mama." Vandra poked her, and Fieta swatted her away. Before they could get into a mock fight, Pietyr sat between them.

"Think you can fix this pylon, Van?" he asked.

"Of course she can!" Fieta said as she sat up. "She can fix anything."

"If it *can* be fixed," Pietyr said.

Vandra shook her head, charmed by the compliment but still worried. Until the gods-cursed syndrium formula had gone wrong, she *could* have fixed anything. "There's so much to do before I can answer that. You have to assess the problem—"

"Before you can treat the problem," the twins chorused.

She had to laugh. "I taught you well."

Fieta gave her a look. "Sometimes, Van, you sound like you're a hundred years old."

Vandra stuck her tongue out. No one else but this sister could manage to make fun of her, praise her, and tease her in under five minutes. Not for the first time, Vandra suspected that living in Fieta's head was an emotional whirlwind.

"We have to assess situations like that in the Watch," Pietyr said as he took a bite. "But just like with people, some problems can't be fixed." He stared at nothing, no doubt worried for the future. If the pylons failed, humanity had nowhere to go. She supposed she should have been focused on that rather than intrigued by the problem itself.

She patted his shoulder. "We managed to build them once. If they can't be fixed, we'll build them again." She hoped she sounded more confident than she felt. She'd failed so many times already. At least the pylons weren't new. "And we're not even fixing anything on this trip. We're to observe and report back."

So that the real alchemists could fix the problem.

The thought made her sigh. Her grandmama had once said that everyone was born with a pool of luck that they drew from all their lives, and one day, it ran out. Vandra had probably used all of hers on her first success creating syndrium.

Her hands squeezed into fists as every ounce of her rebelled against that dark thought. There was no luck, only hard work.

"Whoa, Van," Fieta said. "Did your bread say something ugly to you?"

Vandra looked down to see crumbs raining from her fist and a berry smeared along one finger. She'd crushed her lunch: the perfect end to a string of frustrating thoughts. "I'm…eager to be off. You both ready?"

Fieta sighed and moaned but stood and donned her pack while Pietyr did the same without question. Maybe instead of luck, everyone was born with a pool of foolish, over-exaggerated emotional outbursts, and instead of using hers, Vandra had given it all to Fieta. At least Pietyr could be quiet once in a while.

The next tent city began when Saribelle was a speck in the distance. The fields from Parbeh had ended some time before, and now every clump of bracken or copse of trees seemed home to someone. A trickle of people moving toward Saribelle swelled the closer Vandra and the twins came to the city.

Fieta and Pietyr fell silent and walked closer to Vandra's sides. She could almost feel the tension roiling off of them, as if their entire bodies were coiled. From the temporary shelters, people watched the flood of travelers with curious or hostile looks. Many of the faces staring from their hovels seemed dim or desperate, worn out from fighting to simply exist. There were too many people, had been ever since the human retreat, ever since the spread of the tattered lands.

The tent city against Saribelle's wall was thick with people and dwellings and thin on roads or a City Watch. Vandra and the twins went single file, her in the middle. They stepped over tent pegs and the edges of lean-tos. They picked their way over people lying in the grass. Vandra pressed her sleeve to her nose to try to block out the smell of unwashed bodies and clothing, waste, and sickness.

Before the arrival of so many people, Saribelle had catered mostly to merchants and travelers on their way to and from Parbeh. It had a reputation for fine hotels and shops. She wondered if the whole place looked like this now.

When she and the twins stepped into an open area, a group of children gathered around, begging for coins. Vandra handed out a few while the twins brushed away the eager hands.

"That's enough!" Fieta barked, and the children scattered. She and Pietyr hurried Vandra along. "You can't give away all our cash, Van."

"We have an assignment," Pietyr said. "We might need the money."

Vandra agreed with a frown. The guards around Saribelle's wall let them in without a fuss, their clothing and weapons marking them as someone with money. Inside, the atmosphere changed. The press of people thinned, though there was still a crowd.

She thought of the machines in the fields, tilling as fast as they could until they ran out of syndrium. If she could get her formula to work, she could make all the syndrium they'd ever need, and the machines could run night and day, and there'd be food aplenty.

She just had to make sure they weren't all killed by the tattered lands first. Then she could get on with fixing the world.

Chapter Four

Lilani couldn't get humans out of her thoughts. Her mother had scouts watching the pylons, but Lilani would never be one of them. She couldn't risk herself, or so she'd heard a dozen times. If she wanted to clap eyes on a human, there was only one way to do it.

She'd begun the day wandering the forest and practicing her shrouding, edging ever closer to the border. She thought about turning back several times. Her mother wouldn't approve. Faelyn wouldn't approve. Even her friends and lovers wouldn't approve. Yesterday, *she* might not have approved, but didn't such consideration show that she'd really thought about her actions? After all, her mother wanted to doom an entire species; the least Lilani could do was have a look at them before they were gone.

Plus, she intended to fight her mother's decision. Surely there were other seelie who agreed with her. When they presented a united argument to the empress, Lilani intended to be ready with tales of peaceful farmers or woodcutters or whatever else humans did.

Awith would know. She'd lived with them, saved them, loved them. The thought made Lilani sigh. All her sexual encounters so far had been like slow, seductive dances, where magic flowed over the participants as intensely as kisses or caresses. Sex with a human would probably feel akin to making love to a naked flame, hot and hurried. Humans didn't have time to waste, after all.

With such thoughts, the power inside her rose. She shrouded, holding the magic even while moving. An achievement to be proud of and embarrassed by at the same time. She ran, burning off energy, seeing if she could shroud while at top speed. She stumbled once, but she knew the forest well, and it wasn't long until she reached the border.

She'd never been so close to the human lands. That alone was thrilling. She walked along the tree line as the air turned chill, afternoon bleeding into evening. Lilani peered through the trees, trying to see the road, to catch a glimpse of a human. When no one appeared, her hopes fell. At least no one in the Court would miss her for one night. Maybe the next day would yield better results. She found a comfortable tree with a curved branch that cradled her body and fell asleep thinking about humans.

When dawn woke her, there were still no humans in sight. A pity. If her dreams had summoned one, that would have made a fine story. She sipped from her canteen, scrounged for edible berries, and wondered how long she'd have to wait.

Oh, Faelyn was right; she was too impatient. One day and she was ready to give up? But as she watched the road, her boredom grew. Maybe her mother had made a mistake, and the humans were already gone. A sad thought. No, she wouldn't accept that the humans had disappeared with no one to mark their passing. She'd look harder.

The day stretched on as she walked along the tree line, and still no humans. Should she leave the forest? Too dangerous. After all her practice, she could now shroud while moving, even running, as long as her thoughts stayed…excitable, but while her mother might forgive a trip to the border, she wouldn't excuse a foray into human territory.

Afternoon turned into evening again, and Lilani groaned. She was tired of eating berries, but if she started home now, it'd be dark before she arrived. Better to sleep outside again than spend hours tripping over every clump of brambles in the forest. In the morning, she'd return to the Court in defeat, then she'd press her mother to send scouts to determine if the humans were still alive, and she had all night to think of an argument as to why she should be one of the scouts.

❖

Vandra and the twins left Saribelle at dawn. A bath and a night in a bed had made Vandra's step lighter. They had one more night of camping between them and the pylons, but they'd spend it at the Seelie

Forest. Then they'd turn full north, following the road that led along the massive woods all the way to the pylon.

In the distance, Vandra spotted the lone mountain rising up within the forest, though she couldn't yet make out the dark wall of trees. "Maybe we'll see a seelie."

Fieta hitched her shoulders. "I hope not."

"It'd be interesting," Pietyr said.

Fieta snorted. "Until it kills us."

"Kills you, maybe."

They fell to bickering. Vandra sighed. If any seelie were about, they'd be hidden and would no doubt run away from the twins' childish arguments. There were very few scientific accounts of the seelie, though Vandra heard many "stories." Many histories of human/seelie interactions were lost to the tattered lands. Books hadn't been a priority to those running for their lives, but Vandra never thought of all those abandoned libraries without a sigh of regret. Many claimed that Parbeh had been the seat of human learning long before the tattered lands, but Vandra didn't know how much of that was true and how much was local pride.

If she could perfect her syndrium formula, maybe the tattered lands could be pushed back by a line of mobile pylons, and all that knowledge could be reclaimed. A wonderful thought, but she made herself put it away. One quest at a time.

As evening fell, they reached the Seelie Forest. The road here had been well traveled once upon a time. Now weeds grew between the paving stones, making the surface uneven, but it was still easier to walk on than the bare countryside. Opposite the forest, the land lay bleak and barren, dotted with the occasional clump of bushes or lonely stand of trees. Even with so few places to settle, no one lived here, not with the Seelie Forest and every story that haunted it.

"Should we camp on the road?" Fieta asked softly.

"Too vulnerable," Pietyr said. "According to the stories, if we stay just inside the trees, we should be fine. No need to be afraid."

She rounded on him. "Who's afraid?"

"Hush," Vandra said.

Fieta muttered, and Pietyr grinned before their expressions turned serious. They were probably thinking of their grandmama's tales about people who'd gone far into the forest and disappeared for hours. When they'd returned, they'd told stories of invisible attackers destroying equipment and handing out broken bones as warnings. Vandra thought it a perfect way to send a message to keep out while not angering the humans to the point of invasion.

The twins set up camp inside the trees, out of sight of the road. "I wonder if the seelie know anything about the pylons," Pietyr said as he stared into the woods. "If they can't die, then they were alive for the pylons' creation."

"You could go ask." Fieta gave him a light push. He ignored her.

"It's a shame they won't talk to us," Vandra said as she dug out a small pit for the fire. "I'd like to know if everything we've heard about them is truth or myth."

Fieta cracked her knuckles. "Like if they're exceptional fighters."

"Or exquisitely beautiful," Pietyr said.

Fieta cocked her head as if that idea intrigued her more. "Or both!"

Vandra chuckled. "Your dream lover."

"Anyone can be a dream for an evening," Fieta said with a wink.

Pietyr groaned, and Vandra laughed. If the seelie were watching, she doubted they'd appear simply to provide Fieta with pleasant dreams, euphemistically or not.

Vandra built a campfire, and everyone ate dinner quietly. Once full, Vandra stared into the flames and let them hypnotize her, going through her formula again. When she kept making mistakes, she realized she couldn't keep her eyes open.

Lilani was searching for a comfortable place to sleep when she spotted an orange glow through the trees. She crouched and wrapped her magic around her, shrouding. No seelie would light a fire this close to the human border. That meant…

Her heart pounded, her mouth going dry. Humans at last!

She tiptoed onward, holding her shroud and watching her step. The humans had made camp next to a downed log and a clump of bracken. She couldn't see them clearly, and she wouldn't be able to get close without pushing through the brush and making noise.

At least on the ground.

After moving under a sturdy branch, Lilani leapt and caught hold easily, pulling herself up without a sound. Thank the elders she'd had so much practice hiding from teachers. With her heart pounding, she edged forward until she could get a better look at the three humans crowded around their fire.

All three drowsed, heads bobbing. They'd built their fire so it wouldn't spread if they fell asleep: a cautious act that proved they weren't thoughtless ruffians. Their dark skin seemed a few shades deeper than hers, and their hair was as black as obsidian. It lay still around their shoulders, unmoving without magic.

They seemed…quieter than seelie, duller, like the earth rather than the sky.

The smallest was already asleep. A female, if Lilani was reading the subtle planes of her face and the curves of her body correctly. Humans and seelie were alike in that regard, or so she'd read. The taller two leaned close together, occasionally talking softly. With her eyes closed, the small female smiled, and Lilani couldn't help wondering if she dreamed of a lover's touch.

Lilani chuckled at herself. She needed more hobbies.

When the larger humans stood, Lilani froze, but they only prodded the small female into the tent. After putting out the fire, they joined her, and it wasn't long before all of them snored softly.

Lilani swung down from her branch and stepped close to the tent. From the light of dying embers, she saw that they'd taken all their belongings in with them. She frowned. So much for a chance at snooping. Maybe in the morning, they'd leave something behind. She backed away slowly, holding her shroud as she crept through the brush, making as little noise as she could. When she was far enough away, she let her magic settle and pressed a hand to her abdomen. The cramps were back. Fear and adrenaline couldn't keep them down forever. She let out a long breath and leaned against a tree.

When a touch grazed her back, she leapt, her magic snapping around her. She grabbed the nearest branch and pulled herself up. Terrified, she looked down, expecting to see a surprised human, but Faelyn stood there instead.

His blond hair caught the moonlight as he cocked his head. "I'm beginning to wish I was a worse teacher," he whispered. "You're too good at shrouding now."

Lilani had to calm her thundering heart before she could speak. "You scared the life out of me!"

"I've been tracking you." He shook his head and climbed up beside her. "When I told you to practice shrouding, following humans isn't what I meant."

She licked her lips. "I was curious. I'm the heir; I should know our neighbors."

His bland look said he was unimpressed with the explanation and the haughty grace she tried to adopt. "Well, now you've seen them. Home is that way."

"I don't want to walk home in the dark." She turned from his stare but could still feel it.

"You just want to get a look at them in the daylight."

"So?"

Did he know about the pylons, about the possibility of human extinction? Would her mother want it known? It couldn't stay secret forever.

"Lilani," he said, a warning.

Her temper flared. "I'm being careful. Besides, you can't drag me back, Faelyn."

"Your mother does not want our people consorting with humans."

"Do you see any consorting?"

He rubbed his forehead. "Why do you insist on pushing the boundaries of every rule?"

Lilani waved a hand as if scattering his words to the night. "My mother will want to know what these humans are doing so close to our home."

"We'll tell her that they're currently sleeping. Then she can send scouts to watch them."

"A waste of time. I'm already here."

He ground his teeth, the sound carrying as if he chewed rocks. She'd never pushed him this hard before. "Please, Lilani. Everything you need to know about humans you can find in the library. Isn't that where you'd rather be, hmm? Among the books? Maybe with a little wine?"

She chuckled. "You're cute when you try to relate to the youngsters."

He glared, but after a few moments, he finally sighed. "We can stay until dawn. Just."

She shrugged and settled, making herself comfortable. If he wanted to have a new argument in the morning, that was fine with her.

❖

Vandra awoke before Fieta and Pietyr. Her first thought was to shake them so they could get walking, but it was barely light outside. Better that they rest a little longer. She crept out of the tent, taking one of the packs. She needed to check her equipment and should have done it before falling asleep, but if any gods were lurking the night before, they'd neglected to remind her.

She shivered in the morning air and pulled on a long jacket. With a few quick movements, she unloaded her equipment and arranged it on the forest floor. Her chemicals and powders stayed safe in bottles and jars that were wrapped in cloth and set in leather cases. She pulled out the short-range meter she'd built for detecting syndrium. Only seven inches long, and four wide, the wooden device fit easily in her hand. She twisted the magnets lining the side and made sure the compass in one end read true north. Then she opened a slot that held a tiny ball of syndrium. It rolled along a channel, bouncing between the magnets. With no other syndrium nearby, she expected the compass to stay on north, but as the syndrium ball moved slowly down the slot, the compass needle swung toward the west.

Frowning, Vandra glanced in that direction. The nearest mountain was deep inside the forest, and she was too far from the pylons for this particular detector. A malfunction? She reset the syndrium in its housing and started over, hoping nothing was broken. When she tested it again, the compass rested on true north, and the syndrium ball waited in the middle. She slowly counted to ten, cursing when the same movement happened as before. She shifted the detector slowly, and the needle moved with it. There had to be syndrium nearby.

Vandra took a few steps into the trees, peering into the gloom. She took another reading. Syndrium wasn't normally just lying on the ground, and in the dim light, she couldn't see any silvery-blue gleam. She prayed to any nearby gods to guide her and took another few steps. When the needle began to turn, she stopped. She had to be close; the detector couldn't read far underground. Vandra crouched, searching for jutting pieces of stone. Nothing. Just the roots of a large tree. She put a hand on the trunk. It seemed like a normal tree, maybe an oak. She was good with minerals, some herbs, but trees were not her specialty. She *did* know they couldn't lift syndrium any more than syndrium could climb. She snorted and started to look up into the branches, but someone grabbed her shoulder.

Vandra whipped around, barely keeping in a cry of surprise. Pietyr put a finger to his lips, his eyes wide in warning. After a glance around, he pulled her back to camp. Fieta crouched among the undergrowth, her spear ready as she scanned the quiet forest.

"What's going on?" Vandra whispered. "I detected syndrium out there!"

"Whatever you found, forget it," Fieta said. "You were too far inside."

Vandra looked again. "How can you tell?"

Pietyr shuddered. "I can feel it."

Fieta nodded. Vandra looked between them but couldn't argue. Their instincts for danger were better than hers. And if there were seelie nearby, watching, maybe they used syndrium, and that was what she'd detected. She squinted into the trees, trying to see the oak through the soft light, but the twins pulled her into helping break camp. Even when they were out of the forest, the twins cast glances at the trees as they hurried down the road.

Vandra had to jog to keep up. She couldn't help glancing at the forest and wondering what unnerved them so. If she only had more time to study!

She sighed. There was never enough time to study. But that didn't mean they had to run all the way to the pylons. "Surely we're far enough away to slow down?"

They slowed and seemed to breathe easier after a few more minutes. After setting a brisk but not impossible pace, they even seemed their normal selves again, but Vandra couldn't stop thinking of the unseen syndrium. Maybe the seelie did know something of the pylons if they had syndrium just lying around in their forest. She took out her notebook and jotted a reminder to mention that to Ariadne. Maybe the assembly had an idea about how to contact the seelie. With the future of the pylons at stake, no step seemed too far.

❖

Lilani had opened her eyes when Faelyn gripped her shoulder. It took a moment to remember what they were doing in a tree in the middle of the forest, then she noticed a shimmer in the air where Faelyn should have been. He'd shrouded.

She had blinked and looked down. One of the humans had wandered beneath their tree. Her gray coat rustled softly as she took a small step, her eyes fixed on the device in her hands. Long black hair fell around her shoulders, tousled from sleep. Endearing, even sexy.

She swung the device this way and that but seemed fixated on Lilani's tree or possibly on those hiding in its branches. Lilani fumbled for her power, but it felt sluggish, sleepy, as if she'd overused it the night before, or maybe it was tired of responding to her terror. The human's head angled up. Faelyn's grip tightened, and Lilani wondered if he was readying the knife he kept at his belt. She couldn't let him…

Another human had grabbed this one's arm, making her jump, nearly making Lilani jump, too. They'd hustled back to their camp, and Lilani breathed out slowly. After the humans hurried from the trees, Faelyn faded back into sight, glaring.

Lilani blushed. "I tried to shroud."

He didn't lose his scowl as he climbed down.

She followed. "Did you see that device?"

"I couldn't miss it. It seemed to be leading that human right to us."

"A seelie detector?"

"I don't know. Please, Lilani, go home."

He sounded so earnest that she nodded. She took a step, but when he didn't follow, she turned. "Well?"

"I'm going to follow them," he said, "see if they enter the forest again. Maybe I can get a better look at that device."

"You can't go alone!"

He sighed and seemed more tired than she'd ever seen. Before he could argue, she put her hands on his shoulders.

"I'm not being selfish," she said. "It's too dangerous to go alone."

"Lilani, if you can't shroud when—"

"I can." Her power rose, and she shrouded quickly. "I won't fail again, and I know how important it is to find out if humans are going to start hunting us or…whatever." She tried a weak smile. "If worse comes to worst, I can stall the humans while you run for reinforcements."

He winced, reminding her how hard her death would be on the seelie. She was the heir and the youngest. But nothing about the human woman had screamed threat. She had no weapon. If she'd come hunting, she would have brought something sharp, and she wouldn't have wandered from camp without her armed companions.

Before Faelyn could present another argument, Lilani ran, following the humans' direction but staying inside the forest, never doubting that she'd find them soon enough.

CHAPTER FIVE

On the road going north, Vandra spotted two other sets of travelers, both heading south. One was a group of people pulling a wagon loaded with furniture. They didn't even seem to notice Vandra and her siblings, too busy with their burden. The other travelers were an hour or so behind the wagon: a bedraggled couple with wooden cudgels at their hips. They stared, hands caressing their weapons, but Fieta sneered, and Pietyr stared them down. Vandra didn't know if they were brigands or not, maybe chasing the people with the wagon, but they clearly didn't want to pit their clubs against Fieta's spear or Pietyr's sword. Vandra tried a confident look, one she used on the occasional student, but she doubted she'd warn off any thieves on her own.

Fieta and Pietyr stayed alert, scanning the countryside instead of chatting. Vandra stared ahead, searching for the pylons. The sky seemed darker to the north, a sign they were closing on the border with the tattered lands. On her first trip, the sky past the pylons had been gray and overcast, as if the air itself was tainted. Now the sight raised her spirits; it meant she'd soon be able to get to work on the pylon.

That name didn't do them justice. It brought to mind a simple shard of stone instead of the massive structure Vandra spotted on the horizon. A large, central shaft supported two crossbeams jutting from the middle and the top, making the pylon seem like a large F, but with the top beam pointing in the wrong direction. Even from a distance, the pylons glowed brighter than any syndrium she'd ever seen, the effect of so much of the rare metal in one place, or so the scholars said. A wandering beam of sunlight struck the side, and it flared like quicksilver until the light moved across the barrier and was swallowed by the gloom of the tattered lands.

Like drifting smoke, roiling fog hung along the border of the tattered lands, blocking sight as capably as a wall. When the wind blew from that direction, Vandra shivered. It was always cold there, and the closer they came to the border, the sooner they'd need their jackets.

"Ahead and to the right," Pietyr said quietly.

Vandra glanced at him, but he looked the other way as if taking in the landscape. "What?"

He draped an arm around her shoulders and leaned close. "Don't look, Van. Someone's hiding ahead to the right."

"I see them," Fieta said, scratching her nose, covering her words. "Looks like three or four. I saw them when we crested the last rise."

"Sure you did."

Vandra's heart sank. "Brigands?" She tried to keep her voice as quiet as theirs. "We're so close! What do we—"

"We'll deal with them," Fieta said. "You stop here and pretend there's something wrong with your boot."

Vandra did as she was told, examining her feet even as her heart began to race. Maybe these brigands would hide, intimidated by the twins. Maybe they weren't brigands at all. Maybe they were hiding because they thought the twins were—

"Keep up!" Pietyr turned as he walked but gestured at her to stay where she was.

"There is something in my boot!" She spoke clearly, trying to sound authentic and knowing she was failing. She was bad at lying, but she was worse in a fight. She wanted to tell the twins to be careful or order the brigands to run away. Maybe if she shouted like a lunatic, everyone would be too unnerved to act.

And everyone would stay safe.

The twins continued slowly. Vandra felt along her boot, eyes locked on her siblings' backs. "Gods large and small," she whispered. "Protect them."

Watching from the trees, Lilani tensed. The three humans she'd been following hadn't seemed to notice the other group of humans crouching behind a tangle of brush. Those waiting had weapons in hand, and her group continued blithely forward.

Lilani took a breath, ready to shout a warning.

"Don't even think it," Faelyn said from beside her.

"But they don't see the danger!" When the group of three split, she gasped. "Look! The smallest one has fallen behind. The other two will be ambushed."

"Lilani, don't."

Lilani ground her teeth. The small female who'd almost seen her was now alone and vulnerable. Lilani wanted to protect her, but how? Creep up behind and warn her? More movement from the south caught her attention. Another human ran past a clump of trees on the other side of the road, racing toward the small female's unprotected back. Lilani recognized the newcomer as one of a pair of humans that had gone past earlier on the road. She wore leather, carried a club, and had a focused, cruel look on her dirty face.

The small female was doomed. Her armed compatriots were too far away, and she hadn't noticed the assailant behind her. Lilani shook off Faelyn and ran. Her magic shuddered, but desperation pulled it close. Shrouded, she burst out of the trees.

Ahead, the ambushers sprang at the small female's protectors. The protectors' weapons seemed to fly through the air as they fought together. They'd subdue their opponents in no time, but they wouldn't be able to help the small female. Lilani ran harder, her breath coming in gasps. The wind rushed past her ears, and she tore through the grass.

The small female turned, no doubt drawn by the sound of Lilani's footsteps. She spotted her would-be assailant instead and froze, her mouth open. The assailant grinned. The small female obviously wasn't a warrior. Neither was Lilani, but she wouldn't let herself think about the consequences of her rush at the moment. At least two against one was better odds.

"Vandra!" Pietyr called. "Run!"

Vandra's body wouldn't obey. By the time she'd heard her attacker coming, all she could do was stare. She noted the cudgel and the cruel grin on the brigand's dirty face, but her rational mind refused to catalogue them in any way that made sense.

The cudgel lifted, and Vandra raised her arms. She closed her eyes and tensed for the shock and pain. When the brigand shrieked, Vandra flinched, but no blow came. She opened one eye to see the brigand flying through the air as if blown by a strong wind, her cudgel tumbling from her hand.

Now the world made even *less* sense. The brigand lay in the ditch, cursing, her eyes wide. Vandra looked to her own hands. Had she done something without knowing? An adrenaline-fueled reaction? She took a step forward, and a woman blinked into existence before her.

Vandra gasped, and the mysterious woman's purple eyes went wide as they locked gazes. Their skin was nearly the same shade of brown, but the mysterious woman had dark blue hair, a sight Vandra had never seen. It lifted from her shoulders as if caught in a breeze. She crouched, breathing hard as if she'd been running, and her arms were stuck straight out. Her foxlike features and delicately pointed ears belonged to a creature from another world.

Vandra blinked, and the woman vanished. The twins ran to Vandra's side, weapons pointed at the brigand in the grass. The brigand scrambled up, looking for her cudgel, but Pietyr darted into her path. She dashed out of his way. Fieta leapt to the side, swinging the butt of her heavy spear. It smacked against the brigand's head, and she fell senseless to the ground.

"Van, are you okay?" Pietyr asked.

"I'm fine." Vandra searched for the mysterious woman and saw only scuffs in the dirt by the road. "Did you see…" She looked to the twins, noting their sweaty faces, but neither of them was bleeding. "Are you okay?"

"Not even winded." Fieta clapped her on the shoulder. "And what got into you, Van? She came at you with a club, and you threw her into the ditch? I didn't know you had it in you." She grinned. "Or did she rush you and trip?"

"There was a woman." Vandra strode to the spot where the woman had appeared. She waved her hands in the air but felt nothing.

"Where?" Pietyr asked.

"She disappeared." When the twins glanced at each other, she knew what they were thinking. "I'm not hallucinating, and I don't imagine things."

"Then you've developed the power to manifest mystery women from thin air?" Fieta asked.

"No! She was here. I don't know how she…" The features, the ears, the hair. And she'd vanished from sight. "A seelie." Vandra looked to the woods but saw nothing. "A seelie saved me." A beautiful one, but she didn't say that part aloud. "Why?"

The twins were staring at the brigand, not listening. "What should we do with the thieves?" Pietyr asked.

Fieta glanced around. "We can't march them all the way back to Saribelle, and we don't have time to find a village to take them."

"I don't want them with us anyway," Pietyr said. "We don't have manacles or enough supplies to feed them."

Fieta shrugged. "Let's take their weapons and leave them for Van's imaginary savior."

Vandra glared, but Fieta wasn't paying attention. They took the cudgels and left the small knives so the brigands could live off the land. Vandra didn't know if that was enough for people desperate enough to hunt this far north beside the Seelie Forest. Hopefully, this would force them closer to a settlement.

To prey on the people there? Vandra couldn't think too hard about it at the moment. It was the old problem of too many people living in too small a space. Something had to be done. Maybe the seelie would part with some of their syndrium. She stared into the trees. If the seelie were willing to save her from a brigand, maybe they'd help in other ways, too.

Or maybe they simply hated an unfair fight or took pity on someone who clearly didn't know what she was doing. Either way, Vandra lifted a hand in thanks, hoping the purple-eyed seelie was watching.

Lilani crouched in the forest, but when Vandra waved, she smiled, tempted to return the gesture. One glance at Faelyn's stony face convinced her to keep her hand down. He radiated disapproval.

"I had to," she said quietly.

He kept staring.

"Go on," she said, "tell me how disappointed you are, how foolish I am."

With a sniff, he looked away. "I knew something like this would happen. Why shouldn't it? You and Awith were cousins, after all."

Lilani rocked back on her heels. "We were? What do you know about Awith?"

He gave her a look that was enough to remind her he was centuries older. "I knew her. And yes, you're related. Many seelie are to some extent. Why do you think we keep such careful birth records?"

"Why didn't you tell me about her?"

"Keep your voice down!" He glanced at the road, but the humans were distracted by one another. "If I told you about every seelie I've ever met, we wouldn't have time for anything else." He sighed. "I knew that if you met humans, you'd follow in her footsteps, throwing yourself at them."

"I did not!" But she had. Literally. "I had to help her."

"Any minute now you'll be picking flowers for her and composing a love ballad."

Lilani put her hands on her hips. "I will not." He couldn't know that she'd pictured kissing the one called Vandra after that heroic rescue.

"Give it time."

She glared, but he seemed more tired than angry. If he'd been alone, would he have helped the humans? She didn't have the heart to ask. She'd made the right decision. Vandra and her warriors didn't kill the thieves, disarming them instead. They weren't the paragons of wanton destruction that the stories made them out to be. When they continued on their way, Lilani followed from inside the trees. Faelyn grumbled as he trailed her. Lilani tried to ignore him, watching her humans instead. The warriors seemed lively, smiling together, giving each other playful shoves. Vandra was more composed, more seelie. None were loud brutes. Without the flutter of magic, Vandra seemed quieter than even some seelie.

Lilani cocked her head. She'd thought before that the seelie were like the wind, and the humans were like the earth, but maybe the humans were like water instead: ever changing. Vandra stared into the forest from time to time. She'd obviously deduced what Lilani was and somehow knew Lilani wasn't a threat, but she was also wise enough not to venture into the forest looking for her savior.

Smart and beautiful. The sight of her large, dark eyes and curvy figure would remain in Lilani's thoughts for a long time to come.

She sighed. By the elders, Faelyn was right. That was the start of a love ballad if ever she'd heard one.

Vandra's mind didn't know where to focus. The seelie, the attack? The twins were all right, but Vandra had never been attacked before, and her mind kept flashing to the brigand's awful grin.

Fieta waved a hand in front of her face. "Are you nodding off on us?"

Vandra tried to shake off her gloom and mumbled that she was okay.

"Is it the fight?" Fieta asked. "Cheer up! It's over. We won."

Pietyr put an arm around Vandra's shoulders. "It's all right. We're all okay." He seemed calmer, as if being attacked had broken some sort of anxiety bubble. "Try to look forward. That's what we do."

For once, Fieta nodded, agreeing with him.

Vandra tried to smile for them and focused on the seelie woman. The vision of her was stamped on Vandra's brain, as unshakable as any formula she'd ever learned. Even on her deathbed, she'd know all her calculations and that seelie's face. Her eyes had widened in wonder, as if Vandra was an incredible creature, too, though Vandra didn't see how that was possible. She'd never glimpsed someone so enchanting. Was she following them from the forest?

Vandra shook her head. Now wasn't the time to be thinking of brigands *or* seelie. The pylon loomed in front of them; they'd come close enough to see the iron rungs embedded in the side, the only way to climb to the top of a structure that stood four stories tall.

Fieta gawked. Even Pietyr whistled in appreciation. Vandra hadn't aided in the pylon's construction, yet she felt a jolt of pride. Alchemists had made this. Well, engineers had helped, but the composition had been determined by alchemists like her, and alchemists would breathe life into it again.

Though from the glow, it had life still. When she'd first visited the pylons, she'd noted that they seemed different from regular syndrium: brighter, more…syndrium-like. Her colleagues had put that down to so much syndrium in one place, but Vandra had her doubts.

She took her pack off and approached the vertical pillar, the diameter of which was nearly as long as she was tall. She dug out the notes from her first trip, though she knew them by heart. There was something missing, and she wanted to double-check…

The "hum." As soon as she put a finger on it in her notes, she recalled the feeling. The pylons had a vibration that was felt rather than heard. She'd labeled it the "hum" because that was what the non-alchemists of her party had called it no matter how many times she'd corrected them. And though the pylon still emitted the glow that should have symbolized activity, the vibration was missing, a fact no one would notice until they were close.

Interesting. And disturbing.

"By all the gods," Fieta said as she circled the base. "How did they ever build it?"

Vandra dipped into her bag and pulled out a book on the pylon's construction. "Here. Light on facts and heavy on drama, but better than nothing."

Fieta only held it and continued to gawk.

Pietyr put a hand to his forehead and stared upward. "Maybe they did have a god's help. Or two. The gods of engineers and alchemists?"

Vandra snorted. "Gods that big would want a huge favor in return. I doubt the builders would have risked that."

"Unless the gods wanted to help just to see if it could be done," Pietyr said.

"Yeah, no shit," Fieta said as she tossed the book down by Vandra's pack.

Vandra clucked her tongue, picked up the book, and brushed it off before putting it away and unpacking her instruments. First, she tried the small syndrium detector, knowing it would tell her there was a great lump of syndrium right in front of her, but she had to start with the smallest experiments. She adjusted the magnets, slid open the syndrium compartment, and waited.

The compass pointed north. She nodded and walked several steps to the east, but the compass stayed on north. Vandra frowned and turned the detector, willing the needle to swing toward the pylon, but it stayed stubbornly fixed in the ready position.

"It can't be." Walking a few more steps, she tried again, but the detector didn't lie. The pylon was as dead as a common lump of stone.

"No, it…it can't…" With fear carving a pit through her insides, Vandra hurried to her pack, pulled out a hammer and chisel and knocked a fleck of stone from the pylon's side.

"Whoa, Van!" Fieta called.

"It won't miss a sliver." She unpacked the leather satchel with her chemicals, sending some of the jars rolling in her haste. She placed the sliver of stone into her basalt mortar and added a drop of acid.

No blue froth. Nothing but some quietly dissolving bits of stone. She had to be doing something wrong. It was the failure with her formula all over again. It had followed her here.

"Shit!" She dumped some bicarbonate of soda into the mortar to neutralize the acid and set it aside. She took a deep breath. This wasn't her experiment. These were tried and true methods for detecting syndrium, and this pylon, supposedly *made* of the stuff, wasn't registering any. Standing, she faced the pylon with her hands on her hips.

"What is it, Van?" Fieta whispered. She and Pietyr were both staring at the pylon as if expecting it to attack.

"I don't know, but I'm going to find out." Alchemy would save them, not worry. She took out her notebook and wrote about her readings as quickly as she could, trying to keep the writing legible.

"Van?" Fieta asked.

"Shh," Pietyr said. "Let her work."

Vandra pointed her pencil at the pylon. "It has to be some sort of natural phenomenon. Help me look for cracks or damage." She shut her book with a snap and moved to investigate the pylon's base.

"Besides what you just did?" Pietyr asked.

"Yes," Vandra said through her teeth. She took a deep breath. "Large damage."

They spread out, running their hands over the pylon. Both the twins were up the ladder quicker than her, calling down that nothing seemed out of place along the arms or top. She followed them to the topmost arm, sitting when she got there and not looking down. The twins paced easily back and forth, careless of the wind tugging at their clothes and hair, seemingly oblivious of the long drop to the ground.

Even from this height, Vandra couldn't see far into the tattered lands, not through the drifting haze that covered the miles like a blanket. There was still a good fifty meters of empty land between the pylons and the haze, but that ground was bare and yellow, as if nothing could live this close to the tattered lands. As Vandra looked along the wall of mist, it seemed to be straining forward the closer it came to this pylon. She could see a dot on the horizon, the next pylon, visible only because of her current height. Maybe it was only the curve of the world that made the mist seem closer here. The ten pylons were built close enough to one another that their protective fields overlapped, and the mist shouldn't be nipping at the edges of the Seelie Forest now. Beyond the trees, somewhere in the distance, lay the line of the coast. Or had the mists of the tattered lands already engulfed that?

Pietyr and Fieta sat on either side of her. "Want to tell us about it?" Pietyr asked.

"We're not completely stupid," Fieta said. "We might understand."

Vandra breathed a chuckle, though she felt close to tears. "You're not stupid. I just can't believe it. This pylon is dead. It's not syndrium anymore."

They were quiet for a moment. "How?" Fieta finally said.

Vandra had to shrug. "That's what we have to find out."

Silence reigned for a few more moments. "Could someone have taken the original pylon and put up a fake?" Pietyr asked.

It seemed impossible, but so did the idea of syndrium being turned into useless stone. And what about the glow? Vandra crawled along the pylon's arm, peering at it closely. The silvery-blue gleam was less apparent up here, not nearly as impressive as it had looked from below. She lay down and scooted toward the rounded edge.

"Van, what are you doing?" Fieta cried.

"I need to get a sample from the side." She scooted farther, forcing herself not to look down. She could be brave if it meant…

Her body jerked, and she yelped, but it was only Fieta kneeling on her legs. "Be careful, curse it!" Fieta said.

"Let us do it," Pietyr said. "Our arms are longer." They pulled Vandra back, and she yelped again, trying to protest when Fieta lay along the pylon, head dangling over the edge while Pietyr held her legs.

"What am I doing?" Fieta called.

Vandra handed down her knife. "Take some scrapings!"

"That'll ruin this knife," Fieta said.

"The gods take the knife! I need samples."

Mumbling, Fieta obeyed. They repeated the process several times along different levels of the pylon, Vandra making a note of each location. When she was on the ground again, she performed several tests before sitting back on her heels.

"It's trickery. Paint mixed with some phosphorescent compound!" Vandra was tempted to fling the mortar into the tattered lands. "Who would do such a thing?"

"So, someone *did* replace the pylon?" Pietyr asked.

"More likely, they did something to make this pylon inert then painted it to look like it was still functioning," Vandra said. "The question is, how and why?"

Fieta shivered and looked toward the tattered lands again. "This close, I can feel it. Like a pit opening in my stomach."

"And smell it," Pietyr said. "It's like rotten trees. Or a swamp."

Vandra nodded. Now that they'd pointed it out, she was aware of a creeping sense of dread and a foul smell. She'd been too absorbed by what she *wasn't* feeling from the pylon to notice before. Could the very proximity of the tattered lands have sapped the syndrium out of the pylon? But then who had painted it? The well-meaning government of Citran trying not to cause a panic? Wouldn't Ariadne have warned her of that?

She looked into the tattered lands again. The mist seemed to roil in places as if straining to get out. The dead ground between here and there was pockmarked by holes and the remains of trees. Vandra's eye was drawn to a plot of turned earth. She'd glimpsed it from above but had dismissed it. This close, she noticed that the soil was darker than the baked-looking dirt around it.

She pointed. "Someone's been digging. Recently."

They all exchanged a look. To see what it was, they'd have to walk beyond the border, closer to the drifting, hungry mist.

CHAPTER SIX

Vandra stared toward the recently dug earth before glancing at the wall of moving mist. "I have to see what's out there."

Fieta shook her head. "We shouldn't."

"I didn't come all this way to go home empty-handed."

"It could be nothing." Pietyr watched the mist. They all did, scanning for the twisted creatures said to live inside. Nothing moved; nothing called out. The only sound was the wind sighing around the pylon. Maybe the denizens of the tattered lands didn't need to communicate with each other, but the stories spoke of unholy cries in the mist-shrouded darkness.

Vandra swallowed and tried to sound more confident than she felt. "I'll be the judge of that." She retrieved her syndrium detector, her gloves, and a few specimen jars. With a shaky hand, she noted the relative position of the disturbed earth in her journal.

Then all she had to do was walk out there.

At the edge of the dead grass, she paused, breathing deep. Now or never. When she stepped forward, the twins went with her, weapons out. She wanted to reassure them that the neighboring pylon was keeping the tattered lands back, but she didn't *know* that.

Vandra tried her detector, but it didn't point toward the patch of disturbed soil. She slipped it into a pocket of her jacket and wiped her sweaty hands on her trousers. She knew they should be hurrying, but they took careful steps, the dry, brittle grass crunching under their feet. If something was prowling inside the mist, maybe it wouldn't notice them if they were quiet.

She tried not to remember *all* the stories she'd read, those about mutated creatures and plants, but her mind kept going back to one journal in particular that spoke of a creature with teeth all over its body and no eyes. The author thought it might have been a bear once, but she couldn't say for certain. How could someone mistake a bear?

Vandra bit her lip to stop thinking about mutant bears. She took a deep breath and kept going.

They reached the overturned earth at last. Up close, it didn't seem carefully dug, more like someone had pried up a lump of turf with their foot. Vandra fumbled into her heavy gloves. "Get ready to run."

The twins tensed. Good. She couldn't be sure what she'd find. Any number of elements and chemicals were volatile—who would leave such things casually in a hole?—or there could be a buildup of gas. The twins each put a hand near her shoulders, ready to pull her away; they wouldn't be badgered into thinking of their own lives first. A sweet thought, though their parents would blame her if any of them were hurt.

She paused. Her brother and sister might be hurt. Maybe she should say she loved them? With another breath, she told herself to stop being silly. Nothing was going to explode, and the hole wasn't covering a mutant bear. If this blasted land had any gods left, they were probably laughing at her.

Vandra gently turned the soil and spotted a glint of metal. Slightly dull, it might have been specks of lead. She used her pencil to nudge a few of them into a specimen jar. Several smells drifted up from the soil, and she took multiple samples of dirt that was nearly the color of clay. Interesting. She took off one glove and got her journal out, wanting to make a small drawing and note where she'd taken the samples.

"Van." Pietyr's whisper made her remember where they were. Twenty meters ahead, the mist billowed, agitated.

Vandra put her journal away, but as she began to stand, she saw a thin piece of metal poking out of the dirt. When she prodded it with her boot, it came loose, about half the size of her palm. She put her glove back on and reached for it as a ray of sunlight struck it. A sickening tingle went up Vandra's arm, setting her teeth on edge. She paused, queasy, and shuddered as if invisible oil was sliding over her skin.

"What is that?" the twins asked at the same time.

Vandra shook her head and forced herself to reach for the metal again.

A howl went up from the mist, an unearthly shriek that rattled Vandra's bones. With a cry, she froze. The twins wrenched on her shoulders, hauling her toward the pylon.

"No! I have to get that metal!"

The mist parted, and she caught a glimpse of…something: a bit of fur, rent and torn, dripping blood, and a mouth so large she could have crawled inside. It snapped out of the mist then darted back again.

Vandra's mouth went dry. There were still gods in this land, but they were as twisted and terrible as everything else. Still, she had to get that metal. She tried to plant her feet. "Wait, wait!"

The twins pulled harder as the thing dashed into view again. It weaved in and out of the mist, managing to come closer to them each time before the magic of the pylons pushed it back. She had to get that piece of metal before it broke free. She needed a clue. Her feet left furrows in the dirt as the twins dragged her. "I can get it, but I have to go now!" With a final twist that wrenched her shoulders, she broke free. The tattered thing shrieked again, still nothing more than a blood-covered ball of fur. The twins cried out for Vandra to run.

In one gloved hand, Vandra scooped up the metal. The tattered thing lunged, wide mouth gaping, and rows of needle-like teeth straining forward. Again she froze, hypnotized by that cavernous maw, the writhing purple tongue. Deep in the back of its throat, she saw what looked like a tiny face. Part of it, or something it had just eaten?

Vandra screamed. Cramps wracked her body, and the tattered thing roared as if it sensed weakness. Hot, foul breath washed over her.

She was going to die.

Fieta's spear streaked past, cutting a line across the tattered thing's jaw. It reared back, squealing as it turned for the protective mist. The world spun as Pietyr hauled Vandra over his shoulders. She cried out again. "Fieta! We can't leave her!"

Pietyr ran, and Vandra tried to push up on his shoulder, searching for her sister. Fieta grabbed her spear and ran after them. A wave of relief washed over Vandra, and her vision faded in and out. When Pietyr passed the pylon, not stopping for her pack, she yelled, "Wait!"

He didn't even slow. Jerking and bouncing on his shoulder, Vandra didn't know whether to hold on or try to stop him. Fieta scooped up Vandra's instruments without care, stuffing them in the pack.

They'd gone well down the road before Pietyr finally stopped. After lowering Vandra, he leaned on his knees and breathed hard, glaring.

"I needed the metal." She wanted to feel grateful, but there were too many emotions fighting for supremacy: fear, anger, relief, fear again. She decided to focus on anger. Anger could get things done. It could fight through the waves of nausea coming from the metal in her jacket pocket.

Fieta dumped Vandra's bulging pack on the ground and gasped for breath.

"Careful!" Vandra opened her pack and pulled out a lead-lined box. Still wearing her gloves, she dropped the metal inside, dampening its odious presence to a dull, annoying feeling, like a mosquito whining in her ear.

"You could have been killed!" Fieta said.

Vandra ignored her as she took off her gloves and unloaded the pack. She reached into her other pocket and heard a tinkle; one of her sample bottles had broken. Trying not to curse, she took off her jacket and emptied the pocket over a handkerchief. The soil sample had been contaminated by broken glass, but maybe she could do something with it.

Her hands shook as she went through the pack. She willed them to stop. She had work to do. She did not have time to think about...

Reeking breath and the teeth, and oh gods, that tiny face!

"Hope everything isn't broken," she muttered.

"We just escaped death, and that's what you're worried about?" Fieta yelled.

"Fieta—" Pietyr started.

Fieta waved him off. "Saving the pylon isn't worth your life, Van!"

"Yes, it is!" Vandra jumped up and reared toward her sister's face. "It's worth all our lives!" She was yelling, the aggravation of her recent failures mixing with terror and fatigue and worry until her insides felt like a knotted chain. "If the pylons fail, we die! Everyone dies! Mama and Papa, little Sita..."

Anger clouded her vision, or maybe it was tears. Gods, now she was so angry she was crying like a child throwing a fit, but the tears wouldn't stop, rolling down her cheeks even as she shouted. "I have to stop it!" She pressed her hand against her mouth. With her formula, she could have helped, but she'd failed. Even with that failure, humanity would survive, but now there was more at stake than making people's lives easier; if she failed in fixing the pylons, she'd be killing every human left in the world.

"They'll all die," she said between sobs.

The twins' arms went around her, but she didn't want their comfort, didn't deserve it. She shrugged out of their embrace and went back to packing, trying to be careful, but the rotten tears kept blinding her. She hated that she had to keep sniffling, but her handkerchief was full of dirt and broken glass. Where in the gods' names was her canvas sheet? Nothing was where it was supposed to be. Her set of scoops were bent. The acid wasn't in its place next to the bicarbonate of soda. Did her sister want the pack to melt?

And why in the names of all gods, large and small, had that thing had a *face* in the back of its *mouth*?

Pietyr knelt beside her. "Van, you cut your hand."

She hadn't even noticed the sting. A line of blood dribbled across her knuckles. Not deep, but it oozed. She shook her head. "I have to repack."

He offered his handkerchief. "You know how important it is to clean a cut, especially after digging through *your* bag."

Yes, she'd taught him that. He poured water over the cut, and she wrapped the handkerchief around her hand. The kindness on his face shamed her.

The tears flowed again, and she wanted to say she was sorry, but all that came out was, "I have to save the world, and I can't even protect my hand." It was stupid, but she felt very stupid at the moment. When the twins held her again, she let them. She rested her head against Pietyr's chest. Fieta left off hugging them and repacked Vandra's bag very carefully, stowing the heavier things on the bottom as Vandra had taught her.

"Thank you," Vandra said softly.

Fieta smiled. Her eyes seemed a little misty, too. Vandra felt as if her whole face was on fire. She hated crying, never mind sobbing.

"Sorry I yelled at you," Fieta said, the words rushed together and nearly inaudible.

"Me, too," Vandra said.

Pietyr helped her stand. After a deep breath, Vandra looked toward the pylon, to the line of mist in the distance. She would be brave. She had to be.

Fieta stood, arms crossed. "Well, at least I can say I stabbed something from the tattered lands. I'll be the toast of the Watch."

Vandra barked a laugh but brought it under control quickly, worried it might turn into another sob. She couldn't have that, not after she'd decided to be brave.

❖

Lilani could scarcely believe what she'd seen. The humans had crawled over the pylon, but by their reactions, it wasn't telling them what they wanted to know. Even from a distance, the pylon should have been humming in Lilani's brain, the feel of it tingling her skin, but she felt nothing. It seemed…dead, even more lifeless than regular stone. And she didn't need to see the mist to feel the taint of the tattered lands creeping toward her with ugly fingers.

"Well," Faelyn said, "we can tell your mother she was right about this pylon. If the others fail, the tattered lands will be past here in a heartbeat."

"We can't let that happen," Lilani said. "And not just for the humans. How could we live next to this feeling for the rest of our lives?"

He shook his head. "There's a reason we fled south when the neighboring human lands were engulfed. Even being close to the tattered lands feels as if the sun will never shine again. Right next to them, we'd have to tiptoe through life as if our home was made of thorns." He sighed. "Your mother knows that."

"She wants us to build pylons of our own," Lilani said.

"That might not be enough."

When they glanced at each other, she knew he felt the same way she did. Hopefully, his voice added to hers would be enough to sway Lilani's mother.

Lilani watched the humans again, and when they risked being attacked by a denizen of the tattered lands to retrieve something from a field, Lilani nearly ran to help, but Faelyn grabbed her.

"I will sit on you if I have to!" he said.

Her heart hammering, Lilani watched the trio's narrow escape, eyes locked on Vandra. When the warriors carried her away, Lilani wanted to cheer. What in the name of the elders could be so important that she'd risk being devoured by that…thing?

Lilani and Faelyn shrouded as the humans ran past. Even in the distance, Lilani could feel something wrong about them, as if one of them carried a piece of the tattered lands with them.

"Do you feel that?" she asked.

He nodded, and when she followed the humans, he didn't argue and seemed as intrigued as she was. When the humans stopped to first yell, then weep, then hug one another, Lilani pressed a hand to her chest, feeling for them and their narrow escape.

"They certainly are…noisy," Faelyn said.

They were perfect, but she didn't dare say so. No seelie went through emotions so quickly, but the display fascinated her. They were more like the water than she'd thought.

Vandra had taken something from her pocket, and that feeling of uneasiness surged through Lilani's veins until Vandra put the thing in a box. Then the very air felt lighter.

"It looked like a bit of metal," Faelyn said as he craned his neck. "Why would they want a souvenir from the tattered lands?"

Lilani glanced north. She couldn't see the pylon through the trees, but she felt the lack of it. Whatever Vandra had taken, it hadn't brought the pylon back to life. Now Vandra seemed intent on carrying the tainted metal deeper into human territory. Lilani would have argued for her to throw it as far into the mist as she could. "How can they stand being so close to it?"

Faelyn shrugged. "They're probably desperate to study it in order to fix the pylon. We need to tell the empress."

"You go. I'll watch them."

He ran a hand down his face. "Are you going to make me go through my entire argument again?"

"No, that's a song I know by heart." She sighed. "Are you going to make me repeat all the reasons we should watch them until they're gone from our borders?"

He frowned so hard, she was tempted to chuckle. "I'll only watch!" she added. "And I'll run if they bring out that…device again. I have to make sure they don't leave that piece of metal here."

"Will you rush to their rescue if they need you?"

She knew the answer was yes. He had to know that, too, but she kept her face very calm as she said, "I will take every precaution."

"That's not a no!" He seemed torn, but she'd already proven he couldn't stop her. No matter what he said, he wasn't strong enough to hold her down, and she could shroud if he tried.

And by the myriad of expressions crossing his face, he knew she was right to stay. Neither of them wanted to let that tainted metal out of their sight.

She patted his shoulder. "One of us needs to stay," she said, "and one needs to go, and I won't go. Therefore…"

"I taught you logic, thank you, not the other way around." He drummed his fingers on his knees. "I know you'll do whatever you want, but please, *please*, keep in mind that if you die, it will take more from our people than their heir. You are the youngest of us, Lilani, the last born, and you represent hope that there'll be other children in the future. Do not take away our people's hope, I beg you."

She found that slightly overblown and more than a little manipulative, but she had to agree. "I have no intention of throwing my life away."

"Remember, no matter what you've seen, you *do not know* these humans. You can't predict how they'll react to you or anything else."

Predict, no, but she could imagine and dream. She wondered if Vandra ever wandered off by herself. From the vigilance of her guards, Lilani thought not, and that seemed a shame in one way and a relief in others. If they *did* meet alone, Lilani was certain Vandra would want to talk rather than fight.

Probably.

"Go, Faelyn," Lilani said. "Mother will send the Guard, and I'll be waiting." After a final nod, he departed. The thought of her mother's guards didn't bring Lilani any particular comfort. They'd collect the information she had then take over. She wouldn't be *ordered* back home, but she would be politely encouraged until she wanted to scream, and she'd end up obeying just to stop all the *suggestions*. If she didn't, her mother would come collect her, and the ordering would begin in earnest.

But Lilani had more to worry about than what her mother might say. She followed the humans to their camp and climbed high in a tree to watch them. Moving slowly, her magic tight around her, she tried to get close enough to hear. All seelie children learned some of the human language, enough to recognize it and run. She'd made further studies, learning from those who'd actually spoken the human language of Citran at one time. She knew enough to converse on a variety of topics.

But only if she had to.

Probably.

❖

After they made camp, Vandra hesitated before opening the lead box. The metal's mere presence was enough to turn her stomach, but she would push through in the name of alchemy. She donned her gloves again, hoping they would help. She bit back her disgust as she turned the piece of metal over in her hands, suppressing the urge to throw it away.

Fieta grimaced at it from where she and Pietyr cooked dinner, but she didn't say anything. After the yelling and then the crying, they'd tried to be cheerful but had finally lapsed into silence. Everyone was polite, but Vandra sensed fragility between them. She didn't know how to fix it, but she couldn't wait for it to pass.

Vandra opened her pack and pulled out her metal shears. She set the metal between them and squeezed hard, teeth gritted. The metal was thin; she should have been able to dent it, but nothing happened. She set the shears on the ground and brought her hand down hard on the grips for extra force. The metal piece shot away with a loud *ping* that echoed through the trees. Vandra blinked, trying to stop her ears from ringing. Shockwaves traveled up and down her arms, and the shears fell over, the tips blunted.

Pietyr jumped to his feet. "What in the name of the gods was that?"

Vandra shook her head. "It's tough."

Pietyr swore and walked a tight circle as if he had too much energy. And he was the calm one. If he was upset, Fieta should have been shouting and grousing and all but rolling on the ground, but she only frowned in concern.

Vandra crawled into the brush and found the metal piece unmarred, resting tranquilly against a clump of grass and gently pulsing with malevolence. She wanted to try to score it with acid, but if it resisted a strong hit, it might resist the acid, too.

Or it might fly around the forest and kill them all, or anything else in the entire realm of possibility. No, the place for experiments on the unknown was a laboratory. With a sigh, Vandra put the metal away. Pietyr had gone back to cooking and grumbling. Fieta still stared with that slightly constipated look. Vandra wanted to yell at them to be normal, but of course, such behavior from her wouldn't be normal either.

"I want to check the next pylon," Vandra said. "If we hurry, we should be able to get a look at it and then get home only a little after we're expected."

The twins nodded and said nothing.

Vandra fidgeted, unable to stand so much silence. Strange. She usually loved it. "Ariadne would tell us to check, even though she also wants us to hurry. It won't do any good to walk all the way back to Parbeh then have her send us out again."

Another nod.

"So...we'll do that. Maybe whoever tampered with this pylon started here and is moving their way inland, just...replacing pylons as they go." Vandra scuffed at the dirt. "Who knows how many pylons they'd have to take down to open a large breach? Single creatures are clearly able to come through now, at least for a little while."

Fieta snorted. "By single creatures, do you mean the hideous monster with the face in its mouth?"

"You saw that, too?" Vandra said. "I wondered if my eyes were playing tricks!"

"Oh no," Pietyr said. "Face-mouth was real."

Vandra grinned, relieved, though she couldn't explain why; maybe because they were talking at last, even though it *was* about something ludicrous and repulsive. She burst out laughing, a reaction caused by mental and emotional exhaustion and a depletion of adrenaline.

It felt so good that she didn't care.

The twins joined in, laughing like fools until they were wiping tears from their eyes. When silence descended again, it felt nice, comfortable, and they smiled as they ate, brought together by thoughts of a nauseating creature from the tattered lands.

Vandra supposed that was irony.

"Are you sure this weird metal is connected to the pylon going out?" Pietyr asked. "It's not just something from the tattered lands that appeared out there."

Vandra had to shrug. "I won't know until I can do more tests, but bits of metal don't appear from the air."

Fieta frowned as she chewed. "Could something have thrown it out of the tattered lands?"

"It was partly buried," Vandra said. "If it was thrown, it would have been on the surface. Besides, could something like that creature even throw an object?"

"Face-mouth does whatever it wants," Pietyr said.

Vandra snorted a laugh. "It didn't have hands. At least, I don't think it did." She tried to remember, but the memory caused too many shivers.

"If it does have hands, the gods only know where it keeps them." Fieta seemed about to take another bite, then frowned and set her bowl on the ground.

Since the piece of metal was outside the tattered lands, someone from this side of the border had to have buried it. Unless another creature had broken out just to bury a bit of metal. She shook her head. The tattered lands corrupted the outsides of creatures as well as the insides. Even a corrupted human wouldn't have the wherewithal to break the pylons, disguise them, then bury the evidence.

But how had someone from this side of the border gotten metal that felt as tainted as the tattered lands? Vandra sighed loudly and set her own bowl down.

Pietyr gave her a sympathetic look. "You hate not knowing."

"I love working on a complex problem, but there's too much at stake here."

"We'll check on this pylon tomorrow before we go to the next," Fieta said. "Maybe spending a night away from that metal will have it back to normal."

Unless the field was full of such metal, but Vandra didn't say that. It was a nice hope. Completely impractical, but nice. She also didn't mention that if this one hunk of metal was enough to destroy a pylon, they shouldn't be carrying it around with them, although it seemed part of a larger piece. Maybe it had been broken off during…

What? And what could break something so strong that it dented her shears?

"Pietyr, can you hang this from a nearby tree?" Vandra said, tipping the lead box into a sack. "I don't want to sleep next to it."

"Good idea." He cinched the bag with rope. "I like the number of faces I have."

Fieta laughed and chucked a stick at him as he walked into the dark. "Another face might be an improvement on the original!"

"Ha ha," he called back. "We look almost exactly the same, dummy."

She snorted. "Van, are you sure we should be taking that metal anywhere with a lot of people and syndrium?"

"I don't see another choice." The university would want to study it, even if they never found out what it might have done to the pylon. And if Fieta was right, and the pylon was fine tomorrow, they'd never *have* to know. There'd be no need to tell this story, just the need to make sure it never happened again.

Lilani sat in a tree and listened to the humans' plans. They were going to seek out the next closest pylon. That lightened her heart. But they didn't say they were coming back to this campsite afterward to have another conversation so she could listen. If there was a road close to the next pylon, they'd probably take that home. Then Lilani's mother would have to send a seelie expedition to the next pylon, and *that* group might be drawn into a confrontation, especially if their shrouds failed.

So, in order to prevent a catastrophe, she *had* to follow these humans. She didn't think Faelyn would appreciate her logic, but he wasn't there.

Lilani laid her head along the branch. She smiled when the humans laughed. Even in the midst of a crisis, these three seemed vibrant, animated. She wanted to sit with them, share their fire, and ask questions. They were so much better than books, realer than any tale.

She knew the stories about the hurt that humans could do; she'd heard them often enough. But every human from every story was long dead. Humanity was ever changing, even over the course of one human lifetime.

Lilani couldn't help but feel as if she was changing, too. Maybe humans were what her people needed to keep them from becoming living statues like the elders. Humans would give the seelie much to think about, and animated human lives might spark something in the seelie, a new need to learn, to explore. Children might be born who would know humans over the course of their whole lives, meeting generation after generation. Lilani imagined humans inheriting seelie mentors who would guide them and keep them from the mistakes of their forbears. She pictured the delight on seelie faces from seeing human children scampering in their midst. It would provide them an excuse to exercise their famous patience.

Faelyn would have sneered at every one of those thoughts. She almost sneered at herself. She could hear him calling her naïve, asking when she'd gotten so twee and jolly, and sarcastically offering to tie her hair up in ribbons so she could caper properly.

She rolled her eyes both at the imaginary retorts and her own need to romanticize the humans in order to justify what she was about to do. She would keep her promise to Faelyn tonight. But if the Guard didn't arrive by the time the humans left, she'd follow them. Faelyn and her mother would just have to understand.

CHAPTER SEVEN

They woke early the next morning, and Vandra couldn't shake the feeling of unseen eyes staring at her. After taking the box containing the tattered metal down from where Pietyr had secured it, Vandra dropped it into a second bag, then wrapped that up in a third, but the feeling didn't fade. Maybe there weren't enough bags in all the world to cover it.

Or maybe the feeling stemmed from something else. As the twins packed, Vandra watched the forest, the image of the seelie female large in her mind. Purple eyes and blue hair wouldn't have made sense on a human, but on that delicate face with its high cheekbones and pointed ears, the color worked. At the time, Vandra hadn't paid attention to the seelie's clothing, but as usual, her unconscious mind had captured the image and replayed it for her, showing the seelie in a green wrap top and tight, doeskin trousers. The sleeves on her shirt had scalloped edges that fluttered in the breeze with her hair. Every inch of her seemed soft to the touch.

Last night, Vandra dreamed that she and the seelie woman had shared a cup of hot chocolate under an ocean of starlight. Few women could drive Vandra to whimsy, and it'd been a long time since she'd dreamed about anyone. Her past three lovers had been just like the rest of her life: practical. She was always too preoccupied to pursue objects of fantasy.

And now? Vandra shook her head. She already had one quest. She couldn't go roaming the woods looking for romance.

The packing done, the three of them set out again. Vandra couldn't look for the seelie now, but maybe the opportunity would arise someday.

The seelie had to know something about the pylons. Ariadne would eventually contact them, and Vandra could make certain she was part of that mission. She'd already met a seelie, after all. Sort of. And Ariadne would owe her a favor. Maybe there was a way to let the seelie know she'd be back.

"We should leave a message," she said, staring at the trees from the road.

"For your imaginary woman?" Fieta asked. "That doesn't sound insane at all."

Vandra gave her a dark look. "You grew up with the same stories as me. You know seelie can vanish."

Pietyr shook his head. "If it was a seelie, why save you then disappear?"

"A fleeting moment of kindness?" Vandra recalled the look of wonder on the seelie's face, wonder directed at her, as if they were equally fascinating. Heat rushed to Vandra's cheeks, and she breathed deep, trying to slow her heart before the twins noticed her embarrassment.

Pietyr crossed his arms. "I guess you could call out and hope she hears you."

Vandra tried to imagine what would happen, but there were too many variables. "Maybe she'll answer."

"Or attack us," Fieta muttered.

Vandra walked toward the trees. "It's worth a try." She cleared her throat and tried to think of what to say, what would move her if their positions were reversed. "Hello?" she called.

When only the wind sighing through the branches answered, she was almost relieved. She might have jumped out of her skin otherwise. She had no idea what to say to a woman who could knock her senseless.

But now she was just talking to trees. "Ah well," she said softly. "Might as well fully commit." She cleared her throat and called, "Is anyone there?"

The twins had gone quiet, flanking her. They had their hands on their weapons but didn't draw them. Vandra hoped that if the seelie was watching, she wasn't put off by the show of wariness.

"My name is Vandra Singh," she said, feeling foolish introducing herself to a forest. "I'm an alchemist from Parbeh. These are my siblings, Fieta and Pietyr. We've come to check on the pylon. It seems it has…died."

She couldn't help another blush, her embarrassment growing. And now she was talking to trees about a *dead* lump of stone. Special, magical stone, but still. "We're trying to fix it. Please, if you know anything, have seen anything, will you tell us?"

No one answered. Vandra didn't want to go on yelling at nothing. And it was possible there were other humans hiding nearby, listening. The brigands from the day before had vanished, but they might be close. She couldn't go shouting all her plans to the world.

"Well, that's that." With a strange mix of disappointment and relief, Vandra started toward the pylon they'd visited the day before, anxious to see if a night without the cursed metal had brought it back to life. Best to put the seelie out of her thoughts. She had enough to worry about.

As soon as they reached the pylon, and she felt no hum, Vandra knew nothing had changed. She took a few readings to confirm and found only lifeless rock. If the metal in her pack had done something to the pylon, it appeared to be permanent.

"On to the next," she said, taking comfort in properly repacking. With a great deal of effort, she avoided looking at the mist, though she caught Fieta and Pietyr staring at it. She could go her entire life without seeing it again, but they had to follow the border to the next pylon.

And looking at it was inevitable. Vandra sneaked glances from time to time. As they traveled farther from the dead pylon, the wall of shifting gray shrank farther into the distance but still seemed closer than she remembered. No sound came from within, not even the hum of insects. Nothing moved within the roiling mass, and Vandra tore her eyes from it. She smiled when the next pylon reared into view. Taking out her syndrium detector, she picked up the pace, grinning when the needle swung in the pylon's direction.

She opened her mouth to tell the twins, but the needle slowly swiveled. Vandra stumbled to a halt, despair rising. Was the pylon dying before her eyes?

"What is it, Van?" Fieta asked, looking over her shoulder.

Vandra frowned as the needle pointed at her briefly before swinging toward the pylon again. "What?"

"The tattered lands?" Pietyr asked.

Vandra shook her head. "I need to get a better reading." She took off her pack and put it to the side. The needle stayed fixed on her, ignoring the pack.

Not on *her*. *Behind* her. She turned, and as she thought, the needle pointed to the pylon, then swiveled to pick up something back the way they'd come. It couldn't be the other pylon. She'd taken a reading an hour ago, and it had given her nothing. Plus, it was too far away.

"Are we moving, fighting, or what?" Fieta asked.

Vandra didn't answer, glaring at the detector. No one was standing nearby with a load of syndrium. The land was so barren, she could see the pylon in the distance and the forest beyond that. No one stood in between.

The forest. She'd detected syndrium inside. Then the seelie female had saved her, so the seelie had no doubt been watching the entire time Vandra had been in the forest.

Then she'd felt someone watching her that morning.

Vandra raised a hand, pretending to cough. "The seelie are following us."

Fieta and Pietyr exchanged a glance, but they were smart enough not to say anything. When she knelt beside her pack, they followed, leaning close.

"I thought I detected syndrium in the forest, but I must have been reading the seelie somehow." Vandra clenched a fist. "I should have taken more readings last night!"

Fieta's hand rested on her spear. "What do we do?"

"How do we defend against an invisible person?" Pietyr asked.

"Let me think." Vandra chewed her lip. Maybe the seelie female had heard her plea and was trying to determine if or how to help. Vandra recalled the sight of her and fought the urge to sigh as a tingle spread through her body. "If they meant us harm, they'd have attacked while we slept. All we can do is keep going."

The twins nodded, but they seemed stiffer as they walked. All three of them tugged at one another whenever one tried to glance over their shoulders. Vandra kept her detector out. As she came closer to the pylon, its signal held the needle longer, but there was still that little tug to the west. The hypothetical seelie was still with them.

Toward the end of the afternoon, they reached the pylon, and Vandra felt its hum from a distance. She sighed, so relieved she nearly forgot the seelie. Shaped like the first, this pylon gleamed in the sun, the silvery-blue glow strong enough to wash them in indigo. Vandra dug out her notebook and scribbled a few hurried notes.

Would the seelie follow them to Parbeh? Vandra picked up her detector, but the needle didn't swing away from such a mass of syndrium for long. Indeed, the readings became sporadic, pointing behind her and even out into the tattered lands. She gave the field a quick scan and had the twins climb up to look for patches of disturbed earth. When they reported nothing, she noted the readings as anomalous and possibly tainted by her proximity to the pylon.

The readings behind her, though… She walked a few steps back. If the seelie was going to reveal something about the pylons, she should do so now, before Vandra and the twins started home. Vandra waited, counting the seconds.

Lilani lay flat in the grass and tried to breathe shallowly. She'd held her shroud for miles, and every muscle cramped on and off. Now she had to hide in the grass in case her shroud failed. She'd already cursed herself several times. She should have listened to Faelyn. The forest was far in the distance, too far to run if she needed. What would Faelyn do when he found her gone? Track her with the Guard? What would they do to Vandra, Fieta, and Pietyr?

"Idiot," she whispered. But at least she could report that this pylon lived. She'd felt the magic emanating from it for quite some time. She should have turned around when she'd first felt it, but stupidly, she'd kept on these humans' heels, enjoying watching them though the sight of the tattered lands made her skin crawl.

She'd seen the device Vandra used before, but if it detected her now, the humans didn't seem to know what to do with that knowledge. Such unknowns should have sent Lilani scuttling back home, but she kept hearing Vandra's plea for help, for knowledge. Vandra and her siblings had traveled to the pylons in search of a way to save their lives, to save all humans, and Lilani couldn't ignore their plight.

How could she help, though? They seemed as if they were getting ready to travel again. Vandra was staring toward the forest as if willing help to appear. Lilani couldn't follow them all the way home. Even if she wanted to see Parbeh—which she did—she didn't have supplies for a long journey through unknown territory. And as much as she suspected Vandra wouldn't hurt her, she couldn't say the same for other humans. She wasn't as naïve as Faelyn thought, but she still had to do *something*.

Vandra seemed disappointed as she took up her pack again. The three turned south, just as Lilani feared. Vandra's cry for help rang in her ears.

Now or never.

Lilani stood, still holding her shroud. What should she say? Her heart pounded, and with each beat, the humans walked away. Lilani's mouth worked, but no sound came out. What would Faelyn say? Nothing. He'd tackle her and put his hand over her mouth, but there was a time for caution and one for action. With a thousand thoughts whirling in her head, she cried, "Hello!"

It was a proper response to Vandra's initial words, just a half day too late. Embarrassment flooded Lilani in waves, but she swallowed it.

Fieta barked, "Who's there?" She whipped her spear off her back. Her brother moved to Vandra's other side and drew his sword.

Even from a distance, Lilani could see Vandra breathing hard, eyes searching. "Who is it?"

Right. The shroud. Now that Lilani wanted it to go, it resisted. She took several deep breaths and made the magic settle, but it felt like slipping out from under a blanket on a cold day. The shock of it made her gasp.

Vandra stepped closer, eyes wide. Her gentle face lit up in a wondrous smile. "You're the seelie who saved me."

"Shit!" Fieta said. "She's real."

Vandra muttered something to her while Pietyr said, "You owe me a beer."

Lilani chuckled as Vandra had a sharp word with him. She cleared her throat. Excitement after holding her shroud for so long was making her lightheaded. "Yes, that was me."

"Thank you." Vandra's head cocked as if doing so better accessed her memory. "Your voice is different from any I've ever heard, sort of echoing." Her eyes widened, and she looked down as if that wasn't what she'd meant to say. "It's nice to meet you. I'm Vandra Singh." She gestured to the others. "Fieta and Pietyr." She waved at them to put their weapons away, and they seemed to do so only grudgingly. Lilani tried not to hold it against them, happy Vandra was protected.

"Lilani." She gestured to herself. Vandra's smile took her from lovely to beautiful, shining with hope. A kind heart showed in that smile. Lilani cleared her throat. Now was not the time to be focusing on anyone's beauty. "I heard you in the forest, and…" And what? Admit her curiosity, her attraction? Her ears burned at the thought. What had Vandra asked for? "I've come to speak with you about the pylons."

❖

"Wonderful!" Vandra couldn't help beaming, and it thrilled her to see her smile returned.

Lilani was as beautiful as Vandra remembered. Tall as the twins, the seelie had a trim, athletic figure. Her hair was midnight blue, a shade darker than in Vandra's memory, and her eyes were deep violet. The lyrical, slightly echoing quality of her voice only enhanced her otherworldly image. And like her soft clothing, her hair ruffled slightly, though there was no breeze. Another peculiarity of the seelie, perhaps, like their ability to disappear.

Vandra only wished she had her journal in hand, though she didn't know how easily she could have torn her eyes away to make notes.

"Van?" Fieta whispered. "What do we do?"

"Just be ready for anything," Pietyr said.

Fieta swatted at him. "No shit."

"Stay calm," Vandra said. "And watch your language." She called to Lilani, "What about the pylons? Do you know about the one closest to your border? It's lost power."

Lilani nodded, and Vandra was glad to see their two peoples had gestures in common. And they either shared the same language, or Lilani had learned the human tongue. The idea that she might have learned it hundreds of years ago flitted through Vandra's mind, and she felt even more flustered.

So, she should focus on the alchemy. "We're trying to figure out what happened." Vandra fumbled in the pocket of her jacket and took out her journal. "Anything you can tell us would be appreciated."

Lilani glanced behind her. She probably feared being out in the open, so far from her forest, and that feeling was justified. The village of Shanston wasn't far south; it had turned into a rough place since the tide of humanity had swept into Citran. Who knew how they'd react to a seelie? And Lilani might not have to go that far to encounter a party of brigands. A trading road ran north of the village, and all manner of criminals might be lurking nearby. Vandra shuddered just thinking about it.

"It's all right," Vandra said, daring a step forward. The twins didn't follow, but Vandra could feel their tension. Fieta didn't like unknowns, even if this particular unknown was unarmed, and Pietyr didn't trust anyone out of hand. "There shouldn't be any other humans around. You're safe here." She bit her lip. "Well, I can't promise that. You're safe from us."

Fieta snorted. Vandra wanted to give her a dirty look, but she didn't take her eyes off Lilani, trusting Pietyr to keep Fieta from doing anything rash.

"And we'll protect you." Vandra swallowed hard, feeling the blush in her cheeks. "The twins will protect you. I'll…" She wished she could think of something dashing and romantic, but all she came up with was, "Help you run away." It sounded even stupider outside her head.

Fieta snorted a little louder.

Lilani smiled. "If I must run away, it'll be nice to have a friend." She winced as if fearing she sounded stupid, too.

Vandra grinned, thoroughly charmed. "If you like, we can walk toward your forest and talk on the way." It seemed a better plan than turning south if it meant she'd get more information about the pylons.

And she'd get to spend more time with Lilani.

No, she had to keep her mind on the task at hand. She started walking toward the forest, gesturing for the twins to stay a few steps behind. Lilani fell in beside her but not so close that Vandra could have easily touched her.

"So." Vandra paused. She was usually so good at saying what she wanted, but now the words kept getting tangled. She wished she could sidle closer to Lilani, see if she could feel that invisible breeze, but she didn't dare do anything that might scare Lilani away.

"My people are looking for me." Lilani glanced over her shoulder at the twins. "If we meet them, please, do nothing. I'll convince them that I'm in no danger."

Her tone was reassuring, but her hands fluttered, and while that might mean something different to a seelie, to a human, it meant she was nervous.

"We won't antagonize anyone," Pietyr said.

"But we will defend ourselves," Fieta added.

Vandra waved for them to be quiet. "If we meet your people, I'll stay with Fieta and Pietyr while you greet them."

Lilani smiled again as if that was exactly what she wanted to hear. Vandra knew she should be asking about the pylons, but the idea of meeting more seelie triggered her curiosity. She thought of a hundred questions but couldn't bring herself to ask them. Every one of them seemed…rude.

By all the gods, the quest for knowledge was never rude! Why was this situation so weird? Politics? She much preferred gaining knowledge to practicing flowery words, but then she imagined Lilani's beautiful, foxlike features turning disdainful or furiously offended. Something inside Vandra would die if that happened.

That began to sound a lot like poetry, a bunch of nonsense. If Vandra passed up this opportunity to learn about the seelie, she'd be kicking herself forever. "Um…"

Lilani glanced at her. "We knew one of the pylons had gone out, but I'm afraid we don't know why."

"Ah, right. Good. I mean, not good, but…" She nearly groaned. "Look, I don't want to offend you." That seemed a good place to start.

Lilani blinked. "Good. I…don't want to offend you either."

Vandra breathed a laugh. "But I'm dying to ask some questions."

"About the seelie?" Her smile faded, but it wasn't a frown, not yet.

Still, Vandra's stomach sank. "Nothing personal, I swear! If I ask something personal, but I don't realize it's personal, tell me, and I won't ask again." Her ears were on fire.

And Fieta had the nerve to snort *again*.

"It's all right." Lilani's touch grazed Vandra's shoulder, and Vandra didn't know whether to lean in or jump away from the small gust of air that accompanied the touch. "You're the first humans I've met, too, though I've read about your people."

Vandra's thoughts exploded with images of seelie tomes and texts. With so much time on their hands, the possible number of books was staggering. "Your libraries must be amazing!"

"Do you like to read?" When Vandra nodded, Lilani's smile brightened so much it almost pained Vandra to look. "Me, too! What are human libraries like?"

Pietyr muttered, "Great," while Fieta said, "Wonderful," both of their voices heavy with sarcasm.

Vandra didn't care. For what seemed like only a few moments, they spoke rapturously about the books they'd read. Lilani seemed to favor stories over alchemical or engineering texts, but everything she said was fascinating. Vandra forgot why they were there or even where they were.

"Van," Pietyr said. "Keep it down."

Vandra glanced over her shoulder to see his frown and Fieta's leer. The pylon they'd just visited was far in the distance. How long had they been talking about books?

"Sorry," Lilani said. "I get a little carried away when it comes to reading."

Vandra shook her head. "It was my fault, really."

"You can share the blame," Fieta said.

Pietyr sighed. "Just share it a little quieter, all right?"

Lilani's smile and the twinkle in her eye said that the caution amused more than insulted her.

"Maybe we can visit each other's libraries," Vandra said. She pictured the two of them among the shelves. In the back. Snuggled together under a blanket. Her cheeks burned again, and she ducked her head. "For diplomacy."

"Diplomacy's nice." By her sly glance, Lilani might be thinking about secluded corners and blankets, too.

Vandra's insides lurched. Could it be? An immortal creature of beauty and…her? "Are your people really immortal?" When Lilani frowned, Vandra shook her head. "You don't have to answer that. I shouldn't have asked."

"To humans, we must seem so, but when seelie reach a certain age, they stop living, yet they're still alive." She waved a hand. "It's hard to explain without seeing it."

Vandra nodded, bookmarking that bit of information for another time, some other seelie. She told herself to turn the conversation back to the reason she was standing there now. "Do you know anything about the pylons' construction?"

"Not much. When my people helped build them—"

Vandra stumbled and stared, all the questions she'd lined up blowing away to be replaced with a hundred new ones. "You helped build them?"

"I know human memories are short, but surely someone wrote that down?"

Vandra went through everything she'd read but came up empty. She shook her head even as her mind raced. Was that why the pylons seemed so different from regular syndrium?

"If Vandra hasn't read it, it's not written down," Fieta said.

Vandra started walking again slowly. "I..." She shook her head. "Forget what I might or might not know. Please, start at the beginning."

"A seelie named Awith, who knew many humans before the tattered lands pushed them south, helped with the pylons' construction." She waved as if making room for her story. "Well, Awith knew them and loved them." She glanced away as if the idea embarrassed her.

Vandra's heart sank. Maybe Lilani considered humans beneath the seelie? Then what about their animated conversation or the shy looks they'd shared? After a deep breath, Vandra wrapped her academic curiosity around her like a shield. She couldn't afford embarrassment with lives on the line. "Please, go on."

"Awith gave her life helping activate the pylons." Lilani clasped her hands together and released them as if unsure what to say. Perhaps there were seelie secrets at work.

Vandra thought through the tales of the pylons' construction. Details were vague. At the time, no one had the opportunity to write anything down, and many had been killed. Vandra had always assumed that people had forgotten much of what happened by the time they put pen to paper, but maybe they hadn't wanted to mention a seelie woman who gave her life for the humans she loved.

"It was such a hurried time for humanity," Vandra said, ashamed of her people if they'd left out the seelie because of anger or jealousy or some other emotion that had no place in alchemy or engineering. "Some things just didn't get written down. And as you said, human memory is short."

Lilani nodded. "I didn't know of Awith until recently. Of course, I wasn't alive when the pylons were created."

"That makes two of us," Vandra said.

"Four of us," Fieta added.

Lilani gave them all a smile. So, she was at least under fifty.

Vandra didn't know what her people would think upon hearing that a seelie had contributed to the pylons. Some might not believe it. She didn't know if she believed it exactly. Any proof would have to come from the seelie, and some would never believe that.

Unless…

"Would anyone who was alive at the time be willing to speak with me?" Vandra asked. "Or do you think I could read Awith's tale?"

Lilani stared at nothing. "I can ask, but…" She sighed. "I don't want the pylons to fail. I don't want your people to die."

Vandra smiled. "So, you'll be our Awith?" She blushed again. "I mean…" She wasn't sure if she'd just propositioned Lilani or suggested that humanity would be the death of her. "I'm sorry."

Lilani laughed, a musical sound that echoed even more than her voice. "I understand. And yes, I will help you if I can."

Vandra forced herself to stop staring and think about those words, but her professional distance always ran away when she wanted it the most. "If you can? Your people don't agree?"

"Like everything else in the world, it's very complicated. Seelie memories are long."

And the history between their peoples wasn't always a happy one, though the books Vandra read slanted toward humanity being the injured party. She imagined it had been hard to grow old and infirm alongside people who stayed beautiful forever.

Or did they? Lilani's words about living while not living hinted that the seelie had their own problems, but maybe a human couldn't comprehend them.

Vandra didn't intend to let that stop her from trying. "Do you think I could visit your people? Or they could visit Parbeh, the city where I live."

"Van," Pietyr said, a warning in his tone. She knew what he meant. She wasn't an ambassador; she shouldn't be setting up meetings with other species.

Vandra glanced at him, noting his warning glare. Even Fieta seemed concerned now. "This isn't politics. It's alchemy."

Fieta barked a laugh while Pietyr sighed, but they both quieted.

Vandra looked ahead again, seeing not only the dead pylon but time slipping away. "I found this piece of metal—"

Lilani held up a hand, keeping Vandra from taking off her pack. "I can feel it."

Interesting. Vandra let her pack swing back behind her and wondered how long Lilani had been watching. And since Lilani had broached the subject… "Can you feel syndrium, too? My detector seems to know when you're around."

Lilani's face scrunched up as if she feared what she might say. Vandra felt a spike of annoyance. Not wanting to talk about personal issues was one thing, but she didn't have time to tread lightly around anyone's sensibilities where the pylons were concerned, even very attractive people whom she desperately wanted to know better.

That thought kept her from barking out any demands. "Please."

Lilani sighed. "It's probably the magical field that surrounds all seelie, that allows us to shroud." She gestured to her hair moving on its own around her shoulders. Before Vandra could ask, Lilani said, "I need to speak with my mother, the seelie empress, before I say more."

That put Vandra back on her heels. She hadn't realized she was talking to royalty.

"Wait," Fieta said. "Did she just say her mother is the *empress*? Of the seelie?"

"Who else would she be the empress of, dummy?" Pietyr asked.

Before Fieta could fire back, Vandra glared at them both. "I'm regretting bringing you two along!"

"I'm surprised you remembered us at all when you have books to talk about," Fieta said, returning her glare.

Pietyr cleared his throat and nodded toward Lilani. She was staring at nothing, and Vandra wondered if she realized what a risk she'd taken by telling them who her mother was, how valuable a hostage she'd make in the wrong hands. Vandra would never do such a thing, but if the fate of humanity grew darker, and the seelie held the keys to keeping the pylons intact…

Vandra stepped close. "Don't mention that your mother is the empress to anyone else." Lilani looked at her curiously, but Vandra shook her head. "Trust me."

Lilani nodded slowly. She seemed about to speak again, then stopped and held up a hand, her eyes wide with fear. "Don't move, Vandra, Fieta, Pietyr. They've come."

CHAPTER EIGHT

The grass rippled, the movement too uniform to be the wind. Lilani swallowed her fear for Vandra and took a few steps forward. She couldn't spot a shimmer no matter how hard she searched. Only the Guard could shroud so definitively.

Cobbled from soldiers of all the seelie enclaves, the Guard had at least a millennium's worth of experience between them. Lilani didn't know any of them *well*, though she'd spoken to all at one time or another. And none was exactly easygoing.

"I'm unharmed," Lilani said in the seelie tongue, repeating it in human speech. She gestured to Vandra and her siblings who'd wisely halted, weapons sheathed. "They were escorting me home."

Fieta muttered something. Vandra shushed her. All three stared intently into the grass, but they had less chance of seeing the Guard than Lilani did. Still, along with fear, Vandra also had an intense curiosity in her gaze that reminded Lilani of herself.

The grass ceased moving, but no seelie appeared. Lilani stood between the two groups, her hand out to keep Vandra from following.

"I'll speak to my mother on your behalf," Lilani said with a last smile for Vandra. "You *will* hear from me again."

Vandra seemed torn. "We can't wait here. We have to get back to Parbeh." She gestured to the distance. "It's the large city to the southeast."

Lilani thought for a moment. Her mother would never approve of her inviting humans to the Court. And with the shrouding magic inside the bones of the Highpeak, she didn't know if they would make it, anyway. But she needed to say something. She tried to think like her mother. Even if the humans fixed the dead pylon, more would come to make sure nothing happened to the others. Humanity wasn't going to go away. Change was upon the seelie whether they liked it or not.

"We'll come to Parbeh." Now that Lilani had said it, her mother would have to agree. "A delegation."

Vandra's shoulders relaxed as if she'd anticipated a far worse answer. Her smile faded as she glanced beyond Lilani at an invisible Guard that could kill her without showing themselves. "We'll watch for you." She chuckled a little at the joke, but Lilani's mother might very well send a group of shrouded seelie before an actual delegation. "And I'll have a word with…" Vandra's mouth worked as if she didn't know how to finish that sentence. "Someone important."

Lilani had to smile. Human politics were probably a lot like seelie politics, except debates couldn't rage for centuries with the same participants. "As will I."

Then the only thing to do was say good-bye. Lilani didn't want the Guard to become nervous, but being close to Vandra had been so much more fulfilling than seeing her from afar. Strands of her thick, dark hair had come undone from its tidy braid, and Lilani had to stop herself from stepping forward and tucking it back where it belonged. She'd be so beautiful with her hair free as she ran, as she and Lilani tumbled to the forest floor together…

Heat rose in Lilani's cheeks. She gathered her magic, shrouding. Vandra's eyes widened, but Lilani didn't stay to watch her gawk. She hurried toward the Seelie Forest, hearing faint shuffling as the Guard gathered around her.

Inside the trees, Lilani let the magic fall, happy that Vandra wouldn't witness her embarrassment as she leaned on her knees and breathed hard. She'd shrouded too much lately, and cramps clutched at her from feet to crown. Six members of the Guard appeared, including Captain Lucian. He stood head and shoulders above her and arched a thin blond eyebrow in her direction. His intricately carved leather armor could be mistaken for a dress piece until one looked closely and saw the scratches and worn edges along the dark brown surface; it had seen nearly as many battles as the seelie who wore it.

His pale face remained mostly inscrutable as he looked at her, his mild green eyes without reproach or commendation. That was a bad sign. He usually had a friendly word; that raised eyebrow was probably a question about her state of health.

"I'm all right," she said.

He nodded. When she was a child, he'd knelt before her, cautioning her gently about climbing certain walls or trees. She'd often woken up to find him in her house, though a few years passed before she realized that meant he'd spent the night with her mother. One night, in the midst of some crisis or another, he'd read to her from her favorite book as her mother rushed around.

Now he nodded toward the forest, and Faelyn stepped out from behind a clump of trees. When their eyes met, he opened his mouth, but before the lecture could come, she spoke over him.

"I need to speak with my mother."

Faelyn's mouth shut with a snap, and he drew himself straighter. "Exactly what I was going to suggest." He fell into step with her as she strode past. Lucian followed with the other guards fanning around them.

"Your new friends came very close to death today," Faelyn said.

"I know." Lilani eyed Lucian's weapons, all black-flecked steel imbued with syndrium. It was said that even the sight of such a weapon caused a human to quake. "It was worth the risk to meet Vandra and her siblings. They're only trying to help their people."

The Guard stayed silent, but they were no doubt paying attention. Lilani spoke briefly of what Vandra had said, stressing that she hadn't known the seelie were involved in the construction of the pylons. Faelyn's expression went grim, and by the way he eyed her, he wasn't certain she should have told the humans about Awith. She didn't want to argue; she'd get all the disagreement she needed from her mother.

Daylight was failing by the time they reached the Court, but the Guard didn't disperse until they came within sight of Lilani's door. That didn't bode well; her mother must have given them very specific instructions. Maybe they'd linger outside to make sure she didn't leave again.

Faelyn waited at the door as she went inside. Another bad sign. He'd seen her receive more than a few lectures. She must be in for something truly embarrassing this time. Lilani closed the door gently, listening. No sound came from the stairway to the second level, but she heard the sound of pacing from the solarium to the right. She tiptoed that way, peeking into the glass-ceilinged room crowded with plants and comfortable divans. It was a perfect reading room, completely relaxing, but after tonight, Lilani doubted she'd see it that way for a long time.

Her mother paced, wringing her hands, her hair a whirlwind around her shoulders. Lilani wanted to run away but made herself step in and clear her throat. Her mother whirled around, eyes wide. Lilani steeled herself, but her mother ran toward her and pulled her into an embrace.

Lilani paused before returning the hug. Her mother had never been cold, but physical shows of affection had become rare as the years went by. Before Lilani could sigh in relief, her mother stepped back.

"What were you thinking?"

Lilani almost asked, "About what?" but now was not the time to try her mother's patience. She launched into her tale, not giving her mother time to ask questions or censure her. She emphasized how the tattered lands made her feel, how they couldn't live with such corruption surrounding them. She said the pylons should be repaired, adding that Faelyn agreed with her. Silently, she hoped he would forgive her for using him.

Her mother stared when the tale was done, seemingly stunned. At last, she sat on one of the divans, her hair only fluttering now. She rested her hands on her knees and leaned far forward, staring at the floor.

"You told them we would come to them, help them." She breathed deep and stared at Lilani with eyes like bottomless wells.

"I had no choice! The tattered lands—"

"Do not lecture me about the tattered lands!" Her mother stood and paced again, so much magic swirling around her that it fluttered the drapes and turned the plants into a roomful of whispers. "I know how it feels to walk among the corruption. I fled south with my enclave before my father's death, then I *returned* to rescue the injured from other enclaves. I carried them on my back through miles of despair!" She shouted, and Lilani could nearly feel the chill winds of the tattered lands gusting around her. "I remember the eyes of those who could not shroud and were twisted into nightmares, their own magic used against them!" She turned furious eyes in Lilani's direction.

Lilani fought the urge to look away. She swallowed hard, letting the pain of a dry throat center her. "I know what you sacrificed,

Mother. And you know what's at stake far better than me. You know that living next to the tattered lands, trying to keep them out after they have consumed everything, will be a far worse fate than living next to humanity."

Her mother spread her arms as if taking in the whole world. "So, she has met some humans and is now an expert, so much more knowledgeable than those of us with centuries behind us. She knows more than the maimed, than the relatives of those who have been murdered."

Patience, Lilani tried to tell herself, but her own magic was edging up. She hated it when her mother spoke as if she wasn't in the room. She thought they'd left that particular tactic behind years ago. She arched an eyebrow. "Yes, I know more about *these* humans than anyone."

Her mother's mouth slipped open. She blinked as if she hadn't heard correctly.

Lilani held up a hand. "How long has it been since anyone else has spoken to a human? Were there any after Awith? Because every human she knew is likely dead. So yes, I'm the current expert because my humans are *alive*. They are nothing like any human who came before them because—as you have often told me—humans are always changing. And this current crop has asked very politely for our help." She lowered her tone, stepped close, and took her mother's hand. "I'm not suggesting we open our borders. I will remember the stories. I'll keep my eyes open and my heart closed." She swallowed, seeing a flash of Vandra and not knowing if she could keep that promise. "I will remember what Awith *and* those who criticized her said. The point is, we have to work with the humans if we're going to keep the tattered lands from surrounding us." She swallowed and launched ahead with something her mother might more easily embrace. "Maybe after we help them, we can expand our borders, make more cautious forays into the human lands. Maybe we'll grow again."

Her mother frowned but didn't take back her hand. She had to be thinking of the book of births and deaths, how the numbers rarely moved. "I should never have shown you Awith's journal. You're far too young and impressionable. You wouldn't see what I wanted you to see."

Lilani chuckled. "I thought that was *why* you gave it to me."

Her mother only shook her head. "And I suppose you want to be part of this delegation?"

More than anything, but she tried to keep her face neutral. "Like it or not, my feet are already on this path. I need to see it to the end, Mother."

"I will not have humans here." Her finger stabbed at the floor. "No matter how amiable they may be. If they see what we have, they will want it. Oceans of them will beg for us to shroud them, and we cannot possibly host them all." Her eyes went distant again. "They try to take what we won't give. They can't understand that without us, there is no magic."

Lilani squeezed her mother's hand, unwilling to let this conversation become lost in the past again. "I made it clear we'd come to them."

"By the elders." Her mother put a hand to her forehead. "A group of my people in human hands." She stared hard at Lilani. "My only child."

Lilani tried to hide her excitement, moved by her mother's worry and wanting to acknowledge it but also wanting her mother to hurry up and agree. "I already know three of them. How hard can it be to win the others over?"

"Is this the time for jokes?"

Probably not, but Lilani had never felt so close to getting something she desperately wanted, something important. "Slaughtering the delegation won't help them at all. Surely they'll see that."

Her mother sighed. "That won't stop them from imprisoning you and trying to force you to teach them how to shroud, and they won't believe you when you tell them they cannot. Or they'll use you as a hostage against me."

Lilani thought of Vandra's chilling words about revealing her identity. She wouldn't tell anyone else and hoped Vandra didn't either. "They won't need to threaten us if we're already helping them." She sighed, hoping her chances to be part of the delegation hadn't entirely slipped away. "These are not the humans of old. Even if they're no better, they're generations removed from old grudges. All they have are stories, and we can combat those with new tales of helpfulness and camaraderie."

"And a host of guards carrying enough weaponry that even the stupidest human will keep their distance."

That sounded reasonable, though Lilani didn't think it would be wise to march with an army's worth of seelie. She needed enough guards to make their party a respectable, intimidating size, but she said nothing, seeing the way before her brighten.

"And Faelyn will go to keep you in check."

Lilani nodded at that, too. She could get around him when she needed, and he was sympathetic to her cause. The Guard would be harder to manage. They wouldn't be moved by pleas or good humor. She supposed that was for the best. She didn't know her way around this city of Parbeh. She would need protection, and the human leaders might not be as accommodating as Vandra. A show of force would be required to show that the seelie meant business.

With a smile, Lilani put her arms around her mother again and resisted the urge to squirm when minutes slipped past, and her mother's embrace didn't loosen.

Never had traveling felt so grating to Vandra. Her wish to remain gone from Parbeh for an extended period seemed years in the past. Now, she wished there was some formula that would let her return home in an instant. There was so much to do. She had to speak to Ariadne, study the tattered metal, research whether or not someone could have replaced the pylon without anyone knowing, and find a way to either reignite the dead pylon or build a new one. And she'd authorized a seelie visit to Parbeh! She'd didn't have that authority. Ariadne didn't even have that authority, but the seelie were still coming.

As they made camp that night, worry twisted Vandra's stomach. By the gods, there were so many stupid ways a human might react to a seelie visit. The seelie were coming to help, so it didn't make sense to treat them badly, but in Vandra's experience, people who worked outside of the university rarely made sense.

Even the ones inside spoke nonsense now and again.

"How many invisible warriors do you think there were?" Fieta asked.

Vandra blinked at her, at the camp. She'd nearly forgotten the physical world existed. They'd hurried away from the Seelie Forest, stopping in a secluded copse before nightfall. It reeked of whatever animal had used it before them, but Vandra supposed it was easier on the twins' nerves than being inside a forest surrounded by invisible opponents.

Staring into the fire, Pietyr shrugged. "More than one. I could see the grass moving, but it was hard to tell. I smelled leather oil."

Fieta shook her head. "I knew they could do that, but…" She tossed the dregs of her mug into the fire, making the flames spit. "It was so much easier on the nerves when I thought you were making up women, Van."

Vandra snorted. Maybe the populace of Parbeh would also refuse to believe the seelie existed. Though how they could be presented with a creature as lovely as Lilani and still want to deny her existence…

When she looked up, the twins were grinning, though Pietyr's look was far kinder. "When you make up women, Van, you don't do it by halves," he said. "She's lovely."

Vandra shrugged through her embarrassment. "As if that matters."

Fieta's grin widened. "You sure noticed. Babbling like a schoolgirl."

Heat rushed to Vandra's cheeks. "I was not!"

The twins glanced at each other as if they'd scored a point. Vandra glared at them then crawled into the tent. Even with the teasing ringing in her ears, she was happy Lilani followed her into her dreams.

The next day, Vandra wanted to bypass Saribelle and continue on, but the twins reminded her that they'd never make it to Parbeh before the day was through. And the deeper they went into habitable areas, the more likely they were to run into trouble. They stayed at the same inn, and while it felt lovely to have a bath, Vandra's mind worked too hard for her to enjoy anything. She longed for past days of research, when she could ignore pesky concerns like time and sleeping and eating.

Then her thoughts would tip toward Lilani: her hair, her aura, and the pointed tips of her ears. The distance between them was an uncomfortable ache, like a freshly pulled tooth she couldn't stop searching for.

When they reached Parbeh the next day, Vandra made directly for the Assembly House, knowing Ariadne would be there. Even though she was tired, with an aching back, she couldn't wait. She felt the pressure of the tattered metal inside her pack, had felt it oozing into her consciousness.

When they marched into the Assembly House, they were directed to an antechamber, the only area open to the general public. Everyone stared at their dusty clothes and large packs. When a junior clerk approached them with a disdainful sniff, Vandra was ready to yell at him simply for being alive, but Pietyr introduced them as guests of Ariadne. The clerk's sneer turned into a look of such surprise as he checked his list that Vandra nearly laughed at him. Ariadne had left orders that Vandra be admitted to her office. There they had to wait again, and Vandra refused to sit, wanting to pace if she couldn't start her research.

When Ariadne finally came through the door, Vandra started talking, and the entire tale spilled out in a rush. To her credit, Ariadne didn't seem as perturbed as Vandra would have been in her place. She sat behind her desk and took everything in without expression. Vandra supposed she'd had plenty of practice doing that while listening to political opponents.

Once Vandra finished, Ariadne stared over her interlaced fingers. "You have this piece of metal with you now? Is that what this…miasma about you is?"

Vandra shifted as if Ariadne had said they smelled bad. Which they probably did. "Yes."

Ariadne scribbled something on a piece of paper. "This order should get you all the equipment you need to study the metal, but I want you to wait until the students and other professors have gone home for the night." She scribbled another note and handed it to Fieta. "And this will get you two more time off so you can guard Vandra's door."

Vandra swallowed hard. "What about the seelie? What if I can't run the experiments I need in time? What if the other pylons…" She took a breath and tried to relax, but her back felt like a sack of knots, and a headache that had been threatening for hours was pounding through her temples.

Ariadne smiled, calm as ever, though the dark circles under her eyes said she was tired, too. "I'll send some trusted runners to the other pylons." She took a deep breath. "And the monarchs will need to know what's been going on now that we have proof, and now that we'll have visitors. Tomorrow afternoon, I should be able to bring you before the assembly."

Vandra's stomach burned just thinking about it. "Great."

"Don't worry," Ariadne said with a grin. "They'll have lots of questions, but I'll be with you the entire time. Stick with the facts."

Except this wasn't just about facts. She'd heard that some in the assembly wanted everyone around them to fail so their successes looked even more impressive, and others might dispute everything Vandra said just because she was tied to Ariadne. Some professors acted the same way. They wanted any supposed rivals to be discredited, no matter what.

Ariadne got up and laid a comforting hand on Vandra's shoulder. "You'll do fine. Just tell the truth."

"About everything?" Vandra asked. "Even the seelie?"

Ariadne sat on her desk. "They're already coming, so yes. I'll send a message to the head assemblyperson, and she'll tell the five monarchs before the assembly meets. We'll stress that the seelie volunteered to come. You did not invite them on anyone's authority. There might be some political maneuvering, but we'll have to hope that most of the assembly will see an opportunity rather than a slight."

Vandra nodded again. "Sounds like very murky waters."

"Get some rest," Ariadne said as she stood. "And maybe don't tell your parents you've come back just yet."

Vandra chuckled tiredly. They'd shared many parent stories, and Ariadne was right. If Vandra's parents found out she'd returned, there would be demands for dinner and information. Better that they found out what had happened as the city did, never mind that it would take them weeks to forgive her for holding back the juiciest gossip of the century.

Chapter Nine

When Lilani went outside the next morning, the seelie Court had a murmur running through it. It hadn't taken long for word of her trip to Parbeh to spread, and whether people supported her or not, everyone was talking about it.

Her mother hadn't given any orders to keep quiet, so Lilani answered questions freely, trying to gain information on humans as well as spreading stories about Vandra's curiosity and friendliness. She tried to speak as eloquently as possible, but after too many concerned or shuttered looks, she felt as if she was trying to walk unaided up the side of the Highpeak.

She heard tale after tale of murder and deception, many of them familiar. Even the seelie who'd never met a human, who never cared to, felt the need to reiterate how nasty humanity could be. Most said she shouldn't go. They spoke calmly, and that made Lilani's teeth ache more than if they'd yelled or panicked. But extreme reactions weren't the seelie way. Instead, they had endless discussions with calm, cool voices saying the same things over and over. Lilani finally fled into the orchard behind her house and climbed a tree just in case any of the worriers followed her. She didn't think her mother would take it kindly if she left the Court again.

"Lilani?" Faelyn's voice soon called.

She opened her mouth to reply then shut it. She'd rather eat glass than hear another lecture.

"Don't make me search every tree in the forest."

She smiled. If he could joke, he couldn't be that angry. "Up here." When he climbed up beside her and settled in, she said, "Please tell me you're trying to get away from all the naysayers, too."

"I'm not going to lecture you, if that's what you're asking. I've met some humans I liked." He nudged her shoulder. "And some I didn't. But I wouldn't try to convince a relative of Awith's that humans can't be in her future."

She sighed. "Why do our people have to talk everything to death?"

"You'd rather they used their fists?"

"Like the humans?" she asked, rolling her eyes.

"Some of them. You have to be prepared for the bad with the good."

She rested her head on his shoulder. "That sounds dangerously close to lecture territory."

"I'm a teacher. We teach."

"I won't disobey the Guard. I won't…deliberately disobey you."

He snorted. "Yes, your mother told me I was going. *Thank you* for bringing me into it." He nudged her. "And don't think that 'deliberately' floated right past me either."

She sighed. "I'm not going to run off and—"

"Even if *Vandra* invites you to do a little sightseeing?"

She blushed, happy she couldn't look him in the eye from her position. "You can come along."

"Very gracious of you. And the Guard will come, too. You and your intriguing new friend will *not* be getting any alone time."

She leaned back, giving him an appraising glance, trying to see if he was really upset or if this was just his usual sarcasm. "Aren't you curious at all?"

He shrugged, and she didn't know if that meant he was or wasn't. Like he'd said, he'd known humans in the past. If she'd had some history with humans, meeting new ones would have made her even more curious to see how they'd changed. The thought excited her, but he seemed calm as ever. Maybe she could shake him up, get some real feelings out of him, something that wasn't a rehash of the past.

"I want to see them use their fists," she said.

He blinked at her.

"Not on me," she said. "Or any seelie. I want to see them argue, to get mad or excited, anything. I think they can help us as much as we can help them, Faelyn. We can keep our eyes open for treachery; we can learn from our mistakes. Maybe we can finally forgive, too. And their capriciousness can breathe new life into us."

"There are many who won't want that."

She nodded. "But once we break our forced exile, those who want to get to know the humans will be free to do so. Surely there will be humans who want to get to know us, too. We can explain to the humans why they can't come here. The magic makes it too hard for them. And if that means they won't let us into their cities, either, maybe we can make new places where humans *and* seelie are welcome."

He gave her a kind but patronizing look. "Beginning a relationship by saying someone isn't welcome in your home? Sounds like something I might do." He sighed again. "Most probably won't mind us coming to them. Some won't want us to leave, especially when they learn about our natural magic. They have a hunger for syndrium. They may want to wring it out of us."

She shuddered at the image and remembered what she'd said to Vandra about her magical field. Maybe she shouldn't have done that, either. "We'll have to be careful about what we say."

"Lying *and* saying they can't visit us? Better and better."

"If you keep being cynical, I will shove you out of my tree."

He chuckled and held up his hands. "Teachers also make up problems for the students to solve."

"*Incidents* will happen," she said. "But we can't let that stop us. I have to believe that the good will outweigh the bad." She clenched a fist, willing that statement to be true.

"And if it doesn't?"

Then humanity was doomed, but she didn't say it. They hadn't made the pylons without seelie help. They might not be able to repair them without it, either. Once they knew that, they'd *have* to accept seelie in their lands while also accepting seelie boundaries. She supposed some might want to take hostages and demand help, but if it was already being offered…

"We'll be friendly but wary," she said.

He smiled. "My thoughts exactly."

Now she really did want to push him. "Then why didn't you say so? Why all those doom-laden questions?"

"To make sure you've thought about them."

"So, it was a lecture! You're just like everyone else no matter what you say. You'll be inviting me home to tea in no time."

He grinned. "Unlike the others, I'm firmly on your side. That's why I'm hiding up here with you."

He could have said that from the beginning, but apparently, he had to keep justifying why he was the teacher in their relationship. And glaring at him wouldn't help. Instead, they leaned together and watched evening fall around them, turning the orchard into shadows. One of the Guard checked on Lilani, but she made sure to ask that no one but her mother know where she was hiding. The murmur of voices drifted over the short orchard wall as the streets were set for dinner, and lanterns bobbed hypnotically in the dark.

Lilani hadn't realized she was drowsing until the wind gusted over her. She blinked sleepily. The street in front of her house stood abandoned, with only a few hanging lanterns driving back the shadows. Groups of fireflies flashed through the orchard, and the leaves fluttered gently in the breeze, calling her back to sleep.

A soft snore woke her again. Faelyn had fallen asleep, too, resting his head on her arm. She moved to wake him but spotted someone below their tree, tiptoeing through the orchard.

Lilani froze, watching. The figure continued toward the back of her house. Maybe it was one of her lovers thinking to climb in a window as if in some romantic poem. She shook her head. No, she would *not* enjoy someone randomly appearing in her bedroom. Her friends would know that. Besides, she had too much to think about to relax into lovemaking.

And Vandra kept coming to mind.

Someone wanting to see her mother then. In secret? Maybe they were going to discuss something Lilani's mother would be reluctant to share. About humans? She had to know. Lilani gently shifted Faelyn's head onto the tree trunk and slipped down. She drew her magic around herself and shrouded, wondering why the shadowy figure didn't do the same.

The figure climbed the ivy clinging to the house, heading for the second level, the bedrooms. Lilani gained speed, keeping her shroud tight. Perhaps this poetic lover/conspirator wasn't good at shrouding and couldn't do it while moving, let alone climbing.

Lilani grinned. All the easier to follow them, then. Maybe this had nothing to do with her trip to Parbeh and was only someone who was trying to win her mother's heart. If they paused outside her mother's bedroom and crooned a romantic song, she would collapse with laughter. Her mother would toss them both out on their ears.

Lilani went in through the back door and hurried through the dark house, knowing the way by memory. She ran up the stairs and paused on the landing, listening.

A faint scuffle from down the hall. She edged closer to the window nearest the sitting room. If the nocturnal climber didn't go directly to her mother's window, the sitting room was closest. Another noise came, farther down the hall. Lilani took a few steps, straining to listen.

The sound came again. Her room.

She frowned and moved to the doorway of her bedroom. The shadow eased over the window ledge. Several fireflies drifted through behind it, sparks in the darkness that tantalized more than revealed. Lilani opened her mouth to speak, but the figure tiptoed toward her bed, and she wanted to see what they would do.

Her bedclothes were as rumpled as always. She never saw the wisdom in straightening what she'd only sleep in later. The figure touched their waist and reached for the edge of the bed. Lilani saw a glint of metal, a knife. She pressed her hand to her mouth, her heart pounding. She couldn't move. The knife glinted as it tore into the cloth of the pillow with an awful shredding sound. Lilani uttered a little cry, and the shadow turned.

And vanished.

Lilani stumbled back as pounding footsteps echoed toward her. Lilani's magic held tightly, nearly suffocating her as she stumbled away. The shimmer of the enemy's shroud collided with her shoulder, their shroud flickering, and the knife gleamed again. Lilani fell, knocking into the hall table as the knife sheared into the wall with a dull crunch.

The table clattered and collapsed, sending Lilani and a handful of figurines crashing to the floor. She scuttled backward, hands raking over shards of pottery that bit into her palms like tiny knives.

The pain brought home the notion that she should shriek, alert her mother, but then the enemy would know exactly where she was. Or maybe they could see better in the dark, and they were following the trickle of blood and her path through the shards.

"Lilani?" A light flared under her mother's door.

"Mother!" She rolled, keeping her shroud as she hit the wall and felt along it, looking for a way up, a way out, anything.

The footsteps pounded away, heading down the stairs.

"Lilani!" Her mother appeared at the end of the hall in her long, pale nightgown. She had a needle-like rapier in one hand and a lantern in the other. Her hair whipped around her shoulders. When she spotted the broken figurines, she set the lantern down then vanished, wrapped in her own shroud.

Lilani couldn't even see a shimmer, and the other form had fled. She let her own shroud drop. "Here."

Her mother blinked back, still searching the hallway as she skirted the mess and hauled Lilani upright. "What happened?" She stepped between Lilani and the staircase, sword on guard.

"The door," Lilani said, still struggling to breathe, to have the world make sense. "They headed for the door!"

Her mother took her hand, grabbed the lantern, and headed down the stairs. The front door stood open. Lilani's mother shut it quickly. "Light the other lamps."

When the room was awash with light, her mother turned to her. "Tell me what happened." She glanced toward the stairs as if expecting trouble to rush at them again.

"Someone stabbed the bed, Mother. They thought it was me, and they stabbed it, and then they shrouded and came after me." Tears began to flow as she saw it happening again, and she clutched her mother's hand more tightly than she ever had.

Her mother went still, thinking. Lilani nearly cried out for her to move, to offer assurances, protections. She jerked her mother close, forcing an embrace.

"There now." Her arms went around Lilani's shoulders, but she didn't drop the rapier, not yet. "I have you, my heart."

"Wanted…wanted to kill me."

"No one will harm you. Not while I live." She kissed Lilani's temple. "You must tell the story from the beginning."

Lilani clung to her mother and sobbed, seeing the knife in the dark here, in the safest of all places. How would she ever be able to sleep again? She shifted as her mother moved them close to the wall, then a deep, hollow thrum filled the small space. She risked a look. Her mother had struck the gong that sat in an alcove to the side of the foyer. It had been installed to summon the Guard, but when had they ever needed it before?

Lilani took a step back and wiped her eyes. She didn't want the Guard to see her falling apart, but that accursed knife wouldn't leave her memory. Was this because of her recent adventures? Maybe she should have never gotten involved with humans, never met Vandra, none of it.

But she had to take the good with the bad. Hope for the best; prepare for the worst.

No! That was with humans, not her own people.

The door flew open, and five of the Guard burst in, all in their nightclothes with weapons ready. Lilani had known they took turns manning the nearby guardhouse, but it was for show. They *laughed* about it. Lucian often sat outside of it, feet propped up on the railing, ready in case his empress wanted him for more than guard duty.

His face was tight with worry now, his eyes flicking to Lilani's hands, and she only then remembered she'd cut herself. She'd left bloody handprints on her mother's nightgown.

"Search the house," her mother said. "Detain anyone you find. Watch for shrouds."

The Guard fanned out, Lucian staying with Lilani and her mother. He guided Lilani to a chair and knelt to examine her hands. Her mother stood over them, rapier at the ready.

"Empress?" Lucian asked, so formal when he had a job to do. But he gave Lilani a calm smile as he gently plucked a shard from her hand.

Lilani's mother rested a hand on her shoulder. "Tell him, my heart."

Stammering, focusing on the pain as Lucian tended her hands, Lilani told the story, trying to hurry through as if that would push it further into the past.

The Guard finished the search, and one of them brought Lilani's shredded pillow. Her lip quivered when she saw it. No one had ever wanted to harm her before. As much as she'd feared speaking to Vandra and her siblings, she'd never really believed they'd hurt her.

She took a deep breath, then another. When Lucian finished with her hands, she clasped them together and tried to stop herself from trembling. She wasn't really sitting there. None of this had happened to her. Instead, she imagined standing at the edge of this room, listening to someone else tell the story of a nighttime lurker. Lucian relayed the details to the Guard, and their faces grew even grimmer. They stood as still as statues, and for once, Lilani was grateful. If they'd hugged her or offered comforting words, she would have burst into tears again.

When Faelyn stepped into the doorway, the Guard rounded on him, weapons up. He raised his hands. "What happened?"

Lilani's mother waved him in. Since he'd been sleeping beside her in the tree, he couldn't be the person they were after.

"There has been an attempt on my daughter's life," her mother said with a voice like steel. She turned to Lucian. "Summon the rest of the Guard and find this person."

He nodded, told two guards to remain at the house, and asked Lilani's mother to keep the door shut. It didn't have a lock. Her mother moved to have a quiet word with him before he left, and Faelyn sat at Lilani's side, looking at her wounded hands. Most of the cuts were shallow; they'd stopped bleeding. She rubbed her thumb over one that had already scabbed.

"Are you all right?" he asked softly.

No one else had really asked, not the way he meant it. "No, but I don't want to…" Tears threatened again. She breathed and looked to the ceiling.

He took a deep breath and let it out slowly. "Breathe. Like that."

"What if… Faelyn, what…"

"No, not right this moment. Now, all you have to do is breathe. Then there can be action. Right now, you're just living."

She took his advice, doing nothing but listening to her own breath and her heartbeat pounding in her ears.

It had passed midday, and Vandra's steps through the city were dragging. She wasn't certain if the twins slowed in solidarity or if they were as tired as she was. Seeing the arched edifices of the university had her sighing in relief. At last, she could get to work. Even though the university was the site of all her recent failures, it was also a place she knew well, with instruments and chemicals she was familiar with. Given time, she could crack the mystery of the tattered metal. She was the expert on syndrium, no matter how many times she'd failed. Others had tried to duplicate her one success, and they'd failed, too. It brought some comfort to know it wasn't just her.

Vandra hurried through the halls, dodging students and faculty. Fieta visited the kitchen stores while Pietyr went to the equipment lab and gathered the tools Vandra needed. When they met in Vandra's office, she saw that Fieta had also acquired three cots.

"Where did you get those?" Vandra asked.

Fieta only grinned. Vandra sighed and hoped she wouldn't be hearing about three freshmen who'd suddenly found themselves without beds. Between the cots, Vandra's desk, and her worktable, there wasn't much room to maneuver, at least until Vandra lay down. Ariadne had told them to wait for dark, and the only way Vandra could think of to put off anyone who might come looking was to pretend no one was here. They all lay down and blew out the candle. Her office had no window, so the room plunged into blackness, and since afternoon classes were nearly done, the hallway stayed quiet. Vandra fell into a fitful sleep with visions of the seelie following her into her dreams.

That night, Vandra lit every lamp in her office as the twins set the cots to the side. She rubbed her hands together before she took the tattered metal from its containers and set it on her worktable with a thump. She stared at the jagged edge before fetching a clamp and securing the metal to the table. She tried her shears again, and the same ringing feeling as before nearly vibrated the tool out of her hand.

Fieta stuck her hands in her ears and frowned from near the door. "You already tried that!"

"You can talk or you can stay. Not both." Vandra made a note that the same experiment failed under controlled conditions.

She tried acid next and noted that the metal seemed resistant, though she did get a hint of foam, but unlike the blue of syndrium, this was nearly black and foul smelling. She quickly dumped bicarbonate of soda over the acid then placed the metal under a glass dome. When they had to stand outside the open door and let the room air out, Fieta gave her another look.

"Am I allowed to talk in the hallway?" Fieta asked.

"No," Pietyr said. She shoved his arm. Vandra hurried back inside to make another note, excited that *something* was finally happening.

She succeeded in scraping the metal with a chisel edged in diamond, but it didn't react with any other chemicals. She sprinkled a small amount of syndrium on top and stared in fascination as the syndrium faded from its normal silvery-blue to the gray of common slate.

Vandra took a reading with her detector, but it ignored the metal, honing in on the syndrium scattered through the university, the city. The bit of metal didn't seem to affect any other syndrium unless it was sitting right on top.

So, it was part of something larger, an experiment or apparatus. She put it back in the lead box anyway and ran tests on the soil samples, finding traces of inert acid and lead as well as flecks of iron, and some other metal, the traces of which were too small to identify. Someone had been performing alchemical experiments in that field. To affect the pylon? She'd entertained the absurd idea that someone had dismantled the pylon and erected a new one made of stone without anyone noticing, but now that she'd found proof of alchemy, there was more to this puzzle than brute strength. Someone had found a way to turn syndrium into stone.

Like her formula in reverse.

Vandra drummed her fingers on the table. She put the samples away and sought her books, reading until her eyes grew bleary. There were so few facts about the tattered lands, but there were plenty of stories. Anyone who ventured inside to run experiments risked being corrupted. She tried cross-referencing the tattered lands research with stories about the seelie but didn't find much there, either, save that the seelie had innate magical powers. Vandra had seen that firsthand. And their magical fields read as syndrium. Maybe they had it running through their veins somehow? That could be a clue to their longevity.

Vandra started writing that down then stopped, her hand hovering over the page. She'd never been in the position where her work might harm someone, but if she hinted that the seelie were made of syndrium, she'd be putting Lilani and her people in danger. Her alchemist heart wanted to write everything down, but if she became a source of pain to Lilani…

Was that why no one had made this "discovery" before?

"Van?" Pietyr asked. "Are you finished?"

She shook her head and wished she had the knowledge humanity had lost when they'd fled the tattered lands. Were the books still out there somewhere, lingering in abandoned libraries? Or did the tattered lands corrupt inanimate objects as it did living ones, and in some ancient library, feral books roamed the hallways?

It was getting too late.

Pietyr was still watching her. She smiled. "Almost done."

Fieta leaned against the door in a chair, her eyes shut, arms crossed. Their nap seemed a long time in the past. Vandra stretched; maybe they should all sleep. She didn't want to be groggy for the assembly.

But one pylon was still dead, and whoever had done it might be trying to sabotage the others. Had Ariadne said she'd send guards or scouts to check? Now that Vandra had confirmed alchemy and not a natural phenomenon, Ariadne had to send guards without delay. And since sending a messenger across Parbeh with such secret information was out of the question…

Fieta came awake with a start when Vandra touched her shoulder. "Is it…" She blinked around her. "Are we done?"

"Nice guarding," Pietyr said as he buckled on his sword.

"At least I was blocking the door," she said.

"We have to run an errand," Vandra said, "and then I promise, there will be sleep." She put the lead-lined box into her pack and hoisted the entire thing over her shoulder, not wanting to leave any evidence lying around.

For all their grumbling, the twins came alert more easily than she ever did, and soon the three of them hurried through the night. The twins knew the Watch patrol routes and easily avoided them, not wanting to answer any awkward questions. When they reached Ariadne's house, Vandra paused outside the door. The servants had no doubt gone home for the night. Ariadne would be asleep. If they knocked hard enough to wake her, they might alert the neighbors *and* the Watch.

She debated for a few moments, her tired brain trying to reach a decision before Pietyr said, "Come on," and led them behind the row of houses to where an alley ran between the small garden walls. Pietyr scaled Ariadne's wall with ease and unlatched the gate from the inside. Vandra was tempted to ask if he'd learned that from the Watch or his brief gang days.

"I don't want to break into her house," Pietyr said. "Do you know which window is her bedroom?"

Vandra shook her head. She'd never been here before, but she assumed it would be on the second floor. She hoped Ariadne lived alone, and they weren't about to wake her *and* her lover. Vandra had no idea what she'd say then, picturing herself rushing to explain that she wasn't some paramour.

Well, not anymore.

Fieta tossed pebbles at all the windows until Vandra was certain the neighbors would be stirring, but Ariadne remained asleep.

"Maybe she's not home," Vandra whispered. "She might be sleeping in her office, working late."

Fieta struck a match and tried the back door. It opened easily. "Unlocked." She and Pietyr *tsked*, their inner Watch officers peeking out.

Vandra stepped inside the darkened house, her throat dry. It wasn't like Ariadne to leave a door unlocked. They'd both grown up with lots of siblings and an exaggerated need for privacy. "Let me wake her," Vandra said, hoping the door was just a tired slip on Ariadne's part. "There's less of a chance she'll scream if it's me." She hoped Ariadne hadn't learned any fighting moves since they'd been lovers. It wouldn't do to be nursing a broken arm on top of everything else.

The house remained eerily still. A ball of dread bloomed in Vandra's stomach, growing by the second. She struck a match as they tromped upstairs. Only two rooms waited above, the first with a desk inside, and the other with a bed along one wall, a lump lying in the middle.

"Ariadne?" Vandra whispered loudly, but even then, she knew she'd get no answer.

The lump didn't move. Too still. Vandra tried to swallow, but her mouth had turned to sand.

"I smell blood," Fieta said, not bothering to keep her voice down.

"Careful, Van," Pietyr said.

Vandra's wooden steps carried her toward the bed. The tangle of blankets didn't stir, not even when Vandra held the match close. She couldn't look past the foot of the bed. Only Pietyr's gasp and Fieta's murmur made her follow the pale coverlet upward.

The blood covering Ariadne's throat and chin glinted ruby red. Her wide, dark eyes stared at nothing, and her mouth hung slack. One hand had been flung across her body, the other lay on her breast, fingers curved toward her throat as if she'd been trying to hold in the lifeblood that had been stolen from her.

CHAPTER TEN

Pain flared in Vandra's fingers as the match burned down to her skin. She dropped it, cursing, plunging the room into darkness. Somehow, not seeing Ariadne was so much worse. But when Fieta struck another match and lit a candle on the bedside table, Vandra turned away, but the image of Ariadne's ruined throat followed her.

"Van?" Pietyr's voice. He guided her to a chair. She couldn't thank him, couldn't do anything. Memories kept resurfacing: Ariadne laughing back when the bickering of her colleagues amused rather than annoyed her, little noises she'd made during lovemaking, the sight of her dashing from a room while still pulling her clothes on. She lived on the cusp of being late.

Had lived.

Dimly, Vandra heard the twins moving around the room, investigating, discussing the crime in hushed, business-like tones. She wanted to tell them that whoever wanted to destroy the pylons had done this; they'd probably been following Ariadne all over the city. To her office, her home.

To Vandra.

She jumped out of her chair. "They know we're back!"

The twins gawked, but she was already moving. Why kill Ariadne unless the enemy knew Vandra had returned and that she'd discovered something?

"We have to report this," Fieta said as they rushed downstairs. "Van!"

"Ariadne wanted to keep everything secret," Vandra said.

"Not her own murder!"

"Fieta, we have to get home," Vandra said. "Whoever killed her might be looking for us, too." If the pylons failed, everyone would die, but that felt less important than making sure her family was safe. Vandra's rational mind tried to tell her that didn't make sense, but emotions ruled her at the moment. Even so, part of her found her behavior both fascinating and annoying.

The tidy row of houses in their neighborhood stood dark and silent; the sight made Vandra's chest constrict. Ariadne's house had looked the same, but only horrors lay within. She rushed toward the short fence that protected the tiny front yard. The gate opened easily, the latch still broken after so many years. Why hadn't her parents ever fixed it? It was one more barrier between them and…

She paused. A dark shape lounged on the front steps. Bess, one of the many cats who'd frequented their property over the years, lay before the door, flicking her tail. If there were horrors, she wouldn't be so calm, would she? The other cats would raise an alarm, too. She pictured sleek Ruffy, her little sister's cat, removing the face of anyone who threatened his favorite person. He frightened large dogs.

However.

Vandra stepped over Bess and tried the door. Locked. The cat stood, gave each of them a sniff, then rubbed against their ankles.

"For the gods' sake, Van." Fieta stepped past and used her key. Now that Vandra had given her sister the image of a dead family, it seemed she couldn't rest until she'd made sure. The house was dark and quiet, but Fieta didn't pause as she headed upstairs. Vandra went through the small sitting room and toward her parents' bedroom.

She heard them snoring as she reached the door. With a sigh, she rested her head against the doorjamb, relief coursing within her. It smashed against grief for Ariadne and turned to guilt for forgetting her. Why couldn't emotions be managed as easily as alchemical formulas?

A shout and a thump came from overhead, followed by a child's cry. Vandra turned from her parents' room and raced up the stairs. Two dark forms writhed in the hallway. The twins had caught someone in their little sister's room. All of Vandra's emotions darkened into anger. She leapt the wrestling forms and went into Sita's room, fumbling for a match.

Her sister blinked away from the sudden light, her cries ceasing as she recognized Vandra and launched forward. Vandra caught her and held the match out as she turned to the hallway.

Fieta had forgotten about Ruffy, too. The cat's front claws balled in her shirt, his teeth snapping toward her face. Pietyr was trying to pull him away, but Ruffy twisted and turned, scoring Pietyr's arms with his back claws.

Vandra barked a laugh as she lowered Sita to the bed. By the time she lit a candle, she was guffawing, and Sita joined in, both of them cackling like mad as Ruffy finally left off his attack and leapt nimbly off Fieta's chest. He strolled to Sita's bed and sat in the middle, licking himself.

The twins lay in the hall, both breathing hard. Vandra's parents stumbled upstairs, Papa holding the small fireplace bellows, and Mama brandishing a candlestick. Everyone started talking at once, and they were soon joined by three more of Vandra's siblings, all those who still lived at the house, and everyone wanted to know what was going on.

"Hush, hush!" Mama called. "Everyone back to bed." Papa led the twins downstairs, looking over their scratches. Mama crooked a finger in Vandra's direction and picked up the candle from the bedside. After she kissed Sita and tucked her in, she led Vandra downstairs.

While Papa tended the twins, Mama made a pot of tea and handed cups around. When she was settled, she gestured toward Vandra. "Now, I always knew you children snuck out of the house from time to time, but sneaking in?"

Vandra couldn't smile, and she couldn't lie to them, not with a five-year-old sister upstairs who might have been murdered. After a deep breath, she started with Ariadne walking into her office and sending her on a quest and ended with the news that Ariadne had been murdered.

At the end, Mama gave her a long look but said nothing. Vandra bet she'd hear about the lies one day when everyone was less tired. Papa came around the table and embraced all of them in turn.

Their cuts clean, the twins checked the rest of the house, and when they returned with grim faces, Vandra's stomach shrank again. She thought they might try to hide whatever they'd discovered, but Papa noticed their looks. "Tell us."

"The back door was unlocked," Pietyr said.

Fieta stared at nothing, rage on her face. "And one of the bushes was flat where someone scaled the back wall."

The blood roared in Vandra's ears. While they were coming in the front, someone had been picking the back door? Maybe they'd already been inside. Maybe they'd watched her listen to her parents breathe. The thought chilled her to the core.

She breathed deep, telling herself that everyone was all right. She could picture the enemy's movements: finding her apartment empty, they'd come here, seen that Vandra wasn't present, and left, smart enough not to go into Sita's room and alert the cat. But everyone was all right.

Everyone but Ariadne.

Vandra felt a warm touch. Mama held her hand. "If you don't want to do anything more with this, you don't have to."

Vandra had to smile, knowing her mama was offering to hide her from her responsibilities, no matter that hiding might destroy the world. "I can't stop now. I don't want anyone else to be hurt."

Mama smiled. "I'm proud of you, Vandra."

Vandra had to duck her head, pleased but so undeserving of praise.

"I need to go before the assembly like Ariadne wanted," Vandra said. "I'll tell them everything. Maybe people won't oppose Ariadne for political reasons now that she's…" A lump moved in Vandra's throat.

Pietyr put a hand on her shoulder. "We should leave now, get there before the assembly opens."

"The Watch needs to know there's a murderer on the loose," Fieta said. "Captain Killian can be trusted."

Vandra had heard the name before, a commander both of them liked. "I want to check Ariadne's office in the Assembly House. If she had any proof to present, it's there."

Mama offered to go with them, and by the looks she exchanged with Papa, they were thinking about bundling up the entire family and taking them along. Going to a Watch House didn't sound like the worst idea, but now that they were awake, Vandra knew they could guard their own home, especially since she wouldn't be there to put them in danger.

After many promises to stay in contact, Vandra and the twins took their leave, sneaking through the streets again. Their first stop was the Watch House. Vandra waited while the twins spoke with Captain

Killian, going on about clues and such. They asked the captain about the best way to get past the guards on the Assembly House and up to the offices, but those guards were part of the official Palace Guard, separate from the Watch. Cooperation between the two groups could be iffy, but the captain offered to go along and see if he could talk their way into the offices while one of his trusted lieutenants held Ariadne's crime scene.

The Assembly House was part of a larger, imposing structure, even at night. The bottom half was boxy, designed more for business than beauty, but the rectangular structure helped support four impressive spires, the twisting cones topped with graceful statues, each depicting the goddess of justice in her four forms: child, adult, elder, and the winged soul that existed in all people.

Vandra wondered where Ariadne's soul had gone, if it stared uncomprehendingly at her body. Priests and priestesses said that the soul couldn't remember how it died, but opinion was divided on whether a soul focused on the good or bad parts of its life as it lingered on earth for three days before flying to the stars, free to explore other worlds. Some said that souls never departed, torn because they hadn't finished all they wanted to do on this world.

If Ariadne had the choice, Vandra bet she would go to the tattered lands and find out the cause of the pylons' destruction in the hopes of telling the living. If anyone could find a way to communicate from the afterlife, it would be Ariadne.

The thought made Vandra dip her head from more than fatigue. Their love had never set the world aflame, but it had been good. Real. Each had been what the other one needed. And their relationship had real affection behind it, just not enough to make either of their hearts leap, not like when Vandra thought of Lilani.

She sighed at the thought of the seelie delegation. Without Ariadne, was there any hope of the seelie being received well? Vandra would have to will the spirit of Ariadne to speak through her. She'd have to make the assembly see the benefits of cooperation. They'd want to talk and talk, and she'd have to make them act.

Captain Killian talked the assembly guard into letting them wait inside the public receiving room instead of on the street, but he didn't seem happy about it, and he wasn't inclined to let them go farther. Captain Killian himself left to attend to Ariadne's crime scene.

As the assembly guard led Vandra, Fieta, and Pietyr to the waiting room, he grumbled about people who didn't want to follow the rules. Vandra's temper spiked. Their world might be on the brink of ending, people had been murdered, and this useless donkey was worried about following the rules?

She looked to the twins, wondering if they could knock the man unconscious, but he'd arrest them when he woke up. On the other hand, Ariadne's enemies wouldn't wait for a lawful way into the assembly offices. Time was the enemy.

Vandra spied a small kitchen to the side of the room and put on a smile, hoping it didn't look too false. "Why don't I make us all a cup of tea?" she said brightly.

The guard fell silent, blinking at her.

"Unless you'd prefer coffee?" she asked as she poked her head into the kitchen. She tried to summon the way Ariadne could feign cheerfulness. "It's the least I can do for interrupting your night."

The guard fidgeted and muttered something about the contents of the kitchen being for guests, not guards.

Vandra didn't let her smile slip. "We won't tell anyone." She decided to try a wink. "Maybe I can find a few cookies as well."

The guard grunted, but a smile tugged at the corner of his lips. Fieta looked back and forth between them. Pietyr frowned until Vandra waved for him to follow. She gave Fieta a pointed glance and nodded to the guard.

"Um, let me help," Pietyr said as he followed. Vandra found the kettle while Pietyr lit a fire in the small stove. "What's the plan?" he whispered.

She looked through the tins of tea until she found a strong blend. Then she dug in her bag, glad she hadn't unpacked. Her reagents box had ground poppy and valerian root. She sprinkled a bit of both into a mug.

Pietyr looked at her in shock. After a glance out at the guard, he stuck out his tongue and let his head loll to the side, miming death. When he focused on her again, his eyes held a question.

She gave him a dark look, mouthing, "Of course not." She put her folded hands to her cheek, closed her eyes, and put on a dreamy smile. Pietyr seemed relieved, and she wanted to kick him for even thinking she'd casually commit murder. Instead, she dug through the cupboards and found a tin of cookies. When they had the tea brewed, she and Pietyr carried everything back.

"Here we are." With a smile, she handed the guard his cup.

He bit his bottom lip. "Sorry I was so…" He cleared his throat. "I really shouldn't. We have our own kitchen."

Vandra felt her smile go brittle. Pietyr leaned around her, holding out the plate. "Our mama taught us better than to hog the brew. If anyone asks, tell them we insisted."

"Please, join us," Fieta added as she took a cup. "Then we won't feel so bad for disturbing you."

With a shy smile, the guard took the tea. Vandra fought the urge to sigh. They'd wasted too much time already. She eased out of the conversation, and soon everyone fell silent. Dawn was still some ways off. Vandra set her cup to the side and put her head back as if drowsing. The guard began to yawn, saying, "Excuse me," each time, but everyone else pretended to sleep. When at last his head leaned back and didn't rise again, Vandra sat up.

The guard began to snore. Vandra waved for the twins to hurry. Hopefully, the guard would be so embarrassed when he woke up that he'd say nothing. They took his keys then ran through the door, hurrying through the darkened halls of the Assembly House.

As a junior assemblywoman, Ariadne's office was on a higher floor, and Vandra's legs cramped from running up the stairs. The twins had to put a hand under her elbows and haul her up the last few flights. At last, they were behind Ariadne's office door, and Vandra leaned on the desk and breathed hard. She wasn't built for this much running around.

They risked a candle. Fieta stuffed a small rug into the crack beneath the door, trying to block the light in case of patrols. This room was as tidy as before. Maybe whoever had killed Ariadne hadn't gotten in here. Or they'd straightened up before they left. Vandra sat at the desk and began going through papers.

"What are we looking for?" Fieta asked.

"I'm not sure. Anything that has to do with the tattered lands or the seelie or…" She didn't know what else. The reason Ariadne was murdered seemed simple. Whoever had sabotaged the pylon didn't want her to tell anyone else about it. Vandra was her proof, so someone was after Vandra, too. But how had Ariadne learned about the pylon in the first place, before everyone else? If she could find out, she'd have more proof to back up her claims tomorrow.

But would the assembly assume she was lying? Maybe because of politics. It might have been politics that led to Ariadne's murder, and Vandra felt justified for hating them.

She scanned paper after paper. The twins pulled books off the shelves and leafed through them, but Ariadne wouldn't keep secrets where anyone could find them. The desk drawers held nothing save pens and ink, pencils, and sheets of parchment. Vandra pushed aside blotting paper and Ariadne's seal and wax. She found spare candles, a magnifying glass, and a clean cup and saucer. Ariadne had always been particular about her drinkware. This one had a pink swirl amidst the cream-colored clay. It bore the mark of Ariadne's mother, a potter from Westside. Ariadne could have afforded something with gilt, but she'd never forgotten where she came from.

Vandra felt the heavy hand of grief as she put the cup back. She'd met Ariadne's mother once, a chance meeting at the market. She'd seemed friendly, happy to see her daughter out from behind her books. Vandra tried not to picture her face when she found out one of her children had been murdered.

Vandra glanced up and spied a painting on the opposite wall. She hadn't noticed it earlier. A watercolor, it depicted Westside in all its dank glory, with the houses crowded together, but the artist had focused on splashes of color: a cart selling flowers, a few pots and vases, an orange cat lying in the sun. In the distance were gulls and the tall masts of ships in the harbor. Through a gap in the buildings, the sun winked off the water. The artist had managed to find the beauty in Ariadne's childhood home. It seemed a perfect hiding place for something important.

Carefully, Vandra took the painting down and turned it over. Brown paper covered the back, but it had a slit along one edge. "Look here." She shook it gently and heard the soft sound of paper sliding inside.

Fieta cut a bigger hole in the back. A letter slid out, and Vandra caught it. The script was flowery, dramatic. The paper seemed old though the ink looked new.

"It's about the pylon dying," Vandra said as she read it. "The sender heard of Ariadne's interest in the pylons and thought she was the person to tell."

"Who's it from?" Pietyr asked.

"It's unsigned, and the language seems…archaic. Some of the grammar's old, too." She turned it over, but the other side was blank.

"Some of us aren't as good at spelling and such as you are, Van," Fieta said.

Vandra ignored that. "The handwriting is perfect, even beautiful."

"So, the sender is used to writing, but not in the language of Citran?" Pietyr asked.

Vandra nodded. "And since there aren't any other human languages anymore, I don't think this was from a human. It's seelie, but Lilani acted as if her people hadn't contacted ours for years."

"Maybe she doesn't know," Fieta said.

Pietyr shook his head. "She said her mother was the empress. Wouldn't she know everything?"

Vandra turned the letter over and over. "Seems like everyone is keeping secrets lately."

Outside the window, the sky was lightening, and Vandra fought the urge to lie down under the desk and sleep for the rest of her life. But the assembly would be gathering soon for a long day of bickering, and Vandra had to be there. She stuffed the letter in her pack beside the lead-lined box. She didn't know when Ariadne had put her on the schedule or if she was meant to be a surprise. Should she return to the waiting room or barge into the assembly chambers? The guard would miss his keys as soon as he awoke. Best to give them back, then. Vandra couldn't start the day with yet another person wanting to murder her.

Vandra didn't know whether to laugh or weep at the macabre thought. She was too tired for either. "Come on. Let's get back to the waiting room."

The guard was still asleep when they arrived. They put the keys back on his belt, then Fieta and Pietyr sat, pretending to sleep while Vandra shook the man awake. He snorted and sat up, his eyes bleary. He smacked his lips and tried to focus on her, but his pupils were dilated.

"The building will be open soon," she said. "You'd better wake up."

He blinked before his eyes widened, and he sat up hurriedly, looked at the sleeping twins, then at Vandra again. "What happened?"

"We all drifted off. Must be these comfy chairs. Don't worry," she said as he stood. "We won't tell."

He seemed confused as well as embarrassed, and she hoped that was enough to keep him quiet. He hurried out, and a moment later, the inner door opened, and a secretary stepped inside. She stared as if she hadn't expected to see anyone waiting so early.

"Assemblywoman Ariadne Bahn added us to the schedule," Vandra said, her voice shaking a little over Ariadne's name. "It's important." When the secretary still seemed confused, Vandra put her hands on her hips, too keyed up to wait anymore. "One of the pylons has gone out. I think the assembly needs to know that."

Chapter Eleven

When everyone gathered together in the Court, Lilani was reminded of how few of them were left. Nearly a thousand sounded like a lot in her head, but to see them together, she realized how much trouble they were in if they'd truly stopped breeding.

Especially since someone seemed determined to murder at least one of them. Lilani shivered. Would the killer have gone after her mother, too? Did they want the seelie to be without leadership? Lilani had cousins, both close and distant, but none had ever expressed interest in claiming the throne.

The trail from the night before had led into the square then disappeared amongst the traces of everyone else. Now that the entire Court had awakened to investigate the fuss, the trail grew even colder. The last attempted murder among the seelie was far in the past, and everyone seemed mystified about what to do. Lilani peered at all the people she thought she knew. In the dim light, all of them seemed sinister, capable of being anyone else at a moment's notice.

When a hand rested on Lilani's shoulder, she jumped, her magic roaring within her.

Faelyn held up his hands, eyes wide. "It's me."

She breathed out. Yes, him and her mother, the only two people who certainly didn't want to kill her, at least not at the moment. Faelyn had been asleep when she'd seen the shadowy figure, and her mother had come rushing to defend her. She didn't think it could be any of the Guard, either. One of them had known she was sleeping in the orchard, and the others were too good at shrouding to have been the bumbling seelie who'd attacked her.

Unless they *wanted* her to think they were bumbling, when in reality—

She put her head in her hands. "I'm going crazy."

"Breathe. The Guard is questioning everyone, but it's been a long time since they've had to conduct an investigation, and no one is happy to be accused. The last crime we had was a theft, and that stemmed from a feud a long time in the making."

"If someone was angry with me, they'd have spoken to me rather than try to kill me in my bed!" She fought the urge to bite her thumb, a nervous habit she'd done away with years past. "I can't stay here. I won't need to be guarded if the murderer can't find me."

"So, you propose to camp somewhere *away* from the Court?" he asked. "Oh good, then if the murderer does find you, they'll have no trouble killing you without any pesky witnesses."

"They won't find me."

"That's the trouble with hiding. If you need help—"

She rounded on him, hands curled into fists. She wanted to scream. The entire Court would be appalled by such a display, but she wanted to tear down the walls with her bare hands. And since she couldn't do that…

"Come with me." She grabbed his arm. "If I need help, you'll know what to do. Please, Faelyn, you're the only one I trust, you and Mother."

He put an arm around her. "All right. We'll tell a guard, then we'll sneak away." He had a quick word with Lucian, who frowned but nodded. Faelyn held tight to Lilani as they slipped into the shadows of the orchard again. "Shroud."

Lilani let her emotions free; her magic washed over her. Faelyn vanished, but she could still see a shimmer when they passed a lantern. He didn't let go of her hand and didn't speak until they left the orchard and climbed out of the Court, heading up the trail along the Highpeak.

When they were high up, both of them panting, Faelyn called a halt behind a boulder that shielded them from the trail. They sat and watched the sun rise in the east. In the face of the beautiful view, Lilani rested her head against Faelyn's shoulder and wept. He put an arm around her and murmured soothing nonsense.

As the light grew, she noticed a figure in the shadows above them along the trail. She leapt to her feet, but when the figure didn't move, she exhaled slowly, realizing it was one of the elders sitting inside a shallow crack. Even in shadow, Lilani could make out the elder's striking features, her high cheekbones, and her long dark lashes resting closed. She sat still as a statue, hands in her lap. Her dark hair fell loose about her shoulders, barely moving as her magic focused inside instead of out, keeping her alive.

Lilani plucked a bit of cobweb from the elder's hair. She'd seen this one before, had been struck by her beauty. Lilani often volunteered to range up and down the Highpeak, making sure the elders stayed free of dirt and grime. Someone had laid flowers at this one's feet. Deeper in the shadow behind the elder, another pile of flowers was strewn upon the ground, but whoever they were for had shrouded, fading from life almost entirely. Lilani was tempted to reach out to see if the elder was still there or if they'd somehow managed to vanish from reality.

She turned away, too saddened by the thought to see if it was true. "Well, I wanted our people to change, Faelyn. I got my wish."

"Not what you were hoping for, I know."

She nodded toward the elders. "At least the murderer felt something, unlike..." She didn't finish the thought, angry as well as frightened and tired. "All this because I want to help the humans?"

"Are you certain that's the reason?"

"What else could it be?" she asked. "Why such an extreme reaction? If they'd wanted to frighten me, why not a...strongly worded letter?"

Faelyn snorted, but it had no humor in it. That was fine; she didn't feel like laughing either. She paced, unable to banish the thought that if she'd been in that bed, she'd be dead. But she couldn't let herself be stopped.

Someone called from around the corner, Lucian's voice. When Faelyn answered, Lucian blinked into view at a bend in the trail.

Before he could speak, Lilani rushed forward. "You caught them?"

"No." His gaze was sorry but steady. "Most have alibis, and those that don't say they were asleep."

So, she could rule out those with alibis. Unless her would-be murderer was part of a cabal. Lilani took another deep breath. She couldn't let herself get paranoid. One erratic seelie did not equal a cabal. "Was anyone loudly anti-human?"

He grimaced. "Loud enough to scream, 'I'd murder for this'? No. As for being anti-human, that's almost everyone. I can't say I approve of consorting with humans, either. I just don't see any other choice right now."

"I bet it's a youngster," Faelyn said. "Under two hundred. I can't see anyone older acting this impulsively."

"The lack of shrouding ability could point to someone younger," Lucian said. "But that's still a big pool of suspects."

"And almost all of the *youngsters* are my friends." Laughing with her one moment and wanting to stab her in the face the next? Lilani wanted to throw up just thinking about it.

Lucian had her list her friends anyway. She thought back to the evening before, trying to recall anyone who'd seemed panicked or unreasonably angry. Several had been anxious, but one or two had even been excited, wanting to go with her. The recitations of old wrongs had come from the older seelie. She cursed herself, wishing she'd paid more attention to who said what, but the warnings had all blended together. That was why she'd hidden, overwhelmed. Now she tried to separate the complaints. She thought of three in particular, not friends but people she knew, but as the youngest, she knew everyone. They'd watched her grow up. How could they ever want to kill her?

Before she could think too hard about it, Lilani told Lucian what she remembered. He listened intently, his stare so serious, she thought it might burn a hole through her skull.

"But don't..." She stopped, not knowing what to say. Don't bother them? Don't hurt them? He wouldn't do either without cause. She pictured their faces as he accused them. If they were innocent, she'd be breaking a bond with them forever. And if they weren't...

It was already broken.

"We should return to the Court," he said. "Your mother decided that your delegation to the human city should leave immediately. That should get you out of harm's way. I'll be one of your Guard, and while I'm gone, one of the others will look into the names you've given me."

Well, at least she wouldn't have to watch. She could have hugged him. Instead, she held her head high and followed him back. Her mother met them on their doorstep. Her face was grim, and the Guard surrounded her.

"We're questioning everyone," her mother said. She didn't seem happy at the thought, but she didn't seem angry at Lilani either. She stared into the street as if the very world offended her.

"Lucian told me. People are angry?"

"Some are worried, both about the attempted murder and the fact that we seem to be focused on those who are anti-human. They worry that expressing their opinions will be enough to make suspicion fall on them."

"Maybe I shouldn't have said anything." Lilani felt an odd sort of guilt, as if she'd brought this unrest. Maybe she had.

Her mother took her shoulders. "It's not your fault."

Lilani fought the urge to weep again. As if reading her thoughts and taking pity on them, her mother walked her into the house and stood over her as she packed. The Guard went to assemble their own baggage, then everyone met in front of the house again.

Lilani felt hollow. She'd wanted change, but this felt too fast. As she donned her pack, her mother hugged her, and Lilani realized they were going *now*. Her mother wouldn't have a last cup with her; their final words would be rushed.

"This is only good-bye for now," her mother whispered as they embraced. "You will return to me soon, and I will make certain your home is safe." Her lips pressed to Lilani's cheek, then she stepped back, misty-eyed.

It was almost enough to undo Lilani. She had to whisper a farewell and turn to the others. Lucian, Faelyn, and five other guards were all she had. Part of her had imagined a huge march on the human city with banners and finery, not this little, fast-traveling company. She didn't doubt they'd be safe, but they weren't exactly intimidating. As long as they could shroud, though, she supposed they wouldn't have to be.

As they left the Court and ventured into the forest, Faelyn tugged on Lilani's arm. "As far as the humans know, I'm your advisor," he said. "And once we get close to Parbeh, two of the Guard will shed their armor and act as your personal attendants."

Lilani couldn't help a chuckle. "That should surprise anyone who thinks they'll make easy targets."

"That's the idea." He winked, and even with all the heaviness surrounding them, he seemed cheerful. Maybe it was only for her benefit. The Guard seemed serious, but they always were. Lilani wondered why Lucian had chosen these few, if they were curious about humans rather than frightened or angry. Whichever, they'd been doing their jobs for a very long time, and Lucian trusted them, so she could, too.

Lilani forced herself not to look back.

❖

The assembly room seemed smaller than Vandra remembered. That was probably because she'd seen it empty when Ariadne had once given her a tour. Now it was full and stifling. The room was shaped like a half-moon with three tiers of curved benches loaded with people, and the tables in front of them sagging under paperwork. The straight edge of the room was open, with only a small, heavy table and a raised platform with a podium in the center. A group of chairs sat off to the side for visitors like Vandra and her siblings.

The shuffling and murmuring as people took their seats and spoke to their fellows put Vandra in mind of a stream muttering through the countryside. But a stream had never stared at her curiously or suspiciously. Everyone seemed to know why she'd come. Word had spread like plague. She expected that was why there were so many people in attendance. Even major bills might not see this many, but everyone wanted to hear from the alchemist who said one of the pylons had gone out.

If the spirit of Ariadne still lingered, Vandra hoped it was with her now.

An attendant strode toward them and leaned close to Vandra's ear. "Nata Rahvi is the head assemblyperson," he said, gesturing to a woman sitting at the small table. She was surrounded by a herd of aides. "She'll open the session and make a few remarks, then she'll call on you to come forward." He pointed to the circular dais and podium. It had a half-rail around it, making it seem like an ineffectual cage.

"You'll be given a few minutes to speak," the attendant said, "then the assembly will have questions." He gave her a reassuring smile. "They'll all start talking at once, but don't worry. Rahvi will bring them back to order."

Vandra nodded. It sounded like it worked well, but Ariadne's numerous complaints rang in her ears. The room often descended into chaos. Sometimes it had to be cleared. Vandra supposed that if things got out of hand, the twins could carry her away, but she wanted everyone to hear what she had to say. Their future depended on it.

Nata Rahvi called the assembly to order. Like her fellows, she wore a red sash that cut across her clothing, but she had a cap that sat far back on her head, pinned to her hair. Some of the others wore the same sort of hat, but she had the only gold tassel, and she wore a heavy gold chain around her shoulders, a marker of how long she'd been in office. No other chain was nearly as impressive. Rahvi's hair had gone white in service to Parbeh. The lines around her eyes gave her a permanent squint that Ariadne had said made many a first-year assemblyperson squirm in their seat, but the wrinkles around her mouth said she laughed a lot, too. Maybe her fellows didn't get to see that as often as the squint.

She wasn't smiling as she brought a heavy stone cube down on the table, sending an echo through the room. The thing sounded as if it might crack the wood in half, and Vandra could see a dent in the table where it had been struck many times.

When the hall fell silent, Rahvi placed the cube in a shallow dish. She stood and looked around the entire hall. Ariadne had told her the assembly called this, "Taming With the Gaze," but Ariadne suspected Rahvi did it in order to have time to line up her remarks in her head.

"We gather today to hear grave news," she said, her voice tinged with age but still clear and powerful. "The murder of one of our own and a possible threat to our very survival."

Murmurs erupted, but Rahvi didn't take her gaze from her fellows, letting the swell die. Vandra expected her to elaborate, to say more about Ariadne, about the pylons, but her eyes rested on Vandra.

"Professor Vandra Singh," she said, holding out a hand.

Vandra tried to stand, but her legs wouldn't work. Panic bubbled inside her as time seemed to stretch out. She wet her lips with a tongue dry as dust and tried again. This time, one of the twins gave her a little push. She'd never been so tired and so wide-awake all at once.

She walked quickly to the dais, wishing it had a chair. The rail helped her to the podium, which she clutched so tightly her fingers went white. As soon as Vandra was in place, Rahvi sat, trusting her, Vandra supposed, to make her own case better than anyone else.

But looking at all those expectant faces, silent now except for a note of fidgeting and a stray cough or two, Vandra couldn't remember anything she was supposed to say. She was Vandra Singh; that much she knew. And she was there to talk about...

Pylons. Yes. She took another moment to breathe, picturing herself in her office, delivering a lecture to a handful of students and fellow alchemists. She shifted her gaze to a point on the wall where the bottom of one tier was held by a metal brace. Perfect. She would speak to that brace and pretend no one else existed.

"Recently," she told it, "I received a visit from Assemblyperson Ariadne Bahn." With no more room for secrets, the whole story came bubbling out in fits and starts until it morphed into a real tale. She used her memory like a lifeline, skipping over parts that seemed unimportant, keeping to the pylons and her discovery of the tattered metal, letting the alchemy be the star.

She pulled out the piece of metal and heard the chairs creak as people leaned forward to get a better look. Even Rahvi came half out of her chair. Vandra left the metal in sight as she continued, letting its tainted miasma fill the hall and reinforce what she was saying.

Then she came to the seelie. She didn't mention that Lilani was the daughter of the empress, just that the seelie claimed they were also worried about the pylons and that they'd helped construct the magical barriers in the first place. Mutters and murmurs followed until Rahvi banged the cube again. Vandra said that Ariadne had been told about the pylons by a seelie and that the seelie were sending a delegation to Parbeh.

After a slow breath, she told them about finding Ariadne's body. Sadness threatened to overwhelm her, but she couldn't let it, had to be as unemotional as the metal brace. She could pretend this wasn't her story—only a tale from a book—and when she walked away from the podium, everything and everyone would be all right.

At last, there was nothing left to say. When she fell silent, the hall stayed quiet, too. Vandra took a chance and glanced at the stunned assembly. No one had questions? That was fine; she was more than happy to leave early.

When Vandra reached to put the piece of metal away, the room erupted in shouts. Vandra nearly jumped out of her skin. The cube pounded down once, twice, a third time, Rahvi shouting for order with the last bang. People were still talking, but softer now, to those sitting beside them. Vandra tried to skate over all the eyes, looking for the brace she'd addressed before.

Rahvi called on one assemblyperson, and the questions began. What methods did she use to test the pylons? How did she know for certain the pylon had ceased functioning? Why did she only check two? Did she send someone to check the others? They kept wanting to know about things she had no knowledge of or authority over. She answered as best she could, trying not to get angry at every question that sounded like an accusation, including one demanding to know why she didn't simply fix the problem, as if she possessed a fountain of syndrium.

At last, one smirking man stood near the back, and Vandra knew what was coming. He addressed his opening remarks to the assembly rather than her, always a bad sign. "Honored brethren," he said, "let us not panic about the words of one failed alchemist."

Vandra clenched her jaw.

"Is this not the same Vandra Singh who started out with such promise then produced one failure after another? If we are truly worried, let us send another team of carefully selected, well-respected alchemists, who can study this problem and give us a satisfying solution."

So many retorts flew through Vandra's head, but she kept them down. After all, she *was* a failure. She'd let down a lot of people. But by the gods, Ariadne had chosen her for a reason, and it was more than just their past. Ariadne had died for that choice, and Vandra couldn't let her be shamed in her grave.

"Send them," Vandra said. "If you're a fan of wasting time. They'll tell you the same thing, and they'll be no closer to offering a solution. My latest projects might not have gone as planned, but my one success, my 'promise,' as you called it, was with syndrium. Ask any alchemist you like, and they'll tell you that no one knows more about syndrium than I do. I wrote a book about it, the only book people use now."

She let that sink in. She glanced at the twins to see them smiling. Rahvi had a faint smile, too. The grumpy assemblyperson frowned down at Vandra, still standing, maybe waiting for her to slink off and let him have the day.

"I suggest you send everyone you can think of to the pylons," Vandra said. "Especially soldiers. Someone is doing this, and I don't know why, nor do I know where this piece of metal came from. More people *should* study it. But the pylon is still dead, and the seelie may be our only way to reignite it."

"You had no right to invite them!" the grumpy assemblyperson shouted.

Another stood. "One person always has the right to speak to another," he said smoothly. "Besides, it sounds as if they offered to come."

"And any one of us would have agreed to an initial meeting," another assemblyperson said as she stood. "Now it is in our hands and in the hands of the five monarchs. Professor Singh did what any envoy might have done, make an initial plan then put the issue in the hands of leaders."

Rahvi banged the cube again, and everyone sat.

Another assemblyperson leaned forward, and Rahvi indicated him with a nod. "Professor, why did Ariadne not send you directly to her seelie contact in the first place?"

Vandra shook her head. "I don't think she knew who it was."

"She should have come to us in the first place!" someone shouted, and the bickering was back on.

The cube came down again. "Clearly, Assemblyperson Bahn wanted movement on this issue before the sun dies, and the world turns to dust," Rahvi said. That got more than a few chuckles, but there were also scowls in her and Vandra's directions. They couldn't see outside their own sphere. Vandra imagined she'd been as bad at other times, but this was life and death.

After a deep breath, Vandra answered a few more questions, and then it seemed they had enough to argue about without her. After taking the tattered piece of metal from her, they sent her from the chamber without further orders.

"Bed," Pietyr said when they stood outside. "Now."

Fieta nodded, and it made Vandra yawn just thinking about it.

"Where?" Vandra asked.

"Home," Fieta said. "Not yours, Van, and not your office. We're going to sink into the welcoming bosom of our family."

She didn't say it, but she knew the twins wanted to be present if their family needed protecting. Vandra suspected that her presence would put her family in danger, but if she shared that thought with the twins or her parents, they would *insist* she stay as close as possible. And running off would only put everyone in more danger. By the flat looks the twins gave her, maybe they could read her mind.

"All right." She pitied any assemblyperson or murderer who tried to get through them unscathed.

CHAPTER TWELVE

Even shrouded, the seelie gave the first human settlement they came across a wide berth. Lilani craned her neck, watching humans come and go from wooden walls. The town sat in the middle of a field with no way to blend in with the surroundings. Instead of building *with* nature, the humans seemed to take it as an affront. They'd cut down all the trees and didn't live close enough to a water source. Maybe they only wanted to be surrounded by their own kind rather than nature. A group of temporary looking structures squatted on the southern side of the town, all slanting metal and tin. Sleeping in the trees would be more comfortable than those shanties…if the humans had left any.

She wanted to get closer until the wind changed, and she caught a whiff of all the different smells, not many of them good and nearly all unidentifiable. She changed her mind, deciding they were close enough. She was going to have to get used to human smells eventually.

But not yet.

They stayed off the road, following it at a distance and shrouding whenever anyone came into view. They camped that night without a fire, lying together in a shallow, limestone hollow nestled in rolling hills. The Guard took turns on watch, but they passed an uneventful night.

The next day, the great human city of Parbeh came within view. Lilani had to stop and gawk, and she wasn't the only one. Lucian had a calculating look as if figuring out the best way to approach. Faelyn sighed as if reliving a memory before he dug in the packs and unrolled clothing for himself and Lilani. For their initial meeting with the humans, he'd brought long frock coats to wear over soft, doeskin trousers. Her dark amethyst coat was silk; his was blue brocade. Each had eight carved wooden buttons at the front. Her lapels and the edges of her pockets were sewn with silver thread, and tiny beads in the silk sparkled when they caught the light. His blue coat had a mild shimmer, and with their polished black boots and their hair stirring gently over their shoulders, they made quite a striking pair.

"Hmm," Faelyn said as he looked her over. "I think we should all wear our hair up. From what I remember about humans, the magic surrounding us disturbs them the first time."

"But they'll be able to feel it if they get close," Lilani said.

He shrugged. "They can explain away a vague feeling, but we might tap into their primal fears of the unknown if we walk around with hair that has a mind of its own."

"Very well." She twisted her hair behind her head and secured it with a few pins before helping the Guard do the same. The two who would masquerade as her attendants donned shorter, plainer coats. The other four remained in leather armor, Lucian included, though they polished the dark, intricately carved suits to a high gloss. No one wore jewelry, not yet, not wanting to flaunt such things in front of ordinary humans. They hoped their clothing and weapons were enough to imply they were capable of helping others and defending themselves.

After a few deep breaths, Lilani stood in the middle of the Guard with Faelyn, her two false attendants behind her. They carefully walked toward Parbeh, not wanting to mar their fine clothing with dirt. Lilani began to wonder if one of the Guard should have gone first to announce them, but when the walls of the city came into view, it seemed too late.

Just like the other human place, a temporary looking settlement had collected along these walls as if it had been washed up and abandoned by the sea. As the seelie came closer, a crowd of humans gathered to gawk.

The smell was almost a living thing.

With waste, cooking food, dirt, unwashed bodies, and other smells she was happy not to identify, Lilani barely managed *not* to hold her nose. Maybe it was the sheer bulk of humanity; Vandra and her siblings hadn't smelled like this. Maybe only people of a certain class had the ability to bathe? There were so many humans, after all.

Children crowded around the Guard with no one to attend them. Lilani stared, grinning. She'd never seen another child. All the other seelie had been grown when she was born. She touched one gently on the head before the Guard shooed them back, though they continued to flock around the seelie without fear. What could be better than an escort of happy children? Maybe the adults would learn from them.

Lucian bent close to her ear. "If something goes wrong and we must separate inside the city, we will meet here." He gestured toward a nearby tin dwelling that seemed a little more permanent than the others. Lilani nodded but tried to put that option out of her mind, hoping they wouldn't need secret meeting places.

By the time they reached the walls, the shanty-dwelling humans had made a parade in their wake. Besides armed guards, several others had gathered at the gates to Parbeh, probably brought in haste after the seelie's slow march through the shanties. Lilani spotted finery and flashy metal armor. As she approached, one of those in green brocade stepped forward and bowed. His light brown hair curled around his forehead and ears. He had deep lines around his mouth and small ones at his eyes, a sign of human age. Lilani wondered how old that made him, how old the lack of lines made Vandra.

She returned the bow, feeling Faelyn do the same.

"Welcome to Parbeh, honored guests," the brocade wearer said in badly accented, nearly unrecognizable seelie.

Lilani couldn't help a little jump. She glanced at Faelyn, who shrugged. So, some knowledge of the seelie had survived. The words were mangled, though. This man had clearly never heard the language spoken aloud.

As he stumbled over another greeting, Lilani interrupted. "We speak the human tongue." Unlike his teachers, hers had actually *heard* the language they taught, even if they hadn't spoken it for many years.

He smiled smoothly and switched languages. "We are pleased to have such esteemed visitors gracing us with their presence. I am Wurabi, seneschal to the five monarchs of Citran." He bowed again.

"I am Lilani, envoy of Empress Dyrana, and this is my retinue. We have come to see your monarchs and to speak of grave matters." She cast a glance at the people behind them. If they weren't allowed to bathe, she imagined they weren't privy to most information, either. She'd have to ask Vandra whom she could speak to about what.

Wurabi nodded slowly. "Of course." He stood aside. The guards around him moved aside, leaving room for Lilani's group while glaring at the humans behind them.

So, the shanty dwellers weren't allowed in the city, either. Lilani started forward, and when her group passed, the human guards fell in place behind her.

Wurabi nodded at the seelie Guard. "Are these your only companions?"

"Are we not enough?" she asked with a smile.

When he still looked around, she realized he was looking for shrouded seelie, but he didn't mention them. "We are honored to have you." He returned her smile, and it even reached his eyes. Either he was simply a pleasant person or he knew enough to fake it.

As they wound through the streets, more crowds gathered, curious, mumbling. Lilani tried to smile and not be intimidated. The buildings crowded together, cutting off views of the city, though she spotted tall structures in the distance. She could smell the people again as well as a million other tiny aromas: fish and cooking meat, refuse and offal, sawdust and metal polish. The roads were a mixture of dirt and brick, and some of the buildings sported tiny plots of grass or trees. The entire place was alive with noise: voices, the call of birds, the ring of metal on metal, and more sounds she couldn't separate from the din.

Wurabi led them to an area of the city where the buildings were larger, the clothing more ostentatious, and the plots of nature larger, though the smells were as strong. Thankfully, the noise was less. Wurabi stopped in front of a house that sat behind an iron fence and had a stone path leading to the dwelling. The wooden walls were painted blue with hints of white. It stood on two levels, the same rectangular shape as those on either side.

Wurabi gestured them through the gate then opened the door and beckoned them inside. "This will be your home while you're in Parbeh, if it meets with your approval."

Lilani glanced at the interior curiously. "I thought we would meet with the monarchs."

He gave her another charming smile. "Such a meeting is being arranged, but like everything in government, it takes time." He smiled wider as if that was a joke.

Before she could ask questions, he bid her farewell, asking her to remain inside for the time being. Lilani frowned after he'd gone. She'd expected him to take her to the monarchs right away. Surely Vandra had returned and told them what she knew. But human guards waited at the gate, keeping away those who'd gathered in the street. When Lilani looked out the rear windows, she saw another small plot of greenery surrounded by a high stone wall with a metal gate in the center. She spied movement beyond and knew human guards were watching that side of the house, too.

"Charming as a prison," Faelyn said.

Lilani gave him a dark look. "It's a courtesy while we wait for the monarchs to prepare for our visit."

He rolled his eyes. "They know we can shroud. Traversing that flood of humanity would be difficult but not impossible. We could leave or sneak up on their monarchs whenever we like."

She winked. "So, not a prison, then?"

He shrugged and sat while the Guard went through the house, looking for spy holes or secret doors. Lilani and Faelyn readied their other finery should they need it. The rugs in the bedrooms were soft and plush, and the bedclothes were fluffy. Everything seemed comfortable and thick. Lilani often slept outside with no covering, but these beds were heaped with blankets. Maybe humans were always cold? The thought that Vandra might want to snuggle for warmth was intriguing.

The kitchen was stocked with bags of fruit and vegetables, pots of flour, and several dead animals hanging in a larder. Had someone been bundled from this house to make room for her, or had the humans rushed to make it ready? She supposed it didn't matter, though it bothered her that someone might be burning with resentment at her presence.

In the sitting room, Faelyn lounged on a heavily cushioned divan, sipping a glass of wine. "If it's not a prison, we might as well relax and enjoy it."

"I don't want to relax," she said. "I want to see—"

"Vandra?" Faelyn asked.

"And why not? At least she was..." She trailed off as she spotted movement through the windows. Someone was at the gate. "Something's happening."

Faelyn was at her side in an instant. "Lucian!"

"I saw them," Lucian said as he clomped down the stairs.

He didn't order Lilani back so she stood on her tiptoes. The guards at the gate were speaking to someone, and as they stepped apart, Lilani caught a glimpse of a familiar face.

She was out the door before anyone could stop her, and their warnings didn't keep her from jogging up the stone path. She didn't try to stop her grin. A similar smile bloomed on Vandra's face when their eyes met.

The human guards turned, hands on their weapons. Lilani pulled up short and continued at a more sedate pace. "Vandra! I'm so glad you've come."

Vandra's smile widened. "I..." She looked at the guards as if unsure what to say. Her siblings remained in the street, both of them staring at the guards with irritated expressions.

"My apologies for not sending word," Lilani said. "Please, come in!"

The guards glanced at one another. They had a quick, muffled conversation before one of them hurried away. Lilani sighed. Word of Vandra's visit no doubt had to wing its way up the chain of command. How seelie of them.

"We're not supposed to admit anyone without the seneschal's approval," one guard said. When Lilani raised an eyebrow, he added, "For your protection, madam."

"By all the gods!" Vandra cried. "I'm not an idle tourist. I was the one who first met them. I've *spoken* to the *assembly*. Has no one told you?"

The guards stared, stone-like. Lilani's jaw dropped. That did not sound like the calm woman she'd met, but Vandra had dark circles under her eyes and a stoop in her shoulders. She hadn't rested easy since she'd been home. Lilani wanted to reach out to her.

"We *know each other*," Vandra said. "And I'm not afraid of going in there, so..." She gestured to the gate, but the guards didn't move.

Lilani took another step, hands out for everyone to see. "It's all right, Vandra. Protocol, no doubt." As she reached the gate, she gave the guards a look, and they scooted to the sides, giving her and Vandra a little room. Vandra wrapped a hand around one of the iron bars. Lilani rested hers above. They were close enough to speak without being overheard, close enough to kiss if they wanted, but Lilani put the stray romantic thought out of her mind.

For now.

"Are you well?" Vandra asked.

Lilani nodded. "It's a very comfortable house. I hope the monarchs will see us soon." Even if they didn't know or believe about the failing pylon, they'd want a chance to gawk. "And you? Your siblings?"

"All well." Her smile seemed sad.

Lilani's grip tightened on the gate. "What's happened?"

"A friend of mine…passed not long after I returned."

"Passed?" Lilani asked softly. By Vandra's sad expression, there was only one place the friend could have gone. "I'm sorry." Lilani had to wonder how old a friend it was, how close they were. They must have known each other well for Vandra to be so sad. "Was it sudden?"

Vandra nodded. "And connected to the trouble with the pylons."

Lilani's stomach tied up in knots. So, people were dying already. But humans became infirm when they aged. Could they die from worry? She risked moving her hand onto Vandra's and giving it a squeeze.

Vandra took a sharp breath and seemed as if she might pull back. Embarrassment bloomed inside Lilani, and she tried to pull away, thinking Vandra didn't want to be touched, but Vandra leaned forward, lips parting and gaze darting toward Lilani's mouth.

Was that desire? Lilani felt an answering heat rise within her, but she couldn't indulge it here, not with the guards and the curious onlookers.

"Vandra," Lilani said softly.

Vandra's gaze jumped to Lilani's eyes before she glanced away, stammering, the color in her cheeks deepening. "Sorry."

"I'm glad you're all right," Lilani said.

Vandra smiled again, but before she could speak, Lilani tightened her grip. "When the seneschal comes back, I can tell him I want you with us. He asked if we needed anything; I can lay claim to an alchemist." Vandra brightened, but Lilani shook her head. "Before you say yes, consider that it might make your own people suspicious of you."

Vandra shook her head. "That doesn't matter. We need to be able to speak whenever we want."

Lilani nodded, proud and pleased. If after this, Vandra's people wanted nothing more to do with a friend of the seelie, Lilani would take Vandra and her family with her when she left. She could bring her mother around to the idea of having a few humans in her midst, and there had to be a way of getting past the magic of the Court.

After another glance at the guards, Lilani let her hand drop. She had no doubt this incident would be reported to a superior, but if Vandra was going to become part of Lilani's retinue, that didn't matter. She had no doubt she could get what she wanted. She was used to arguing with immortals. She'd heard it all.

❖

Vandra didn't know what to do. The guards weren't letting her pass, but she didn't want to leave, not with Lilani so close. When their hands touched, heat seemed to radiate from the contact, and Vandra felt the flutter of Lilani's magical field. Vandra's first instinct had been to pull away, not wanting to give the guards a show, but Lilani's presence drew her forward as if they had opposing charges. After the surge passed, Vandra was glad the guards hadn't let her in. She might have draped herself all over Lilani then died of embarrassment.

Now Lilani had come up with the perfect solution to their predicament, but she was right that claiming Vandra and the twins as part of her retinue might alienate their own people. Still, no matter what, Vandra *had* to work with the seelie. Even if certain assemblypersons wanted to oust her because of her ties to Ariadne, she *was* the syndrium expert. Perhaps being listed as an associate of Lilani's would get her back to where she needed to be: fixing the pylon.

Torn by indecision, Vandra stood there stupidly, staring as Lilani smiled. They couldn't say anything real with an audience, but what would Vandra say if they were alone? Admit she'd been thinking about Lilani? That she looked forward to sleeping so Lilani could appear in her dreams? Not only was it not the time for such musings, what would she do if Lilani dismissed her feelings? Vandra shuddered. Lilani seemed kind, incapable of such boorish behavior, but Vandra wasn't the best at reading people, and she hadn't even confided how she felt to the twins.

"When is the seneschal coming back?" Vandra asked.

"It might be a while." Lilani glanced behind her. "I wish you could come in."

"It's all right," Vandra said with a little chuckle, though she burned with impatience inside. She glanced at Fieta and Pietyr. Their captain had agreed to let them stay with Vandra, but that luck wouldn't hold forever. Someone higher than the captain might take exception to their special duty, then they'd have to go back to work or risk losing their jobs.

And if they were assigned to the seelie? That could be very bad for them.

"Excuse me, Lilani," Vandra said. "I need to talk to the twins."

"I'll be here."

Vandra grinned at her then headed for Fieta and Pietyr. She tried to ignore the stares of the crowd. Not only were the residents of the restricted Garden District interested in the seelie, but people had wandered over from all corners of Parbeh. Guards at the district entrances tried to shoo away non-residents, but people still managed to slip in.

Vandra put her arms on the twins' shoulders and pulled them close. "Lilani is going to claim me as part of her retinue so we can work together. That'll likely put me in conflict with a few people in the government and the university, maybe the city in general."

"And?" Pietyr asked when she didn't continue.

"*So*," she said, "you should leave now before you're also seen as pariahs."

"What?" Fieta asked. "Not a chance!"

"You're not safe on your own," Pietyr said.

Vandra shook them slightly. "Listen! If the Watch thinks you're tied to the seelie, you could lose your jobs."

After a glance, they both said, "We're staying."

Vandra rolled her eyes. Pietyr had been lucky the Watch accepted him with his gang tattoos. He might never find another job, and Fieta wouldn't stay in the Watch if he left. She was aimless without him. "Your jobs are important to you. Don't deny it."

They frowned, looking so similar in that moment. "This is important, too," Pietyr said. "And not just because we love you."

"Yeah," Fieta added. "You have to repair the pylon, and we have to watch your back. Someone in this great muddle has to be looking out for you, Van."

She wanted to hug them and hit them, but they were right. "I love you, too, dummies. But at least tell your captain and ask him to assign you to the seelie so it's official."

Pietyr rubbed his chin. "Those are Palace Guard at the gate, not City Watch."

"But the Watch *will* want to be included," Fieta said. "Especially since the seelie aren't being housed in a government building. There might already be a squabble going on."

They looked at each other again. "You go," they said at the same time. Both pulled back, frowning, before they said, "He likes you better."

"Oh, for the gods' sake!" Vandra said. She lowered her voice and leaned in. "Fieta, pick even or odd."

"Even."

"You're going," Vandra nodded toward the edge of the crowd.

Grumbling, Fieta took off at a sprint. Pietyr nudged Vandra's shoulder. "You were going to make her go no matter what."

Vandra shrugged, but it was true. Lazy as she pretended to be, Fieta fidgeted too much if she had to wait. Pietyr was more content. They were often assigned together to balance each other out.

Vandra didn't go back to the gate, giving Lilani a friendly wave instead. Lilani faded back but hadn't gone inside. The whole street seemed to be waiting. When the seneschal marched into sight, the Palace Guard around him, the crowd fell silent. He opened the gate to the seelie house, smiling when he saw Lilani waiting. He bowed with a flourish and offered her something. Lilani replied then nodded toward Vandra.

Vandra nearly held her breath. The seneschal's cheerful mask didn't slip, but there was something predatory in his eyes as he looked at her. He said something to Lilani then walked from the yard, heading toward Vandra. Her heart hammered in her ears, and she told herself to be calm. She'd faced down the tattered lands, and this was just a man.

Who held her future with Lilani in his hands.

The seneschal stared at her. She wasn't wearing her scholar's robe or any sign of her status, but she had no doubt that he'd find out everything about her within the hour.

"The seelie have requested your presence at their welcoming ball this evening." He held something out, and she took it without thinking. Thick paper, it had handwriting so flowery and dense she could barely read it.

"An invitation?" She squinted at it. "To a ball?" She blinked several times. With all the work that needed to be done, they were having a party?

"Someone on my staff can tell you where to purchase suitable attire."

"Attire?" Confusion was tipping into anger. A pylon had failed, and the monarchs wanted to celebrate?

"Attire means clothing," he said slowly.

She almost hit him, but Pietyr poked her sharply in the back. "She will be suitably attired," he said with a small bow.

The seneschal smiled graciously as if happy to finally be speaking to someone with brains.

"And suitably guarded," another voice said.

Vandra turned to see the twins' captain Killian, Fieta at his side. She sighed in relief. The seneschal stared at the captain, but before he could say anything, Killian stepped forward. "Since the seelie are guests of the city as well as the five monarchs," Killian said, "I'm assigning these two to guard them as well as provide escort for Professor Singh."

The seneschal flushed, but his smile didn't slip. She wondered if he coated his teeth in something that wouldn't let his mouth close. He had to bow, but Vandra had no doubt the commander of the Palace Guard would be meeting with the commander of the City Watch soon enough. That was fine with Vandra. She wouldn't be involved.

When the seneschal marched away, one of his retinue, a young man with long, fair hair, stopped in front of Vandra. "Begging your pardon, Professor," he said. "Would you like me to show you some shops as the seneschal suggested, or do you have yourself well in hand?"

His smile seemed genuine, and he offered help instead of demanding, so Vandra's temper cooled a bit. And now that she was thinking, she realized that neither she nor anyone in her family had anything suitable for a ball at the palace.

"I don't suppose I can wear my scholar's robe?" she asked quietly.

The servant frowned in sympathy. "I'm sure we can find something that conveys the dignity of your office and nods to the pageantry of the evening. And since you're part of the special party," he glanced at the seelie, "there will be a substantial discount."

Well, she was happy he brought it up instead of making her say it. She sighed. While there was a *crisis*, she was going to go *shopping* rather than meet with other alchemists and the seelie to keep humanity alive. From the gate, Lilani nodded, smiling happily. Vandra nodded back. At least seeing Lilani was something to look forward to.

CHAPTER THIRTEEN

And now Lilani had a ball to go to, which sounded like quite a spectacle, if the flowery invitation was to be believed. Strange that the monarchs didn't want to talk about the pylons right away, but perhaps this celebration was part of their customs, and the conversation would come after the dance.

Faelyn took the invitation and turned it over. "It even smells nice. We better put on our best."

"Are you talking about clothing or fake expressions of happiness?"

He gave her a relaxed, blissful, completely artificial smile. "Both."

She chuckled and went upstairs to change into a coat of deep indigo. After brushing out her hair, she piled it on top of her head, leaving some curls to cascade around her ears and neck. Her magic shifted them around, but she'd be surprised if any of the humans noticed. Even if they did, they'd have to get used to the magical field that surrounded all seelie sooner or later.

Faelyn switched to a bright green frock coat and braided his hair tightly, tucking the tail under the rest. They both decided on a little jewelry; no doubt the humans would be decked out in full finery. Faelyn chose silver cuffs that curled over the entire length of the ear. Lilani dangled gold ornaments from the pointed tips of her ears. Metallic thread chased through her coat and Faelyn's, and their guards' armor was once again polished to an almost metallic shine.

The two guards posing as attendants, Maegwyn and Burani, would stay in the house, watching for intruders, though Maegwyn didn't seem pleased to be left behind. By her scowl, Lilani bet she lamented volunteering to be an attendant.

"We'll bring you some sweets," Lilani promised. "Or whatever they have during a celebration."

Maegwyn gave her a grateful smile. Burani only snorted a laugh.

Then all Lilani had to do was wait for their escort. Vandra would be part of it, thank the elders. When lanterns paused at the gate at dusk, Lilani nearly ran up the path, anxious to greet Vandra without a barrier between them.

Lilani took a sharp breath as she reached the gate, her eyes pinned on the vision before her. Vandra wore a crimson skirt embroidered in gold thread. It flared when she turned, displaying depths of sparkling decoration. The neckline of the tunic dipped low, and the hem didn't quite meet the skirt, revealing tantalizing glimpses of flesh. Embroidery covered the scarf that hung backwards across Vandra's throat. Sparkling with clips of bronze and copper, her thick dark hair had been pinned behind her head, the longest pieces left to cascade down her back.

Her dark eyes widened as she looked Lilani up and down, and Lilani couldn't hide her grin. Vandra's siblings stood behind her, dressed in similar costume, though with plainer designs, no scarf, full shirts with higher necks, and simple, flaring skirts that only reached their knees. They also carried daggers at their hips, and she supposed the flared skirt would be easier to fight in if it came to that.

By the elders, Lilani hoped it wouldn't.

When the seneschal Wurabi opened the gate, bowing, Lilani hurried past and went to Vandra with her hands outstretched. Vandra took them, and they didn't speak for several moments, grinning at each other like fools.

Faelyn cleared his throat. Lilani tore her eyes off Vandra and looked to her siblings. "Fieta, Pietyr, nice to see you again."

They smiled, Pietyr's more welcoming than Fieta's, but both seemed happy enough. Lilani turned. "This is Faelyn, my advisor. My guards Lucian, Alonse, Carisse, and Selgwyn."

The guards inclined their heads, and Vandra and her siblings followed suit before saying hello.

Lilani shook her head. "Not all of them speak the human tongue, I'm afraid." She turned so that her gaze included Wurabi, too. "Only Faelyn and I are fluent."

Wurabi bowed and gestured ahead. "Shall we?"

The seelie guards surrounded Lilani, Faelyn, Vandra, and the twins in a loose circle, and the human guards, headed by Wurabi, spread around them all. Lilani tried not to think of them as a wall, trapping her in. It was enough to make her long for home.

If it didn't have a murderer in it.

Lilani leaned toward Vandra, anxious for a change of thought. "I'm counting on you to tell me how to behave at this ball."

Vandra snorted. "You're out of luck. I've never been to one."

Lilani frowned. "It's not a human custom? The party before the serious conversation?"

"Ha!" Vandra covered her mouth and lowered her voice. "It seems like typical human foot-dragging if you ask me. All anyone ever wants to do is talk."

Lilani sighed. "That's a seelie problem, too." But the humans couldn't carry on the same argument for hundreds of years. She touched the scarf that fluttered behind Vandra. It was as soft as she imagined. "But I'm grateful for any occasion that lets me see you in this."

Vandra ducked her head, and Lilani bet her cheeks were burning. "You look lovely, too. I'm so glad to finally be spending time with you."

Lilani took Vandra's hand, wanting to forget the pylons and the politics for a little while and simply stroll with her crush. Vandra's smile sparkled like a star, and Lilani wondered if her lips would be as soft as her scarf.

Lilani's magic pulsed within her, and she concentrated to make it behave.

Soon, Vandra pointed out a rectangular building with four massive towers. "We're close to the center of Parbeh. The tower on the left is above the Assembly House, next to that is the treasury, then the Courts of Law, and the farthest right is where we're going: the Monarchs' Seat."

"And the assembly rules all of Citran?" Lilani asked.

"With the five monarchs."

Lilani frowned. Her mother ruled the seelie alone, but maybe the humans needed many rulers because there were so many of them. "Are there five monarchs because there were five human kingdoms before the tattered lands consumed them?"

"There were seven," Vandra said. "Two are…not around anymore." She shook her head as if the idea of two entire kingdoms being wiped out was more than she could utter.

Lilani squeezed her hand, her heart aching for all the dead. "Very gracious of the monarch of Citran to welcome the other rulers as equals."

Vandra gave her a sidelong look. "Well, Citran is full to bursting with humans from those kingdoms, enough to overpower us if they wanted. Best if they have someone looking out for their interests, though some people are still upset that they don't have their own kingdoms anymore."

"I see." How long had the humans debated before they settled on a plan that wouldn't rob refugees of their leadership while maintaining the rights of the humans who'd lived in this land first? And even after they'd made decisions, some still weren't happy. That was also a seelie problem. "And as an alchemist, you work with the assembly?"

"I work for the university." She pointed, but it was too dark to see far. "It's in that direction, a place of teaching and learning. Mostly alchemists, engineers, and scholars."

Faelyn stuck his head between them. "You teach?"

Lilani chuckled. "If you're a teacher like Faelyn, you've made a friend for life."

Vandra grinned. "I teach a little. Mostly, I study and experiment. The great library of Parbeh is also at the university."

Lilani's heart fluttered. "All the human knowledge is there?"

"Well, all that wasn't lost to the tattered lands."

Lilani sighed. "Yes, many books were left behind when my people fled, too."

Vandra bit her lip, and the next words burst out as if she couldn't contain them. "Why didn't the seelie stay where they were? They can hide from the tattered lands, right?"

Lilani shivered at the thought of living within that cloud of dread. "We can hide from the creatures, and our magic protects us from the taint, from being corrupted, but the feeling of the tattered lands... unnerves us. We don't like to be near it."

Vandra brightened. "But with your magic, your people could mount expeditions to their former homes? You could retrieve your lost books as well as...anything else." She ducked her head, and Lilani knew what she was thinking. If the seelie could get their own books, they might be able to rescue the humans' as well.

"Let's save that until after this current crisis," Lilani said. "The decision wouldn't be up to me, anyway."

When they reached the entrance to the Monarchs' Seat, Lilani gave Vandra's hand a final squeeze before letting go. From a distance, the walls had seemed solid and bare, but they were actually carved from street to ceiling with statues and frescoes. Lilani wished she could linger, but Wurabi kept them moving to a set of iron-studded wooden doors which stood open to admit a throng of people.

The human guards cleared the way to the front, and the partygoers stared at the seelie, covering their mouths with fans as they whispered to their neighbors. The dress varied wildly: dresses and trousers and skirts of all colors and lengths. Lilani supposed it was a sign of each land the humans originally hailed from. It might be several generations before everyone fully assimilated. The seelie had never had very separate cultures, another product of their long lives. They changed only slowly, old ideas replaced at a glacial pace. Her frock coat had been her mother's and probably her grandfather's, but the stitching had changed as fashion evolved. She took comfort in that sort of repurposing, as if she carried a bit of history on her back.

Inside the doors, strains of music came from a raised platform, but the notes were nearly lost in the noise of conversation. People spun and swayed in a dance, pairs breaking off to dance in circles of six or ten before separating into pairs again. The moving mix of color, the swells of noise, and the gusts of perfume nearly overwhelmed the senses.

Those nearest the doors caught sight of the seelie and stumbled. Word spread through the room more quickly than fire, and soon a path cleared between the seelie and another raised platform that held a long table and a handful of ornate chairs. As the guards escorted Lilani's party forward, the five people on the platform stood, gathering in front of the table for a closer look.

The five monarchs. At last. Lilani's heart lifted. At the moment, any step in the right direction seemed like a leap.

The hall had gone quiet. Wurabi halted on the first step of the dais and spoke loudly. "Esteemed monarchs of the five kingdoms, protectors of this, our human race, I present, Lilani, representative of the seelie Court."

Lilani bowed her head, her shoulders following a little. As Faelyn told her, the seelie were not subjects of this monarchy and did not owe it fealty, but she wanted to be polite. After what Vandra had said about not telling anyone she was the daughter of the empress, she didn't want the monarchs to think she held the same rank as them.

The five monarchs nodded. "Monarch Nimah Pentari," Wurabi announced.

Nimah Pentari was dressed like Vandra, though her dark green skirt and tunic glimmered in the light, and her sandals glittered with gold and jewels. She wore gold netting over her black hair, and the point of a crown rested on her brow, dangling a green gem in the middle of her forehead. "Welcome, Lilani," she said with a smile, "envoy of the seelie, to Citran, our combined kingdom."

Lilani supposed that as the leader of Citran itself, this monarch always got to speak first. At least Nimah Pentari seemed glad to see her. Before Lilani could respond, Wurabi continued.

"Monarch Metran Van Hurans." The man next to Nimah Pentari was dressed in a coat similar to Lilani's, but the front hem reached his knees instead of ending at the waist. It was heavily embroidered, and he had tiny jewels woven into his black beard as well as a heavy gold circlet on his dark brow. He glared as if the very presence of the seelie offended him.

"Monarch Bora Daelsdotter." A bored-seeming pale woman with hair the color of copper, she wore a dark, heavily patterned skirt that reached her knees and a dagger at her belt. The fabric of her skirt matched a heavy scarf that ran around her waist and up the front of her blousy white tunic, dangling over one shoulder. Tattoos covered the right side of her pale face, bold patterns in dark blue.

"Monarch Falla Sett." An olive-skinned man stood next to Bora, his costume similar to hers, except that he wore trousers, and the scarf had been separated into a belt and a matching patch on his shoulder. And he gave Lilani, Vandra, and probably everyone else a slow glance and a leer so bold, Lilani was tempted to chuckle. The pattern of his clothing was softer, a mix of brown and gold. He had only a small beard and a slim circlet of silver on his brow.

"Monarch Shyn Harra Rhys." The last monarch was small in stature, and Lilani could not see any obvious signs of their sex. For hair, they had no more than a fine dark fuzz, and the planes of the face were sharp with high cheekbones. Their coloring was a shade lighter than Vandra's or Lilani's, and their clothing was simple: a plain tunic and trousers made of maroon fabric. Dark red rubies glittered from both ears, and they sported intricate tattoos that started on their hands and disappeared up their sleeves. They looked on Lilani and the rest of the seelie with a small, welcoming smile.

"Our august and wise leaders," Wurabi said. "May their rule last forever."

The room erupted in applause, even though they had to know that nothing human lasted forever. Lilani waited for the roar to die down before she offered another bow. "Many thanks from myself and my people for allowing this visit. After so much time apart, I am sure we have much to share."

Polite applause followed. Lilani feared saying anything more. She expected the monarchs to whisk her away to some private room, but the music began again. People pushed forward, held back by the Guard, but Lilani heard several people calling her name as well as calls of, "Ambassador!"

Lilani wondered if she should acknowledge the cries, but Vandra nudged her. The monarchs were staring as if waiting. She looked to Wurabi who nodded for her to mount the dais. She stopped on the third step, unsure of the protocol. Faelyn stayed at her back, leaving the Guard on the lowest step. Vandra shifted from foot to foot before Lilani gestured for her to come, too.

Falla Sett was the first to approach. "Well, well, a seelie after all this time. You must tell us, Ambassador Lilani, what brings the seelie out of hiding?"

Shyn Harra Rhys gave him a bland look. "What my esteemed colleague means is, welcome. And I'm sure he would then add a polite inquiry as to the well-being of your people."

Nimah Pentari laughed. "I second both of those thoughts."

Lilani chuckled, glad they had a sense of humor. "My people are well. And we thought it time to be reacquainted with humanity after the possible trouble on the horizon."

They nodded, and the other two moved closer. So, they all knew, but it seemed as if they were waiting for her to continue.

"The pylons—" she said.

"There will be time enough to speak of those on the morrow," Bora Daelsdotter said. She hadn't lost her frown. "Did your…leader not want to come and speak with us personally?"

"The empress meant no offense," Lilani said, trying not to dislike this monarch at once. "She never leaves the Court."

"Never?" Shyn Harra Rhys asked.

Lilani shook her head. Her mother never even went for a walk in the woods or up the Highpeak.

"What happens if she does?" Metran Van Hurans asked. "If it would not be unpolitic to reveal it."

Lilani blinked, at a loss. She had no idea.

Faelyn cleared his throat. "Forgive me, Monarchs. My name is Faelyn. I am advisor to the empress and Lilani. No magical compulsion requires the empress to remain in the Court. It is simply that she has always been there, and there is little value in upsetting a routine that is so comfortable, just as when one knows one should be working but spends all day relaxing instead."

That got a couple of chuckles, as well as a frown from Metran Van Hurans. Falla Sett smirked as if his idea of relaxing involved something incredibly licentious.

Nimah Pentari gave him a dark look and gestured toward the party. "Please, enjoy yourselves. And feel free to shoo away any pests that seek to monopolize your time." She didn't look at her fellow monarchs as she spoke, but Lilani got the feeling she was talking about them. She glanced at Vandra as if wondering about the connection there but turned away instead of asking, towing Falla Sett with her.

Lilani stepped down, and Shyn Harra Rhys joined her, offering a smile and gesturing toward a table in the corner. The human guards had mostly dispersed, with only one staying at Shyn Harra Rhys's side. The seelie guards stayed with Lilani and Vandra.

Shyn Harra Rhys seemed not to notice when their passage disturbed the dancers, who bowed at the monarch's passing. "How do you like Parbeh?"

Lilani just kept herself from mentioning the smells. "What I've seen of it seems wondrous, Monarch."

"Shyn, please. I've not yet met your alchemist friend."

"Professor Vandra Singh," Lilani offered, not able to help a smile. "We hope to work together."

Vandra bowed, her mouth working as if she couldn't decide what to say. "A…pleasure."

"Do the seelie practice alchemy as well?" Shyn asked.

"We have herbalists, but I don't think it's the same."

"Is there a seelie university?"

Maybe Shyn was as interested in books as she was. "No, though we have a library. We are taught by our elders."

"Who never die, yes?" Shyn asked. "They must be fonts of knowledge!"

Lilani couldn't help a laugh. If Shyn was only interested in seelie immortality because of the knowledge, they would make a good ally. "Some more than others. And some are only fonts in their own minds."

When Shyn threw their head back and laughed, Lilani nearly jumped. She hadn't expected such an overt display of joy. "The same is no doubt true for many, both seelie and human. Imagine if we bonded over mutual irritation about pretention in both our peoples."

That would be better than all of them dying together. Or running from the tattered lands and throwing themselves into the sea. When they reached a table loaded with food, Shyn moved off to speak with someone else.

"I have never been so close to the monarchs in all my life," Vandra said. "Even when they congratulated my graduating class."

"Did it change your opinion of them?" Lilani asked.

"Well, I like some better and some worse."

"I know you were hoping for a chance to speak about the pylons. I was, too."

"Or at least to be alone for a while."

Lilani glanced at her in surprise, delighted by the idea.

Vandra stiffened and covered her mouth as if just realizing what she said. "To...talk...that's what I meant. I didn't... Oh gods, I'm so sorry!"

Lilani waved to stop the flow of words. "It's all right. I know what you meant."

Vandra had turned several shades darker. By her own burning cheeks, Lilani had joined her. "I can't believe I said something so stupid," Vandra said. "Not that I wouldn't...I mean, you are very..." She went darker still, verging on purple.

Lilani felt compelled to lay a hand on her shoulder. She fought her own blush and leaned close. "I think you're *very*, too."

Now Vandra looked at her with gratitude and admiration as well as something else, a smile that seemed torn between surprised and intrigued.

Before they could say anything more, Faelyn said, "Perhaps some mingling is in order." When they both looked at him, he gave Vandra a kindly smile. "Diplomacy is important."

Vandra quickly grew tired of having to fend off one nosy person after another. She'd been unnerved after meeting the five monarchs, but since most of them acted like ordinary people, she'd lost interest. As for the regular crowd, she'd *started* without interest. It became harder and harder to keep a hospitable smile plastered on her face.

If they couldn't work, she at least wanted to be alone with Lilani, but it didn't look like she'd get the chance anytime soon. And no one really wanted to talk to her. She let the crowd around the seelie push her to the edge and moved to the buffet, Fieta and Pietyr behind her.

"This party is boring," Fieta said. "And my thighs are chafing under this skirt."

Pietyr gave her a look. "You aren't wearing the little shorts?"

"What little shorts?"

"The undergarment that goes under here." Vandra twitched her skirt. "They were in the bag."

Fieta's expression darkened. "No one told me about any shorts!"

Pietyr barked a laugh. Fieta gave him a shove.

"Children, behave," Vandra said. "Hopefully, this ball won't last much longer."

But the crowd around the seelie didn't seem likely to break up any time soon. Vandra sighed, wishing Ariadne was here to guide her. She'd have known how to excuse herself gracefully and get some work done.

Thinking about her spawned a wave of dread in Vandra's stomach. Ariadne could have navigated all the diplomacy with complete aplomb. How was Vandra supposed to do the same?

"I think those shrimp were bad," Fieta said, rubbing her stomach.

"I didn't even have shrimp, and I feel it," Pietyr said.

Vandra frowned at them. "Like a pit of dread in your stomach?"

They nodded. Vandra glanced around. The feeling was too sudden to be something they'd just eaten. It felt similar to the emanations of the tattered piece of metal. Had someone from the assembly brought it here? Why? She didn't see anyone flashing it around. The nearest people were two blank-faced palace guards who stood on either side of a door past the table. They didn't seem queasy, and she didn't spot anyone else holding their stomachs, but the feeling persisted, growing stronger by the moment.

The hair on the back of Vandra's neck stood up. She shivered, every primitive instinct telling her to flee. She backed away from the buffet, tugging Pietyr and Fieta with her. On the table in front of her, a puff pastry rolled off a dessert tower, seemingly blown by the wind.

Or knocked away by the passage of an invisible hand, one that had been reaching for Vandra.

"Van," Fieta whispered. She pulled the scarf from Vandra's neck. It had been slit in the center.

Vandra felt her neck and winced at a slight, papercut-like pain. Fear froze her to the spot.

"It's a scratch," Fieta said. "Hardly any blood."

"Because she stepped away," Pietyr said as he moved in front of her. "Otherwise, she would've been…" He swallowed and pulled Vandra back farther, knocking into some of the partygoers and causing a bit of a stir.

"What now?" Fieta asked.

Vandra could barely speak, fighting the image of Ariadne's ruined neck. She told her brain to work; she needed to think. "Someone just tried to kill me. Someone invisible."

"Seelie," Pietyr said.

Vandra swallowed hard and looked for Lilani. All the seelie she'd brought were still with her. And why would they want to kill Vandra here? They'd had better opportunities. Why wait for a crowded ball? So, if it wasn't anyone with Lilani…

"Head for the seelie," Vandra said. "They can tell us what to do."

Pietyr frowned hard. "One of them just tried to kill you."

"They're all still there! It had to be a different seelie."

Fieta shushed them. "If they know who the killer is, they won't do anything while we're standing in the middle of them, and if they don't know, they can watch our backs."

Vandra tried to still her trembling, but the glittering throng seemed sinister, a distraction for murderous intent. Lilani's guards parted to let Vandra and the twins through, and something in Vandra's expression made Lilani's eyes widen. She had a word with Lucian, and he pushed out all the curious humans. Then the guards closed ranks and maneuvered everyone closer to a corner.

"What—" Lilani started.

"An invisible seelie cut Vandra's scarf." Pietyr thrust it under Lilani's nose.

Selgwyn took it instead, examining the hole.

"Are you all right?" Lilani asked.

Vandra nodded. "We were standing over there, and we all felt… something rotten, like the tattered metal I picked up at the border, so I backed away, and then…" She gestured at the scarf.

Lilani paled and looked to Faelyn. He frowned and glanced about. "Someone tried to kill Lilani at the Court, too."

Vandra sucked in a breath, afraid for both of them now. Had her would-be murderer followed Lilani to Parbeh in order to kill everyone she knew? Or had they beaten her here and murdered Ariadne, too?

"The friend I told you about, the one that passed away," Vandra said. "She was murdered in her bed, her throat cut."

Lilani gripped her hand. "Vandra, I'm so sorry!"

Vandra squeezed her hand. "What do we do now?"

"This is beginning to sound like a conspiracy," Faelyn said. "Do we tell the human guards?"

"Will they believe us?" Lilani asked.

"If they did," Pietyr said, "they might think one of you is the murderer." And by the way he and Fieta frowned, he wasn't ruling that out.

Lilani's eyes had gotten wider, her breaths shorter. She seemed one second away from bolting. Her fear dampened Vandra's, stoking a protective urge.

"You'll be all right, Lilani," Vandra said. "I'll…" She wanted to promise protection, but what could she actually do? "We'll help each other."

Lilani took a deep breath and seemed calmer. Vandra admired her so much in that moment, it was hard not to kiss her, a reward for being brave.

"I don't feel queasy right now," Fieta said. "So, if that had something to do with the murderer, they're probably gone, right?"

Lilani had another word with Lucian. He strode to the buffet, scanning the crowd, the doorway. When he returned, he shook his head and said something in seelie.

"He felt nothing," Lilani said.

When she and Vandra sighed in unison, they chuckled at one another, though Vandra heard an edge in her own voice. The image of Ariadne wouldn't leave her, and she rubbed her throat, her heart still thundering.

"We should leave with a crowd," Faelyn said. "And hurry back to the guesthouse."

They met up with their human guards again and timed their departure to coincide with another large group. Vandra thought it must be midnight or thereabouts. When they reached the guesthouse, should she and the twins stay the night? There was safety in numbers, and Lilani would no doubt want Vandra to be safe.

And maybe her family would be safer *without* Vandra for the time being. That should have made her feel better, but terror still clawed at the edge of her consciousness. She tried to focus on something else, like the fact that she might very well be about to spend the night with Lilani.

Nothing sexual would happen, of course, not in the midst of a crisis. And they could finally work on a solution to the pylon without distractions. She tried to picture it, tried to morph her fear into something else. They'd work hard, but they'd eventually have to take a break, which would leave them alone together. Finally.

That was so much more pleasant to think about instead of someone trying to kill them, so much better to picture than Ariadne's death. Vandra's adrenaline sought a new outlet in fantasy, and when Lilani's hand closed over hers, Vandra's heart raced both from the danger and from the enchanting woman at her side. She met Lilani's gaze and had a vision of those purple eyes dark with desire. What would that melodious voice sound like as it was crying out in ecstasy?

Vandra tried to clear her throat and speak about anything else, but her libido wasn't listening now that it had been roused. She needed a release from all this tension. Lilani's touch caused tingles all through her, and Vandra clearly did something to Lilani, too. Their gaze hadn't broken, and Lilani leaned toward Vandra, coming so close that her features blurred. Even with all the danger and pain, Vandra let her eyes slip closed and felt Lilani's breath on her face.

"By the elders!" Faelyn cried.

Vandra's eyes flew open. Lilani's did the same. They leaned away, and their hands came loose. The street ahead was lit with an orange glow, and as the wind shifted, Vandra smelled smoke. Cries of alarm drifted down the street. The guards moved them faster, heading deeper into the Garden District. The smoke became denser, the glow brighter.

"Oh gods," Vandra said.

Waves of flame engulfed Lilani's guesthouse. Bucket brigades tossed water into the blaze and over the neighboring houses. A firefighting machine lumbered down the street, spraying bursts of water from its huge tank, and Vandra heard the sound of another one rumbling nearby.

They wouldn't be in time. Vandra didn't know if there was enough water in Parbeh to put out a fire so massive. All they could do was hope to save the houses around it.

"Maegwyn, Burani," Lilani whispered.

Vandra glanced at her. Those weren't the names of any of the seelie around them. There must have been two more in the burning house. "Oh, sweet gods." After years without communication, the seelie had finally come to Parbeh, and it had killed two of them within a day.

CHAPTER FOURTEEN

Vandra's mind raced as she tried to think of a way to stop the blaze. She grasped Lilani's hands. "I'm so sorry."

When Lilani gave her a stricken look, Vandra clenched her jaw. She might not be able to fight the fire, but she could find out if anyone made it out alive. The commander of the human guards was shouting at the bystanders, demanding to know what happened, but Vandra couldn't hear him, so she grabbed her own passerby. "Did any seelie come out of that house?"

When he only gaped, she repeated the question, turning and addressing several people. The question passed through the crowd, and people shook their heads. Fieta followed her lead while Pietyr stayed with Lilani. They heard several stories of humans being injured by smoke or cinders, but no one had seen any seelie.

But the seelie could have been invisible. Vandra moved back to Lilani. In a short time, her face had gone from stricken to stone.

"No one saw them," Vandra said. "But that doesn't mean—"

"We set a meeting place among the shanties." Lilani said, so softly Vandra almost didn't hear. She scanned the crowd, brows drawn. "If they survived." Her voice choked.

Vandra wanted to hold her, but with so many people watching...

Screw it. Maybe the gods would shield her. She put an arm around Lilani's shoulders. "I'm so sorry."

Lilani leaned into her, and her magical field rushed over Vandra like a warm breeze, comforting and tingling all at once.

When Lucian gestured toward them, Lilani pulled away. Vandra stepped back reluctantly, missing the feel of Lilani's body, her light scent of jasmine. The seelie guards were eyeing the street as if memorizing the exits. Vandra's heart thudded. Were they thinking of running? Would they ever come back? She opened her mouth to ask, but the human captain butted in.

"You're all coming with me." He took a deep breath as the seelie regarded him coolly. "Honored guests, please. We don't know what happened, and we need to ask questions. The five monarchs will have other…accommodation for you."

Vandra frowned. The way he paused before "accommodation" could mean another house or a prison cell.

"We must find out if my attendants are alive," Lilani said, glaring. Everyone else shuffled as if preparing to square off.

"We'll look for them," the captain said. "One of your guards can come along." He glanced around. The crowd seemed torn between watching the fire and whatever was happening with the seelie. "Please, I'm very sorry, but we have protocol."

Instead of bunching up as Vandra would have suspected, the seelie took a few steps away from one another, loosening their circle. Lilani cast one look at Vandra and smiled sadly; she seemed on the verge of saying something, but before she could, one of the human guards took a step toward the nearest seelie guard, reaching for her weapon.

All the seelie vanished.

The human guards leapt back almost in unison. Even Vandra froze, and she *knew* what the seelie could do. She felt a rush of wind as someone dashed past, and she had to keep from shouting. If the alternative was capture, the seelie had to get away. The palace guards brought their weapons up and waited, but the seelie didn't strike. Vandra could barely breathe, her lips clamped shut. After a few long moments, the guards probed the air with their weapons. Nothing. The seelie were gone.

The captain swore and turned on Vandra, eyes blazing. "Where did they go?"

Vandra shrugged, not wanting to lie, but she didn't know the whole truth. She did know that Lilani had left her. There might not have been any choice, but it stung.

"We know as much as you, Captain," Pietyr said.

The captain turned his glare on Pietyr, proving a lack of intelligence; he should have been more concerned with Fieta standing behind him. "You're coming with me," he said. "Don't run."

"We're stuck being visible, Captain," Fieta said.

The captain whirled around, gave her a glare, and pointed back the way they'd come. "If you please," he said through gritted teeth.

For the next few hours it was questions, questions, questions in a tiny room deep inside the Courts of Law. With her, Fieta, Pietyr, and a handful of guards, the room didn't have air. Vandra grew tired of repeating herself and very tired of hiding what she couldn't say. Yes, she knew the seelie could vanish; she thought everyone knew that. No, she didn't know where they'd gone. It was partly true. She didn't know exactly where the "shanties" were that Lilani had spoken of, but she could guess.

She wouldn't guess, though. She was bad enough at lies of omission; she didn't want to try to invent something. As it got later, it was hard enough to keep the facts straight. One kept bubbling to the surface, though: Lilani was gone.

Vandra didn't want to see her locked up and questioned. And Lilani had seemed stricken; she hadn't wanted to leave. Still, her absence left an ache in Vandra's chest, even though moping wouldn't help anything. As if fine-tuning a formula, Vandra turned her depression into anger, a much more useful emotion.

When the seneschal came in, Vandra thrust her scarf at him and told him about the attack during the ball, adding that they hadn't reported it because they hadn't been sure what had happened. The seneschal stuck his hand through the hole in her scarf and seemed lost in thought. Finally, he gave the scarf to one of the guards, and the questions went on.

Vandra's anger carried her until the third hour, when she wanted to scream. She was tired, worried about Lilani, trapped in a closet, her intelligence was being wasted, and she still hadn't been allowed to work on the gods-cursed pylons! She rubbed a hand down her face and tried to control her rising temper. Under the table, her leg bounced like a piston, and she wished the vibrations could shake the building down.

"Why did the seelie flee?" the seneschal asked.

Vandra couldn't keep the sarcasm out of her voice. "I suppose they didn't take kindly to two of them being murdered."

"Who said anything about murder?" The seneschal waved casually. "More likely, it was a cooking accident from someone unfamiliar with human homes."

"Right," Fieta said. "They took the wood out of the stove and built a campfire in the sitting room."

The seneschal kept his oily smile, but his eyes seemed to be thinking about murder even if the rest of him wasn't. He turned his gaze to Pietyr, who smiled blandly and shrugged.

Vandra fought the urge to pace. "This is a waste of time." She wanted to be with Lilani, comforting her, working with her, talking with her, demanding an apology from her for leaving, anything but this.

The seneschal stared for a few moments until another guard came in and had a word in his ear. He smiled wider. "This way, please."

"Thank the gods." Vandra nearly leapt out of her seat and followed him, more than ready for some fresh air, but he led them to a room where the five monarchs waited. Vandra's stomach lurched to the side.

"Fuck," Fieta whispered.

Vandra didn't even have the energy to reprimand her for such a serious swear word. She could only hope the monarchs hadn't heard.

The head assemblyperson, Nata Rahvi, asked questions this time while the monarchs listened. They looked almost as tired as she felt. And they wanted to know the same things, all about her involvement with the seelie and how close she was to them. As if she'd ever betray her own kind!

But as she went through the entire story of that night again, Vandra didn't shout or swear or even invoke the gods. Even Fieta's and Pietyr's answers were less flippant in the face of royalty. They deserved medals. The thought nearly made her howl with laughter. She didn't think it was possible to be so tired that she'd risk breaking into hysterics in front of the leaders of the entire human race.

Rahvi stared at Vandra as if able to read her mind. If by some magic she could, Vandra hoped she appreciated the humor.

"What progress have you made with the pylons, Professor Singh?" Rahvi asked.

Vandra blinked, mind racing to catch up. An actual question about her *work*? Would they mind if she did cartwheels? She cleared her throat as another wave of anger drove away some of her fatigue. "My tests on the tattered metal were inconclusive, but if I might be permitted to resume work, I would be grateful." She put on a smile that she hoped didn't look too fake.

Fieta nudged her and frowned, giving her head a little shake.

Vandra sighed and let her face go blank. The smile must have looked very fake indeed.

The monarchs bent their heads together and whispered, all except Shyn Harra Rhys, who stared at Vandra with an unreadable expression.

Nimah Pentari had a word with the seneschal, then the monarchs left.

The seneschal gestured for Vandra and the twins to follow, pushing them out into the street before closing an iron-bound door behind them.

Vandra breathed deep, put her arms over her head, and stretched. The sky was lightening with the first hints of dawn, and she reveled in it, feeling as if she'd been buried alive for the past few hours.

"Come on," Pietyr said. "Let's go home. I hope the seelie made it out all right, the non-murderous ones, anyway."

Fieta snorted. "I second that."

Vandra sighed, hoping any nearby gods would keep Lilani safe. To argue with later? Yes, among other things. "When we go back to the pylon, we can find them again."

Fieta gave her a pitying look. "Van, they're not going to let you work on the pylon anymore."

Vandra stopped, stomach clenching. "What?"

"Did you miss those looks, the whispers? They think we're part of some seelie plot. They're not going to let us anywhere near the pylons."

Vandra looked to Pietyr, expecting him to disagree with their sister, but he gave her a sorry nod.

The ground seemed to fall away. Vandra clenched her hands, willing the street to stop going in and out of focus. "But surely they wouldn't throw away knowledge just because of…" She'd been about to say "a few setbacks," but the death of two seelie and an attack on Vandra's life was more than that.

Ariadne was more than a setback.

Vandra shook her head. "People have died, but even more will die if we do nothing. Who else will the monarchs get? Anyone from the university would consult me." She felt a sting of pride, but this was more than that. This was *common sense*. "Surely…surely…"

The twins kept their apologetic looks.

"No." Vandra stalked toward the university, her mind on fire. When she reached the grand building with its delicate spires and welcoming atmosphere of learning, she skidded to a halt. Guards waited at the doors, studying every early riser who passed.

She tried to look as if she was supposed to be there. Confidence was key when you were going where you didn't belong; Pietyr had taught her that. And she did belong here. She had only ever belonged here.

One of the guards looked at a sheet of paper and barred her way. "I'm sorry, Professor Singh."

Dark red spots swam in Vandra's vision, and she nearly screamed. Her hands began to cramp as she curled them tight. Pietyr pulled her away. Vandra's breath came in gasps as the twins guided her back home. She couldn't go to her apartment. That was university property, too. They'd be pawing through her things, boxing them up. They had her equipment. They had the tattered metal. There was nothing for her.

Tears almost broke through her rage. The world was still at stake, and they were going to force her to do *nothing*?

At home, Papa made her a cup of tea, but she didn't hear anything he said, didn't acknowledge Mama's embrace. As soon as she could get away, Vandra slinked to her old room at the top of the stairs, changed into a nightshirt, and crawled into a bed that now belonged to a sister who wouldn't need it until nightfall.

Sleep wouldn't come, no matter that Vandra was exhausted. She wept for a while, clenched her fists, and railed inside her mind, but no amount of emotion could quiet her brain. This was another in a string of dismal failures. The university would fire her; they wouldn't want her scandal clinging to them. One of the mining corps might take her. She'd spend her days figuring out how to wrest syndrium from the ground and waste it on whatever scheme the corporation dreamed up. But even that wouldn't last for long, not with the pylons going out.

Ariadne was dead, sacrificed and buried in bureaucracy.

Lilani was gone, never to be seen again.

And the world was still ending.

Vandra pulled the blanket over her head, trying to shut out the light along with the thoughts. And someone wanted her dead. Gods supreme, they wanted to murder the entire human race.

Vandra sat up. That was *insane*, as twisted as that creature from the tattered lands with a face in its mouth. And feeling sorry for herself wouldn't stop it. She balled a fist and struck the mattress. If everyone but her had gone mad, so be it. She wouldn't let the pylons fail.

She knew what her family would say: she'd done enough. Others could figure it out. She needed rest. But they didn't understand. She could find a way to stop this, and if it could be done, it *had* to be done. Everyone else might be content to talk; she would act. She'd find Lilani. She would save the gods-cursed world.

Vandra threw off the covers, rubbed the grit from her eyes, and donned the clothes she'd left there the day before. A glance in the next room revealed that Fieta and Pietyr had fallen asleep, no dark thoughts keeping them awake. They were used to getting sleep whenever they could when they pulled back-to-back shifts. She watched their peaceful faces, torn between the desire to have their help and let them rest. If she woke them, Fieta would grumble, and Pietyr would make a sensible argument about why they should stay in the house, but if Vandra insisted, they'd come with her.

Vandra shut their door quietly. She'd have to beg funds from her parents for some ingredients and equipment, but they would oblige. Hopefully, it would be enough. And while she was out, she'd make a quick stop in Lowtown to see if she could spot the seelie.

More likely, they'd spot her first. Lilani might have left her a message. Vandra was the first to admit she wasn't an expert at translating feelings, but *something* had passed between them. They'd almost kissed. That was a fact. Even the thought of Lilani could bring heat to Vandra's cheeks.

And Lilani would probably want to apologize for leaving so suddenly and dooming Vandra to be questioned by idiots all night.

After borrowing money from Papa's satchel, Vandra hurried out of the house. She kept thinking of her cut scarf—which she hadn't gotten back—but it was light out, and Parbeh had never been so unsafe that people feared walking the streets in broad daylight. She'd be quick in Lowtown, surrounding herself with people the whole time, and then she'd buy what she needed in Parbeh. Even if Lilani hadn't been able to wait or leave a message, Vandra knew she'd end up back in the Seelie Forest. All Vandra had to do was get there and Lilani would come.

Simple.

❖

Shrouding had been the easy part.

After Lilani had let her magic flow over her, she stared at Vandra's shocked face and wished they could both vanish and run away together for a little while.

Then Faelyn touched Lilani's arm, and she ran. She hadn't thought of anything but escape, blocking out Vandra and the fact that Maegwyn and Burani were likely dead. The streets of Parbeh looked so different after dark, but Lucian's touch steered her. When they'd gotten a few streets away from the fire, he'd pulled on her arm, slowing, no doubt getting his bearings.

They'd gone slowly then, seeking to remain silent as they slipped around the few people who stumbled into their path. Once the fear wore off, Lilani was left with grief and anger. Why would the humans do this? Or had it been a seelie? The one who'd sought to murder her, or the one who wanted to murder Vandra?

In the dark streets, Lilani felt alone even though she was surrounded by seelie. They walked for hours. Lilani began to think they were lost when the gates to Parbeh finally appeared out of the gloom. She wanted to cry out in relief until she noticed the gates stood closed.

Faelyn cursed. Lilani was tempted to do the same, but she was too tired. Even the emotional intensity of the past few hours wouldn't help her hold her shroud much longer. Cramps wandered from her belly and down both legs. It wouldn't be long until pain vibrated up her knees all the way to her neck.

"Here." Lucian tugged on Lilani's sleeve, leading her into a deeper patch of darkness, an alley off the brighter street.

Standing so close, she felt him drop his shroud. She did the same, her magic not so much fading as oozing down around her. Not a good sign. The others followed suit, but Lilani could barely see them in the dark.

"Do we climb over?" Faelyn asked.

"Too high," Selgwyn said.

"There must be a way through." Alonse's voice. "What do the humans do if there's an emergency in the night?"

"I think the gates are to keep the emergencies out," Lucian said. "Carisse, get a closer look at that smaller door set in the gate."

Lilani felt her move past. She was happy all the guards were so capable, but it made her miss Maegwyn and Burani. Even though she hadn't known them well, it felt as if there was a hole in their group. Lilani took a deep breath and wondered if she'd grieve every time she paused from now on, if only exhaustive running could keep her mind occupied.

When Carisse reappeared in the dim alley, Lilani jumped. Faelyn touched her arm, but she couldn't take any comfort from him. She was far too tired.

"There is a door," Carisse said softly. "Also shut and barred from this side, and two guards wait on either side of the gate within small stone huts. One guard is asleep, but the other seems wakeful, and there are many torches in the wall."

Faelyn sighed. "The wakeful one would probably notice an invisible person unbarring the door."

"We can't kill him," Lilani said in case anyone was thinking it. Even if some human had killed two of them, violence wouldn't be cured with more violence. No one responded, and Lilani couldn't bring herself to ask if anyone had even thought of that solution.

"We wait for daybreak," Lucian said. "If Maegwyn and Burani survived, they'll be stuck inside the city, too. We'll look for them in the shanties."

Lilani leaned against the wall. Faelyn pulled her close. "Sit down and close your eyes," he said. "We can take turns on watch."

"I wouldn't be able to sleep," she said, "not out here in the open."

"Standing and worrying is better?"

She sighed, feared that would turn into a sob, and slid down to the wet stones. Her coat was doomed, all its history ruined, adding to the veil of sadness around her along with grief for Maegwyn and Burani, her faith in her people, and her hope for the humans.

And any chance of seeing Vandra again.

Lilani hoped the human guards wouldn't blame Vandra for Lilani's disappearance. If Vandra remained free, she'd keep working on the pylon, and Lilani would see her again. Even if both their peoples were against them, they could hold back the tattered lands themselves.

Somehow.

Selgwyn grunted in pain. Lilani sat up as someone else cursed. "What—"

Faelyn grabbed her arm. "Shroud!"

Lilani's magic stuttered but pulled together, making her feel as if a blanket was pulled too tight around her. She froze, listening, no longer able to see anyone in the dim alley.

Slowly, Lilani stood, silent. She didn't reach for the others, not knowing what had happened. But why would Faelyn call for her to shroud unless there was a threat? No bodies lay on the ground, so everyone was alive.

Lilani leaned forward, ears straining. If she stepped into the street, maybe she could see footprints in the light of the torches. Farther into the alley, something fell over, making Lilani jump. Several footsteps smacked wetly against the stone, and Lilani raced into the torchlight and whirled around, watching the ground.

A scuff appeared on a muddy stone, followed by a skidding pebble: someone walking. Friend or foe? The alley had gone silent again. Lilani breathed shallowly, waiting. Whoever stood before her seemed to be waiting, too. Something swiped through the mud on another stone, and a small lump of dirt squished to the side, headed straight for her.

Her shroud was tight. How could they still see her? As she spotted the outline of a boot on the wet ground, realization dawned, and she looked to her own feet.

She stood half in a puddle, leaving a void with one foot.

Lilani leapt to the side as footfalls smacked against stone. The puddle splashed when the runner hit it, and Lilani rolled, hoping she wasn't leaving too much of a trail through the muck. Other footfalls ran toward her. She tried to rise, but a telltale *whoosh* of air made her go flat. Feeling around, she grabbed the first thing that came to hand and flung it with all her might.

A small wooden box hit someone invisible and crashed to the ground. The footsteps stumbled back, skidding. Other footfalls spread out around the street.

"I'm here!" Lilani said.

"Come this way." Faelyn's voice, still in the alley.

Lilani stood as the footfalls converged on the wooden box. The sound of tearing cloth, followed by a grunt, made Lilani wince. Then the street went quiet again save for the sound of dripping. Blood splashed amongst the puddles, staining them crimson.

Lilani reached the alley, and her shroud fell. A dark shadow flickered in the street, and Burani appeared, holding a bleeding wound in his side.

"Oh elders, no!" Lilani took a step toward him. He'd escaped the fire, and they'd repaid his bravery by stabbing him?

"Wait." Someone gripped Lilani's elbow. She turned, expecting Faelyn, but Selgwyn stood there, a line of blood across her brow. "He attacked me."

Lilani glanced back, but Burani was gone. No one else appeared, but the wakeful human guard now stood outside his little hut, staring at the street with a frown.

"Run," Lucian said. He grabbed Lilani's elbow, and she coaxed her reluctant shroud over herself again. If the guard realized what had happened, the entire city would be looking for the seelie, if they weren't already. And dawn was almost upon them.

CHAPTER FIFTEEN

Vandra wandered through Lowtown but didn't know what she expected to find. She'd hoped the seelie might find her, but they hadn't shown themselves. Maybe they'd gotten over the wall. That seemed the best case even though it meant Lilani was gone.

No sign of a message, either, but that had been a long shot. Most of Lowtown's denizens seemed too consumed with their own problems to notice her or anything else, but she'd seen a few greedy glances. The twins had told her that criminals often mixed with the poor, hiding from the City Watch.

Vandra hurried toward Parbeh again. As she made way for a group of people walking together, she happened to glance back. Someone stopped exactly when she did. A green mantle hid their face, but Vandra's suspicious mind went on alert, and she realized how foolish it had been to go out without the twins. No doubt they'd say the same thing later in a louder tone.

She walked faster, taking peeks over her shoulder. The green mantle followed, head down. They might simply be going in the same direction, but Vandra couldn't trust that. She didn't want to try to lose them in Lowtown, so she picked up speed, hoping nothing would happen in a crowd.

Up ahead, the stream of people stalled behind a herd of sheep. Vandra reached one of the shepherds and nodded ahead. "I need to get through."

"We're all goin' the same way in the same time," he said, his voice tight with irritability.

She pushed past, walking among the sheep. The shepherds cried out as others followed Vandra's example. She looked for the green mantle but could see nothing past the sheep and the crowd. When she got to the head of the herd, a shepherd practically flung her from their midst, making her stumble, but she kept her feet. The green mantle couldn't follow her through that, not without attracting too much attention. Vandra hurried past the guards on the gate, who let her through after a glance. Vandra relaxed a little. If the green mantle got past the sheep, the guards would stop them.

She relaxed even more when she was far into Parbeh, listing off the ingredients she needed in her head. A few turns from home, she made way for a wagon and happened to look back. Her heart thudded hard at a flash of green.

Lilani hoped Lucian remembered the way back to the gate; she was almost too tired to keep putting one foot in front of the other.

"There," Lucian said, nodding ahead.

A squat, gray building, it seemed like some sort of barracks. Lucian wanted to hide in the midst of guards? He pulled Lilani to the building, and as dawn crept over them, she peeked in a window. All the guards were leaving for their shifts, and a barracks would be the last place anyone would look for runaway seelie.

The last guard left, locking the door behind them. Lucian revealed hidden talents by picking the lock. Lilani could barely hold her shroud as the door opened. She slipped inside, and the rows of bunks seemed like paradise.

Provided no one came back for a nap.

Alonse wrapped a bandage around Selgwyn's black hair. It was a wonder she'd managed to hold her shroud after Burani hit her.

"How did you know who hit you?" Lucian asked.

Selgwyn stared at nothing. "I know his scent."

Lilani nearly gasped. So, they'd been close, probably intimate. Selgwyn had to feel so betrayed.

"Why would he do this?" Lilani asked.

Faelyn sat on one of the bunks with his head in his hands, getting the blanket dirty. The barracks was going to be filthy after they left;

hopefully, no one would connect that with a pack of missing seelie. "There are so many questions. Did Burani set the guesthouse on fire? Did he kill Maegwyn, or is she also trying to kill us?"

Selgwyn glanced at Lilani. "I think he was after you, Lilani."

Lilani didn't think she could feel worse, but somehow, she managed.

"It doesn't matter," Lucian said. "If he comes back, I'll kill him." He had to feel as betrayed as Selgwyn. Burani had gone bad under his watchful eye.

"Do you think he attacked Vandra at the ball?" Lilani asked. "He could have followed us while Maegwyn burned down the guesthouse."

"Then why didn't she attack us, too?" Faelyn asked.

Lilani lay back on her bed. Who was she supposed to grieve for, and who was she supposed to hate? No one seemed to have any answers.

Some of the guards lay down while others kept watch. Lilani's worry and grief and anger took turns washing over her, but her eyes closed anyway. She knew what Faelyn would say: it was best to sleep while they could.

Vandra stumbled in shock. The person in the green mantle should have been stopped at the gate. Unless she'd been wrong, and they were innocent, just in town for business. Vandra looked again. The green mantle slowed and made a small gesture against their chest, as if they were trying to hide the movement from everyone else on the street. A wave? No, it had been up and down, like a stabbing gesture. A threat? Her mind worked overtime, running through one dangerous scenario after another.

The gods could figure it out later. She ran, thinking of the slit scarf, the seelie burned to death in the guesthouse, the attempt on Lilani's life, and poor Ariadne slain in her bed. Her heart thundering, Vandra looked for a Watch officer, but saw none. Just her luck. Fieta and Pietyr hated jokes about how the Watch was never around when needed, but that was certainly the case now.

Vandra barreled past people who cursed in her wake. She wanted to shout for help but barely had the breath to run. She dashed for home, for Fieta and Pietyr, taking a shortcut down an alley.

Fool! Such dim, close surroundings would be the perfect place to murder her, but there was nothing to do except run faster. Vandra skirted a pile of rubbish and leapt another. Footsteps pounded behind her. She willed herself to go faster, but her foot skidded, and her shoulder bounced off one wall. She pushed off, banged into the opposite wall, and nearly slid down. Her back throbbed, and she couldn't get enough air. She turned, wanting to see any attack coming.

Nothing. No one stood in the alley but her. Her heart still beating wildly, Vandra barked a slightly hysterical laugh. She pressed a hand to her chest and almost panted. Maybe the gesture the green mantle had made *was* a wave, a simple acknowledgement that they'd seen each other before. Vandra turned for home again, relieved to be laughing at herself rather than lying in a pool of her own blood.

A figure blinked into view ahead of her. Vandra cried out, staggering back. She began to turn, but the figure pushed back the hood. Still, Vandra took a few steps away before her rational mind convinced her of what she'd seen: pointed ears and a face she'd glimpsed behind Lilani at some point.

One of her attendants. He must have escaped the fire. Vandra stumbled to a halt, trying to calm her heart. "Who…"

He put a hand to his chest. The other was pressed to a wound in his side. "Vandra Singh? Lilani friend, yes? My name is Burani."

"Burani," Vandra said with a sigh. She trembled, too much fear and anxiety after too little sleep. She was going to fall down soon. "You're alive!"

He smiled sadly. "I escape. Maegwyn…no."

He spoke the human tongue haltingly, his accent much thicker than Lilani's or Faelyn's. And besides the wound in his side, Vandra noted marks near his collar, the edge of a burn peeking out from under a hasty bandage.

"I did not mean frighten you," he said. "I try…" He made that same gesture she'd seen in the street, the one she hadn't understood, waving up and down his body before hiding his eyes.

"Disappear? Vanish?"

"Yes. Vanish. Then I come close, show my face, and you know me."

She nodded. He hadn't dared speak to her until he could be sure no one else would see his features. His brown hair hung lank and sweaty around his neck and pointed ears. Dark circles under his eyes stood out starkly against his pale skin. He needed help.

"Come on," she said, waving him forward. "My family's house isn't far. You can rest, and we can tend your wounds." She spoke slowly, trying to help him understand with gestures. When he hesitated, she stepped around him. "You can trust us. You'll be safe."

After a sad nod, he put his hood up and followed. Vandra hurried him as much as she could, and when they were inside the house, she called for help.

Papa came out from his weaver's workshop. "Vandra? What are you doing—" He gasped as he caught sight of Burani. "Who's this?"

"Burani. He needs our help." She stepped aside, and Papa clucked over Burani's injuries. Fieta and Pietyr emerged a short time later, both of them yawning. Everyone sat at the kitchen table and listened as Vandra told them of her adventure.

The twins frowned at her story. Vandra thanked the gods that her youngest siblings were either playing elsewhere or at their lessons. She didn't need more accusatory glares.

"Van," Pietyr said once she finished her story. "What were you thinking?"

"Other than a bruise on my shoulder where I hit a wall, I'm fine." Except for the fatigue that left her feeling hollow.

"You were lucky," Fieta said, but her voice was distracted as she stared at Burani.

He stripped to the waist, and Papa wrapped a bandage around his belly. Burani was fit, all lean muscle under pale skin, but Vandra preferred Lilani's athletic curves. Papa dabbed at the burn mark that crossed Burani's shoulders and muttered about how it could have been worse.

Fieta stared at Burani with an appraising smile before biting her lip. Vandra nudged her arm and whispered, "You can't jump on him until he's healed."

"Says you."

Pietyr rolled his eyes and dug a plate of chicken out of the cold store. "Let her practice her own version of diplomacy, Van."

Fieta barked a laugh. Vandra gave them both a glare before taking a large piece of chicken. She hadn't realized she was so hungry.

Pietyr grabbed her hand. "No food until you promise never to leave the house without us again."

She wondered how she'd ever get anything done under that promise, but at the moment, the food was more important. "Sure." Through a bite of chicken, she asked, "How bad is it, Papa?"

"Not as bad as I feared," he said. "You had good luck, Burani."

"Not Maegwyn," Burani said sadly. "A lantern broke…" He gestured toward the window. "She is cut here." He touched his neck. "I try, but so much fire."

Vandra imagined a lantern flying through the window, the flames surrounding the seelie, one of them wounded in the neck. She shivered. Fieta took one of Burani's hands. He gave her a tiny smile, and she grinned, thoroughly tactless.

Burani looked away. "More lanterns, more fire." He gestured toward one of the naked beams on the ceiling. "Those fall with fire." He touched the burn mark. "And I fall…" Another wave at the window before he indicated his side. "Hurt. I…try Maegwyn again, but I run from…" He looked at all of them in turn.

Vandra nodded. "You couldn't go back inside, and you didn't know who had started the fire, so you had to hide? To vanish?"

"Vanish, yes. Such hurt. Find this to help." He plucked at the green mantle where it lay on the table. "Sleep, then you."

Sorrow filled Burani's voice, but he didn't weep. Maybe seelie never wept, or maybe he'd done so already. When he looked at Vandra, he seemed resolved, even angry, as if action was called for before grieving could begin. "Lilani? Lucian?"

She shook her head. "When they saw the fire, they vanished. They must have fled the city. Word would have spread if they'd been caught." He stared, and she didn't know how much he understood. "I'm sure they're safe. If they get caught, they'll be all right. I mean, they should be, though, sometimes the monarchs don't know what they're doing. They want me to abandon the pylon, but I'm not going to."

Burani blinked at her. "You…go against monarchs?"

"When they're wrong? Sure," Vandra said. "If they won't hurry up and save the world, I will."

Papa cleared his throat, giving her a warning look. "They just won't know you're helping, that's all."

Vandra chuckled, happy her family was on her side. "I still need to buy a few things."

Papa finished with Burani's shoulder. "There now. I'm sure someone has a clean shirt you can borrow."

"I'll look." Fieta hurried upstairs. "No one get injured again without me," she called over her shoulder.

"That means you, Van," Pietyr said. "Give me a list, and I'll shop for you."

Vandra handed over a list. Papa announced he was going back to work, and in the space of a few moments, Vandra was alone with Burani. Awkwardness descended.

"I'm very sorry," Vandra said, fighting the urge to fidget. "About Maegwyn. I know it probably doesn't help, but most humans are good people."

"I knew her two…" He waved a hand.

"Years?" But that probably wasn't right. "Twenty years?" When he shook his head and held his hands far apart, Vandra swallowed, her belly going cold. "Centuries? Two hundred years?"

He nodded. A heavy weight settled around Vandra's shoulders. Two centuries. After so long, no doubt they knew everything there was to know about each other. What a blow that had to be, an eternity snuffed out by some idiot with a few lanterns and a grudge.

"I'm sorry," Vandra said again. Grief for a friend of two centuries seemed so much weightier than her grief for Ariadne, a friend of less than a decade. What a sad day when someone had to ponder the difference between the two. "You should rest, sleep," she said, not knowing if sleep would come to him.

He nodded, and she led him upstairs. After claiming a shirt from Fieta, he settled in Vandra's old bedroom.

"Time for you to sleep, too," Fieta said.

Vandra sighed. She'd given up thinking that sleep even existed, but now that someone had said the word, sleep seemed to be taking her by the shoulder. Fieta guided her to a bed and saw her lying down before leaving. Vandra closed her eyes, knowing Fieta was probably standing guard on the other side of the door.

CHAPTER SIXTEEN

Vandra woke up a few hours later with a head full of ideas. She'd dreamed of silver lakes of syndrium. She often did, but these dreams felt different, with more promise. It didn't hurt that she'd also dreamed of reuniting with Lilani and fixing the pylon, saving the world, and kissing until they swooned.

First things first.

As luck would have it, she'd left her notebook at her parents' house. She wouldn't be surprised if she'd managed to leave copies all around the city. She rarely went anywhere without something to make a note on. Now she scribbled hurriedly. Replacing the pylon would be impossible. She didn't have the syndrium and would never convince anyone to give it to her. All she had was some old equipment she'd left here, whatever ingredients Pietyr managed to get, and her wits.

Added up, it didn't seem like much.

She went downstairs, running possibilities in her mind and discarding them. In her dreams she'd been so hopeful, but when confronted by the reality of just how little she had…

"Vandra, you have a visitor," Papa called from the kitchen. "One of your friends from the university."

Which friend? She'd never been close with any of her colleagues. And how did Papa always know which of his children was moving around? Maybe he'd befriended a little god in the area and used it as a spy. She shuffled to the kitchen and stopped, gawking at Shyn Harra Rhys, who sat at the table drinking tea as if monarchs did such things all the time.

Papa stood. "I must get back to work. Nice speaking with you."

Shyn inclined their head and waited until Papa left the room before saying, "Professor Singh, I'm happy to see you again." When she still gawked, Shyn smiled. "Please, forgive my lie to your father. I did not wish a…big reaction."

Vandra's mouth worked, and she fought to get her brain working. "What can I do for you?"

Shyn reached down and picked up a large, paper-wrapped package, setting it on the table. "I've come to give you this."

Vandra walked forward woodenly. There was a monarch sitting at her kitchen table. At least her hands seemed to know what to do. She clipped the string holding the paper and whisked it away. It took a moment before she realized what it was: a bundle of equipment and ingredients, all carefully boxed and labeled, including exactly what she needed for her syndrium formula.

"How…why?" She cleared her throat, remembering that she was supposed to be intelligent. "Thank you."

"You're welcome. As to how, I have money. The why is a little more complicated." Shyn sipped their tea and sighed. "Some of my colleagues think you should be barred from the pylons because of your connection to the seelie, and some think you should be barred because you have *no* connection to the seelie." Shyn tilted their head. "At least, not the right kind of seelie."

"I don't understand."

"And I don't have enough proof to name names at the moment." Shyn stood. "I won't tell you to be careful; you already know the danger you're in. I will tell you that there are some in the monarchy who want their kingdoms back by any means necessary, even if a great many people are killed." Shyn spread their hands. "Perhaps they've taken to heart an old saying in the lost kingdom of Farisse: better to have an estate in hell than rent a room in heaven."

Vandra shook her head, trying to think of what that might mean, what unscrupulous people could help the monarchs get their kingdoms back and how. By pushing back the tattered lands? That would be good news, wouldn't it?

But having an estate in hell implied that the tattered lands would remain as they were, only with people living inside them. "They want to return to their old kingdoms as they are now? Tattered? They'll all be corrupted or die!"

"Until I know more, it's better to have the pylons in working order, and I believe you're the one to keep them so." Shyn stepped around the table and took one of Vandra's nerveless hands. "Please, thank your father for the tea."

She was still staring at nothing as Shyn left, and Fieta and Pietyr came in. "Van, was that a monarch?" Pietyr asked.

"In our house?" Fieta added.

Vandra nodded numbly before she smiled. The why didn't matter. Now she had real equipment, a host of ingredients, her wits, and the support of a monarch!

And she had a seelie. She'd nearly forgotten about Burani.

She answered the twins' questions as quickly as she could and tried to ignore their rampant speculation. She had work to do. "Help me convince Burani to do some experiments with me."

"What sort of experiments?" Fieta asked.

"It's time we found out how that magical field around the seelie can help us." They gathered up the equipment and ingredients and trooped upstairs.

"These experiments won't hurt him, will they?" Fieta asked

Vandra gave her a dark look. "We also don't have time for your crushes, Fie."

Pietyr snickered, and Fieta grumbled. Vandra knocked on Burani's door but forgot to wait to open it. Luckily, he was up and dressed, staring out the window. He turned when he saw them, hand going to the knife at his belt. Even after he saw them, he hesitated before straightening, as if making certain they weren't going to rush him. Vandra couldn't blame him.

"How are you feeling, Burani?" Vandra asked.

He smiled softly. "Better, thanks."

"Good. I need to run a little experiment." She set some equipment on the bed, found a syndrium detector, and used it, gratified when it detected both the syndrium in the ingredients and Burani, but how could that information help with the pylons? Maybe the presence of a seelie helped in the pylons' creation? Could they affect alchemy just by being nearby?

One way to find out.

Vandra went through a list of possible experiments, but once she'd seen that her ingredients included those needed for her syndrium formula, it stuck in her brain. Well, if she was going to start somewhere…

She set up on the nightstand. "Come stand here, please."

"Why?" Burani asked.

"It's all right," Fieta said. "It's not going to hurt, I swear." She moved into the position. "See? Vandra's never hurt anyone. Come stand with me."

He frowned but moved to stand slightly behind Fieta. She turned to face him with a wink.

"You'll be fine," Pietyr added from out in the hallway. Very reassuring.

"Don't move." Vandra went through her formula, adding all the ingredients and heating it. She went faster than last time, not expecting this to work but curious to see if Burani's magical field affected it at all.

Five agonizing minutes passed, and they all leaned close. When the mixture puffed with smoke, they jumped back. Burani nearly fell over the bed. Vandra waved her hand through the smoke, her heart not knowing whether to lift or sink. When she saw the glint from the bowl, she blinked, not daring to believe.

"What is it?" Fieta stepped around Burani, staring at where the jumble of common materials had turned into a bowl of syndrium. "Van…we're going to be rich!"

Vandra barked a laugh, but it had happy tears behind it. "That's not the point, Fieta."

"She can fix the pylon," Pietyr said. "She could make a million pylons!"

Fieta whooped and grabbed Vandra, swinging her around. Vandra laughed and clapped her on the back. After she set Vandra down, Fieta ran to Burani and grabbed his hand, but he leaned away as if torn between the desire to stay or leap out the window.

"It's all right, Burani," Vandra said. "It's better than okay. We have a chance now."

He gave her a smile that seemed kind of sickly, but she wasn't in the mood to explain. All she had to do now was find Lilani, and everything would be okay.

Two thoughts nibbled at the back of her mind. Would the syndrium she'd created be as powerful as the syndrium that made up the pylons? Maybe, like her colleagues claimed, the pylons' power simply came from so much of it being in one place. If so, and she could create enough, it might be all right.

Also, if it took a seelie to make her formula work, why did it work the first time? Could there have been a seelie in the room when she'd first experimented with this formula? Her stomach went cold. How long had they been following her?

She shook the thought away. Unnerving as it was, it was a puzzle for another time. "We should leave for the pylons now."

The twins fell silent as if she'd thrown cold water on them. "It's already well after noon," Pietyr said.

"We don't have time to waste. Lilani is gone. A murderer is hunting us, and if someone has been sabotaging the other pylons while we've been gone…"

They glanced at each other and nodded. It would take them an hour to pack, and they could be on their way. Burani seemed relieved, no doubt in a hurry to get back home.

When Lilani awoke, the sun streamed in the windows of the barracks. She'd slept longer than she'd wanted, though nearly everyone else was still asleep. Lucian guarded the door, casting the occasional glance toward the back door and the barrack's small yard. He offered her a tiny smile, one with the weight of disappointment and fatigue.

She moved to his side. "You should take a break," she whispered. "I'll watch."

"No, thank you."

She shrugged, knowing he wouldn't change his mind.

"We can't stay here much longer," he said.

"At least Burani will have moved on by now."

"I hope he died from his wounds."

Lilani fidgeted, not knowing how to comfort someone so much older than her. Best not to try. "Should we try the gate again?"

"Yes, and sooner is better than later."

She took the hint and gently woke Faelyn. By the time he'd risen, the other guards sat up, roused by the activity. Carisse and Alonse raided the small pantry, stuffing whatever they found in a sack and filling two canteens from a rain barrel in the yard. When everyone was ready, Lucian had them line up and shroud.

Lilani wrapped her magic around her. The door opened under Lucian's invisible touch, and Lilani gaped at the sight of a human standing there, key in hand. He froze, blinking at a door opened by no one. He seemed young, no lines on his face or gray in his hair.

He scratched his neck and stepped inside. "Hello?"

Lilani stepped to the side and almost chuckled at his confusion. She heard a soft tread and followed it to the door, keeping contact with the seelie in front of her. The confused human turned as Lilani passed, and for half a heartbeat, she looked into his eyes, dark like Vandra's and thoroughly spooked. Then she went wide around him and through the door.

In the daylight of late afternoon, the gates of Parbeh were bustling. Lilani wound through the humans, bending or gliding out of the way. She imagined the seelie as an invisible snake darting between hustling feet. When they were through the gates, Lilani began to feel as if she'd been dancing for hours, her muscles overtaxed from all the ducking and creeping, all while keeping a hand on the fellow in front of her. They strayed from the main road through the shanties, having to step over tent ropes and refuse, the occasional sleeping human. Lilani became as lost as she'd been in Parbeh, too tired to watch where she was going.

At last they stopped, and Lilani recognized the dwelling, a large one made of tin, the rendezvous point. The door creaked open, and Lilani followed the person in front of her inside.

Boxes, baskets, and all sorts of possessions littered the insides. No humans stood to confront them, and Lucian blinked into view, followed by Faelyn. Lilani dropped her magic and turned to find the rest of them there as well.

Lucian sighed. "Good, we didn't lose anyone."

"We should rest a little," Lilani said. "Maegwyn might find her way here if she…lives. And we should watch for Vandra. I told her we were coming to the shanties. She'd follow the road, looking for us."

Lucian nodded, and everyone spread out, Selgwyn watching the door, the others waiting in the shadows. Light flooded through many holes in the shanty walls; anyone coming in would be blinded temporarily, giving the seelie time to hide. Lilani sat on a pile of flotsam and watched the road through a gap in the tin.

"I hope Vandra hasn't been captured," she said when Faelyn settled beside her.

"If she has, she can be rescued."

Lilani pictured herself returning to Parbeh with as many seelie as would come. She could rescue Vandra, they'd fall into each other's arms, then venture forth to breathe life into the pylon once again.

Or something like that.

A few hours passed, and Lilani knew they couldn't stay any longer. They hadn't found Vandra or Maegwyn, and Lilani's heart felt even lower than it had after Burani had attacked.

"Lilani," Faelyn's voice said. The others had already shrouded.

"I know." She let Vandra's image linger in her thoughts, whispering, "I will find you again." Her magic flowed around her.

"One by one." Lucian slipped past, brushing her arm.

She followed, dodging humans as best she could, but there were too many people in the shanties to avoid them all, and as it got darker, the numbers seemed to swell. She bumped into a few, and most seemed to forget the touches after they happened, but some made a sign on their forehead before fleeing. None raised an alarm, and after a few, slow, agonizing hours, Lilani was free of the great human mire, and she could breathe again.

When Parbeh was far in the distance, Lucian led them away from the road and dropped his shroud. With a sigh, Lilani did the same. Between only a few hours of sleep, overusing her magic, and all the emotions twisting inside her, she was exhausted. They'd have to sleep again soon, much as Lilani wanted to hurry home.

Of course, someone back home was trying to kill her, too, and that clumsy attempt couldn't have been Burani, who was a member of the Guard. How many confederates did he have? Just one more or others among the Guard?

Lilani eyed Alonse, Carisse, Selgwyn, and Lucian. None gave off a feeling like the one Vandra had described: an aura of nauseating dread. That meant there were other seelie lurking in Parbeh, maybe working with Burani, and they could have other spies.

How did that help her now? She couldn't shroud and run away, not without Faelyn. These guards had already had many opportunities to kill her and hadn't. Unless they'd been waiting to find out exactly *what* she knew about them, and now that they knew she was completely ignorant...

Faelyn rested a hand on her shoulder, and she jumped, clamping her teeth together to keep from crying out. Everyone turned, alarm on their faces.

"Lilani?" Faelyn asked. She wondered if he could hear her heart thundering. "Are you all right?"

Lilani sighed. "No, but keep walking."

They'd reached a small forest not far from Parbeh. Inside the trees, Lucian had the others spread out to search for possible campsites. Lilani leaned against a tree, knowing she should be helping but unable to do more than wish for the boredom she'd lamented a week ago.

"What's going on?" Faelyn asked.

She barked a humorless laugh. "Where shall I begin?"

"Besides the obvious."

She glanced around to make sure none of the guards stood too close. "Do you think Burani was the only traitor in the Guard?"

His lips pressed into a thin line. "Out of all of them?" He shrugged. "Out of those with us? Well, Lucian is the only one I know well, and he's one of the most loyal people I know. And he trusts Selgwyn."

"Alonse and Carisse?"

"Don't panic. Last thing we want to do is let paranoia drive us into the wilderness by ourselves."

She sighed and closed her eyes, trying to quiet her busy mind. "Or maybe that's the last thing a cabal of murderers would expect us to do."

"Let's talk to Lucian and Selgwyn. They'll know who's capable of belonging to a *murder cabal*." He sighed. "I want the answer to be, 'no one.'"

They found Lucian and Selgwyn together, and Lilani told them of her suspicions while Faelyn kept watch for Alonse and Carisse. Lucian stared for several minutes after she finished. She couldn't read his expression, but then, she never could.

Finally, he nodded. "I'm glad you told me." He offered a smile, probably pleased she didn't suspect him, even though she had at first. She'd decided to leave that part out. He glanced at Selgwyn, who shrugged.

"Before Burani," Lucian said, "I wouldn't have believed any of the Guard capable of murder."

"The question is who to suspect now," Faelyn said. "If anyone."

Lucian rubbed his chin. "Neither Alonse nor Carisse have ever been personally harmed by a human."

"And Alonse cared for Maegwyn," Selgwyn said. "He wouldn't have had a hand in her death."

"Good to know," Faelyn said.

Lilani wasn't relieved. "There's still whoever tried to kill Vandra at the ball, and whoever is waiting to kill me at home."

"Problems for the future," Faelyn said.

She gave him a dark look. "I guess now we just try to get home as fast as we can."

He hugged her. "And not be murdered in the process."

She was too tired to kick him.

Despite Lucian's attempts to allay her fears, Lilani watched everyone closely as they set up camp. She jumped at every snapping twig or rustle from the surrounding trees. It felt nice to be inside a forest again, but it wasn't *her* forest. It may as well have been on the moon.

And Lucian seemed to watch Alonse and Carisse more closely than usual. Alonse added a deer to their meager supplies, and Carisse and Selgwyn built a fire and roasted the animal. Lucian and Alonse dragged in brush to shield their campsite. Everyone seemed normal enough.

Faelyn sat beside Lilani and nodded at the branches above. "A pity these trees aren't big enough to sleep in."

"I wouldn't want to," she said. The branches grew too close together, with many spindly twigs sprouting among them. "It'd be like sleeping in a pincushion."

"Still, it's not so bad on the ground. Plenty of dead leaves for a soft bed."

She grunted a reply, craning her neck to keep everyone in sight.

"Still not feeling trusting, huh?"

She sighed. "That obvious?" He didn't have to answer. She nodded at Lucian. "He's watching Carisse and Alonse, too."

"I noticed."

"Good to know I'm not the only paranoid one."

"He takes his job very seriously." With a sigh, Faelyn sagged down a tree trunk as if all the energy had gone out of him. "And that means he and Selgwyn will be taking turns on all the watches. They'll be exhausted by the time we reach home."

Lilani tipped sideways to lay her head on his chest. "Won't we all?"

He poked her lightly. "The leaves are your bed, Princess, not me."

She laughed, her first real laugh in what felt like days. By the time dinner had cooked, she felt calm enough to eat, though the unflavored meat sat in her stomach like bits of clay. Afterward, she lay in her pile of leaves and stared at the darkness. Alonse had banked the fire into a pile of glowing embers. Luckily, it wasn't cold enough to need the heat. Faelyn had once complained that it never really got cold this far south. He'd told her stories of valleys filled with snow, peaks so high they froze solid all year round, and a great sea of drifting ice.

Lilani's hand tickled as an insect meandered across. The sound of them filled the forest with a comforting din. No matter her strife, the world still turned. She willed herself to be one with the forest, the sound of the wind through the branches and the soft leaves beneath her. She'd missed this feeling in Parbeh. Humans were a part of nature like everything else, but the way they shaped the world drowned out the natural flow. Instead, they made their own flow, and they never had to fear being drawn so far into it that it overwhelmed them; they'd never fade from the world like the eldest seelie.

Vandra especially was warm and alive with her bright smile and the thick, dark flood of her hair. In the street, her chest had risen and fallen so becomingly as their lips strained to meet. Visions of Vandra's skin in the warm candlelight followed Lilani into her dreams. Their near kiss became full body contact, their lips sliding over each other, tongues mingling. Lilani could almost feel Vandra's breasts pressed against her, could feel Vandra's hips under her hands. Clothing vanished in the haste capable in dreams, and Lilani kissed a line down Vandra's neck, desperate to hear more of Vandra's throaty moans.

A twig snapped.

Lilani's eyes flew open. She could still feel Vandra's heat from her dream, and her eyelids wanted to flutter closed, hurrying back to imagined ecstasy, but she forced herself to stay awake. She counted her breaths: one, two, three…

She closed her eyes, putting the sound down to over-imaginative nerves when it came again, a footstep by something heavy enough to be a threat. The closest insects fell silent. The sound came from inside their circle of brush. Selgwyn on watch? If it wasn't, she had to have heard it, too, would leap into action any moment now.

A rustle, then nothing. Lilani sat up slowly. A leaf crunched beneath her, as loud as a boom in her ears. She touched Faelyn's arm, and he gave her a squeeze, signaling that he'd heard something, too. The fire had dimmed too much to see. Lilani could barely make out the shape of trees, darker shadows against blackness. The tangle of branches overhead blocked the stars, and if the moon was out, it wasn't high.

Lilani opened her mouth to call out when she heard another crunch, closer this time. Her heart raced in her ears, and she had to force herself to breathe slowly. She felt Faelyn shift, no doubt sitting up. She was about to ask him what to do when he shouted, "Lucian!"

Sounds of movement erupted around them. Lilani shot to her feet with Faelyn, glad he'd done something.

Lucian called, "Faelyn? Lilani? Are you all right?"

Faelyn pulled Lilani toward Lucian's voice. "Here."

Other voices demanded to know what was wrong. Lilani's searching hand found the trunk of a tree near Lucian, and she pressed her back to it, keeping Faelyn with her. The tall shadow of Lucian moved to stand in front of them.

"Selgwyn, bring the fire back up!" Lucian called.

No answer came, and the fire stayed dark.

"Selgwyn?" Lucian called. "Alonse? Carisse?"

They answered, and he ordered them to rebuild the fire. It came slowly to life, stirred by Alonse. Carisse stood next to him, no sign of Selgwyn. Lilani gripped Faelyn's hand, her heart hammering. Everything felt so *wrong*. The very air felt heavy, stinging, as if she was trying to breathe through a stand of nettles.

Was this what Vandra had felt at the ball before someone tried to slit her throat?

Carisse stepped around some brush and shouted, "Here!"

Lucian dashed forward. Lilani and Faelyn stayed with him. On the ground by Carisse, Selgwyn lay facedown, the back of her head torn open in a bloody gash.

CHAPTER SEVENTEEN

Burani shrouded for the journey through Parbeh and Lowtown while Vandra and Fieta walked on either side of him. Pietyr kept in front, shielding Burani's invisible form. The first few times Burani's hand touched her shoulder, Vandra jumped, but when he pulled her out of the way of a stumbling drunk, she began to see him as a good luck charm. He definitely made her reflexes look better.

Once in the country, Burani blinked back into view. He'd kept the green mantle—though Vandra noted that someone had laundered it—and he wore the hood up just in case. He scanned the countryside constantly, no doubt searching for his people. Vandra wanted to offer comfort but had no idea what to say. She hoped he felt safe with her and the twins, but he had a right to be mistrustful. He didn't know them well, and it might have been a human who killed his friend. The thought made her ashamed of her race.

Of course, she couldn't maintain that feeling, given how many idiots she knew. She'd be drowning in embarrassment.

"Lilani seems very capable," Vandra said. "Smart. She'll be fine; they all will."

He gave her a small smile, but it seemed a bit forced and diplomatic. "Yes."

Fieta still eyed him appreciatively, though she'd ceased trying to seduce him under the circumstances. Pietyr watched him, too, though with a suspicious frown. Vandra supposed it was a good thing that they watched him so closely. No matter what happened, he wouldn't lack help or hindrance as the situation warranted.

They headed directly west instead of slightly north as they had on their first trip. Everyone wanted to get to the Seelie Forest as quickly as possible, but it would still take two days. By the end of the first, they'd marched so hard Vandra's feet ached, and she stumbled.

"We have to stop, Burani," Pietyr said. "We need to make camp before dark, and we're exhausted."

"He means I am," Vandra said. "My pack feels like a boulder."

"I second that." Fieta left the road and headed over a small rise. The trees in this area weren't very dense, but they found a small, skinny stand that was better than nothing.

Burani paused on the rise and searched the distance in the failing light.

"You can keep going," Vandra said softly. "Since you can vanish, you'll be in less danger."

He seemed as tired as her but didn't reply. He glanced at her then looked toward the twins as if weighing his options. Fieta was setting up camp, but Pietyr stared at Vandra and Burani and nodded toward the camp as if urging them to join it.

"Even if you walk all night," Vandra said, "you won't reach the forest. Then you'll have to camp alone."

He sighed. "Thank you."

"Fieta is going to keep watch first," Pietyr said when they joined him. "Then me."

Burani shook his head. "We safe here, yes? Why watch?"

Pietyr narrowed his eyes, but Fieta chuckled. "Better to be careful," she said.

When Pietyr didn't lose his scowl, Vandra leaned close. "He was Lilani's attendant, not a soldier. He just doesn't get it." She smiled at Burani. "Listen to Fieta and Pietyr. They have a lot of experience; we'll be fine with them around."

His lip quirked as if she'd made a joke. She supposed the notion of a human having lots of experience would be funny to someone who'd lived for centuries.

After they ate, Burani settled in his bedroll near the roots of a tree. Vandra crawled inside the tent with Pietyr; she hoped that when Pietyr got up, he didn't wake her, too. It was a selfish thought, but she was too tired to care.

❖

The seelie stared at one another. Lilani thought in vain for something to say, but another of them had been murdered, and even with all the recent strife, she still didn't know how to respond to death.

Lucian knelt by Selgwyn, but she lay too still, and the wound in her head didn't stream so much as ooze. Lilani pressed a hand to her mouth. "Was it Burani?" she whispered to Faelyn.

"I don't know."

But there had been that feeling, the same as Vandra had described from the ball.

"What happened?" Lucian demanded.

"I heard someone moving," Lilani said. "She didn't cry out." And Lilani hadn't heard her fall. She imagined someone ghosting through the dark, bashing Selgwyn's head in, and lowering the body softly to the leaves. She shuddered, and her dinner threatened to arise.

Lucian stood, glaring at everyone. "She didn't attack herself. So, either someone crept up on her from elsewhere—"

"Or one of us is a murderer," Faelyn said. "Lilani and I were beside each other. Neither of us could have moved without the other knowing."

Everyone exchanged a glance, and Lilani could guess what it meant: she and Faelyn could have done the killing together. Well, she knew they hadn't, and the others seemed stunned, but a killer would be good at blending in, a truly callous heart.

If they had to defend themselves, Faelyn had his belt knife, but Lilani had nothing. Not that it would have helped her much in a fight. She didn't even know if she *could* stab someone. But she could shroud and run. By the wary looks on the others' faces, they had to be thinking the same thing. If one of them was a murderer, there was only one sure way to defend themselves.

Almost on cue, the three guards vanished. Lilani shrouded, too, grabbing Faelyn just before he blinked from sight.

"Go!" he whispered.

Lilani ran, and the two of them crashed through the brush gathered to protect them. Forest flotsam clattered and crunched as everyone else sprang into motion, too. Lilani heard someone behind her and kicked a stray branch in their path. She and Faelyn ran on. Soon, the light from the fire was lost in the distance. Lilani breathed hard, choked with fear, nearly blind in the darkness. Trees loomed out of the black without warning. She and Faelyn pulled each other around four of them, but on the fifth, they hit dead center, and it broke them apart.

Lilani stumbled, crashing through undergrowth and sending twigs skittering away. She spun, trying to maintain her footing, then crouched with one hand on the ground to steady herself. She forced her mouth closed and took hard breaths through her nose, her pulse rushing in her ears and her stomach tight. No night had ever been filled with such horror.

Lilani couldn't make out the glow from the fire. The forest had gone silent save for insects in the distance. Faelyn must be straining to listen, too. The murderer would be doing the same.

After a long moment, the chirp of nearby insects returned. Lilani shifted, trying to wriggle her foot under the leaves to make less noise. She stood slowly, gritting her teeth as she reached for a tree behind her. She couldn't stay here all night. Bending, she found a chunk of wood and flung it into the darkness, listening for the rustle as it landed. Another noise came from nearby, someone moving behind her. Faelyn? He should have been to the left, not behind her.

Lilani nearly growled in frustration. There had to be a way to know if there was someone out here besides her and Faelyn. She spotted a branch within reach above her and leapt up to catch it. "I'm here," she said breathlessly. "Show yourself." She pulled upward, out of harm's way.

For a moment, silence. Then, "Lilani?" Faelyn's voice to the left as she thought. Behind her, she heard another noise before Faelyn called, "Are you moving?"

"No, that's not me!" A feeling of dread washed over her, making her stomach do a nauseating turn. She hooked her legs around another branch and swung over as something smacked against the trunk of her tree where her head had been.

"Faelyn, run!" she cried, struggling up through the dense branches. They snapped and snagged at her clothes, her hair. She heard a *whoosh* of air below her, and one of the limbs broke away. She pushed higher into the tangle as the dense twigs gouged her flesh. With terror clogging her throat, she closed her eyes and tried to climb higher, but the limbs were as thick as a basket.

"Lucian!" she shouted. "Help!" By the elders, she hoped he wasn't already here and trying to kill her.

Someone cried out below her. She peered down. Another shout, then another. Three people? The brush rustled as if someone was rolling over the leaves. Lilani fumbled for a match in her belt pouch and lit it against the side of the tree. The underbrush below her waved and twisted. When the match burned down to her fingers, she swore and let go. A pile of old leaves beneath her tree ignited.

"Let go! It's me!" Faelyn's voice.

An *oomph* came from the tangle below, followed by a cry of pain. Faelyn popped into view, holding his stomach and breathing hard. The crackle of leaves spoke of someone fleeing into the night before Lucian blinked into life. He leaned against the trunk of Lilani's tree, holding one hand to his chest while the other held his sword. Blood trickled over his fingers.

Lilani clattered down, dropping her shroud. "Lucian, how bad is it?"

He lowered his hand. Lilani raised his shirt to find a slash, the blood trickling down his belly. It didn't seem too deep. She hoped. He pressed a hand to it as Lilani turned to Faelyn.

"Are you all right?" she asked.

"Just punched in the gut." With a few swift steps, he stomped the fire out of existence. "Are you trying to burn the forest down?"

"Yes, I hate it." He snorted as if she'd made a joke, but she meant it. The scratches and gouges on her face and hands stung. A cut across her jaw bled slowly, and she wiped it with her palm.

"Follow me." Lucian turned to the darkness again. Lilani kept a hand on his back, and he kept his weapon out. She hoped he'd managed to wound their attacker, whoever it was. She kept thinking of that feeling of dread that had washed over her, the feel of the tattered lands.

By the time they broke out of the forest, the moon had risen. The road wound in the distance like a pale ribbon. The forest was a wall of blackness behind them.

"Can you shroud?" Lucian asked.

When they both answered yes, he vanished. Lilani summoned her magic again, using her fear as Faelyn shrouded, too. They kept hold of one another and moved toward the road, then along it. Lilani was tempted to look back, but she resisted, knowing she wouldn't be able to see anyone. They had to return home before their attacker, before Burani. They couldn't have him spreading lies about how they'd struck first or something like that. She didn't need her people chasing their tails questioning her while they needed to repair the pylon and flush out any conspirators in their midst.

When someone shook her awake, Vandra grumbled, muttering about how she'd just gone to sleep, but her eyes were gummy, and her mouth tasted of grit. When she crawled out of the tent, the rising sun cast just enough light to see. Burani was already up, his gear packed. Vandra rubbed the sleep from her eyes, ate the rations handed to her, then pulled her pack over her aching shoulders. She was still half asleep as she walked, the pack making her stiff and clumsy. And grumpy.

Late in the day, they finally spotted the Seelie Forest on the horizon. Burani picked up speed. Vandra tried to match him, but the twins held her back.

"If he wants to run, let him," Pietyr said quietly. "We're not headed all the way inside."

Vandra gritted her teeth, but he was right. The pylon was their true destination. She wanted to see Lilani, but she wasn't welcome deep in the Seelie Forest. Even with Burani, the seelie might still take her prisoner. It was a delay she couldn't afford.

"Burani!" Vandra called. "Will you ask the empress to send Lilani to the pylon? We'll still need assistance. Help."

He turned and grinned, the first full smile she'd seen from him. "I come, promise." He pointed farther north. "Go that way. Meet you."

Then he left, walking fast, one hand held to his side—which was probably aching like fire—but it didn't slow him down.

By the time the sun was going down, he was long gone. Vandra and the twins reached the Seelie Forest, and Fieta turned north, but Pietyr stopped her.

"What?" she asked. "Burani told us he'd meet us to the north."

Pietyr shook his head. "That's exactly why we should camp here, in the southern part of the forest. Then we head north tomorrow and find Lilani and the other seelie."

Fieta rolled her eyes. "You're always so suspicious. Burani's all right."

"You say that about every cute guy, Watch Officer Singh."

"And I've never been wrong!"

"Because I've always been there to arrest the bad ones!"

"Enough!" Vandra said. "We're camping here in the south because I'm too tired to keep going." She really wanted to see Lilani again, but she doubted the seelie would venture out at night to find her. Everyone would be waiting until morning, and Vandra's feet were overruling even her heart.

❖

Lilani, Faelyn, and Lucian walked through the night. Lucian had to travel slowly, his hand pressed to the wound in his chest even after Faelyn bandaged it as best he could. By dawn, Lilani had never felt so tired and knew the others felt the same. She'd thought she'd known what fatigue was. Now her head swam, her thoughts scattered, and her feet hurt. Her back ached even though she carried nothing, and she was beyond thirsty. She hadn't had enough water in the past few days, and they'd had to leave what they'd taken from the barracks.

She'd given up shrouding, not able to hold her magic. Faelyn and Lucian had dropped theirs, too, and Lucian had bled through his bandages.

"Lucian," Faelyn said. "Stop. I want to look at your wound."

Lucian shook his head, probably too tired to speak.

Lilani stumbled to a halt. "None of us can shroud," she said, the words coming out in fits and starts. "And any murderers *must* be as tired as we are. We have to stop."

Lucian frowned but stopped. In the dim light, Lilani spotted a human village in the distance, but they couldn't seek shelter there. Where were they? At the first hint of dawn, Lucian had led them out of sight of the road.

"Let's keep as close to that village as we dare," Faelyn said. "Let our tracks mingle with theirs."

Lilani nodded, but she barely noted his logic as she looked for a place to sleep. If some murderer caught her right then, she might welcome death.

The only cover within stumbling distance proved to be a clump of bushes. The center had been dug out by some creature, but it had abandoned its den. Lilani desperately wanted to take her boots off, but Faelyn and Lucian didn't remove theirs. The only reason they had footwear at the moment was because they'd fallen asleep fully clothed the night before. They might have to flee again, and she didn't want to go trekking in her stocking feet.

Lucian glared at nothing. Faelyn shifted through the dirt. Lilani hoped he wasn't planning to eat whatever he found. They weren't that desperate.

Yet.

"So." Lilani's voice was a wheeze. She licked her lips with a dry tongue and tried to swallow.

"Here." Faelyn handed her a leaf and placed another in his mouth. "This will help."

She did as he suggested, grateful he knew about plants. The leaf was almost sweet against her tongue, but the edges felt sharp enough to cut her dry mouth. She bit down gently, and the feel of the fresh-tasting liquid oozing from the leaf was like concentrated happiness. Lucian took one, too, and after a long moment of silence, Lilani spoke again.

"Who do you think killed Selgwyn?"

Lucian glanced at her with an ugly look. She couldn't blame him for being bitter. Alonse or Carisse could have killed her, and they'd been under his command, people he thought he could trust. Like Burani. Deception lurked in every corner.

Or maybe everyone in the world besides them was a murderer. No, if that was so, she would have been murdered long before now. The bleak thought nearly made her chuckle…or scream.

"I don't know," Lucian said at last. The words sounded rusty, and she didn't know if that was from thirst or if he had trouble getting them past his lips. "I trusted them."

"You did not," Faelyn said. "I saw the way you watched them."

The two of them turned dark looks on each other, but Lilani kept herself from snapping at them. They couldn't fight amongst themselves on top of everything. "Did you notice that feeling of dread when you were wrestling with the person who hurt you?"

Lucian nodded. "But how could an outsider have gotten past our perimeter without anyone knowing? I…suppose it could have been Carisse. She never socialized like the rest of us."

"And you didn't mention that before we left the Court?" Faelyn asked.

"Being quiet is not a crime." Lucian looked away, jaw tight.

"None of us can read minds," Lilani said, hating that she had to play peacekeeper when she wanted to knock their heads together. Her mother would quip about how resisting the urge to punch people was what being a leader was all about. "There's some group at work here, and there are unknown seelie among them. We would have noticed anyone with that…miasma hanging around them in the Court. And who knows how long they've been planning? Our people can afford to wait centuries for a conspiracy to come to fruition."

"But how could they hide such a thing?" Faelyn said loudly. Lilani touched his arm, and he brought his voice down. "We don't hide from one another."

She would have agreed before the whole mess had started. "There are more seelie than your enclave from the north and the original Court," Lilani said. "Some might have been planning before they even fled the tattered lands." Her mind raced, trying to recall all the ancestral groups, but no one brought up those differences anymore, not wanting to create factions within the seelie.

Faelyn and Lucian listed old enclaves. Some had retreated to the Court before Lilani was born. Not all had been rousted by the tattered lands. Some had gotten into conflict with their human neighbors and fled south. One had been driven out of their homes by a volcano. And not all came south immediately. Some went to other colonies. They'd been moving among one another for thousands of years. And some had been left behind in their old enclaves, elders who'd shrouded, their locations forgotten. They might still be alive in the tattered lands, their magical fields protecting them.

"Did any of the enclaves try to live beside the tattered lands or among them?" she asked. "Could they have been…twisted in some way even through their magical fields?"

Lucian and Faelyn frowned, each consulting his own long memory.

"There was an enclave to the southeast of mine," Faelyn said. "They had to march through the tattered lands on their way here. My own enclave skirted large portions of it."

"There was an enclave who lived near the sea," Lucian said. "They refused to leave their home at first. They'd formed a kind of symbiotic relationship with the creatures of the waves."

Faelyn nodded slowly. Lilani thought over her lessons. She remembered learning about them. Nothing stopped the spread of the tattered lands, but water and cold slowed it down. The seelie near the sea had retreated to an island, but the tattered lands eventually reached ugly fingers out to them, corrupting the sea creatures and the waves themselves. The enclave couldn't find enough food to sustain them, so they'd fled in canoes, hoping to find a new place to settle on the southern coast, but those waters were deeper and more tempestuous. Few survived to reach the Court. They'd never struck Lilani as unfriendly or murderous, merely sad.

"Why would anyone want to taint the last place left to live?" she asked.

"And why wait all this time?" Faelyn asked. "They could have disrupted the pylons long before now."

"Unless they just discovered how," Lucian said. "And they had to wait until all the humans were gathered in one area."

"But the humans didn't drive all the seelie away from their homes," Lilani said. "Most fled the tattered lands!" This time, Faelyn had to remind her to be quiet.

"Many seelie believe the humans caused the tattered lands," Faelyn said. "Though they don't know how."

That sounded crazy to Lilani. Who would design their own demise? Unless it was an accident. Humans were endlessly curious, and from what she'd seen, they didn't care about what they did to their surroundings as long as they got what they wanted. She admired their spontaneity, but it could get them into trouble, too.

A seelie set on revenge might not care about the truth, anyway. And they had plenty of time to nurse a grudge, imaginary or not. No wonder Lilani's mother insisted on every problem being talked about in the open. Arguing until they achieved a solution was better than dark feelings festering for hundreds of years.

"What about that feeling of dread?" Lilani asked. "I've never felt it from anyone in the Court."

They shook their heads. Maybe that feeling was new, and it only enveloped a seelie when they turned murderous. Then why had she never read about it? No murders had happened in her lifetime, but there were some in seelie history, and no one had mentioned a miasma of dread surrounding the killer.

Lilani pressed a hand over her mouth and imagined that pall of misery settling over the whole Court. Maybe even with the pylons, the Seelie Forest was too close to the tattered lands, and it had infected some of them. Maybe she'd return home to find the Court in chaos. The cabal could have murdered her mother, maybe more of the Guard.

Maybe everyone.

Faelyn wrapped an arm around her shoulders, but he looked as sick as she felt. "We'll figure it out when we get home," he said. "Your mother is smart; she won't let anything catastrophic happen."

"And the taint of dread gives the murderers away," Lucian said. "People can feel when they're nearby and be on guard."

If anyone figured out what that awful feeling meant *before* they were murdered.

And Burani hadn't had it. There could be more like him.

"Sleep," Lucian said. "I'll take first watch."

"You need sleep more than us," Faelyn said.

Lucian frowned as if he might argue, but Faelyn had years of staring down unruly students. He matched him glare for glare.

"You're the fighter among us, Lucian, and you're wounded. We need you at your best." His expression softened. "If you promise to sleep for four hours, I promise to wake you and let you take the next watch."

Lucian sighed, but Faelyn's commanding tone coupled with his sensible kindness cracked many an opponent. With a nod, he lay down. Lilani squeezed Faelyn's leg and gave him a grateful smile. He nodded for her to join Lucian. She half hoped he would wake her in four hours so Lucian could rest longer, but he never broke his word.

Lilani closed her eyes. So many dark thoughts whirled in her mind that she didn't know if sleep would come, but the ground was strangely comfortable, and all the fear in the world couldn't keep sleep from her exhausted body.

CHAPTER EIGHTEEN

Lilani awoke with a shiver. The shadows in the den were on the other side from before, and she realized the sun had moved all the way across the sky. Lucian peered through the breaks in the bushes, and Faelyn lay by Lilani's side, one arm flung across his eyes.

When she sat up, Lucian nodded to her. She smiled and shifted away from Faelyn, not knowing if he'd gotten his fair share of sleep. Or maybe Lucian intended to hide until dark. If Lilani didn't return to the Court before Burani, what would he say? That she'd turned on her people? Her mother would never believe it. He might tell everyone she'd been killed, then he'd send someone to turn fiction into fact.

But she knew the Seelie Forest well. If she could get there, she could avoid any attack long enough to reach her mother. Then the cabal's plans would come undone, and Burani and his cronies would be arrested. If Lilani could figure out exactly who those cronies were.

Faelyn woke at dusk. He checked Lucian's wound, which had slowed considerably. The three of them shrouded before they crept out of the bushes. With Lucian guiding her, Lilani hurried from one batch of cover to another. She didn't want a repeat of yesterday's exhaustion, so she dropped her shroud whenever possible. Faelyn followed suit, but Lucian seemed content to stay hidden.

At one copse, they stopped to rest, Lucian blinking into sight. Faelyn rooted around and found edible plants as well as a few more leaves that held unexpected water. Lilani had never thought she'd use the nature lore Faelyn had tried in vain to teach her. Now she was more than grateful for his knowledge.

As they hurried on, her anxiety rose. It felt as if the whole world held its breath, poised for an attack. Instead of being a beacon, the rising moon and stars threw a spotlight over them and created more places for danger to hide. The wind picked up, dragging in clouds from the north. Lilani pulled her filthy coat tighter around her. Lucian kept a brisk pace, and even while shrouded, Lilani could feel Faelyn pulling at him to slow down.

"If you push too hard, your wound will reopen," Faelyn said.

"It's getting colder," Lucian said. "Keep moving."

Dawn couldn't have been far off, though the clouds made it seem a lifetime away. With the meager light came a slight drizzle, and fog lifted from the ground like the fingers of a hungry ghost.

Lilani shivered and wiped the mist from her face. She could see the hazy outlines of the others as the rain slid over them, making shrouds useless.

"We might as well give our magic a rest," Faelyn said. "Anyone can see us."

Lilani was happy to do so. As her shroud lifted, she sighed with relief. The cramps had begun, though they were far less painful than the day before. Maybe she was building her shrouding muscles. At least the trip to Parbeh had yielded one good result.

Besides seeing Vandra again.

Lilani let thoughts of Vandra warm her. When a gust of wind parted the fog and revealed the dark wall of the Seelie Forest, she was tempted to believe that warm thoughts could affect reality. She picked up speed, reaching for Lucian and Faelyn, urging them on. They were almost home!

Something whistled past Lilani's ear. She turned with the others, searching. A bird? An arrow? Common sense came to her slowly, fighting through exhaustion. "We should run."

Her feet had barely begun to stumble toward the forest when a crack from her left made her world explode into brilliant, white-hot agony. Her legs gave way, but she barely felt the fall. Pain shot through her skull with a roar that nearly drowned out Faelyn's and Lucian's cries. Streaks of color stabbed across her vision, and her stomach rebelled.

"Faelyn?" Her words were a slur.

She heard him close. Her mouth tasted foul. Vomit or blood? She felt over the ground, looking for Faelyn, but the world wouldn't stop spinning. Her magic had blown away like cobwebs in the wind. She could sense a taste of it hanging limply around her, but it fell apart as she tried to pull at it.

Someone seized her arm. "Faelyn?" The brightness faded, and she glimpsed a shadow. "Lucian?"

Agony bounced from her shoulder up her neck as someone wrenched her arm behind her back. Her stomach twisted again, but this wasn't pain. She'd felt it in the forest, and this close, it carried an echo of the border near the pylons. This was the taint of the tattered lands.

"Welcome home," a voice breathed in her ear.

A foreign sound roused Vandra from sleep. She thought that the shouts had followed from her dreams, but as she heard another, she realized they came from outside. She scrambled for the tent flap, trying to blink away the fog of sleep. When she poked her head outside, someone hauled her roughly into darkness. She twisted, flailing blindly, fatigue blown away by fear. A hand clapped over her mouth, but before she could sink her teeth into it, Pietyr whispered, "Stay down."

Vandra let him lower them both to the ground. He took his hand away, and she breathed hard, her heart pounding. "What's happening?"

Beyond the trees, someone shouted. Leaves rustled, and someone yelped in pain. A dark shape stepped over Vandra and Pietyr: Fieta, barely visible in the gloom as she hurried through the trees toward the sounds.

Someone cried out, a woman's voice, Lilani's voice. Vandra tried to stand, but Pietyr held her tight. "Stay here!" he whispered. Then his shadowy form followed their sister.

Vandra ground her teeth. All the gods in the world couldn't have gotten her to stay. She pushed up and hurried toward a gap in the trees. In the clearing between the trees and the road, several dark shapes wrestled on the ground. Vandra squinted, trying to make certain it was Lilani before she hurled herself into danger. One of the wrestlers broke away, dashing for the trees. They sprinted past Vandra's hiding spot, and she caught a flash of blond hair and a face that could have been Faelyn's. When another of the combatants tried to follow, Pietyr leaped from the darkness and tackled them.

The unknown combatant cried out, and Vandra shuffled away. A nauseating feeling roiled off the newcomer, a gut-punch of despair and putrescence that reminded her of the creature from the tattered lands: Face-mouth. She'd barely gotten a taste of it at the ball in Parbeh, but it was unmistakable now.

And it had her brother in its grip.

What could she do? Hit it with a stick? She looked around for one, but Fieta dashed from the shadows and joined Pietyr's fight. No one could match the two of them together, and Lilani still needed help. Vandra looked back to the field.

Empty.

She stepped closer, scanning the road, the trees. Everyone had vanished. That made them seelie, but why would the people they'd attacked disappear with them? She hurried to the camp and lit a lantern as fast as she could. Holding it high, she ran back for the twins.

Fieta stood with her hands on her hips, breathing hard. At her feet, Pietyr knelt over a still body. Vandra came closer, the light picking out the body's slender limbs, and his pale, gaunt face; the bones stood out like blades beneath slightly shimmery skin. His silver-white hair had been pulled back from his pointed ears, and the face was spotted by crimson stains. One large red pool covered a bright blue eye. He was seelie, though different from any other she'd seen, much paler and thin enough to have led a hard life. A red-stained rock lay under his temple.

"I didn't mean to kill him," Pietyr said weakly.

"You didn't," Fieta said. "It was me." She hauled Pietyr to his feet.

"But…" His eyes shone as he stared at her, stricken.

"It was me," she said again, louder. "I rammed his head against the rock. That was the blow that killed him. Mine."

Vandra looked from the dead seelie into the field. Still empty. When a twig cracked, she spun around, her heart rate ratcheting up again as the light tilted crazily off the trees.

Faelyn put his hands up. Blood dribbled from his nose and streamed down the side of his face. "You? Did they…did they…" He swayed as if he might fall over.

Vandra steadied him. "What in the name of the gods is going on?"

Faelyn glanced at the dead seelie. "I tried to get them to follow. So she could get away."

Vandra gripped his arm. "Lilani? What happened?"

He shook his head slowly. His eyes seemed unfocused.

"I think he's concussed," Vandra said, trying to see his pupils. She looked to the twins. Pietyr couldn't take his eyes off the dead seelie. Vandra looked to Fieta, who flicked her eyes in Pietyr's direction.

Yes, both he and Faelyn needed tending. "Come on, Pietyr," Vandra said. "Help me with him."

Pietyr shook as if trying to wake himself, then he took Faelyn's arm and led him toward camp. Vandra dug out her meager medical supplies and examined Faelyn's wounds while Pietyr kept watch.

Vandra was the first to admit she'd never had to patch up a serious injury. She took comfort in the fact that she knew how to do it in theory. Faelyn had taken a hit to the nose, but it didn't seem broken. The head wound was scarier. Nearly two inches long, it ran along his hairline and was already swelling. He hissed in pain as she examined him but seemed more confused than anything. On closer inspection, one of his pupils *was* slightly larger than the other. A fellow professor had the same look after one of his experiments exploded in his face.

And Vandra had no idea how to treat a concussion besides making sure the patient didn't fall asleep. "Faelyn," she said after she'd bandaged his head. "Think. What happened?"

"Attacked," he said with a frown. "They came for Lilani. I tried to lead them away." He blinked as if trying to clear his mind through sheer willpower. "Couldn't see, couldn't think…"

If only Vandra had woken up a little sooner. "A group of seelie? Why did she shroud and go with them?" Even if they'd carried her off, Vandra should have been able to see her unconscious body floating away. The magical field surrounding a seelie couldn't mask everything around them, too, not from what Vandra had seen.

Faelyn shook his head. "What?"

"Van?" Fieta's lantern bobbed through the forest as she jogged over. "I took a look at the field and found some soot." She held out a hand, presenting Vandra with a bunch of burnt soil and grass. "Barely spotted it through the fog."

Vandra gave it a sniff. "Sulfur and…" She sniffed again. "I'm not sure. Something very acrid. An explosive?" She turned to Faelyn. "Something exploded? Is that why you couldn't see?"

"A white light."

Vandra sat back on her heels. "I thought your people didn't practice alchemy."

He frowned again and seemed as if he might topple. Vandra caught him. "We have to keep him awake," she said. "If he falls asleep, he might not wake up again."

Pietyr nodded and helped Faelyn to his feet. When he tottered, Pietyr put an arm around him. "Come on. We need to walk."

"Don't go far," Fieta said.

When Pietyr didn't have a smart comeback, Vandra and Fieta exchanged a look. He was taking the seelie's death hard, even though Fieta had claimed the kill. Vandra wondered if Fieta ever killed anyone before. By the way she'd insisted she'd done it, Vandra doubted she'd killed anyone *now*, either, but they'd both spare Pietyr the guilt if they had the chance.

"There was nothing on that body but a canteen and a knife." Fieta held it out, but Vandra shied away as the dread feeling radiated from it. "Yeah, I feel that, too. We're not keeping it. But it was sheathed, which means he wasn't wielding it while chasing Faelyn. I think he was going for capture, not kill."

The worry worming through Vandra's stomach lessened. If that was true, Lilani was probably alive. She'd make a much more valuable hostage than Faelyn. *If* ransom was why these unknown seelie wanted her. That seemed the best possible scenario at the moment.

"We have to follow them," Vandra said. "Is it light enough for tracking?"

Fieta frowned. "Probably. But we're not trackers, Van."

"You hunt criminals!"

"In a city! Not in the wilderness."

Pietyr walked back, Faelyn held tight against him, though by the way Faelyn stared at their surroundings, he seemed to be coming back to himself.

"Van is right," Pietyr said. "Whoever took Lilani has to be the same people trying to sabotage the pylons. We need to find out more about them."

Fieta put her hands on her hips. "And what do we do with him?" She nodded at Faelyn.

"Take him with us," Pietyr said. "We can't leave him on his own."

"I want to go with you," Faelyn said. "For Lilani."

Vandra smiled and nodded. Fieta sighed loudly as if the world was made up of idiots. "Oh, fine. Let's go get killed."

❖

Lilani's vision went in and out of focus. Flashes of memory came to her: struggling with someone, shouts, a whisper, and grunts of pain. Faelyn had crashed to the ground, blood in his hair. She'd cried out, thinking him dead, but he'd struggled to his feet and ran for the forest.

She'd shouted, "Go!" or something like that, willing him to get help. Then something had cracked against the back of her head. Now the hazy dawn was moving around her, the overcast sky growing brighter each time her eyes drifted open. Someone held her close, but that gave no comfort. They reeked of the tattered lands.

She saw no one. A shrouded seelie. But she couldn't see herself, either. Had she shrouded? No, her magic hung around her like wet paper, useless. The miasma of the tattered lands covered her like swamp ooze. It trickled down her throat. She coughed, and pain billowed through her head, her eyes, her shoulder. She tried to curl around the pain but couldn't.

"Be still." A seelie voice, rough and ragged.

She tried to ask who it was, but her tongue felt like lead.

The arms shook her slightly. "Do you want another crack on the head? Be still!"

"Kill her," someone else said. A human voice? It had the same flat quality. But humans couldn't shroud.

"She's the blood of Awith," the seelie said.

The human snorted. "Her body will still be full of blood after she's dead."

"No." Another seelie voice, deep, feminine, sultry. A touch glided along Lilani's brow. "We need her magic, not her blood." Lilani smelled a whiff of perfume, a musky scent that drove away a bit of the dread. "It was a mistake to try to kill you, lovely Lilani. Don't worry. I'm in charge now. All will be well."

Lilani doubted that, but she didn't struggle, drawing what comfort she could from the touch. She let her eyes slip closed and waited for her senses to return. Faelyn had gotten away. He would tell her mother. The Guard would come for her. She hoped Lucian lived, too, but as the sky seemed to roll past, she still saw nothing. Did these seelie have some power to shroud others, even humans? Could humans be taught to shroud? Her mother said it was impossible, but the impossible seemed like the everyday now.

At last, the movement stopped, and the arms lowered her to the ground. She lay still, pretending to be senseless. She didn't have far to pretend. Pain bounced through her skull and along her neck. She wondered if her head was as bloody as Faelyn's had been.

"Why did you bring her here?" a new voice asked.

She knew him without seeing him. Burani. She wanted to scream at him for his treachery, but she forced herself to be still except for opening her eyes just a little.

He stood visible, hands on his hips, facing down empty air until four people blinked into view: one human and three seelie, though it sounded as if more stood behind her. Pale as corpses and with a slight shimmer to their skin, the seelie squinted in the meager light straining through the clouds. Their white hair was pulled tightly from their harsh, angular faces. Their bare arms were corded with lean muscle, and their black leather clothing seemed to absorb the light.

The human was as pale as the seelie, but his red hair and beard stood out starkly against his skin. He wore a leather belt with many pouches, two hanging down his legs. He glared at Burani while the two male seelie seemed entirely disinterested.

The female smirked. Her hair was longer than the others, a cloud of white that danced along her back. She stared at Burani with shining turquoise eyes. "Why did you lead that group of humans to attack us?"

Group of humans? Lilani's heart sped. From Parbeh? Could it be...

Burani bared his teeth. "I sent them right to you so you could kill them!"

No!

Another group of the strange seelie blinked into view behind Burani. "We were waiting where you said the humans would be," one said. "They weren't there."

"They were waiting to attack *us* instead," the long-haired female said.

Lilani closed her eyes briefly, hoping the humans had survived.

Burani frowned and swallowed as he looked between the two groups. "They must have changed direction. That's not my fault. I told them to go north."

"You should have killed them yourself."

"I never got the chance! There were three of them!"

Three! Vandra and the twins?

One of the seelie spat at Burani's feet. "Coward."

Burani put his hand to his sword and turned to keep everyone in sight. "Where is Remus?"

"Dead." The long-haired female glided closer, spreading her hands. "All hail Camilla, empress of the tattered seelie."

The other seelie laughed. The sound sent shivers down Lilani's spine.

Burani drew his weapon. "You'll have no allies in the Court if you kill me."

Camilla sighed. "Maybe." She turned her back on Burani. He breathed out, letting his sword dip toward the ground. "But who cares?"

The seelie behind Burani leaped, catching him as he vanished. Their blades stabbed forward again and again, the tips disappearing into Burani's invisible body, staining the ground crimson. He blinked back into view as he sagged, falling to his knees and then to the ground, his sightless eyes staring Lilani's way.

She could barely breathe. Another of them dead, and he hadn't even named his co-conspirators before he died. When Camilla knelt at her side, Lilani tried to pull away.

Camilla caught her tenderly. "Now, now, my sweet. There's nowhere to go. Let's sit you up."

As she moved, Lilani's head ached in time with her pulse, and her stomach rebelled as vertigo rolled through her. She squeezed her eyes shut, but Burani's face followed her.

"Deep breaths, child." Camilla's soft hands stroked Lilani's hair, her face, and the sides of her ears. "He was a traitor and a coward, and I have dispatched him for you, yes?"

"What…" Lilani took a deep breath. "What about Lucian?"

"This one?" She gently turned Lilani's head. Lucian lay on the ground behind her. His hands and feet were bound, and his body was slack, but his chest still moved. "He lives. For now. Look at me." She was as beautiful and as cold as an elder seelie, with the same air of immovability. "I'm afraid the other one perished."

Lilani couldn't hold in a sob. Faelyn! No, he'd run, he'd gotten away. Or had he? What were the chances of that? She put her head in her hands. She didn't want to weep in front of these monsters, but Faelyn!

Camilla held her close. "There now, there, dear Lilani." Her skin was soft, but there was so much strength in her arms that she felt like velvet-covered steel. Lilani fought the urge to push away, not wanting to antagonize her. This close, Camilla's perfume couldn't quite overwhelm the miasma that surrounded her. Lilani drank in that despair, letting it bring her back to herself. Faelyn would want her to be strong.

When Camilla pulled back, she smiled like a cat with a lizard. "You have a chance, dear Lilani, to save this one." She nodded toward Lucian. "If you do as we say, you'll both remain unharmed, and we'll return you to your mother safe and happy."

She spoke as if she hadn't just had someone killed, as if she hadn't killed this Remus who'd been in charge before her, as if Faelyn hadn't been slaughtered. As for Vandra…

Dare she ask? No, if Vandra had perished, Lilani didn't want to know. She took a deep breath. "What do you want me to do?"

Camilla's smile widened. "See, Maruk?" she said to the human. "I was right about her. She's a good girl."

Maruk snorted. "We'll see."

"Come along, darling," Camilla said as she helped Lilani stand. "Let's go meet the others."

Two of the seelie hauled Lucian up between them, and Lilani stumbled along at Camilla's side. Her head pounded, and her body was sore. If she ran, she wouldn't get far, and by the ease with which Camilla held her, she'd never be able to overpower these seelie.

She risked a look around. There were ten of them, and they were leading her toward others, lessening her chances of escape. But even if she got away now, they'd kill Lucian. Maybe among more of them, she'd find a chance to untie him and slip away.

The pylon loomed through the haze in front of them. Her stomach shrank. There were no tents at the pylon's base, no signs of a camp. Single-file, the other seelie continued past the pylon, into the shifting mist and the pall of dread that was the tattered lands. Bile rose in Lilani's throat, and fear made her head pound harder. She dug in her heels.

"I can't," Lilani said, her breath coming in gasps. "Please!"

"Hush, darling." Camilla held her closer. "I'll protect you." Her lips nearly brushed Lilani's ear, tickling, terrifying. "If you stay close to me."

Lilani shivered, her insides going cold. When Camilla started forward again, Lilani had no choice but to go with her, each stumble taking her closer to the wall of mist.

❖

The light rain that swept through the night before proved to be a boon. The seelie left tracks so clear, even Vandra could see them. Maybe they didn't expect anyone to follow them. They might have thought they'd encountered some random group of humans rather than those who were trying to undo their plans.

Vandra's rational brain told her this pursuit was stupid. She wasn't a fighter. Even as good as Fieta and Pietyr were, they couldn't defeat a host of enemies on their own. They had Faelyn, who was currently stumbling along on her arm. No help there. And whoever these seelie were, they either knew about alchemy, or they'd found someone to help them.

Fieta kept muttering about how they were all going to be killed. Pietyr didn't say anything, but he had a pinched, worried look as he followed the tracks. Vandra called a halt. The others gathered around her, and she spoke in a whisper, even though no one was in sight.

"I know this is dangerous, but if we go looking for help now instead of following Lilani, the trail will grow cold. We'll find out where she is and then…"

"Yes?" Fieta asked.

Faelyn rested a hand on Vandra's arm. He'd thrown up twice already, and he had that queasy, greenish tinge again. Pietyr gathered Faelyn's hair behind him and turned him away from the others. Oh yes, they were a rescue party worthy of song and story. Vandra rubbed her temples and tried to think.

"Thank you," Faelyn said after dry heaving. "I can probably make it to the Court and get help."

Pietyr frowned and shook his head. Fieta snorted.

"Not on your own, Faelyn," Vandra said. "You can barely walk. If you pass out in the forest, you might never be found."

He nodded then winced as if that little movement pained him. "You can't come with me. Seelie magic makes the land unwelcoming to humans."

Vandra had suspected as much. "Maybe by the time we catch up with Lilani, you'll feel better."

It was all they could hope for. Fieta shrugged, and Pietyr shook his head, but they didn't argue. Vandra thanked the gods for that small favor. They continued on the trail, and Vandra wasn't surprised to see the pylon rearing through the misty morning. Of course, the trail headed straight for it. Everything led back to the pylons.

"There's someone lying in the grass ahead," Fieta said.

Pietyr stood on tiptoe. "They're not moving."

Vandra halted with Faelyn. She couldn't see what the twins could, and her heart wrenched. "Is it…" She couldn't even finish the sentence.

"I'll go check," Fieta said. "Wait here."

"I'm coming with you," Pietyr said.

Fieta stabbed a finger in Vandra's direction. "Stay with them!"

He seemed as if he might argue, but after a glance at Vandra and Faelyn, he stayed put. Vandra held tight to Faelyn as Fieta bent double, keeping as low in the tall grass as she could. She streaked forward, spear in hand. Vandra fought the urge to hold her breath. Any moment, she expected Fieta to whirl around and pit her skills against invisible foes. Pietyr would run for her, and Vandra would, too. Faelyn had managed to distract one of the seelie that had attacked Lilani. Maybe Vandra could do the same.

Fieta knelt then glanced up again quickly before she dashed back. "It's Burani." She swallowed hard. "He's been stabbed."

Vandra didn't ask if he was dead. The haunted look in Fieta's eyes said it all. She spat to the side, her expression dark.

"Good riddance," Faelyn said.

Vandra looked at him in shock. "What?"

"He's a traitor."

Vandra glanced at the twins. Fieta stared at Faelyn with murder in her eyes. Pietyr frowned, looking between everyone. "No," Vandra said, "he was with us yesterday. These enemy seelie must have caught him."

Pietyr shook his head. "But he was heading straight for the forest. What's he doing all the way out here?"

"They probably captured him like they did Lilani," Fieta said, still glaring. Then she looked away as if something occurred to her. "Except he's armed and stabbed in the back."

"I'm telling you, he betrayed and attacked us in Parbeh," Faelyn said.

Vandra went through several scenarios in her head, but she needed more data. "I want to see him."

They all went forward this time, Faelyn grumbling that they should believe him. The mist grew thicker under the dark clouds overhead. Vandra knelt beside the body along with Pietyr.

"Well," he said, "the sword near his hand is his own, but if he'd been captured, he could've stolen it back at some point." He shifted Burani's arm. "There're no marks on his wrists, so he wasn't bound."

Fieta knelt near Burani's head. "No wound here, either. They didn't knock him out."

Vandra sighed, grateful they knew what they were doing. "I'm sorry, Fieta. I know you thought he was..." She cleared her throat. "Whether he was in league with them or not, they turned on him."

"He was," Faelyn said.

Fieta frowned at the corpse as if it had injured her personally.

"We suspected some kind of cabal," Faelyn said. "There might be more."

"Did he start the fire in Parbeh?" Vandra asked.

"It's possible."

Vandra thought back to Burani's words about barely escaping the fire and not being able to save his friend. Maybe he'd injured himself pushing her deeper into the flames. She shuddered. Whatever had happened, they couldn't linger if they hoped to catch Lilani.

As they approached the pylon, Vandra expected to see the soldiers assigned to guard duty, but there was no one. Either they'd never arrived, or they were as dead as Ariadne, Burani, and so many others connected to this awful business.

And Lilani wasn't conveniently waiting.

Vandra wasn't surprised to see the seelie trail continue past the pylon, through the dead field, and into the wall of mist. Her heart sank as she thought of the aura of nauseating despair around the dead seelie. He'd had a deathly pallor, as if he hadn't seen the sun in who knew how long.

The sun never shown in the tattered lands.

"Oh gods," Vandra whispered. "They've been living in there." And they'd taken Lilani inside. Vandra slowed her breathing, forcing herself to remain calm. Lilani could shroud. She'd be all right.

For a little while.

"Why come out if they can live in there?" Fieta asked. "Why break a pylon?"

Faelyn frowned. "I thought I heard a human voice among them, too."

Humans living in the tattered lands? Vandra tried to think how it could be done without them turning into creatures like Face-mouth. "The why doesn't matter at the moment," she said. "Lilani's in there, and we're going to get her out."

Chapter Nineteen

As they passed through the wall of mist, every nerve in Lilani's body burned. She gasped, gulping in air that oozed through her lungs. She could almost feel it corrupting her from the inside out. Then, like the tender folds of an enclosing flower, Camilla's magic flowed around her. It felt nothing like the warm blanket of her own power but drew from the taint around them and turned that malevolent energy back on itself like a mirror.

Lilani's own magic shivered, and she was tempted to pull it around herself even though she was already shrouded by Camilla's power. Better to save it for her escape, though the desire to shroud persisted like an itch in the back of her throat.

She braced herself for Camilla's touch, a guiding hand since they were invisible, but she felt a tingle as Camilla's magic touched those of her followers, all of their power joining like some great bubble. If she concentrated, Lilani could feel where the tattered seelie were standing, marking the edges of their shroud.

So much for sneaking away; they'd feel it if she left.

By their appearance, these seelie had been living inside the tattered lands for some time. They'd clearly adapted, their magic binding them into an unseen horde. Had it also made them murderous or just more casual about the loss of life?

She couldn't bring herself to ask, watching the mist instead. She recalled the hideous creature that had attacked Vandra and imagined it circling them, knowing someone was there but unable to find them. Or could it smell them, maybe tasting Lilani's fear on the wind?

The deeper they walked into the tattered lands, the more cries and gurgles echoed from the mist. Tall black shapes that loomed out of the gray haze proved to be the remains of trees, now bent and twisted. Lilani swore she saw one move, the branches snapping. A crash came from the left, and Lilani jumped, but Camilla's touch on her shoulder kept her moving. No one spoke, and Lilani repeated in her mind that they were hidden. The creatures of the tattered lands couldn't see through the shroud, or these seelie wouldn't be alive.

Something snuffled from the right. The mist swirled and parted, revealing a long snout bristling with teeth. Lilani clamped her lips together to keep from crying out. Camilla's grip on her shoulder turned hard; the strength in those fingers could punch into bone. Lilani couldn't help a gasp, and the snout twitched in her direction. She didn't take her eyes from it as Camilla picked up speed. Before the mist closed over the snout again, she spotted something else between the teeth: little waving tentacles or tiny fingers, all of them pointing in her direction.

The mist closed, and the thing was gone, but Lilani kept seeing it in her mind, wondering what other horrors surrounded her. Even her pain wasn't enough to distract her from the fear. She tried to breathe deep, to keep hold of her sanity. To bolt into the mist would mean death, if Camilla didn't simply crack her over the head again.

They walked for an hour or so, but it felt like days, each moment counted by her racing heart. When she spotted a shadow ahead, she thought it might be another great beast, this one too large to pass, but the seelie kept their course. The shadow was as large as the library in the Court, maybe larger, and nothing that huge could miss their passing.

Lilani's heart thundered, and she tried to pull away, but Camilla's other hand grabbed her arm, marching her forward. Were they going to feed her to this giant monster? Her breath came in gasps, her mind drowned by a fog of panic as thick as the one surrounding them. Any moment now she'd shriek and force Camilla to let go or wrench her arm from the socket.

Then the mist parted to reveal not a monster but a structure. Lilani nearly laughed in relief, even with the danger. A tower loomed above them, rising from a larger mass. The tower's corners were marked by jutting spears of brick. It seemed more like the buildings of Parbeh than anything in the Court, a stronghold inside the border of the tattered lands.

She stumbled as the ground sloped, and Camilla kept her upright. The stronghold wasn't as tall as she'd thought but had been built upon a short, steep, craggy hill, and the path to the tower took them through spires of pointed rock. She didn't see trees or a single blade of grass; what the tattered lands couldn't corrupt, they killed.

Lilani glanced at the spire, and something tickled her memory, an offhand comment inside Awith's tale. The humans had tried many experiments before hitting on the idea of the pylons. This had to be one of a series of watchtowers where humans had experimented with alchemy to stop the spread of the tattered lands. They might have conceived of the pylons in strongholds such as these, but ultimately, the watchtowers had only been observatories to watch a wall of fog and malevolence gobble everything in its path.

The path led to a small door set in the base of the tower. A squat, rectangular building joined the tower on the right, but Lilani could see through the windows that the inside was a ruin. Mist streamed through holes in the roof and walls. The tower appeared solid, and its door opened soundlessly. When everyone was inside with the door shut, the seelie blinked back into view along with the human, Maruk, and Lucian, still unconscious.

Torches illuminated a staircase that circled the tower's interior before disappearing through the ceiling. Lilani let out a deep breath, and some of her fear went with it. Behind the safety of the walls, her ire rose, and she focused on the lone human.

"Why bring down the pylons and destroy your entire race?" If possible, Lilani was even angrier at him than the seelie. At least the seelie could survive in the tattered lands, but Maruk was condemning his kind to death.

He smirked and turned his back without answer. She took a step toward him, ready to kick him in the name of humanity.

Camilla's iron grip didn't let Lilani get far. She laughed, the sound echoing off the walls. "You'd better watch your back, Maruk."

He snorted, and Lilani twisted in Camilla's grasp until Camilla leaned close to her ear. "Don't worry about the humans, dear Lilani. They'll be fine."

Lilani turned, the anger still bright inside her. "How?"

"Well, not all of them," Camilla said, "but those who work with us will be fine. Look around." She gestured around the watchtower as if it were a palace made of gold. "There is safety here, and there are far too many humans packed into Citran. Those who agree not to fight us will have places like this, and they'll be free to spread out as they can and have their kingdoms back, albeit a little smaller than before."

Lilani shook her head. "That's nonsense! They could never go outside, not without seelie to shield them."

"Let them worry about that." She tugged Lilani toward the staircase.

Lilani went with her, not wanting to be carried or knocked out again. From the corner of her eye, she watched as another seelie carried Lucian through a door across from the exit. That left one more door, barred from this side, that probably led into the ruin.

Lilani's hand brushed the stone of the tower, and it sent a tingle up her arm. A glimmer ran through the brick, lines of syndrium wound through the rock. Whatever the humans had done here, it hadn't been enough to stop the tattered lands, but it kept the mists out of the tower itself. Maybe it kept the creatures at bay, too?

Maybe it would even help her.

"What do you want of me?" Lilani asked. They passed a large open room on the second floor with tables, chairs, and a fireplace.

"You have the run of the tower for now," Camilla said, continuing upward. "I hope our walk through the tattered lands was enough to convince you how foolish it is to go outside."

They passed into a third floor, this one divided into rooms with only a narrow space for the stairs. "I suggest not poking around in anyone's room," Camilla said. "I won't let them hurt you, of course, but it's not wise to make enemies in so small a space."

"What do you want?" Lilani said again, trying to keep her voice firm.

The fourth floor was much the same as the third. Lilani couldn't tell one room from another. Camilla's laughter rang like a bell. "It's been so long since anyone raised their voice to me. Except for Remus, of course." Her fingers caressed Lilani's knuckles. "I stabbed him twelve times. An overreaction, perhaps, but I had so many grievances to make up for."

Lilani took the warning and fell quiet. The fifth floor was a large, open space, with windows looking out on the swirling mist. The floor was dominated by two tables bearing different kinds of equipment.

Alchemy, Lilani guessed. Two closed doors stood on opposite sides of the room.

Camilla sighed as she released Lilani and went to stand by the windows. As fearful as she was, Lilani shivered at the loss of contact and crossed her arms. Camilla wasn't exactly friendly, but Lilani felt safer with her.

"You said that you don't want all the humans to die," Lilani said. "So why sabotage the pylons at all?"

Camilla didn't turn. "We're so much stronger now that we've lived inside the tattered lands. It's time the rest of the seelie became strong, too."

Lilani's stomach went cold. "So, you're killing the pylons, forcing the tattered lands on our people, and risking the humans to…make the seelie stronger?"

Camilla winked. "They just don't know what they can become yet."

It was madness. Even with her shroud, Camilla had been driven mad by the tattered lands.

"Remus wanted to kill you," Camilla said. "He wanted to slaughter all the blood of Awith. He feared the power inside you. When mixed with human alchemy, it can do wondrous things."

She advanced slowly, and Lilani resisted the urge to back up. As if sensing her unease, Camilla stopped before touching her, but the look on her face said she was amused rather than concerned. "My room is there," she said nodding to the left. "You will stay with me."

Lilani's heart pounded, and she fought the urge to leap away.

"In your own bed," Camilla said, catching a strand of Lilani's hair where it moved across her shoulders. "Unless you wish otherwise." She laughed again, released Lilani's hair, and strolled toward the table. "Don't touch Maruk's equipment."

"What of Lucian?" Lilani asked.

Camilla shrugged. "Nurse him, bed him, kill him; I don't care. If he attacks anyone, he'll die. If he escapes, he'll die. You already know I plan to use him against you. Can you kill him to avoid that? It would be the most merciful outcome." She laughed as if the idea delighted her.

Lilani fought the urge to sink to the ground and bury her head in her hands. This woman was as twisted as any creature in the tattered lands, and she didn't even know it. Lilani turned, nearly running down the stairs.

❖

Vandra stood at the border of the tattered lands, racked with indecision. She had to believe that Lilani would be all right since she could shroud, but as a human, Vandra had no protection.

"I'll follow them." Faelyn's color was a little better, and he was able to stand on his own, but he seemed unsteady.

Pietyr shook his head. "Not on your own." His lips pinched together so hard they turned white. Faelyn might not know what that meant, but Vandra did. If Faelyn tried to step into the tattered lands, Pietyr would sit on him.

"I appreciate your concern," Faelyn said, "but—"

Pietyr took a step, but Fieta laid a hand on his arm, stopping him. "It's more than concern, Faelyn. You'd get lost or eaten immediately, and we'd have no way to tell your people what happened to you or Lilani."

Whether he saw her side or was affronted by the thought that he'd be eaten if left on his own, he shut his mouth.

"I need you here," Vandra said quietly. If she couldn't go after Lilani, the next best course would be sending Faelyn to gather his people and mount a rescue operation. Vandra wanted to do that, wanted Lilani back, but she had another duty. The pylon was right *here*. She had more to worry about than the fate of one seelie, as much as that pained her.

"With your magical field," she said, "I can turn this pylon back into syndrium. That'll help when we do rescue Lilani." She added that last part for his benefit as well as hers, though she felt like a traitor. She clenched her hands, quelling her desire to see Lilani rescued before anything else. When she looked to the others, Fieta nodded, Pietyr looked at Vandra with such sympathy she wanted to hug him, and Faelyn's chin raised as if he might rebel. Well, why wouldn't he? His friend, the daughter of his empress, had to be more important to him than any human, maybe even all humans.

And part of Vandra wanted him to ignore her and march off to fetch rescuers, but she said, "Please." It was barely a whisper, all the force she could muster. "I want to go after her, but this is all I can do to help right now."

Indecision crawled across his face, and time seemed to creep by, the nauseating feel of the tattered lands washing over them every time the wind gusted.

Fieta sighed, always the most impatient. "Give me some names."

Everyone turned to her as if they were marionettes tied to the same length of wood.

She lifted her arms and dropped them. "Some seelie names, some things to say so they know I'm serious and not some crazy human. I'll go into the forest as far as I can and shout my head off for help."

Vandra grinned. "I'll give you some syndrium. It might help against any measures the seelie have for keeping humans out."

"Are you sure about this, Fie?" Pietyr asked.

"I'll be safer than you. Keep your head up out here." They gripped each other's arms before hugging. Fieta slapped Pietyr on the back and straightened, taking the syndrium Vandra gave her and stuffing it in one pocket as if it wasn't the most valuable resource in the whole world.

Faelyn blurted out a few names, some words that made no sense to Vandra, but she hoped the seelie would understand. He had her repeat them, and they sounded mangled, but maybe they'd be good enough.

"I'll stomp up and down the forest for a few hours," Fieta said. "Then I'm coming back."

Vandra nodded. "I'll be surprised if you last that long."

Fieta gave her a crooked grin before hugging her roughly. "Take care of yourself, Van." She pushed away and put her hands on Vandra's shoulders, looking deeply into her eyes. "Do what Pietyr says."

Vandra rolled her eyes. "Yes, yes."

"If he says, run, you run!"

Vandra shrugged out of her grip. "I said yes! Now, speaking of running…" She nodded toward the forest, but when Fieta jogged away, Vandra smiled at her back, silently asking any gods to watch over her sister.

She turned to Faelyn. "Let's get to work."

At first it seemed impossible. The pylon was huge. Vandra couldn't break it down, perform her formula on each piece, then glue it back together. Maybe she could transform it one piece at a time while it was whole? The best place to start was the top.

Faelyn and Pietyr climbed without hesitation, though Pietyr insisted on tying a rope around Faelyn's midsection and looping that through a metal rung in the pylon's side. As Vandra watched him tenderly tie the rope, she couldn't help a smile. Pietyr had always been careful with anyone who needed his help. As good as he was at his job, he had a tender heart, but there was something more in the particular way he cared for Faelyn. It might have been Faelyn's sorry state or all the people they had to worry about at that moment—like the entire human race—but Vandra saw something else, a subtle darkening of Pietyr's cheeks. To Vandra's knowledge, Pietyr had never been romantically interested in anyone, unlike his sister, who gave her heart as freely as water. Vandra didn't dare ask. If Fieta saw Pietyr's tender looks, she'd tease him enough for everyone.

And if Faelyn noticed past his concussion, Vandra couldn't tell. He chuckled when Pietyr asked him for the fifth time if he felt secure. "With you here, how could I not?"

Pietyr turned away, but Vandra noticed his small smile.

Faelyn sat at Vandra's side. "What do you need me to do?"

"Just be here." She filled him in on the experiment she'd done with Burani, adding that her formula hadn't worked since the first time she'd tried it. He frowned, but if he had specific thoughts about whether a seelie had been present then, he kept them to himself.

Vandra mixed her ingredients, but the problem was how to heat a large portion of the pylon at one time. She could knap a small chunk and turn that back to syndrium, but when she tried to glue it in place or turn it into a rough paste and add it back to the whole, the rest of the pylon stayed dark.

Faelyn sat cross-legged, staring at her eagerly while Pietyr watched the surrounding countryside. "I need heat," Vandra said, talking to herself as much as anyone else. "A blast of heat to complete the transformation."

Faelyn nodded. "Could you apply part of the mixture to the pylon's surface then use a flame as you go? A torch, perhaps?"

She blinked, not expecting that he'd have any ideas, but he was a teacher and an advisor to royalty, so he had to be smart. "Anyone walking along the pylon taking a torch to it would be in danger of burning themselves."

"A pity you can't light it all on fire at once," he said.

She flashed back to the burnt soil Fieta had showed her near their campsite. "Light all of it at once," she muttered, looking around.

Sprinkle her formula over the entire pylon then spread a flammable component? Would Faelyn's proximity be enough to change the entire thing?

It would have to be. She couldn't very well have him standing in the flames. She knocked another chunk from the pylon. "I need to do another experiment."

"If you keep taking pieces, there won't be any left," Pietyr said.

"Thank you, Papa."

He snorted a laugh. They helped each other down, and Vandra tried her experiment, covering the pylon piece with her formula, sprinkling a small amount of flammable powder on top, and dropping a match.

The burst of flame was so large, they leapt back before Pietyr rushed in and stomped out the fire in the grass. Vandra and Faelyn joined him, though Faelyn looked a little woozy by the end. Pietyr helped him sit while Vandra investigated her pylon chunk.

A perfect piece of syndrium. She grinned and looked to the pylon again. Now, did she have enough flammable powder to coat the whole thing? Not in her pack. She glanced around the countryside, focusing on the brown grass from the edge of the tattered lands. She lifted a patch with her shoe: brittle, with the soil underneath soft and spongy. The grass came up in a sheet, almost as if the land was covered with a blanket instead of roots. It reminded Vandra of peat, though she'd only heard of that growing in wet climates.

Despite the moisture, peat was flammable.

She grinned. Perhaps the moisture-rich, fog-shrouded tattered lands had given her a gift after all.

The tattered seelie lounged around their tower as if they weren't bent on destroying the world. Those who bothered to meet Lilani's eyes didn't smile or sneer or display any emotion except mild curiosity. She'd never met any of them, and that alone was enough to make her head spin. She'd known all her people since birth.

If Burani had known these seelie, others at the Court knew them, too. Were they the rest of the island seelie? Did their kin know they were alive? She tried to tell herself it didn't matter at the moment. There were probably more humans and seelie in the tattered lands, huddling in places like this, trapped in the corruption. Why live here instead of fleeing? Perhaps the corruption inside them was as afraid of the sun as normal people were afraid of the tattered lands.

Lilani passed Maruk on the stairs. He read from a book as he climbed, not looking at her. Maybe alchemists always had their noses in books. The thought reminded her too much of Vandra and everything they'd been through, and she fought the urge to push Maruk down the stairs. Vandra had to be alive. Lilani wouldn't accept anything else.

No one waited at the bottom of the tower. The exit stood barred from the inside, but Lilani could easily unbar it and flee. And how would she find her way? She'd never see the pylons through the fog. She fought temptation and turned for the door Lucian had gone through.

Should she knock? What would she say if someone answered? Rebellious at the very idea of having to ask to see her friend, she pushed the latch and opened the door, ready to stare down any guards who stood in her way.

When no one accosted her, she nearly slumped in relief no matter her rebellious thoughts. Lucian lay on a straw pallet, one wrist bound in an iron manacle with a chain that led to a ring in the wall. His eyes were closed, and a bruise darkened one side of his face.

Lilani closed the door and hurried to his side. A pitcher sat next to his head. She sniffed its contents. Water, with the slightly greasy odor of everything in the tattered lands. She rolled up the sleeve of her coat, wet her shirt cuff, and tried to clean Lucian's face so she could better see his injuries. The bandage around his chest had stayed put, and that wound didn't seem worse. His lips twitched, and she leaned forward to hear.

"Are they watching?" he asked.

She tried to look natural as she sat back. So, he wasn't as wounded as he seemed. She glanced around, looking for spy holes. Nothing, and she didn't feel the conspicuous aura of dread that surrounded the tattered seelie. "No."

He opened his eyes and gave her a brave smile. She wanted to throw her arms around him and weep, but she kept that inside. She was the daughter of the empress, and she would act like it.

"I'm going to stay still," he said, "in case any of them come in. Act worried."

She wanted to fall down and laugh hysterically. "That won't be a problem." Quickly, she told him everything she'd seen and heard, not knowing how much he'd caught while being carried around like a slain deer. She skirted around the reason Camilla had kept him alive, but when she finished, he said:

"They want to use me against you." When she didn't answer, his mouth pressed into a thin line. "You know what I'm going to say."

"That I shouldn't worry about you, the same thing Faelyn would say."

"But you'll worry about me all the same."

"Yes."

He stared at her levelly, and she knew that if they were on a cliff's edge, he would be tempted to jump so she wouldn't have to consider his safety. But that would also leave her alone in the hands of their captors.

He squeezed her hand. "We will survive this."

She smiled. "I'm so happy you included both of us in that statement."

"Look around," he said. "Note everything. Look for the keys to this." He pulled at the chain. "Or something I can use to force it. Arm yourself if possible."

She nodded. She should have thought of all that instead of letting herself sink into anger or despair. She'd read enough books about people escaping from impossible situations. She had to have learned something from them.

Lucian stayed still as she stood. Lilani looked back before leaving, but he'd shut his eyes again. In the entryway, the door into the ruin looked promising, but she couldn't go exploring, not without freeing Lucian first. To do that, she needed tools.

A few tattered seelie lingered in the common room on the second floor, eating and drinking. As before, they paid her little mind except to fall silent. The lack of noise felt as great as a deafening bell, and Lilani swallowed, imagining everyone could hear the sound. Her heart pounded, but she forced herself to come closer to the barrels and boxes lining the room, to peer into the cauldron that hung over the fireplace. The cauldron stood empty, but one open box held roughly shaped lumps of oats. Lilani took one and bit in, tasting honey, oats, and fruit. Hard to chew, but it would do for the moment. She put another in her pocket for Lucian.

Conversation still hadn't resumed when she climbed to the next floor, and she shivered when she was out of sight. She didn't want to go poking through the rooms, not knowing who might be where. One seelie left a room on the third floor, and she noted which one, not knowing what might be important later.

The next floor stood abandoned, so Lilani sat between the doors, listening. She used her damp sleeve to wash her face and hands as best she could, but she was stuck with her ruined coat, stained and ripped shirt, and filthy trousers. Her earrings were long gone, but a few pins clung to her hair. She took it down, fighting through the tangles before pinning it back, trying to keep it as still as possible. She chuckled as she imagined trying to make sense of the rat's nest later. She could count herself lucky if that was her biggest problem.

After another deep breath, she climbed to the top of the tower. If there was anything useful lying around, it would be amongst the alchemical equipment.

Camilla was no longer there, and both doors stood closed. Lilani crept past the tables, looking over strangely shaped glass containers, mortars and pestles, bundles of herbs, and rows of jars filled with multi-colored powders. Several metal tools lay strewn about. Any of them might help free Lucian, but they were too large to hide. Between two clay vessels, she spotted a length of metal as long as her hand and as wide as one finger. It tapered to a point on one end and crooked at the other. After a quick glance around, she snatched it up and hid it in her sleeve.

She forced herself to breathe when no outcry sounded, and no horde of tattered seelie descended upon her. She moved to the next table when the door on the opposite side of the room opened, and Maruk stepped out.

His eyes widened before he put on a smirk. "So, Camilla's letting you wander about, eh? Did she warn you not to touch my equipment?"

The piece of metal in Lilani's sleeve seemed to burn like a brand, her overactive imagination at work. She curled her fingers to keep it in place. "Nothing of yours holds any interest for me." She tried to sound bored as she turned to look at the mist. With so many windows, she could see in every direction, but she didn't know which would lead her home to Vandra.

Maruk muttered and fussed amongst his equipment. From what she'd seen, he was proud. He probably wouldn't answer any questions, but maybe she could get him to admit something by feigning disinterest or disgust.

She caught something snide about showing her people and the world enough to interest them for the rest of their lives. She snorted. "I doubt it."

"What?"

She didn't bother to look at him. "Nothing about you is even the slightest bit interesting, like most humans." When Maruk stomped over to glare at her, she knew there was some rift between the tattered seelie and their ally, or at least a fear of inadequacy.

"Is that so?" he asked.

She shrugged.

"Listen, you little…" He stopped, finger in the air, and smiled. "I know what you're doing. I saw you quaking in your boots when we brought you here, and I now see your little manipulations for what they are." He looked her up and down, sneering. "I'm not telling you shit."

She tried to remain bored, inwardly cursing, and shrugged again.

He barked a laugh. "Try all your tricks. None of them will work. You have no power here."

Lilani tried to summon up every memory of her mother staring someone down. She lifted an eyebrow. "Or so you think."

He frowned. She had no idea where she was going with the words, but she had to sow whatever doubts she could. He rolled his eyes, but as he began to turn away, a bloom of fire came from outside, far in the distance. It lit the fog of the tattered lands like a beacon.

Lilani's mouth fell open, but she closed it quickly. Maybe Vandra's gods were granting her a boon.

When Maruk glanced at her, his mouth open, too, she inclined her head toward the fire. The glow had faded a little, but whatever it had been, she was taking credit for it. "See?"

CHAPTER TWENTY

Well," Pietyr said, shading his eyes from the glare. "We lit the pylon on fire. Now what?"

It had ignited faster than Vandra expected. When Pietyr had thrown the torch onto the peat-covered pylon, Vandra had ducked and cried out, Faelyn beside her. Pietyr leapt away and rolled. Luckily, he hadn't been burned, though his hair looked singed.

Now, seeing the pylon lit like a beacon, Vandra grinned. Finally, something had gone according to plan. The fire burned away some of the lingering morning mist, but the tattered lands seemed as close as ever. Vandra frowned. That wasn't *quite* according to plan.

Bits of flaming peat rained from the pylon. "Shit!" Pietyr dashed forward and stomped a fire out. "Van, Faelyn, hurry!"

Vandra joined him, not wanting to set the countryside on fire. Would it spread through the tattered lands and burn the taint away? More likely, the rest of the world would burn, and only the tattered lands would be left.

With Lilani inside.

Vandra shuddered and kept stomping. When the fires burned down, and the rain of peat ceased, Vandra took a deep breath. Time to see just how lucky they were. She opened her pack and found the syndrium detector. After another breath, she calibrated and pointed it in the pylon's direction. The detector zeroed in right away, and Vandra let out a whoop of joy.

Faelyn peered over her shoulder. "Good news?"

"Better than good." With elation coursing through her, she grabbed his hand and shook it, then threw her arms around Pietyr. Finally, something had gone right! Could rescuing Lilani be far behind? She only had to invent a device to protect her inside the tattered lands.

Easy.

As she stared at the mist, her smile faded. The turbulent wall of gray should have been receding if the pylon was working.

"What's wrong?" Faelyn asked.

Pietyr shushed him. "Give her a moment."

Vandra took another reading. Syndrium, without a doubt. She edged closer to the pylon, wincing at the heat that radiated from the silvery-blue surface. A telltale glow coated the entire pylon, enough to pull the detector. Could it be that she'd transformed the outside, but the inside was still rock? She peered up. The top of the pylon seemed duller than the bottom; it had been farther away from Faelyn's magical field. Maybe she would need an entire team of seelie? Standing on top of it as it was engulfed in flames? Suicidal.

She turned to Faelyn. "Do you know how the seelie helped create the original pylons?"

He shook his head. "Awith, a cousin of Lilani's, wrote about helping the humans, but I'm afraid she was sparse on details. She didn't have time to write when the pylons were actually going up. I know that aiding in the construction cost her life."

Vandra gnawed on her lip. "We don't have to resort to killing you just yet."

Pietyr gawked, but Faelyn chuckled. "So glad to hear it. And I don't know how she died or if her death was…necessary somehow. I always assumed the tattered lands killed her."

"At *this* pylon?" Vandra asked. "If she died here, how did she help construct the others? Unless other seelie helped, too?"

He sighed and shook his head. "By that time, relations between the humans and the seelie were very strained. Many of my people blame yours for the creation of the tattered lands, and when our peoples met while fleeing the spread of the taint, well, it wasn't always happy."

"People aren't on their best behavior while running for their lives," Pietyr said.

Faelyn chuckled. "True."

Vandra kept her frown. From what she'd read of the history of Parbeh, seelie-human relations had already been muddy when other humans started flowing into Citran. There'd been several disputes over land and trading, and there'd been some horrible misunderstanding where the seelie leader died. If Lilani was the daughter of the current empress, that meant the leader who'd died was who? Her father? No, she'd been born long after he'd died. Her grandfather?

Vandra sighed, mourning for her. Such a long-lived race could have huge, unbroken chains of family members, generations able to share stories and memories. But Lilani hadn't known her own grandfather. When Vandra's grandparents died, they'd been great-grandparents, and she had fond memories of them.

Well, she couldn't get caught up in embarrassment for her own race again. Especially when it seemed like the current troubles were because of a group of seelie. Faelyn wasn't wasting time being embarrassed.

Pietyr squinted at the forest and put his hand to his sword. "Someone's coming." Before Vandra could even see who he was talking about, he said, "It's Fieta."

It still took Vandra a moment to spot the figure running through the shadowy forest. How could Pietyr know his sister from such a distance? Probably a twin thing. He didn't let go of his weapon, though, staring as if trying to deduce the cause of Fieta's speed.

Fieta didn't slow as she approached, her gaze swinging between all of them and the pylon. When she reached them, she skidded to a stop, leaned on her knees, and glared. "What…the fuck…was that?"

"Language!" Vandra said. "Our parents would be appalled."

Fieta's glare landed on Vandra. "I saw a flash of light. I thought you were in trouble, so I ran." She waved at the forest. "A *long* way. And I'd been shouting, so I was already tired, and when I get here, you're all just standing around!"

"You'd rather we were dead?" Pietyr asked dryly.

She picked up a blackened clump of peat and threw it at him. "What happened?"

"An experiment," Vandra said loudly. "One that only went half right." She put her hands on her hips and looked to the pylon. "I knew something made the pylons different from regular syndrium."

Fieta still glared, but Vandra waved her dark look away. If anger was how Fieta wanted to cover up her fear for her family, so be it.

Vandra had other things to worry about. "So, Lilani's cousin did something to this pylon, or did something with the humans who were building it. And she wasn't just standing here." She looked to Faelyn, who shrugged. Vandra hoped the humans hadn't sacrificed her. Even if it was for the good of the world, Vandra didn't think she could kill in the name of alchemy.

And Pietyr wouldn't let her, anyway.

"Did you speak with the seelie?" Faelyn asked.

Fieta shook her head. "But that doesn't mean they didn't hear *me*, right? And maybe they saw or heard your little explosion."

Vandra nodded. Maybe if enough seelie were gathered around, her formula would transform the pylon. But if that was true, how had Awith done it?

And could anything she was doing now help rescue Lilani?

The murmurs of the seelie echoed through the watchtower, putting Lilani in mind of a buzzing hive. Everyone had crowded onto the highest floor, jostling for a position at the window. The glow from outside had faded a bit. Maruk and a few others had demanded answers of Lilani, but she'd shrugged and kept an enigmatic smile on her face.

Now, as they argued with one another, she crept toward the staircase. Her heart thundered as she willed the tattered seelie to remain distracted a little longer.

Camilla barged out of her room. Lilani froze, but Camilla's gaze snapped to her. The metal tool up Lilani's sleeve seemed to weigh a hundred pounds, and if she thought any harder about it, she was certain it would glow through her sleeve.

Camilla scowled, and Lilani swallowed, her magic roaring within her, but if she shrouded, her escape plan would become horribly apparent. Camilla's loose, disheveled hair whipped around her head. She'd probably been asleep, something that would make her even angrier. Fabulous.

She tore her eyes off Lilani and waded into her people.

Lilani let out a breath, relieved beyond measure. When Camilla's voice rose above the others, demanding silence, Lilani nearly leapt down the staircase, going as fast as she dared before anyone noticed she was missing. She tried to keep track of the glow's direction, using the holes in the floor as a reference as she hurried past the bedrooms and kitchen. She and Lucian had to escape while everyone was distracted. This luck could never hold.

She made it to the bottom floor without meeting anyone. When she barged inside Lucian's cell, he sat up, his eyes wide. "They're all upstairs," she said. "We've got to go now." She handed over the metal tool.

His face fell as he took it. "Is this it?"

She looked from him to the tool and back, fear morphing to anger. "Were you hoping for a broadsword?"

"Maybe a key." While he prodded at the manacle, she opened the door a crack and peeked through. Nothing.

"What happened?" he asked.

"A light in the tattered lands, something to guide us. If we stay left of the tower, maybe we can get…" She didn't know what to say.

As if reading her mind, he asked, "How do you know it won't lead us deeper into the tattered lands?"

She shook her head. All the stress built on her headache, and she tried to keep her voice level. "Since the tattered seelie seemed surprised by it, it can't be a natural phenomenon." Silently, she thanked Faelyn for all his logic lessons.

He grunted in pain. "Help me."

Lilani shut the door and hurried over. He was holding the tool awkwardly, trying to fit it into the cuff.

"If you push right there…" He turned the tool in his hands.

Lilani took it and followed his instructions. When she heard a click, she couldn't help beaming. The manacle slipped free. They had a little luck left after all. But as they moved toward the door, Lilani froze. Dread washed over her, along with a wave of nausea that had nothing to do with her headache.

Their luck was gone.

Lucian gave her a gentle push. "Lilani?"

"Don't you feel it? Their dread?"

"This entire place—"

"No." She sighed, hope fleeing as she opened the door.

Camilla gave her an almost kindly smile. Her seelie stood behind her, silent, eyeing Lilani with cold disinterest.

"Clever Lilani," Camilla said. "Maruk would like to have a word about the recent disturbance. I will admit to some curiosity myself." She glanced at Lucian, an unneeded threat.

Camilla held out a hand. Lilani put the little tool in her palm and stepped out. She tried to shut Lucian inside, not ready to see his life thrown away.

He caught the door. Lilani flinched.

Camilla's smile widened. She lifted a hand.

"No!" Lilani cried, but the tattered seelie rushed around her. Camilla pulled her close in a grip of iron and carried her beyond the press.

Lucian cried out in pain. Lilani pushed against Camilla, kicking her feet uselessly in the air. "Stop!" Camilla's arms were too tight, their bodies crushed together, and Lilani's head flopped uselessly over Camilla's shoulder. "Please." She began to wheeze, her vision growing dark around the edges.

"That's enough," Camilla said, her voice as hazy as if she was yelling in a cave.

The horrid pressure around Lilani's chest loosened, and she gulped in air. She felt the floor under her boots, but her legs wouldn't support her. Camilla held her up and turned her. Lucian lay on the floor, unmoving, his face bloody, but what drew Lilani's eye was the way his right leg turned unnaturally at the knee.

"He won't be running anywhere now," Camilla said. "I warned you what would happen if you tried to escape."

Lilani fought the urge to sob. Lucian wouldn't want her to cry in front of these monsters. And his chest rose and fell. He lived. While he lived, she could save him. She forced her feelings down, deep into the cave Camilla's voice had come from. This was just another story, and what would the hero of the story be doing in this moment?

Taking stock. Waiting. Looking for her moment.

The tattered seelie had a few bloody noses between them. Lilani smiled with grim approval at two split lips and what would become a black eye. If Lucian had a weapon, he would have killed at least one. Of course, then he'd be dead, too. A good hero didn't rely on weapons. She used her wits.

Camilla led her upstairs to where Maruk was waiting.

"Sit," he said, pointing at a chair. He stalked up and down the room like a caged animal, anger radiating from him along with the feeling of dread.

Lilani obeyed, biding her time.

Camilla rewarded her with another smile. "Don't move until I come back."

Again, Lilani stayed. Some of the equipment had been turned over or broken. No doubt Lilani would get the blame. Maruk didn't ask any questions until Camilla reappeared, fully dressed and armed. Lilani wondered if that was for her benefit or if Camilla thought the fireball was a sign of impending attack.

Lilani's thoughts raced, trying to shatter her calm. She'd claimed the glow in the sky, but Camilla wasn't a fool. Even if he'd believed her earlier, Maruk would see through her lies when she had no information to offer.

"Maruk tells me you're responsible for that mysterious explosion." Camilla turned Lilani's chair so it faced the window. The glow had disappeared.

Lilani stayed silent, waiting for a question or something she could build on. Camilla only sat on one of the tables, swinging her legs and smiling.

"Well?" Maruk said.

"Well what?" Lilani asked.

He took a step, fists clenched as if to strike her. Camilla didn't move, and Lilani wondered how far her protection extended. Only one way to find out. Lilani took a deep breath and told herself that a few blows were worth seeing if she could drive them apart. She lifted an eyebrow and held her chin up.

Maruk bared his teeth. "What *was* that?" He nodded at the window.

"A glow in the sky."

He swung. She tried to block, but the back of his hand cracked against her cheek. She flew sideways, her ears ringing. Shockwaves rebounded through her skull, picking up her earlier headache and intensifying it. The dull pain of hitting the floor became buried under the rest, a hurt to be considered later.

The whip-crack of Camilla's voice cut through the waves rushing in Lilani's ears. That strong grip hauled her upright and put her in the chair again. Lilani tried to focus through the pain as a hero would.

Camilla's pale brows were drawn down in concern. "Can you hear me, Lilani?"

"A little." Lilani made her blinking slow, taking a cue from Lucian and playing more injured than she was.

Camilla stroked Lilani's face before turning a glare on Maruk. "Careless fool!"

"We do not have time to be delicate, Camilla. If she won't answer—"

Camilla stood so fast, Maruk staggered back. "There are ways to force the truth without risking her." She stepped closer, making him lean away. "Do you need a lesson?" She took his hand and ran her fingers over the spot where his thumb and palm joined.

Lilani shivered. She was not brave enough to face Camilla's darkest side. She shook her head as if to clear it.

Camilla was kneeling before her again in an instant. "Now, you were telling us about the fire in the sky, darling. Maruk wants to know if you caused it, or if, as I suspect, you were attempting to trick him."

Lilani said the first thing that popped into her mind. "It was a signal from Vandra, letting me know she's coming for me with an army of human alchemists and all the seelie loyal to my mother."

By the elders, she hoped that was true. Either way, she needed a confident expression. She pretended to be her mother again, pressing her back teeth together to make a firmer jawline and ignoring the ache from Maruk's backhand.

Camilla stared for a long while before her smile reappeared. "I very much doubt that, my dear." She stood and crossed to the window.

Lilani rubbed her cheek as Maruk followed Camilla. He whispered to her, gesturing. Lilani rolled her shoulder and flexed her elbow, easing the ache from hitting the floor. She'd never been struck in the face. Not an experience she would recommend.

"What if it's true?" Maruk asked in a loud whisper.

Lilani continued to survey her injuries, pretending she couldn't hear. Camilla's answer was too low, but Maruk leaned away. Lilani fought the urge to smile. He was nervous, scared, and maybe rethinking his alliance with Camilla. Maybe he'd run.

No such luck. He stalked back to Lilani, and she couldn't help flinching, but he merely stared, nearly quivering, his fists clenched.

Courage; it was only a story. "The army *is* coming, and all your careful plans will be undone." She sneered. "There's nothing *you* can do to stop it."

There came the teeth again. Lilani stiffened, ready.

"Maruk," Camilla said, a warning note.

He knelt in front of Lilani. She squeezed her hands into fists, ready to defend herself if he tried some torture technique. No hero could be expected to sit idly by and—

He smacked one fist against the floor as if venting his anger. "You're lying."

She leaned forward, keeping her face still, though her imagination shrieked about what Maruk and these seelie could do to her, to Lucian, to everyone. But the people she loved needed her. "And you're a piece of human garbage who is nothing without the seelie."

He rocketed forward, slamming into her and tipping the chair backward. Lilani cried out, her mind going blank with terror. She slammed into the floor, Maruk on top of her. The air rushed from her lungs, and her head bounced off the stones.

Her body acted on some instinct while pain blossomed again. She writhed, hitting, kicking, slapping, trying to escape the tangle of limbs and chair. Maruk was roaring, a wordless cry of rage. His hand pressed against Lilani's face as if trying to smother her. His palm slid over her nose, creating another arc of pain, but when his hand slipped lower, she sank her teeth into him.

He shrieked and wrenched away as Camilla pulled him to his feet. Lilani scrambled free from the chair and pushed to the wall. Camilla yelled at Maruk, but his eyes were still wild with rage. Lilani's magic roared within her, and she surrendered to it, shrouding. Enough pain. Enough terror. It was beyond time to hide.

Camilla shook Maruk as easily as she would a doll. "Calm down or I will kill you!"

He ceased struggling. She dropped him, and he sank to his knees, cradling his wounded hand.

Camilla's eyes went wide as she surveyed the room. "Now where has she gone?" She strode to the staircase and called down; someone answered that no one had passed that way. Camilla smiled again. "Lilani?" She raked the room with her gaze. "It's all right now. I won't let him hurt you again."

Lilani forced herself to breathe slowly. She didn't think she could drop her shroud if she tried. How far she'd come from when Faelyn first taught her. Weeks seemed like centuries. She wondered if all her life would feel like this from now on, if everything she'd gone through had taught her to count the moments as humans did.

"Come out, Lilani. It's all right. I promise." When Lilani didn't reappear, Camilla turned a glare on Maruk. "Go to your room."

He ground his teeth. "I'm not some sulky child!"

Her calm expression darkened as quickly as if she'd whipped off a mask. She strode toward him. He put his hands up, cowering, babbling. She grabbed his collar, dragged him to his room, and threw him through the doorway, shutting it behind him.

"There!" Camilla turned. "I've gotten rid of him, darling. You won't have to deal with his temper again, but if you stay shrouded, you *will* see mine, and Lucian will pay the price."

Lilani sighed. She couldn't stay hidden forever, anyway. And at least she'd upset Maruk. Maybe he'd rebel and get himself killed; one less enemy to worry about. She forced her magic to calm, letting her shroud drop. Camilla's smile came out like the sun.

"Wise Lilani," Camilla said. "I would truly regret having to kill you."

Vandra knew it had only been a few minutes, but she was tired of waiting for the seelie to arrive. She'd tried to fix the pylon. She'd failed. Again. She'd invented a world-changing formula and somehow still managed to fail.

That seemed an accomplishment in itself.

And she'd tried to do her duty. It was time to rescue Lilani. She thought of the tattered piece of metal, how it had carried some taint with it. And syndrium imbued with the magic of the seelie was enough to keep the tattered lands at bay. So, if Vandra could make enough seelie-infused syndrium to shelter them…

"Help me collect some stones."

"Why?" Fieta asked.

Pietyr bent to look. "Because she needs them, Fie! You know she won't explain until she's halfway through doing whatever it is she's doing."

Fieta sighed loudly, probably rolling her eyes, but Vandra was too busy to notice. Faelyn helped, too, and Vandra noted his curious, excited glances. He seemed to love knowledge for its own sake. As much as he wanted to help Lilani and his people, he was probably curious to see what Vandra did next. A teacher after her own heart.

Soon, they had a nice pile of rocks, and Vandra replicated her formula again. This would nearly deplete her resources, but if she couldn't get enough syndrium this time, she'd have to take more chunks off the pylon. It could afford to lose some, especially for Lilani's sake.

What a different opinion than the one she'd had scant hours ago, but once she'd set her mind to a new task, she found it hard to concentrate on anything else. After igniting these stones with Faelyn nearby, she was ready to go.

She distributed the stones among them, everyone staring at them curiously until Pietyr's eyes went wide. "Van, we can't!"

"Can't what?" Fieta said. "What is going on? So help me, Van, I'll start swearing again if you don't—"

"We're going in, aren't we?" Faelyn asked quietly. "We're going after Lilani."

She nodded, and the wind from the tattered lands gusted across them as if on cue, carrying the chill and the taint. Fieta and Pietyr began speaking at once, Fieta calling her crazy, Pietyr pleading with her to see sense.

Vandra kept her eyes on Faelyn, matching his little smile. "The stones will keep the taint away," she said.

"You hope!" Fieta yelled.

"Van, it's not safe," Pietyr said.

Vandra walked away, striding toward the tattered lands, stowing the rocks in her pockets. She heard the others scramble to keep up.

Fieta appeared at her side as if by magic. "Don't push me, Van. You know I can carry you out of here, and so can Pietyr. He's done it already!"

"I'm going."

"Van, think!" Pietyr said from her other side. "Even if we're safe, how will we find Lilani?"

"There might be tracks. We won't know until we look." She let them babble, knowing they wouldn't grab her unless they absolutely had to, as when Face-mouth had attacked. Her heart felt lighter than it had in a long time. She was doing something; she had a plan. It was a stupid plan, but it was hers, and she was doing it. Sick and tired of being told what she could and couldn't do, what was possible, she kept putting one foot in front of the other and letting the twins argue until she stopped, ready to prove her point.

They stopped too, continuing their diatribe until they seemed to notice where they were standing. No one had even noticed when they'd passed through the mist. Vandra smiled at her work in satisfaction.

The tattered mist formed a bubble around them, the roiling wall of despair surrounding but not touching them, repelled by the stones. Faelyn was as pale as when they'd first found him in the woods. He trembled and wiped his lips on his sleeve as if seeking to cleanse his mouth of the taint.

Vandra took his hand. In the past, Lilani had seemed much more affected by the tattered lands and the piece of metal than Vandra ever had. She didn't know if it hurt him or simply crushed his spirit, but she wanted him to know she appreciated his sacrifice.

As if shaken out of a stupor, Fieta held her spear ready, scanning the mist, and Pietyr drew his sword. Ever practical, he knelt to look for tracks. If they were in the tattered lands, they might as well find some clues.

"This ground is like sand," he said softly. "Except…mushier."

Vandra looked down, her own curiosity piqued. It seemed a little like sand and a bit like mud, though it didn't cling as she lifted her feet. It kept the impression of her boot and put her in mind of a sack full of mud or some other disgusting substance. A sack of blood?

She shook the thought away. "Any tracks?"

"A few." He frowned. "Some…very odd. But some could be seelie."

"Great." She gestured for him to lead on.

"No, we go back," Fieta said, her angry voice low, the words spoken between her teeth.

Vandra started to shiver. The cold from this place sank through her jacket, but the air was so heavy with moisture that a sheen of sweat coated her forehead and the back of her neck. Her skin crawled as if a thousand invisible stares drifted over her, and a litany of dreadful, self-defeating thoughts built at the back of her mind.

But none of that would stop her now. "Pietyr," Vandra said. "Please."

He swallowed and looked her in the eyes. "If I tried to go alone," he asked, "would you follow me?"

"Yes."

"Don't be stupid!" Fieta said.

"I'd follow as well," Faelyn added.

Pietyr sighed. "Fieta, go back and wait for the seelie."

"The gods can take that idea and cram it! Either we all go, or we don't go." She blinked as if hearing her own words and not believing them. "Shit."

Vandra smiled at her brother and sister, worried for them and proud of them at the same time. Keeping Faelyn's hand in hers, she started forward while Pietyr searched the ground, and Fieta watched for danger.

CHAPTER TWENTY-ONE

When the tattered seelie retired to their rooms, Lilani went to see Lucian again. They still hadn't bothered to lock his door. He lay right where they'd left him with his leg broken. Lilani took a few deep breaths, determined not to weep at the hopeless sight. He would want her to act, just like a protector in a story.

But it wasn't a stupid story! Anger mixed with the fear and despair lingering in every crevice of this place. She balled her hands into fists and resisted the urge to scream, not wanting to bring the tattered seelie down on her head. She was so sick of feeling tired, of being hurt, of feeling as if she had to run, run, run from one crisis to the next when all she wanted to do was find a quiet place where her friends and family were safe, and she could snuggle up with Vandra to sleep for the next year.

Thoughts of Vandra had her breathing deep again, her mind calming. She had no idea if the light in the distance had anything to do with Vandra, but ever since she'd first conceived of the idea, part of her had held on to it. Even if the light had nothing to do with Vandra, it could stand for hope. Vandra was out there somewhere, and she wouldn't be giving up.

Lilani muttered an apology before she turned Lucian over, grunting at his weight. He wound up half-on and half-off the pallet. Good enough, maybe, but she wanted him to be as comfortable as possible. She gritted her teeth, grabbed his uninjured leg, and pulled him fully onto the pallet. Her head and shoulder throbbed from the effort, and her cheek clenched at the pain. Lucian didn't stir. Breathing hard, Lilani regarded his leg. She had to believe they were going to come through this ordeal alive, so she had to plan for Lucian to be well in the future; if his leg began to heal crookedly, it might stay that way forever.

She thought through every book she'd read, but she'd never been attracted to medical texts or violent stories. She remembered when one of her friends had dislocated a shoulder; there'd been a sickening pop as Faelyn pulled it back into place. She recalled a few broken limbs among the seelie but hadn't been there when they'd been treated, only seeing the heavy swath of bandages later.

Well, nothing to do but to see what could be done. She felt along his healthy leg, trying to get an idea of how the knee aligned with the upper and lower leg. Maybe she should remove his trousers? No, she might not be able to get them over the injury. She'd have to do this blind. With shaky hands, she reached for his injured leg, her stomach roiling at the feel of the twisted joint. It seemed as if the kneecap tilted sideways, and she felt straining muscles and tendons while others felt unnaturally slack. Not broken then, only dislocated. At least that was something.

"Lucian," she whispered. "I'm so sorry. This is going to hurt so much. Please, stay asleep."

She sat between his legs and braced one foot against his thigh, lifting his injured leg onto her free leg. She put her back against the wall. Then, before she could think about it too hard, she yanked on the lower part of his leg while pushing away with her foot.

Nothing could have prepared for the gut-wrenching crunch and pop as the joint resisted before sliding back into place. She felt the tremor travel up his leg before his eyes flew open, and he sucked in a great gulp of air. She pounced, cupping both hands over his mouth and keeping his screams inside.

"I'm sorry, I'm sorry," she said in his ear. "You have to be quiet, or they'll come back and hurt you again!"

His eyes rolled wildly before they settled on hers. It took a few moments for his breathing to slow, then he nodded, and she took her hands away. He took a great, shuddering breath, his entire body trembling, and Lilani trembled with him. If they lived through this, they'd be as close as siblings, closer even. She'd discovered a part of the seelie she'd always been missing: the connection that came with tragedy. This was why her mother had been so angry when Lilani insisted on visiting the humans; this was why her mother insisted that Lilani was playing with forces she couldn't comprehend. It was something every other seelie knew: suffering.

Now Lilani was part of that, at least a little. She saw Lucian's face turn down in sorrow as if he realized the same thing. The last seelie child had finally grown up.

But they didn't have time for anger or grief or even pain. Lucian's face settled into its normal resiliency. "They're upstairs?"

"Resting, I think."

He sat up, pushing her gently away. "Then we escape."

Her horror only intensified. "No! You can't walk, and if they catch us—"

"That doesn't matter. I'll walk if you help me."

All she heard was that he was still willing to throw himself on the guards while she got away, and she couldn't have that. They couldn't keep trying the same plan and hoping for a different outcome. She stood. Lucian held out a hand, but she backed away, shaking her head.

"Lilani?" He shook his hand as if that would prompt her to take it. "Help me up, and—"

"No, no. Wait. The time will come." She felt behind her for the door, fumbling for the handle.

"Lilani—"

"No." If she was a grown-up, she couldn't rely solely on others to know what to do. "I'll come back." As he called her name again, she backed out the door and shut it behind her, leaning against it, listening to him swear on the other side.

Lilani sank down to the floor against the door, telling herself she was guarding Lucian, but there was simply nothing left in her to climb the stairs. Out of sight of everyone, she thought she might weep, but her chin slipped down to rest against her chest, and when she closed her eyes, sleep rolled over her as inexorably as the tide.

Vandra thought their march through the tattered lands was the slowest on record. They *crept* through the mist, the comforting bubble moving with them through a land of endless fog.

Pietyr's eyes were glued to the ground, and everyone else stayed close enough to touch, Fieta behind Vandra and Faelyn. Several times, Pietyr paused and swore, and Faelyn took the lead with him. He wasn't a tracker, he'd said, but he was more used to navigating the wilderness than either of the twins, both of whom would have been more comfortable seeking robbers along a dark street.

But who would be comfortable here? Vandra was tempted to grab Fieta's hand and hold on out of fear, but Fieta needed both hands to grasp her spear.

"Your knuckles are white," Vandra whispered. "If you hold on too tightly, your hands will go numb."

For once, Fieta didn't have a snide remark. She loosened her grip, nodding as if Vandra's advice wasn't just coming from the need to say something. Vandra rested her hand on Fieta's arm, taking comfort from the touch. Fieta didn't shake her off, another sign that she was as nervous as everyone else. They couldn't see beyond the gray. The sunlight barely penetrated the mist above them; Vandra didn't know what they were going to do when night fell. Any light would be like a beacon. They'd heard various hoots and calls from the mists: strange, unidentifiable animal noises. She wondered if Face-mouth was one of them, if it remembered their scent.

When a rumbling half-scream echoed behind them, they all froze.

"Pick up the pace," Fieta whispered.

Pietyr grumbled, but he and Faelyn peered at the ground again. They moved a little faster, but if they lost Lilani's trail, all the speed in the world wouldn't help them. Vandra tried to breathe slowly, forcing the air through her nose so she wouldn't hyperventilate. Something crashed off to the side. Vandra reached into her pocket and grasped one of the syndrium stones, hoping its presence would scare off any tattered creatures. Even incredibly large ones, by the sound of it. She kept her other hand on Fieta so she could move with them while staring into the mist, her spear ready.

Fieta kept muttering, "Faster," until Pietyr finally hissed at her to shut up.

Instead of her usual comeback, she said. "We either run, or we stand."

Vandra swallowed hard. So, it was as close as that? She supposed Fieta would know better than she did. Maybe she'd hunted a criminal in a fog-shrouded alley a time or two.

Pietyr drew his sword and stood with her as snuffling came from the mist, followed by a horrid grinding that could have been wood breaking or a pair of massive jaws working together.

Faelyn continued to search for tracks, and now Vandra kept a hand on each of her siblings, backing them up as she followed Faelyn, her head whipping back and forth to keep everyone in sight. As she looked back again, she saw a shadow moving through the mist, coming closer, a massive shape as tall as the grand doors of the university, twice her height, at least.

She reached back to give Faelyn a tug. "You should shroud."

"I'm not leaving you!" he said.

"If that thing attacks, find Lilani, then lead your people to her."

He seemed stricken, looking at all of them and watching the massive shape come closer. At last, he gave a quick nod and vanished. "I'll help if I can." Only a rush of air marked his passing as he moved around her.

Vandra set her pack on the ground. What did she have to fight with? Acid? If the bottle didn't shatter, it'd be just like throwing a rock. And she didn't dare fling it open. She couldn't predict where it would land or who it might splash along the way. She could light some peat on fire and throw that. It might make a nice missile, but if the fire went out, that would be like another rock again. Maybe she *should* throw rocks.

The fog had parted enough for a glimpse of a mottled gray hide. Vandra's thoughts were stuck on throwing rocks, but what good would that do? On the heels of that thought, her panic parted like the mist, and she realized what she'd been trying to tell herself. Idiot! She took out one of her syndrium rocks and hurled it at the approaching creature.

It shrieked, the sound echoing weirdly and making Vandra's ears ring. The mist swirled as the creature turned, and Vandra caught two tails thrashing through the air. Fieta pulled her down as the tails whipped over them, and Pietyr knelt, peering into the mist as the sound of running feet pounded away.

Silence reigned for a few moments until Pietyr turned a grin Vandra's way. "Good thinking, Van!"

Fieta huffed. "I'd rather have kicked its teeth in."

Vandra breathed a laugh. If nothing else, she'd given everyone some confidence back. She stared at where her stone had created a hole in the mist. She opened her mouth to say they should go get it, but the mist parted again, and their bubble slowly expanded. Faelyn blinked into view, holding the stone just before Vandra realized it was him. Fear really was a logic killer.

Faelyn and Pietyr went back to tracking, but everyone walked a little easier knowing they could at least scare the tattered creatures away. And maybe some had been drawn to the one creature's pain-filled cry and decided to follow it rather than focus on the strange aura that surrounded Vandra and her party. She supposed she should be grateful the creature hadn't come close enough to be repelled by their bubble. She'd hated to have to carry the image of it in her mind any more than she already did.

When Vandra saw another shadow rising above them, she readied a stone, but this one was much larger than the first; surely no amount of alchemy would chase it away. Still, she wasn't as frightened as before. As large as the shadow was, everything about it seemed unmoving, and she prompted the others forward. "It's either a hill or a building."

"The tracks go toward it," Pietyr said.

She nodded, and they walked more carefully. The shadow proved to be a twisted hill, an area of blasted rock with no signs of vegetation. The tracks became harder to follow as the spongy ground firmed, but after wandering through several craggy twists and turns, they reached a tower, a structure left over from before the tattered lands.

Hope bloomed in Vandra's heart. Lilani could be inside. Every part of her wanted to rush for the door, but she couldn't, not yet, not without knowing what waited for them. Her eyes drifted to the broken-down building beside the tower; the gaping windows looked out on the tattered lands like lidless eyes.

"What now?" Fieta asked. "We bust in?"

"No," Pietyr and Vandra said at the same time.

"The door is no doubt secured," Faelyn said. "But we can't wait out here forever."

Vandra nodded toward the large building. "It doesn't look like anyone's in there."

"I'll scout," Fieta said.

Faelyn tapped her arm. "Let me."

She seemed as if she might object before her brows lifted. "Invisible. Right." She gestured for him to continue.

"Wait." Pietyr tried to hand over his blade. "In case you get into trouble."

Faelyn chuckled. "Thank you, but I'd probably do myself an injury before I wounded anyone else. If I get into trouble, I'll be back here fast."

They smiled at each other, and Vandra hated to break up their moment, but...

"Don't forget about the stones," she said. "I don't know if they'll drive these seelie away, but it's worth a try."

"Right. Throw rocks, then run." He winked and vanished.

Vandra stared, trying to track Faelyn by the ripples he created in the mist.

"Come on, you two," Fieta said as she dragged them behind a jagged outcrop. "I'm going to have my hands full with Vandra not knowing what she's doing and Pietyr mooning around."

"I am not mooning!" Pietyr said.

"I think I'm doing quite well, thank you," Vandra said at the same time.

Fieta grinned crookedly. "We're all going to be moony corpses if we don't stay out of sight and *whisper*."

Pietyr muttered something about Faelyn not being able to find them. Fieta rolled her eyes and elbowed Vandra in the side. "Enough," Vandra said. "Watch the doors. Honestly!"

They settled into silence, and Vandra began to count the seconds, not knowing what would be worse, if those doors opened and let loose a flood of seelie armed against them, or if Faelyn never returned. She tried to shake the grim thought away and imagined him returning with Lilani in tow. The tight feeling in her chest lessened at the thought, and she held on to it as the only ray of hope in this wasteland.

A scratching sound startled Lilani from sleep, her unconscious mind ready for danger even if she couldn't remember where she was or what she was doing on the floor.

It came back in a flash. She and Lucian were trapped in a tower inside the tattered lands, and a group of tattered seelie had made her part of a plot to destroy the pylons and bring the tattered lands into the south, killing everyone who wouldn't go along with Camilla's plan, whatever that was.

She grimaced, wishing she hadn't been able to remember. When she heard the scratching sound again, she sat up straighter. That had woken her up. She looked toward the steps, at the door behind her, at the door to the outside, but it sounded as if it was coming from the barred door that led into the building next door.

She stood, staring, wondering what awful monster had gotten in there and now wanted in here. It had to be something truly awful to be able to resist the syndrium laced into the bricks of the tower. Maybe one of the tattered seelie had gotten lost in there and was seeking a way inside.

By scratching at the inner door instead of coming to the front? Maybe they were injured. She took a step toward the door before her rational mind overcame her need to help. If one of the tattered seelie was injured, she wanted them to stay that way. A dark thought, but one she had to force herself to honor.

And she didn't want anyone else coming to help, either. She headed up the stairs, wondering who else had heard the noise. Maybe she could stop them with idle conversation, find out if anyone was missing.

Several seelie sat around the tables in the kitchen. No one spoke to her, and those she passed near the bedrooms didn't even acknowledge her. She lingered on the stairs, watching where they went, but no one went to the ground floor.

She kept going up, beginning to think she hadn't heard an injured seelie but some other creature. As she reached the top floor and Camilla turned from the window, Lilani had another thought: maybe she'd been right all along, and Vandra had come. The idea froze her, and she barely heard Camilla's words of welcome. Had she just walked away from her chance to escape?

"Just in time," Camilla said. "Maruk has some experiments he's desperate to try."

Lilani took a step back, fighting the urge to run. Camilla would only follow her, stop her. Worse, if that was Vandra or some other rescuer behind that door, Camilla would kill them.

"Don't worry!" Camilla said, lifting her hands. "I'll be with you the entire time."

Lilani's mind raced as she tried to come up with some excuse—needing more time to recover from her earlier injuries, something—but Maruk walked into the room. He glared at Lilani, but he seemed to have lost the monstrous rage from before. Maybe since no rescue party had appeared, he'd calmed.

But the rescue party could be here after all. Lilani held on to that hope as Camilla guided her toward the table. She went with wooden steps. If it was a rescue, what was the plan? How could she help? And if it wasn't, if it was some tattered creature that could resist the syndrium in the watchtower, maybe she could let it in and escape in the chaos. There were no idle vermin in the tattered lands with nothing to do but scratch at the walls, unless some had bred inside these stones, the last cockroaches in the tattered lands. She was tempted to laugh. Her nerves were getting to her.

Maruk laid out several items on the table: a large iron box, several jars of powder. "Brace yourself."

Lilani tensed, but it was Camilla who nodded, and Maruk lifted the lid off the box. Camilla hissed; Lilani felt a peculiar hum along her skin. She leaned forward and saw the silvery-blue glow of syndrium filling the box. It had to be a piece of a pylon.

Maruk grimaced, drew on a thick pair of gloves, and lifted the syndrium free. Using a chisel, he sliced off a chunk before throwing the large piece back in the box and slamming the lid.

Camilla seemed to breathe easier, but she stared at the chunk of syndrium with distaste. Someone called from the stairs, and Camilla yelled, "It's fine. Stay there."

They hadn't locked the box. If Lilani could grab it…

"Put your hand here." Maruk indicated a spot on the table next to where the syndrium chunk rested in a crucible over a small flame. When she touched the table, he said, "No, on the plate."

A metal plate sat next to her hand, and a copper wire led from it to the crucible. She hesitated, fearing a shock or some other pain.

Maruk sighed loudly. "Camilla, please?"

Camilla took Lilani's hand in her iron grip. "Now, Lilani dear, do as Maruk says. We all want to get along, don't we?"

If Lilani didn't move, Camilla would only move her. She touched the plate. Camilla took her shoulders and stood behind her, holding her in place. She didn't have time to ask anything before Maruk began mixing powders and dumping them onto the hunk of syndrium. Sweat dripped down Lilani's brow. Nerves, maybe, but her palms started to itch, and the feeling radiated throughout her body. Her breath came in gasps.

Camilla's grip increased. Lilani put her free hand on the table to steady herself. She couldn't lift her other hand from the plate. Her hair whipped around her as her magic rose, but instead of covering her like a soft blanket, it rushed to her chest, pooling there before it crawled down her arm, rippling the cloth on her sleeve, and scattering crumbs of powder.

"It's working," Maruk said, triumph in his voice.

Lilani gasped for air. Her head spun. She tried to speak, but she could only groan, fighting for words. Spittle flecked her lips, and her eyes felt as if they were on fire. Her chest ached, and she knew her heart couldn't take it. Any moment it would burst. Vandra would break in here in a daring rescue and find her corpse.

"Oh, Van," she wanted to say. "I'm so sorry."

"Look, lovely Lilani," Camilla said in Lilani's ear. She turned Lilani's chin toward the chunk of syndrium. Lilani watched the magic in it die, the silver sheen and blue glow fading to the dull gray of ordinary rock.

So, that was how they'd drained the magic from the pylon. They'd used seelie magic to pull it out. She wanted to be happy that she finally had an answer or horrified at the implications, but she couldn't feel anything except misery.

The pounding in her chest stopped with a jolt. She had no feeling in her legs, and her face still burned; the sweat still dripped. She was powerless as Camilla lowered her to the floor and stepped past her to look over Maruk's shoulder.

"That went more quickly than the others," Maruk said. "And she's still alive! I don't think we even came close to killing her."

"I told you. It's the magic of Awith. We don't need blood when we have this much power."

CHAPTER TWENTY-TWO

Vandra felt a shock from her jacket pocket. She almost shot to her feet, thinking something had stung her, but Fieta clapped a hand on her shoulder, and Pietyr put a finger to his lips. Vandra reached in her pocket and took out one of the stones. It tingled under her touch, and the hair on her neck stood up.

"What in the gods' names?" She touched the other stones; they tingled, too, but the feeling was fading. "Did you feel that?"

Fieta frowned, but Pietyr nodded. "A shock?"

"I didn't feel anything," Fieta said.

"Maybe your skin's too thick," Pietyr said.

She frowned as if she might retort, then stopped as if she wasn't certain whether she'd been insulted or not. "What does it mean?"

Vandra shook her head. She wanted to think it was a good sign, but nothing that had happened recently led her to expect random good luck. She'd spotted the syndrium laced into the watchtower's stones, but it wasn't the same as the syndrium that made up the pylons. The blue glow wasn't strong enough. Maybe the proximity of so much syndrium had done something to her stones?

No, then they would've been reacting to it the entire time she'd been here. She looked up and down the tower, but the mist hid the very top floor. Maybe Faelyn had done something? She glanced at the doorway, then into the mist behind them. The creatures of the tattered lands stayed away from this place because of the syndrium, but it hadn't been enough to stop the taint from spreading around it. Now that she wasn't moving, Vandra felt the tattered lands sliding around their bubble, probing, trying to get in. The very air felt heavier, and it took effort not to let her thoughts turn to despair. Not even her curiosity could break through the miasma of sadness.

She put her stone away. She didn't have enough data to figure out what had happened anyway. "What's keeping Faelyn?"

"I can go look," Pietyr said.

"No," Fieta and Vandra said at the same time.

"If anyone is going, it's me," Fieta added as Vandra said, "If we go, we go together."

Pietyr rolled his eyes. "Which is it?"

"I'll go with going together," Fieta said. "I don't trust your moony love-eyes to watch for danger."

He glared at her. "I do not have—"

"Children," Vandra said, pitching her voice low. "Enough. The tattered lands are fraying your tempers. Fight it."

She didn't know if it was the tattered lands or nerves, but the idea shut them up. "We give Faelyn another five minutes, then we go in after him."

They nodded, and Vandra could almost feel the seconds tick by, thick as the fog around them. After she'd judged that enough time had passed, she nodded to the twins, and they crept out of their hiding spot.

"Slowly," Fieta said. "Until we clear the fog, then dash for the door."

Vandra nodded and moved as stealthily as she could until she reached the cleared space around the watchtower. Then it was time to run, hoping no one was looking.

Darkness reigned inside the abandoned building, and Vandra staggered to a stop, waiting for her eyes to adjust. Pietyr pulled her out of the doorway, and she breathed hard. What she'd thought were windows seemed irregular from this side, as if they were holes in the wall. The only true windows were too high to see out, but they provided soft light, enough to see piles of splintered wood heaped over the floor. There might have been a second or third story at one time, but the flooring had collapsed, leaving the ground a sea of jagged planks and splinters. Inside, the entire structure creaked and moaned as the mist drifted through the many holes like scudding clouds.

Fieta took a step forward, beckoning. Vandra followed her, stepping lightly as Fieta picked her way through the tortured wood.

As they passed through a beam of meager light, Vandra noticed that the wood seemed spongy, rather like the ground outside, and some patches had turned green. Vandra leaned close to one patch, intrigued by the idea that moss could flourish in such a place, but the green mess wriggled, and she nearly leaped away. She hoped anything larger would be kept away by the stones in their pockets.

She glanced around at the dim space, comparing it to the footprint of the building from outside. It was huge. They didn't have time to search every nook, and they wouldn't be able to see Faelyn anyway, though he should be able to see them. Unless he was hurt. Or dead.

Vandra curled her hands into fists. That was the tattered lands talking. Maybe they should light a lantern? It probably didn't matter. If any of the enemy seelie were hiding in here, they were going to spot a group of humans sooner or later.

Pietyr leaned past Vandra and tugged on Fieta's jacket. When she turned, he held up an unlit lantern. So, he'd had the same idea. Vandra imagined her sister frowning as she weighed the pros and cons of a light, but she must have not had any better ideas. She pulled a box of matches and lit the lantern before giving it to Vandra.

There wasn't much room to move in the tangle of wood and brick. The light shone off several things that seemed slimy or shiny, and tiny patches of movement caught Vandra's eye, though they seemed to be moving away from the light, a good sign.

Several cleared paths led in different directions; someone besides Faelyn had been in here since the collapse. One path led to a door that connected to the watchtower. The seelie no doubt knew about it, but Vandra pointed that way. They approached the door warily, and Fieta gave it a gentle push. It held fast, locked or barred.

"Look." Pietyr pointed to a jumble of wood beside the door.

Vandra held the light closer and saw another gleam of wetness, red this time. Blood. Fresh blood.

She exchanged a glance with Pietyr, not bothering to reassure him that it might not be Faelyn's. She'd already come to the conclusion that any luck they found in this place was bound to be bad.

Vandra ran a hand through her hair. Whether the blood was Faelyn's or not, something had happened here recently. Maybe Faelyn had gotten into a scuffle. Maybe he'd been captured. Maybe he'd managed to wound his opponent. Or kill them? No, she would have seen a body. Maybe Faelyn had been wounded and was now somewhere in this building, waiting for help.

Then why not come out? If he'd been captured, the seelie in the watchtower now knew someone had come looking for Lilani. Faelyn wouldn't talk willingly, but anyone smart enough to survive in the tattered lands wouldn't believe he'd come alone.

"Can you break open the door?" Vandra whispered.

"It'd be noisy," Fieta said. "And even with the element of surprise, we three can't take on a tower full of armed seelie."

"Who have hostages," Pietyr said.

Vandra smiled. If the seelie left the tower, the hostages could easily be rescued. "Let's go outside and gather some peat," she said. "It's time we made someone come to us."

Lilani struggled to move. Camilla and Maruk had said they'd used seelie blood as part of some alchemical process to warp the first pylon, and she bet they hadn't used their own. Then whose? The Court would have noticed if hordes of seelie had gone missing.

Unless it hadn't taken hordes but only a few, those whose disappearances could be covered up by traitors like Burani. An overdue scout, someone who preferred camping alone on the Highpeak, an older seelie who liked to visit the elders: any absences like that could be easy to explain away. She had to stop it, but her body wouldn't move.

Camilla and Maruk stepped over her as they tinkered with the equipment. She caught snippets of conversation in between trying to get her limbs to move.

"Can you use this formula to produce a cascade effect on the other pylons?" Camilla asked.

He muttered something, and Lilani heard the clink of glass. "Now I know why all our previous attempts failed. I thought that disabling the pylon that Awith imbued with her life would cause the rest of the pylons to fail, just as absorbing her life had caused the rest of them to activate, but now that I know we need the magic of Awith's line instead of the actual blood…"

"Is that a yes or a no?"

"Yes! I think it will work. If we suck the magic out of one of the pylons using someone with Awith's magic, that should dim all the pylons because they are connected, and Lilani has a powerful magical field."

Cold spread through Lilani's body. They were planning to take all her magic, which would probably kill her. Constructing the pylons had taken Awith's life, but she'd given it freely to save those she loved. Now these seelie were going to use her to destroy her cousin's legacy.

"So, do you *think* it will work, or do you *know*?" Camilla asked.

Lilani heard the threat in those words, but there was something else, too, a cruel bit of thoughtfulness, the same Camilla had used with Burani before she'd had him killed. If Maruk *knew* his device would work, Camilla might not need him anymore, but if there was a chance it might fail…

Maruk shifted toward the stairs as if thinking of running. Lilani hoped with every heartbeat that he would. Then Camilla would kill him. Whether his formula worked or not, that'd be one less person to get away from.

Maruk cleared his throat. "I…*think* it will work. When we get to the pylon, it might need some tinkering."

"Ah." Camilla's voice went back to normal. "Hear that, lovely Lilani? You're going home!" She winked. "For a little while, at least, long enough to see the pylons fail." She bent over, tweaked Lilani's nose, and laughed. "Let me know when you're ready to go, Maruk." She walked away, whistling.

Were they going to leave her on the floor? Maruk didn't seem to be paying her any attention. She willed her limbs to move again and nearly wept with joy when her hands twitched. Now for her feet…

The seconds seemed to crawl by before she could get every part of her body to obey. She could still feel her magic, but it flowed as sluggishly as when she'd been exhausted. If destroying the pylons took all her magic, could she live without it, dead to the feeling of the world around her? Would she want to? She knew what Faelyn would say: anything was survivable except death.

And to survive any of it, she had to get up off the elders-cursed floor!

Lilani strained and propped herself up on her elbows. Her muscles ached as if she'd run for miles. She pushed, trying not to groan, not wanting to attract Maruk's attention. Voices came from the stairs, Camilla calling for the seelie to be ready to march soon. Lilani forced herself to sit up, then rolled onto her knees.

Maruk faced away from her, digging through a large chest. The iron box containing the pylon piece rested where it had been, shut but not locked. Lilani put a hand on the table and pulled to her feet. She was shaky, swaying, but she knew what she had to do. She took one step, then another, keeping hold of the table.

Maruk turned. His eyes widened. "Oh, you're up. That was a lot faster—"

Lilani lunged for the box. He reached for her, but she flung the lid open, and he shied away from the glow, his hands rising to protect his face.

Lilani grasped the pylon piece and pulled it free. Nearly as long and slightly thicker than her forearm, it was heavy, but not as much as she expected. She hugged it to her chest, still holding herself up on the table.

"Put that away!" Maruk yelled.

Lilani backed away. Her steps grew lighter as if the pylon piece helped repair her magical field. She hurried for the staircase as Maruk followed, bellowing for help. A seelie poked his head up, then hissed as if Lilani was carrying a burning brand. She followed, the pylon piece humming against her skin, fortifying her courage. Other seelie stepped from their rooms, asking questions, but as she advanced, they darted out of her way. Still, she felt them gathering around her, saw the weapons in their hands, but they didn't attack, not while they needed her. She hurried on, desperate to get to Lucian before they could use him against her.

On the second floor, Camilla barred the way. She had her hands on her hips, but she didn't seem angry. If anything, she looked radiantly happy, a wide smile on her bright lips.

"Clever Lilani. I won't ever let it be said that you lacked intelligence."

Lilani took a few steps closer. Maybe if she swung the pylon piece like a club, she could drive Camilla into the kitchen. She couldn't shroud; she wanted Camilla to see the threat. Besides, they'd be able to tell where she was while she held the piece, just as their taint gave them away.

Lilani's heart pounded as she went through her options. She clung to the wall, trying to come at Camilla from the side and doing her best to ignore the others. There was no way this was going to work.

Camilla hadn't lost her smile, though her wince increased the closer Lilani came. Her eyes were almost slits, turning her smile into a grimace, as if the top and bottom halves of her face weren't communicating anymore.

"Turn around, and put that rock back where you found it," Camilla said.

Lilani didn't bother to reply. Could Camilla stand the pain long enough to knock the piece out of Lilani's hands? No, she would have done it by now. Lilani's gaze flicked past Camilla to the stairs, to freedom. Her breath came faster, and she could feel the dread surrounding the tattered seelie creeping in on her, smothering her. Soon, they would leap, or Camilla would rush her.

Behind Camilla, Lilani saw a slight waver in the darkened stairway, a hint of fractured light. It could have been a shimmer of heat from the torches, but what if it wasn't? Lucian shrouded so well, she normally couldn't see him, so who...

Camilla shrieked and lurched sideways, her hands flying to a wound that bloomed in her side. She clasped pale hands over the flow of blood, and as she tottered out of the way, Lilani leapt past, following the shimmer down the stairs. She heard steps behind her and spun, swinging the pylon piece. A host of seelie fell back, one flickering into view after he'd shrouded.

Someone pulled Lilani backward, and she let an invisible hand guide her down the steps. Her own magic rose over her, summoned by fear, shrouding her. The door to the outside stood open. Lucian leaned against the doorjamb. As they locked gazes, he stepped outside, and the shimmer ran past him. After Lilani followed, Lucian slammed the door shut, and Faelyn blinked into view. He slipped his knife through the door handle, the blade catching against the bricks, barring it from this side. It wouldn't hold for long, but Lilani nearly wept with joy.

There wasn't time to throw her arms around Faelyn. She ducked under Lucian's arm to help him walk, still holding the pylon piece. When Faelyn took Lucian's other arm, they all shrouded together.

"This way!" Faelyn said. "Down the path."

Lilani braced herself and smiled. The tattered seelie would be through the door in moments, and they had so much dangerous territory to hike through, but they were together. They could keep one another safe. She hadn't given in to despair before; she was not going to start now when escape was so close.

"By the elders!" Faelyn said, anger roughening his voice. "Where did those fool humans go?"

"Humans?" Lilani's hopes soared further. "Vandra?"

Light exploded from their right, toward the bottom of the craggy hill. A fireball raced through the mist, blowing it away like cobwebs. Hot air rushed over Lilani, making her stagger.

"Come on." Faelyn tugged them down the path as if he knew that any explosion must be a good sign.

Lilani grinned. If the explosion was because of Vandra, then the light from before *had* been Vandra's doing also. Lilani had been right. Vandra and Faelyn weren't an army, but the fact that they'd come for her meant everything in the world.

CHAPTER TWENTY-THREE

Vandra shielded her eyes from the flames. As with the pylon, the peat had flared quickly, reflecting off the fog of the tattered lands and suffusing the area with much-needed light. Crashing and shrieking echoed around them as tattered creatures fled, and even the fog seemed to pull away. Vandra grinned, happy to do some damage to this horrible place. With the right alchemical combinations and a controlled burn, could they actually drive the tattered lands back?

A thought to put away for later.

Vandra and the twins crouched behind one of the jagged rocks that shielded the watchtower. The bubble that their magical stones created in the mist no doubt gave away their position, but who would be looking at them while the ground was on fire?

"When they come out, we grab Lilani and run," Fieta said.

"Not without Faelyn," Pietyr added.

Fieta tightened her grip on her spear. "We can come back for him!"

Vandra poked them both. "If the seelie don't bring out their hostages, we'll sneak into the watchtower and grab them in the confusion."

That shut them both up, though it also made their task ten times more difficult.

Frowning, Fieta nodded. "Okay, we'll go in the front door, grab them, then run out the door into the ruin."

"Right," Pietyr said. "Their invisibility won't help them as much in that jumble."

Vandra was glad they were thinking strategically. As soon as she'd said Lilani's name, all Vandra could think about was having her safe again.

"Look!" Fieta whispered.

On the path from the watchtower, the mist whirled, just what they'd been waiting for: the sign of someone moving while invisible. Vandra tensed, but the disturbance didn't seem large enough to contain a cadre of enemies. Vandra fought the urge to swear. If the enemy seelie had sent scouts while the rest of them remained in the watchtower, this plan was over before it had begun.

"Wait," Pietyr tugged on Fieta's shoulder. "There's a bubble."

Vandra squinted. More than eddies, this invisible group seemed to have a small void around it, just like Vandra and the twins. And since the enemy seelie would no doubt be uncomfortable in the presence of the stones she'd made…

She stood. "Faelyn!"

Fieta and Pietyr reached for her at the same time, shushing her, then they stood, too, as Faelyn appeared, holding up Lucian, and on Lucian's other arm…

"Lilani!" Every smidge of awkwardness or embarrassment Vandra had ever felt vanished. All she could think of was the wasted time between when they'd last seen each other and now. Worry and fear and hope and relief mixed up within her, and she couldn't have stopped her feet if she'd tried.

Lilani smiled even as her eyes filled with tears. She ducked out from under Lucian, gave him a large stone she'd been carrying, then opened her arms. Vandra rushed into her embrace and reached up, tilting her head down so their lips could meet in a kiss that pushed the tattered lands back further.

Lilani's magical field covered Vandra in a thousand tiny caresses. She slid her hands into Lilani's hair as their kiss deepened. Vandra leaned in to the silly, sentimental, wonderful thought that this was everything she'd ever been missing. Lilani's grip tightened, revealing her own need.

Faelyn pulled them apart. "Time to run, young lovers. They *are* right behind us."

"Ri…right." Vandra nodded and beat her thoughts back into order. Without Lilani wrapped around her, some embarrassment and fear trickled back in, and she didn't dare look at the faces around her, not wanting to see grins. "Running, not kissing."

Lucian seemed incapable of walking on his own, Faelyn had a wound in his side, and when Vandra made herself look somewhere besides Lilani's beautiful eyes, she noted the bruises and dried blood flecking Lilani's ears and neck. They were all hurt, the enemy was probably steps away, and the fire was fading.

But by the gods, she wanted another kiss.

Fieta turned her around, muttering about lovesick morons. "Let's move!"

Pietyr took the lead, following their own tracks back toward the pylons. Fieta walked behind them, guarding the way. Vandra ducked under Lucian's arm with Faelyn since Faelyn was wounded, and she didn't trust herself next to Lilani.

"What happened to you?" Vandra asked softly. "We saw the blood near the door."

"A trap," Faelyn said. "I was trying to get someone inside to open the door, thinking that if I could lure an enemy out, I could sneak in." He grimaced. "I stood well back, but a tiny blade shot from the door and gouged me in the side. If I was any closer, it would have impaled me. I was so surprised I dropped my shroud, but luckily, Lucian opened the door."

Lilani gasped from Lucian's other side. "Wait, was that you scratching?"

"I was trying to sound suspicious enough to be investigated but not threatening enough to bring reinforcements."

Lilani grumbled in seelie before she said, "I heard you, but I thought it was some tattered creature. If I'd let you in then, we could have escaped nearly unnoticed!"

He barked a laugh. "No matter."

"Still—" Lilani started.

"It's all right," Vandra said, wanting to hug her. "You did well, Lilani. We're free."

Across Lucian's body, Lilani gave her a glorious smile.

Lucian said something in seelie, and Faelyn chuckled. "He says we should save our breath." He shifted, and Vandra helped him adjust Lucian's weight across both their shoulders.

They moved well at the moment, but that couldn't last. The border was too far away, the enemy seelie too close. They couldn't possibly make it. As the mounting dread made her stumble, Vandra's suspicions rose. She'd felt this abnormal fear before, at the monarchs' ball.

Were the enemy seelie closing, or had they already surrounded Vandra's party, waiting for the chance to strike? Vandra glanced to the side, trying to spot telltale eddies in the mist, but her own hurried progress made too much of a disturbance.

"They're here," Lilani said, the words almost a whisper.

Vandra felt a rush of air, then something heavy slammed against her shoulders. She stumbled along with Faelyn. Lucian toppled forward, and the weight was enough to drag Vandra and Faelyn to the ground. Vandra struggled upward in time to see Lilani swinging the glowing piece of syndrium.

Fieta was on one knee, twirling her spear in a wide arc. "Go, Van!"

"Where? The worst thing we can do is split up!"

"I felt someone move," Pietyr said as he pulled in tighter to the rest of them, his weapon moving in a defensive arc like Fieta's.

They couldn't stand there waiting for invisible opponents to find a way through their defenses. Faelyn pulled out one of his stones. He caught Vandra's eye, then vanished.

She gasped. Was he taking the fight to the enemy? Going for help?

Pietyr, Fieta, and Lilani formed a defensive triangle around Vandra and Lucian, though Lucian looked ready to wring someone's neck if they got within range. On the edge of their bubble, something whistled through the air, parting the mist before smacking against an invisible foe. An enemy seelie blinked into view, crying out in pain as one of the magical stones dropped at their feet. Fieta grunted and threw her spear, sticking the enemy seelie in the chest. He sank to the ground, hands wrapped around the shaft.

"Your weapon, idiot!" Pietyr yelled.

"At least I killed one." She drew a knife from her belt.

So, Faelyn was aiming for the enemy. And now their bubble was a little wider. The enemy seelie didn't seem to want to stay within its protection. Otherwise, they could have overwhelmed Vandra and the rest within seconds.

Unless the enemy was simply toying with her. She gritted her teeth. She needed time, needed to keep the enemy seelie at bay, or needed to create some room. Faelyn couldn't keep throwing stones. He'd run out; she'd have to give him more, then they'd have to worry about the enemy seelie *and* the tattered lands itself. But what else repelled the tattered lands and everything in it?

Fire.

Vandra swung her pack around and pulled out several pouches, a bottle of oil, and some matches. She emptied the pouches, scattering herbs to the wind, and stuffed two pouches into one before dribbling oil inside. She tied it loosely, lit a match, and dropped that inside, too. It flared to life, but before the fire could penetrate the outer pouch and burn her, she flung it into the mist, hoping Faelyn wasn't in its path.

She rubbed her hand. Even with the thick leather, she'd still held fire in her palm, and she felt the tingle of a mild burn, but the pain disappeared as fire bloomed in the peaty ground of the tattered lands. This time, several enemy seelie cried out at once. The mist billowed away from the flames, and another enemy appeared. It was a shame Fieta no longer had her spear.

Faelyn appeared next to them, Fieta's spear in hand. Pietyr waved him into their circle, but he shook his head. "Now, while they're distracted, run!"

They ran together, Pietyr keeping them on track. Vandra lit another fire pouch and threw it in their wake, but she only had materials for one more. As soon as the enemy seelie went around the fire, Vandra and her friends would be in the same situation as before.

Lilani shoved the glowing syndrium piece into Vandra's arms so she could better help Lucian. Vandra tucked the piece under her arm and fumbled through prepping her last fire pouch. When should she use it? How far were they from the border? Terror kept trying to beat past her reason, and soon it would win.

In the lead, Pietyr fell. Vandra stuffed the unlit fire pouch in her pocket and raced around Lucian, reaching for Pietyr, Fieta beside her. He rolled on the ground, clutching his leg with his free hand while still trying to swing his blade at an invisible foe. Fieta leapt in front of him while Vandra dropped the syndrium piece and fell to her knees at his side.

"Let me look, let me look," she said, trying to still him so she could see past the blood and the mist and the fear. Oh gods, there were arteries in the leg, tendons that if destroyed meant the leg was now useless, but he wouldn't be still, and she couldn't see, and dread was choking her until she could barely breathe.

Fieta pitched forward, grunting as someone struck her. Her feet tipped up, and she landed on her shoulders. Vandra tried to stand up and pull Pietyr with her. If she could get the twins together, she could fix them both at the same time.

Rough hands grabbed her, spinning her around. Her jacket pulled around her tightly, balled in an invisible grip. She fumbled for her pocket and drew a magic stone. The grip released her, and a pale seelie appeared, hands raised to shield their face as they stumbled away.

"Draw your stones!" Vandra shouted. "Get—"

"Vandra!"

Vandra spun. Lilani reached for her. She had no stones, needed Vandra to protect her. Everyone needed her. Another enemy seelie appeared in front of Vandra and staggered back from the glow of her stone. She could make a space that—

A long blade flicked past her shoulder and sliced the back of her hand. Her fingers clenched as she cried out, and the stone dropped to the ground. She flew backward, yanked with such force that the pain of her hand faded as she slammed into the ground. The air rushed from her lungs, and she struggled to breathe, to see past the spots dancing in her vision.

A seelie pale as death smiled down at her.

Lilani darted for Vandra, shrouding as she went. She hit the tattered seelie who stood over Vandra and knocked him off balance. Faelyn knelt between the twins, but he could do little more than cradle them. On the ground, Lucian grabbed two of Vandra's stones and was holding them as if to bash in the skulls of anyone who reached for him.

But no one did. They were going to be captured, not killed, so Camilla could use them against Lilani.

"No!" Lilani reached for Vandra, but Vandra flailed in her grasp, unable to tell one invisible opponent from another. "It's me! Where is the pylon piece?"

"Lilani? I dropped it."

Lilani spotted its glow at Pietyr's side. She darted for it, keeping hold of Vandra, not willing to let her go again. When Vandra wrenched back, Lilani's hand slipped free as Vandra lifted clear from the ground.

"Let's see you, lovely Lilani," Camilla's voice said.

Vandra reached into one pocket with a bleeding hand, but as she drew a stone free, her wrist twisted to the side, finger-sized dimples appearing in her flesh. She cried out in agony, and the stone fell from her grasp.

"Let her go, Camilla," Lilani said as her shroud dropped, though her magic still roared around her.

Camilla appeared, one hand holding Vandra aloft by the back of her neck, and the other grasping her wrist. Camilla breathed hard, and she seemed even paler, if that was possible. Blood soaked through a hasty looking bandage wound around her. Yet her smile hadn't faded. Her gaze flicked past Lilani's shoulder, and her fingers tightened around Vandra's neck, making Vandra wheeze and scratch at Camilla's hand.

"Faelyn, Lucian, please, stay still." Lilani could barely breathe; she wanted Vandra's pain to stop. They could surrender now and live. They'd escaped once. They could do it again.

Camilla's laughter sounded as pure as ever, even in this blasted place, even with all the blood and horror, yet Lilani wondered if there was anything inside her that could be saved. She set Vandra down and snaked an arm around her. "Back up," Camilla said.

Lilani stepped back to stand even with Faelyn. He'd managed to drag the twins together. Pietyr was still awake, hands curled around his bloody leg, but Fieta's eyes were closed, and a line of blood flowed out of her hair and down her temple. Two more seelie appeared on either side of Lucian but kept out of reach. He'd managed to stand and still held his stones. Camilla would have a hard time convincing him to put them down.

The pylon piece lay beside Pietyr, but Camilla could snap Vandra's neck before Lilani could grab it, before Faelyn or Pietyr could throw it, before anything. Lilani fought the urge to sob, to roar, to fling herself at Camilla and make this all end.

"Now," Camilla said. "Lilani, you and I, and this one"—she shook Vandra—"are going to the pylons. Anyone else who can walk is welcome to come along."

"What is she saying?" Vandra asked, her voice rough.

"What about the injured?" Lilani asked.

Camilla shrugged. "They'll stay here."

"She's going to leave everyone else and take us to the pylons," Lilani said in the human tongue.

Vandra snarled and twisted. "No, Fieta! Pietyr! They'll die!"

Lilani barely detected a flex in Camilla's arm before Vandra's voice cut off. She gaped, mouth and eyes wide.

"Stop it!" Lilani shouted. Vandra's face began to redden. "She can't breathe!"

"If she wants to breathe," Camilla said sweetly. "She'll obey."

"Vandra, please," Lilani said. "Faelyn and Lucian will stay with your siblings. Camilla won't hesitate to kill them to get what she wants."

Vandra managed a nod. She sucked in a gulp of air as Camilla let her breathe again.

"As long as you both comply, I'll give the rest of you a chance," Camilla said. "Otherwise, I'll send someone back to kill them quickly." She tilted her head. "Compared to the death they'll find out here, that seems more of a mercy. Shall I do it?" She glanced between Vandra and Lilani. "No? Suit yourself." She nodded ahead of them. "March."

Faelyn and the others had Vandra's stones; they had the pylon piece. They'd be all right. Lilani wished she could say so, but she didn't want to give Camilla any ideas about taking the stones or the piece away. It seemed the sort of game Camilla would like.

In fact, why would Camilla leave enemies alive at her back? As if she'd seen it written, Lilani knew Faelyn and the others would be murdered as soon as she and Vandra were out of sight. Camilla would use the idea of them to keep Lilani and Vandra in line, but they'd be long dead. They were all dead; they just hadn't realized it yet.

Lilani planted her feet. Better to die here together, fighting. As much as the idea hurt her, it made so much sense. She had to make Camilla kill her, too, so she could go with them into whatever waited after death. She didn't want to live with the sight of their lifeless corpses.

"Move," Camilla said.

"No." Lilani faced the mist. She couldn't watch Vandra die and see a world of possibilities end forever. Would that have shamed a hero in a storybook? Did she care anymore?

Camilla pulled Vandra to Lilani's side. She frowned and seemed genuinely confused as she shook Vandra so hard, Lilani heard the rattle of teeth. "What are you waiting for?"

Vandra gasped as she stilled, and her eyes met Lilani's. Lilani smiled softly, trying to put everything she felt into that one look. Ignoring Camilla, Lilani said, "Somewhere along the way, I fell in love with you."

Vandra smiled back. "Probably a hormonal and psychological reaction to everything we've been through together." She blushed. "But that doesn't change the fact that I love you, too."

Lilani chuckled and felt the tears start. They barely knew each other, and now they'd never get to find out all the little things that meant love could be real and not a passing passion.

Camilla was still frowning. "Last chance, Lilani. Move!"

One of the other seelie grabbed Lilani's arm. She kicked him, and though it felt as if she'd struck a fence post, she kicked again, hitting and slapping. Something primitive rose up in her; if she was going to die, she would do all the damage she could before that final breath.

When her captor cried out, she thought she'd scored a hit. She redoubled her efforts, and he tottered to the side. It was only then that she spotted the arrow in his back. Purple fletching: the color of royalty. Her mother had come.

Vandra twisted in Camilla's grip, but she stood there staring at Lilani as if she couldn't believe anyone would defy her.

Vandra tried to move her left hand, but it flared with fiery pain at every twitch, probably broken. She jammed her right hand in her pocket and felt around for her fourth and last stone. Before Camilla could regain her senses. Vandra smashed the stone over her left shoulder, hitting Camilla in the face.

With a cry, Camilla released her and staggered away. Blood poured from her nose, and the rest of her face gleamed red as if the stone had burned her. She snarled like a mad dog and drew a thin, cruel looking knife from her belt, something that might be used to strip away delicate flesh.

Before she could advance, another stone struck her hard in the chest. Her cry sounded more like a roar as she backed away. Lucian staggered closer, another stone at the ready. Vandra risked a look around. Faelyn held the pylon piece, shielding the twins. Lilani had bested her attacker and turned, her eyes meeting Vandra's in joyous relief. They could do this; they could win. She didn't know how, but—

Camilla disappeared. Vandra swore. There had to be a way to prevent them from doing that! Cries sounded around them, and Vandra heard the clash of weapons coming from the fog.

Lilani hurried over, clasping one arm around Vandra's shoulders. "My mother is here. Stay close."

Vandra let out a sob of relief and let herself lean into Lilani, even with the muck and the blood spattered over them both. They loved each other, and if they could all stand together, they might live through this.

Lucian fell to the side as if pushed. Vandra reached for him, but her ribs howled in pain as something smashed into her. She fell onto Lucian, catching her damaged wrist and making her scream as the two points of pain met somewhere in her middle and compounded each other. Someone called her name, and she tried to roll, to see. Lilani was reaching out, fading by degrees as if shrouded by someone else.

Camilla. Vandra felt the dread, smelled that same perfume. Lilani's cry cut off as she vanished, and Vandra felt a rush of wind as Camilla carried her away.

CHAPTER TWENTY-FOUR

Vandra struggled to her feet, searching for footprints on the spongy ground, for eddies in the mist, anything that might tell her where Lilani had gone. Before she could take more than a few steps, a seelie appeared before her. Vandra stumbled back, the stone she'd used to get free from Camilla in her grasp. She held it up, but this seelie didn't shrink, her glare turning slightly confused as she barred Vandra's path.

She had dark hair, and her skin was nearly the same dark brown as Vandra's instead of the corpse pallor of the enemy seelie. What was it Lilani had said? Her mother had come.

Vandra pointed away. "We have to follow Lilani! They have her; do you understand?"

This seelie only frowned harder. Vandra turned, looking for Faelyn. "Tell them we have to—"

Seelie appeared everywhere, surrounding Vandra and her friends along with a few dead, pale seelie. Several newcomers helped Lucian stand, and more knelt beside Faelyn. He was gesturing to the twins and talking rapidly with a woman who had blue hair.

Like Lilani.

Vandra hurried over. "Faelyn, they took Lilani. We have to go after them."

"They're being pursued as we speak," Faelyn said. He took Vandra's hand. "Dyrana, Empress of the Seelie Court, may I present Professor Vandra Singh of Citran."

Vandra wanted to gawk and bow and stammer about how it was nice but also very awkward to meet the mother of the woman she loved, but none of that mattered at the moment. "Empress, please, I want to follow your daughter, to save her."

The empress tilted her head. She wore intricate leather armor and held a sword that seemed like a long needle. Her hair was pinned up behind her head, but the ends twitched as if it was desperate to be free. She stared at Vandra with eyes as hard as amethysts, and there was something immeasurable in her gaze, as if she had a well of time behind her eyes.

Vandra fought the urge to look away, to be made smaller by that stare. She'd come this far. She'd face whatever stood between her and Lilani, even the accusation in the eyes of someone who seemed more goddess than woman.

The empress's look softened as if she saw something in Vandra she liked. Vandra didn't know if it signaled acquiescence or not, but she'd take whatever she could get. She looked to her siblings again. She hated to leave them, but…

"I'll look after them," Faelyn said. "Go, bring her back."

She squeezed his hand again, wishing she could take Fieta and Pietyr, but the seelie seemed to be treating them well. Her eyes met Pietyr's, and he nodded. Fieta would spit and swear when she woke up, but Pietyr could keep her calm.

Vandra retrieved her stones and tucked them away. She put her wounded hand in her jacket pocket and tried not to jostle it as she moved. A host of seelie gathered around her, the empress with them. Two of them put their hands on her shoulders before they disappeared. Then Vandra felt their gentle push. She kept her eyes pinned on the mist before her and ran.

Lilani remembered struggling, reaching for help. Vandra had reached back, but Lilani drifted farther away. No! She and Vandra had finally found each other, kissed each other. Lilani had admitted the love that had been growing inside her like the light of the rising sun, and Vandra had said she'd loved Lilani, too. This couldn't be the end of them.

But Camilla's perfume and dread wrapped around her like tar, suffocating her. She'd pulled Lilani and Vandra apart and struck Lilani in the head. Now the wind rushed over Lilani's skin. But it was never really windy in the tattered lands. It somehow managed to be cold and humid, the foul air barely moving. Was she falling? No, her body jolted up and down, and something hard dug into her ribs.

Shoulders. She lay across someone's shoulders. For a moment, she dared hope that someone she loved was carrying her. Vandra. Faelyn. Lucian. Her mother. The purple fletching meant her mother had come.

No. The perfume. The taint. Camilla. Her arms curled around Lilani's arms and legs, and she moved swiftly, though her breath rattled. She'd been wounded. If Lilani could stop her, maybe by falling, Lilani's mother and Vandra could catch up. They had to be chasing her. She'd never believe otherwise.

She jerked, and Camilla sucked in a breath, but her grip only tightened. She didn't even bother to speak.

"We have to slow down," someone else said in gasps.

Lilani opened her eyes but saw nothing but the mist rushing by. A wave of vertigo swept over her, and she closed her eyes again. She hadn't seen Camilla or the speaker, but she knew his voice. Maruk.

"Keep running," Camilla said, and she sounded tired, too, but she didn't slow.

If Maruk was here, they were no doubt trying to complete their plan for the pylon. Lilani tried to fight Camilla's grip, but all she could do was shudder. When Camilla's fingers threatened to break her flesh instead of bruise it, Lilani ceased moving. Camilla wasn't going to stop, and if she did speak, it would only be a reminder that Lilani didn't have to stay in one piece or something equally gruesome.

Lilani stilled, waiting, terror and dread clogging her throat with bile. She tried to will it away. As soon as Camilla set her down, she would run, fight, anything she could do to slow them down.

When she felt a bit of heat upon her shoulders, she risked opening her eyes again. They'd emerged from the fog into the sunlight at last. Lilani drew a deep breath, tamped down her fear, and braced herself, looking for the pylon, for the Seelie Forest. Her mother would have stationed someone at the pylon, someone waiting for those who'd gone into the tattered lands to emerge.

But as Camilla flipped Lilani over her shoulders, Lilani gasped. When she hit the ground and the wave of dizziness passed, she glanced around. They weren't at the pylon near the forest or even the next closest one she'd seen with Vandra. She had no idea which pylon this was, no idea where in the human lands she was.

She jolted upward, trying to run. Anywhere in the human lands was better than here with the tattered seelie, but Camilla grabbed her collar, and her legs slipped out from under her. Movement caught her eye. A cadre of human soldiers milled around the pylon's base.

"Hey!" Lilani cried. "Here! Help!"

When Camilla didn't bother to quiet her, Lilani knew it was already too late. The humans turned toward her voice, but they would see nothing. Before Lilani could speak again, the humans began to fall, throats cut, faces slashed. They drew their weapons and shouted, turning in circles, but all of them fell soon after, a pile of dead where there had been life. Lilani fell to her knees and retched.

Three tattered seelie appeared at the pylon's base. Lilani groaned as Camilla jerked her upright and dragged her forward. Their shroud dropped, and Lilani saw Maruk by Camilla's side. He carried a large pack and hurried toward the pylon, unpacking as he went.

"Don't do this," Lilani said.

Camilla didn't bother to respond, all her compliments dried up now that her plan was coming to fruition. Or maybe she was just too tired. Lilani knew how that felt.

"Please, Camilla," Lilani said, willing to make friends with this monster if that was what it took. "You can stay in the tattered lands, and no one will bother you."

Camilla barked a laugh. "Is that what you think I want? To not be bothered?" She sighed. "I want the seelie to be whole again, with room to spread out, to grow, room to breed."

Lilani gawked. It was a speech her mother might have made. "You want…children?"

"For all the seelie. We can't live out here." She squinted at the little sun left in the day. "But the rest of the seelie can adapt to the tattered lands. You'll all be stronger." She shrugged. "Well, maybe not you, Lilani. But soon, everyone will appreciate your sacrifice."

Lilani's bile rose again, along with her fear and anger. So, this *would* be the death of her. "If you think our people will thank you, the tattered lands have twisted you more than I thought. Your shroud protected your body, but your mind is monstrous. How else could you think about sacrificing one of your own and dooming those of us who can't shroud well? And that's not to mention the humans who won't blindly follow you, who won't want to spend their lives cowering in old towers inside a world that wants to consume them!"

Camilla reached the bottom of the pylon and stopped. "That was a pretty speech. I hope it gave you some comfort." She looked to Maruk. "Ready?"

He gestured at a sheet of metal he'd placed on the ground. It was connected to the pylon, and more wires led from the metal to a rod half buried in the ground.

Lilani tensed. If Camilla put her on the metal and released her, she'd bolt. They'd catch her immediately, but she had to—

Camilla shoved her to the ground, Lilani brought her hands up instinctively, right on top of the metal sheet. She tried to cry out, tried to tamp down her magic, but as soon as her hands touched the metal, her body went limp, her magic pouring out of her like a river.

Pain flared, bright and hot, filling every corner of her body. She wanted to scream, but her mouth wouldn't obey. She couldn't stand this; she would burst under the pressure! Thought abandoned her, all except the wish for death, for anything to make the pain stop.

It cut off like a switch, taking vision and hearing with it. In the depths of her mind, she said a thousand thanks to anyone or anything that was responsible for freeing her. Slowly, a blue glow suffused her vision, surrounding her, one with her. Her magic? The magic of the pylon? Awith must have felt something like this when she sacrificed herself, her magic joining with the pylons, with the syndrium, becoming one with it. But Lilani wasn't joining with anything; she felt her own magic pulling power from the pylon and guiding it back into the ground, into veins of syndrium that crossed beneath the land. She flowed with that power, seeing the network of veins that ran from shore to shore.

The light flared brightest beneath the Court and the forest, the syndrium in the land so vital it infused the people who walked over it, who were born among it. Wherever the humans went, the lines of syndrium darkened, interrupted by mining. When they pulled it from the ground, they gave up something precious, the difference between them and the seelie. Maybe they'd been one people sometime in the distant past, and pulling the syndrium from the earth had turned the humans into something else. Maybe the seelie scholars were right, and the humans had even created the tattered lands by taking the natural magic from the ground and bending it to their will.

So, Camilla was actually returning the magic to the land. If Lilani could have laughed, she would have.

Putting the magic back underground wouldn't stop the tattered lands. That took concentrated magic like the pylons, but now they were dwindling. Lilani's power and Maruk's alchemy pulled the magic from this pylon and the others, their power connected by the syndrium running through the ground and now the strength of Lilani's magic, the blood of Awith.

Lilani tried to stop it, to do whatever Awith had done to strengthen instead of drain, but she didn't know what to do, felt as if she was trying to hold an armload of sand. She felt for the veins of syndrium, tried to will the pylon's magic to stop flowing into them, but the magic ignored her as if it belonged to someone else. She cast about desperately, searching for a solution among the humans, among the seelie, anything!

Here and there along the land, she saw sprouts of light, as if the syndrium pushed from the ground like trees. Not pylons, but the lights were hooked into the same magic all over the world, even among the mists of the tattered lands, little blooms of light that held against the darkness.

The elders: those seelie who'd retreated from life, who never moved or spoke, who barely seemed alive, some of them shrouded for so long their locations had been forgotten. They'd tapped into the syndrium of the world, existing as she did now, their consciousness moving slowly along rivers of light.

"Help me," she whispered.

She felt their attention turn to her. They weren't used to thinking quickly, flowing as they did with the earth. They were the consequences of giving in to the magic, the polar opposite of the humans ripping it from the ground, and both options seemed less than ideal.

But the elders were used to working with the magic of the land. They'd know what to do. She felt the congregation of their attention and tried to convey her wishes, but they didn't seem to understand, simply gathering around her as if she was a fascinating anomaly. She shrieked at them, tried to infuse them with her panic, wondering if her body was shouting as it lay on the ground. They drifted around her like a ponderous swarm, and despair nearly overwhelmed her as her magic continued to flow away, taking the magic of the pylons with it.

No, she couldn't give up. She struggled, reaching for the elders again, wishing she could shake them. One light drifted closer as if watching. Was this one of the elders Lilani had seen on the Highpeak? Or was it a seelie shrouded in a distant cave, collecting cobwebs while hidden from the tattered lands?

"Please, help me. I…" She needed to do something, but she'd nearly forgotten what. If she could let go, perhaps she'd exist as one of these streams of light, following the syndrium forever after her body died. Maybe after a hundred years as such, she would cease to care about anything at all.

Even Vandra? Lilani struggled to bring her thoughts back to order. "Please. I want to see her again."

The little light flared, and she felt a sense of kinship, someone who understood, who hadn't retreated like the elders but had chosen this existence for a greater purpose.

"Awith?" Lilani asked. "Is that you?"

The one light guided the others, forming them into a single entity rather than a swarm. This stronger light pulsed, and the magic slowed. Lilani wanted to cry out with joy, but she felt stretched and tired. No, she had to struggle back to somewhere, someone. The light was slowing the magic, and that was good, but she had to open her eyes again. She had to see…who?

Vandra didn't know how many seelie Lilani's mother had brought, but it didn't sound like hordes. She knew many of them had stayed behind to help Lucian, Faelyn, Fieta, and Pietyr out of the tattered lands, and she was glad of that, really, but she wanted legions instead of what sounded like twelve running feet.

Maybe the seelie considered one of their soldiers worth ten human soldiers or something, and so they counted things differently, but they weren't fighting humans; they were fighting other seelie. They should have brought everyone they had.

Unless this *was* all they had. Maybe even the non-soldiers had volunteered to come, and the empress said no. Vandra pictured a score of Faelyns running around, trying to be helpful. They'd probably be as useless as a horde of Vandras.

A nagging pain grew in Vandra's side, and running along the spongy ground caused an ache in her calves. She couldn't see the seelie, but her stones caused the same little bubble in the tattered lands as before. She tried not to think of all the creatures she might be whizzing by, who might be drawn to the noise: a concern quickly outpaced by the pain in her side, which now throbbed with every step and felt as if it might grow large enough to squeeze her lungs shut.

The light around them was failing. They couldn't have come far into the tattered lands before. They should have emerged already. They should have…

The hands on her shoulders pulled back, slowing her. As their run became a walk, Vandra put her arms on top of her head and tried to breathe deep, tried to quiet her pounding heart. The humidity of the tattered lands pulled the sweat from her body as if she were a cloth it could wring out.

Lilani's mother appeared in a blink. "The edge of the mist is ahead." She spoke slowly. It had probably been a long time since she'd uttered the human tongue. She grimaced, seemed pained by the tattered lands now that she wasn't shrouded. "We are far from the forest that holds the Court, near one of the pylons."

Vandra nodded. "Let's go get Lilani."

"There are more enemy seelie there. More than we fought before."

"Reinforcements? Great. Just what we need." Vandra stalked ahead, ignoring the empress's protest. If she was going to help, she needed to examine the situation. She couldn't attack with a weapon, so she'd have to find another way to help, and for that, she needed all the data she could gather.

The mist didn't thin near the border so much as stop. Vandra remembered little curls of it coming from the border before, but it halted like a wall instead of a natural phenomenon. Still, she could see the fading sunlight coming through.

She stopped just inside the mist, catching glimpses as the air from outside the border pushed the tendrils away. The pylon stood ahead and to the right, several seelie arranged around the bottom, ten maybe, but there might be more she couldn't see. Several dead bodies lay among them. She spotted Camilla and a human man.

And Lilani on the ground, unmoving.

Pain spiked in Vandra's uninjured hand. She'd made a fist so tight, her fingernails were digging in. She relaxed, forced herself to think past her fear and sadness, past her indignation that the one person she'd ever fallen in love with was going to be taken from her by a madwoman and a cadre of loons who wanted to destroy the world.

Vandra tried to study the mechanism beside the pylon, but she was too far away. She could feel a hum and an echoing feeling from her stones; the bubble around her appeared to be shrinking bit by bit as if the stones were being drained. A jot of professional curiosity shamed her.

Was this her formula in reverse, as she'd once thought? No, not exactly. Her formula couldn't create syndrium from a distance, yet the enemy seelie had figured out a way to drain the pylon and her stones, even though she wasn't right beside them. By the gods, she needed to be closer to figure this out.

"What are you doing?" Lilani's mother's voice asked in her ear.

Vandra couldn't avoid a jump. She'd never get used to invisible people. "I'm going to get closer and check on Lilani."

The empress breathed in sharply. Maybe she'd just realized her daughter was on the ground. She spoke a few words in seelie then said, "We will distract them. Work quickly. They are stealing the magic."

Vandra turned to ask what that meant, but the air rushed around her as the seelie dispersed. At the pylon, one of the enemy seelie fell. The rest vanished, all but Camilla and the man beside her. The sounds of combat filled the field, and the occasional seelie form blinked into view before disappearing again.

"Come on, come on," Vandra said, nearly dancing in place, ready to run, but she was no match for Camilla.

As if answering her prayers, Camilla leaned far to the side as if avoiding a strike, then she vanished, too.

Vandra ran, not knowing how long the empress could keep the enemy seelie occupied. The man still stood where he'd been, checking the alchemical equipment and ignoring Lilani's limp body. Vandra's lips pulled back as she snarled. She didn't remember anything Fieta or Pietyr had tried to teach her about self-defense. She just kept running, teeth gritted, and anger making her vision flash red. When the man finally looked up, it was too late to scramble out of the way, and his mouth opened as wide as his eyes.

Vandra ran into him at full speed, one arm out. He flew back, and she fell after him, tripping. He knocked against the pylon, and she didn't hesitate to smash one of her stones atop his head with all her strength.

He sagged, not moving, and she turned away, dropping the stone. She reached for Lilani, intending to pull her off the metal sheet but paused, her rational brain crying out for her to think. Lilani's hair didn't flutter. Even unconscious, her magical field should have been flowing. If it was this alchemical contraption that had taken her field away, it could be the only thing that could bring it back.

Vandra's fingers moved to Lilani's neck, and after she found a pulse, she headed for the wires that led from the pylon to the metal and also to some sort of portable lab with a large crucible. She threw her pack on the ground and tossed its contents out until she found her syndrium detector, but it spun around the field, detecting the pylon and all the seelie. No help there.

She gathered the ingredients she'd need to create syndrium, but there were so few left, and she didn't know if her formula would help at all. With a metal scoop, she took some of the mixture cooking in the enemy's crucible and smelled it. Definitely sulfur. She smeared the mixture inside her ceramic mixing tray. Those dull flecks were probably lead. But the other metallic flecks…

"Silver?" It hadn't quite melted, and when she dug out her most powerful, rare-earth magnet, the silver tumbled toward it. "Why would you need a conductor like silver?" she asked the enemy alchemist's slumped body. "To draw Lilani's magic? The pylon's magic?" She frowned. "If you could draw the magic out of the pylon, why would you need…" She looked to Lilani. Maybe the silver wasn't the only conductor here.

She turned to her pack again, digging until she found a pouch of glass rods. "First, stop the connection from the pylon to the apparatus." She found the coil connecting the two and slipped a rod inside. The glow from the pylon ceased fading almost immediately. "Then the apparatus to Lilani." She found the coil at the metal plate and slipped in the other rod.

Lilani sighed, though her hair remained as lifeless as a human's.

Vandra spotted another wire leading from Lilani to a metal bar stuck in the ground. This wasn't the same kind of connection. She touched the metal bar gingerly, following it with her fingers. If Lilani had been their conductor, using her to drain the pylon of power, then that power had to be going somewhere. If she pulled this from the ground, would that help?

Vandra moved to Lilani and shook her gently, wondering if she could even live without her magical field. She didn't stir. Vandra looked to her pack again. If they'd drawn Lilani's magic out, maybe Vandra could put it back as if Lilani were a pylon. She started assembling her ingredients, hoping the proximity of all these seelie would be enough to complete her formula.

She poured her ingredients into her own crucible and set it down beside Lilani, ready to add the heat she'd need. "I love you," she whispered.

As she struck a match, she flew sideways, grunting, her ribs aching again as pain bounced through her like a ball on a string. She struggled to her knees and opened her eyes to see Camilla kick her crucible over, spilling the last of her ingredients over the ground.

CHAPTER TWENTY-FIVE

Crying out in despair, Vandra dove for the crucible, but nothing remained inside. She'd need tweezers to gather everything from the ground while keeping it pure. Camilla smiled. Maybe she understood what she'd done, maybe not, but Vandra surrendered to a fury she'd never felt before.

Her vision darkened, not simply exploding with pops of color as it had with the enemy alchemist. She knew she was moving, but she couldn't see, couldn't hear, could barely feel. Her rational mind blinked from existence like a hidden seelie. She knew she ran toward her death, but nothing in the world could have stopped her.

The ground smacking into her face woke her. Her anger blew away in a gust of confusion; free, her rational mind reasserted itself. She looked up to see the empress standing over her. Whether Vandra had fallen or the empress had tripped her, Vandra didn't know. The empress faced down Camilla, blade to blade. Besides the wound in her side, Camilla had a long tear in her armor. Blood marred the pale flesh of her shoulder as well as her face where Vandra had hit her earlier.

The empress breathed hard through her open mouth. Her left hand hung limply, and her shoulder jutted forward at an unnatural angle. A trickle of red ran out of her armor and down her leg, but Vandra couldn't spot the source. Still, her sword didn't waver.

And she'd bought Vandra more time.

Vandra turned for her pack. There wasn't time to tweeze her ingredients out of the grass and dirt and blood. The ring of weapons sounded all around her, but the empress's seelie were outnumbered. It was only a matter of time before someone else interrupted Vandra. She searched hurriedly, throwing things around the field, searching for a mythical trove of ingredients hidden at the bottom of her pack.

Her rational mind knew the sad truth. She didn't have enough for her formula.

But did she need them? She wasn't trying to create syndrium; she was trying to restore Lilani's magical field. Maybe that wasn't as complicated. But where to start? She gripped the case containing her scraps of lead and fought the urge to scream. This couldn't end here, not so close, not like this! The gods wouldn't be so cruel.

Vandra groaned as she got to her feet, her ribs aching. With nothing else to try, she grasped Lilani's wrist and heaved her one-handed from the sheet of metal.

Now what?

Nothing. Even her rational mind despaired.

Vandra sank down at Lilani's side. "I'm sorry," she whispered, not bothering to wipe away her tears. "I thought I saved you, but I didn't. I'm sorry."

Lilani's eyelids fluttered. Hopes soaring, Vandra stroked her face. "Lilani?"

Her mouth worked, but Vandra heard nothing, and her pulse was still weak. Had she only awakened enough for good-bye? Was that mercy or cruelty from the gods?

Off to the side, the empress cried out. Vandra looked in time to see her fall, one hand pressed to a streaming wound in her stomach. Vandra gritted her teeth. First Lilani, then her mother? She couldn't just let that happen.

Camilla said something to the empress, but the empress looked at Vandra as if seeking a way out.

There was none. Unless… Vandra glanced at the apparatus and metal sheet. She smiled. Maybe she could beat Camilla if she used what she was best at: alchemy and getting in the way. Keeping the empress's eye, Vandra looked pointedly at the metal plate, then at Camilla's back before she made a shoving motion. As Camilla turned away, the empress nodded.

Vandra stood and stepped in front of the metal plate, staring Camilla down. "I'll be your next opponent."

Fieta would have said, "Next kill, more like." Pietyr would have added cautions and tips. Vandra tried to summon their courage. She willed her feet not to move as Camilla stalked toward her. She would make an end of this.

In Lilani's name.

The empress launched up without a sound and rushed Camilla from behind. Vandra dropped to her hands and knees, acting as a fulcrum for the empress's shove. Camilla tripped over her and toppled onto the metal plate.

Vandra sprang for the alchemical apparatus and pulled out one glass rod.

Face and hands stuck against the plate, Camilla groaned. Her head lifted slightly before crashing down again. Her mouth and eyes were wide, but if she tried to scream, Vandra heard nothing. The sight managed to be satisfying and disturbing at the same time. Her eyelids fluttered once before closing, and Vandra didn't know if the device would be an end to her, but it kept her contained.

It didn't help Lilani.

The empress had stumbled to Lilani's side and knelt. Vandra followed. They'd saved the pylons; Lilani would be happy about that. Camilla was likely dying. Lilani might have been comforted by that. But in a moment, Vandra and the empress would be killed, and the remaining enemy seelie would retreat back into the tattered lands to make a new plan.

Vandra smoothed Lilani's hair. The empress glanced at her before looking at Lilani, and something like frustrated resignation creased her face before it settled into grief. Vandra wanted to tell her to run, that the seelie would still need their empress, but her face had gone pale, and she sagged, too wounded to go anywhere.

Vandra clenched her jaw. She was still alive. Lilani and her mother were still alive. While they lived, they had a chance. Her parents would be so ashamed if she just lay down and died. She stood, but what could she do? With one arm, she couldn't drag Lilani and her mother to safety at once. As much as the thought hurt, maybe the enemy seelie would leave Lilani alone—since she was unconscious—and Vandra could help her mother to safety? She stood and pulled the empress up.

"What are you doing?" The words came out with a groan, and the empress nearly slid off Vandra's arm.

"Come on. We're not going to sit and…" She trailed away as she spotted a group of people rushing toward them from the south. Seelie or human? It didn't matter. They were coming from the untattered side of the border.

Vandra beamed. She could save Lilani and her mother. And as before, all she needed was time. "Call your people to pull back to us," Vandra said as she let go of the empress and retrieved her last fire pouch and her bottle of oil.

"Why?"

"Call them! And tell them to be visible!" She emptied the oil in a long line.

The empress took a deep breath, then shouted. Vandra lit her pouch, ignoring the burn as three seelie appeared and streaked past her. She threw the pouch into the line of oil, and it *whooshed* into flame. Several enemy seelie cried out as they fell back. Vandra turned for Lilani and grabbed her arm, dragging her. One of the ally seelie helped, while the two others picked up the empress and began carrying her away.

"We will not outrun them!" the empress cried.

Vandra grinned. "We won't have to!"

When the sounds of combat came from behind them, Vandra turned. Most of the enemy seelie had dropped their shroud, and now the human soldiers that had come up behind them were cutting into their ranks. Vandra had bought them some time. She sank down beside Lilani and laughed, her adrenaline leaving her, and her emotions battering her until she wept and cackled at the same time.

The human soldiers put out the flames, and Monarch Shyn Harra Rhys hurried toward Vandra. "Professor Singh! I'm so happy you're safe."

She wiped her eyes. "I should have known you'd show up here." She looked to Lilani, and the urge to weep reared up again, but she fought it down. "I have to help her."

"Well, then. I'm glad I thought to bring supplies. I sent some with all the pylon teams." Shyn Harra Rhys gestured to a woman carrying a bulging backpack. "Hopefully, we'll now have enough soldiers at each pylon to guard them fully."

Vandra could have kissed everyone, should have been thanking them, but she had to save her energy. "The pylons should be all right for a little while longer, at least until after I help Lilani."

As quickly as she could, Vandra assembled all her ingredients in a crucible and took a deep breath. "Gods large and small," she whispered, "please, heed my prayer and restore my love to me." She lit the flame.

❖

Lilani was tired of drifting in this in-between place, aware of all she was leaving behind one moment and tempted to flow with the syndrium the next. All she got from Awith, from all of the elders, was only a vague sense of existence. It must be so relaxing, like turning into a leaf on the summer breeze.

At the edge of her senses, Lilani heard voices, felt someone touch her old body. Her memory fed her tantalizing glimpses of the physical world.

"Lilani?"

Vandra's voice. Lilani wanted to get to know her in all possible ways. Love and desire beat strongly inside her, but she wanted the chance to test those feelings, to love Vandra and speak with her and lie under the stars with her.

The light that had once been Awith drifted like a firefly, radiating approval. Even if nothing else remained of Awith, she seemed to remember the love she'd once shared with a human.

"I'll need your strength," Lilani thought. "To fight our people's expectations and my mother's disapproval."

Awith's light pulsed and floated away to join the cloud of drifting elders before they all withdrew.

"Wait!" Lilani called. "Where are you going?" She willed herself to follow, but the veins of syndrium rushed past her as quickly as if she'd fallen into a river.

"Lilani!"

Vandra's voice again, insistent, louder. Not a memory. Could Vandra be here with her?

"No, Vandra, tell me you didn't sacrifice yourself!" Lilani was torn between the desire to yell or welcome Vandra. Together forever, they could explore this existence at their leisure, and if anyone could figure out how to communicate with Awith or the elders, it was Vandra.

"Lilani, open your eyes."

The river of magic pushed Lilani faster, yet a sense of heaviness settled around her at the same time. Leave it to Vandra to figure out how to bring the sensations of having a body along with her. She could do anything.

Lilani smiled, feeling the movement of her cheeks along with the amusement. The heaviness increased, and with it came the pain. The network of syndrium faded, the feeling of floating dissipating until she wondered if it had been a dream.

And if she could dream, she could wake up.

Lilani forced her eyes open. Vandra smiled down at her, the planes of her beautiful face lit by the flicker of lamplight. Her hair was muddy and disheveled, and by the way her forehead creased when she moved, Lilani knew she was in pain, too.

But all the pain in the world didn't matter at the moment. "Hello." Lilani covered Vandra's hand with her own. Her magic flowed weakly, but it was there, as tired and wounded as she was but still alive.

"Hi." Vandra ducked her head, and her lips ghosted over Lilani's forehead. "How are you feeling?"

"Confused." She ignored the pain beating in her skull and tried to look around. Her mother lay beside her, torso swathed in bandages, but her eyes were open, and she took Lilani's other hand, giving it a squeeze. "Mother?"

"She'll be all right," Vandra said.

"The twins? Lucian and Faelyn?"

"They will be safe with our people," her mother said weakly. "They are probably waiting for us at the forest."

Vandra smiled, nodding. "We'll see them soon. Rest."

Lilani didn't want to rest. She wanted to kiss Vandra, wanted to go to the forest and check on Faelyn and Lucian and the twins. She wanted to go home, but she could barely move. "Help me sit up?"

Vandra pursed her lips, but she helped, leaning against Lilani's back to keep her upright. Lilani noted her hiss of pain and tried to lean forward, but Vandra held her in place.

"Before you ask," Vandra said. "Yes, I'm hurt, but all of me would hurt more if it wasn't touching you." She frowned. "I mean, I'd rather be touching you than…not touching you." Now she swallowed, looking down as if embarrassed. "I mean, my injuries are inconsequential—"

Lilani rested her head against Vandra's shoulder. "I know what you mean. I'd rather be touching you than not touching you, too. I think that idea is what kept me from drifting away among the syndrium."

There was a long pause before Vandra said, "I want to hear all about it once we're better."

Lilani kissed her gently. "There'll be time enough for all our stories."

EPILOGUE

Vandra watched the towering machines stomp forward, streams of fire rushing from the cannons on top. A handler rode on each, sitting in front of the glowing syndrium batteries. They looked to Vandra, and she nodded, consulting her map. They'd had good results burning patches of the tattered lands and then seeding the ground with blocks of syndrium Vandra had created while in Lilani's or her mother's presence. As long as no one dug up the syndrium "trees," chances were good they could keep pushing the tattered lands back.

Still, it was slow going, and the people of Citran were impatient to expand. Homesteads had already started popping up far closer to the border then they had before, but Vandra thought it was a good thing. They were essentially volunteers to find out if living on previously tattered land was harmful to the inhabitant.

Everyone gave her a funny look when she said that.

She glanced to where the flag of the pavilion tent flapped in the breeze. Lilani and her mother were in there as well as Shyn Harra Rhys and two of the other monarchs, Metran Van Hurans and Nimah Pentari, those who hadn't been part of the tattered seelie's plan to doom the world. The other monarchs had been so desperate to have their own kingdoms back, they were willing to live inside the tattered lands in communities created for humans.

Vandra had doubted that such places could exist, but the existence of Maruk, the tattered seelie's alchemist, proved otherwise. Taken into custody by Shyn Harra Rhys, Maruk recovered from his head injury, and without Camilla to protect him, he answered all their questions.

The tattered seelie had also convinced some in the Court to go along with their plot. Lucian had made it his mission to root them out, though he walked with a cane now. Some of the seelie had been spying on the humans, and Vandra knew one had been in the room when she'd first performed her experiment. That seelie had warned the tattered seelie about what she could do.

It made her shudder. Maruk had also told them that the feeling of dread that surrounded him and the tattered seelie was a side effect of living so long in the tattered lands. But living in such a place had also taught the tattered seelie how to merge their magical fields, creating a bubble much like Vandra's stones. Faelyn was busy experimenting to see if that effect could be re-created without, as he put it, "turning into an evil reprobate." He suspected that the seelie of the Court had done something similar without knowing it, creating the anti-human field that surrounded the Court.

Maruk had also made reference to Remus, the leader of the tattered seelie before Camilla. Lilani said that Camilla boasted of killing Remus, and that the traitor Burani had seemed upset at that turn of events. There were no doubt schisms among the tattered seelie just as there were among everyone else.

That still left one mystery unsolved: who had warned Ariadne about the first pylon going out?

As Lilani emerged from the tent, Vandra's thoughts shifted quickly to the memory of their first night camping together inside the Seelie Forest. They'd already had a few days of resting and recovering by that point. Vandra had made certain her siblings were all right. Lilani's mother had been resting under the care of Shyn Harra Rhys's medics. They'd bathed, thank the gods. Then they'd met again at Vandra's camp.

"Our people seem to be getting along," Lilani had said.

"Yeah," Vandra said, nervous feelings fluttering through her stomach. They hadn't had many chances to be alone since…ever. "There's still so much to do, though. Make sure there aren't any misunderstandings, that we're all on the same side."

"While guarding against any more tattered seelie." The night breeze sent her hair across her face. "Everyone is so tired."

After Vandra's gaze traveled down Lilani's beautiful face to her graceful neck and her wondrous curves, she looked up to find Lilani's own gaze roving over her. When Lilani focused on Vandra's lips, Vandra couldn't help a step forward. "You're tired?"

Lilani matched her. "No. And everyone else can take care of themselves for a night."

"My thoughts exactly." They'd met in a rush of kisses and caresses. Vandra had barely remembered to blow the lantern out before they fell to the forest floor and made love in the soft moss and leaves. Lilani's magical field rushing across Vandra's naked skin like a thousand tiny caresses was a feeling she'd never forget.

In the weeks that followed, Vandra had nearly lost count of all the times they'd made love, and it still felt far too few.

Lilani sighed and stretched. Her mother thought she should be part of every political talk surrounding the humans and the seelie. As Vandra would say, Lilani's rational mind understood this decision, even agreed with it.

But every other part of her found it deadly dull.

And the more suspicious parts of her suspected her mother wanted to keep her occupied and away from Vandra.

Lilani's mother had embraced humanity in other ways, albeit with cautious suspicion, but she still didn't want Lilani romantically involved with one. She hadn't been shy about giving Lilani "advice" meant to turn her from Vandra's side. She'd tried to steer other members of the seelie delegation into Lilani's path by talking up their attributes.

When Vandra found out, she'd grown thoughtful, and Lilani worried that her feelings were hurt, but then she'd gone on and on about cultural factors and generational memory and thinking up experiments until Lilani had grabbed her and kissed her, exclaiming over Vandra's wonderful mind until she became lost in Vandra's wonderful body.

That had silenced both of them. And Lilani's mother's protests had grown feebler as the days went by, especially when Lilani reminded her mother that if it weren't for Vandra, they'd both be dead.

Now, Lilani grinned as she spotted Vandra in the distance, supervising the burning of the tattered lands. Their eyes met, and they both smiled. Light bloomed all through Lilani, making her tingle from fingers to toes. She couldn't wait until Vandra's arm was finally healed and they wouldn't have to be so careful during their lovemaking. She wanted each of them to be able to truly lose herself.

Lilani had been one of those who'd questioned Maruk, prying out all of Camilla's secrets. He hadn't really started spilling his guts until he'd seen Camilla's dead body. Whether he feared the same fate or finally felt safe from her, Lilani didn't know. The only secret they hadn't uncovered was who had written to Vandra's friend, Ariadne. None of the seelie had admitted to it. Out of desperation, they'd asked Maruk, but he'd said it might have been a plan of Remus's to get Vandra out of Citran so they could more easily kill her, but with Remus dead, there was no way to know for certain. If it had been him, Camilla had killed him before the plan could be completed.

Good for Camilla. She'd done one thing right, at least.

Lilani crossed to Vandra and took her hand. The land around them seemed blasted right now, all the vegetation dead and the soil burnt, but the tattered lands had no doubt done that first. They'd encountered several hideous creatures, and Fieta and Pietyr had happily been part of the brigades that killed them or drove them farther into the mist. The twins' injuries were healing nicely, though Lilani thought that even missing limbs wouldn't have held them back for long.

"What will happen when we find an abandoned settlement in the tattered lands?" Lilani asked as she threaded her fingers with Vandra's. "Will we burn the buildings down?"

Vandra shook her head. "And risk any books inside? No way."

Lilani laughed. "I'm glad to know our priorities are aligned." She kissed Vandra's cheek. "Does the most famous woman in Citran have time for lunch?"

Vandra kissed her back. "Only for the most famous woman among the seelie."

"That would be my mother."

"Only for the most famous woman among the seelie who doesn't hate me."

Lilani groaned. "She doesn't—"

"Don't lie to me." She still smiled, but Lilani could tell that her mother's feelings mattered to Vandra. After defeating Camilla together, Vandra clearly thought she had an ally, but she didn't know how stubborn seelie could be. And at least Lilani's mother was entertaining the thought of a human lover for her daughter. If they hadn't defeated Camilla together, Vandra wouldn't have a ghost of a chance.

"She'll come around," Lilani said. "And if she doesn't, we'll have some awkward visits. Either way, I'm not letting you go."

Vandra teared up as she smiled, but she wiped them away and kissed Lilani again. Her eyes held a thousand questions: about their families, about the people, about the spans of their lives. Before she could ask any of them, Lilani kissed her forehead, then her lips.

"Lunch first," Lilani said. "Then everything else in the world."

With a chuckle, Vandra leaned into her. "I can live with that."

About the Author

Barbara Ann Wright writes fantasy and science fiction novels and short stories when not ranting on her blog. *The Pyramid Waltz* was one of Tor.com's Reviewer's Choice books of 2012, was a *Foreword Review* BOTYA Finalist, a Goldie finalist, and made Book Riot's 100 Must-Read Sci-Fi Fantasy Novels By Female Authors. It also won the 2013 Rainbow Award for Best Lesbian Fantasy. She's won four other Rainbow Awards and has been a Lambda Award finalist.

Books Available from Bold Strokes Books

A Fighting Chance by T. L. Hayes. Will Lou be able to come to terms with her past to give love a fighting chance? (978-1-163555-257-7)

Chosen by Brey Willows. When the choice is adapt or die, can love save us all? (978-1-163555-110-5)

Death Checks In by David S. Pederson. Despite Heath's promises to Alan to not get involved, Heath can't resist investigating a shopkeeper's murder in Chicago, which dashes their plans for a romantic weekend getaway. (978-1-163555-329-1)

Gnarled Hollow by Charlotte Greene. After they are invited to study a secluded nineteenth-century estate, a former English professor and a group of historians discover that they will have to fight against the unknown if they have any hope of staying alive. (978-1-163555-235-5)

Jacob's Grace by C.P. Rowlands. Captain Tag Becket wants to keep her head down and her past behind her, but her feelings for AJ's second-in-command, Grace Fields, makes keeping secrets next to impossible. (978-1-163555-187-7)

On the Fly by PJ Trebelhorn. Hockey player Courtney Abbott is content with her solitary life until visiting concert violinist Lana Caruso makes her second-guess everything she always thought she wanted. (978-1-163555-255-3)

Passionate Rivals by Radclyffe. Professional rivalry and long-simmering passions create a combustible combination when Emmett McCabe and Sydney Stevens are forced to work together, especially when past attractions won't stay buried. (978-1-163555-231-7)

Proxima Five by Missouri Vaun. When geologist Leah Warren crash-lands on a preindustrial planet and is claimed by its tyrant, Tiago, will clan warrior Keegan's love for Leah give her the strength to defeat him? (978-1-163555-122-8)

Racing Hearts by Dena Blake. When you cross a hot-tempered race car mechanic with a reckless cop, the result can only be spontaneous combustion. (978-1-163555-251-5)

Shadowboxer by Jessica L. Webb. Jordan McAddie is prepared to keep her street kids safe from a dangerous underground protest group, but she isn't prepared for her first love to walk back into her life. (978-1-163555-267-6)

The Tattered Lands by Barbara Ann Wright. As Vandra and Lilani strive to make peace, they slowly fall in love. With mistrust and murder surrounding them, only their faith in each other can keep their plan to save the world from falling apart. (978-1-163555-108-2)

Captive by Donna K. Ford. To escape a human trafficking ring, Greyson Cooper and Olivia Danner become players in a game of deceit and violence. Will their love stand a chance? (978-1-63555-215-7)

Crossing the Line by CF Frizzell. The Mob discovers a nemesis within its ranks, and in the ultimate retaliation, draws Stick McLaughlin from anonymity by threatening everything she holds dear. (978-1-63555-161-7)

Love's Verdict by Carsen Taite. Attorneys Landon Holt and Carly Pachett want the exact same thing: the only open partnership spot at their prestigious criminal defense firm. But will they compromise their careers for love? (978-1-63555-042-9)

Precipice of Doubt by Mardi Alexander & Laurie Eichler. Can Cole Jameson resist her attraction to her boss, veterinarian Jodi Bowman, or will she risk a workplace romance and her heart? (978-1-63555-128-0)

Savage Horizons by CJ Birch. Captain Jordan Kellow's feelings for Lt. Ali Ash have her past and future colliding, setting in motion a series of events that strands her crew in an unknown galaxy thousands of light years from home. (978-1-63555-250-8)

Secrets of the Last Castle by A. Rose Mathieu. When Elizabeth Campbell represents a young man accused of murdering an elderly woman, her investigation leads to an abandoned plantation that reveals many dark Southern secrets. (978-1-63555-240-9)

Take Your Time by VK Powell. A neurotic parrot brings police officer Grace Booker and temporary veterinarian Dr. Dani Wingate together in the tiny town of Pine Cone, but their unexpected attraction keeps the sparks flying. (978-1-63555-130-3)

The Last Seduction by Ronica Black. When you allow true love to elude you once and you desperately regret it, are you brave enough to grab it when it comes around again? (978-1-63555-211-9)

The Shape of You by Georgia Beers. Rebecca McCall doesn't play it safe, but when sexy Spencer Thompson joins her workout class, their non-stop sparring forces her to face her ultimate challenge—a chance at love. (978-1-63555-217-1)

Exposed by MJ Williamz. The closet is no place to live if you want to find true love. (978-1-62639-989-1)

Force of Fire: Toujours a Vous by Ali Vali. Immortals Kendal and Piper welcome their new child and celebrate the defeat of an old enemy, but another ancient evil is about to awaken deep in the jungles of Costa Rica. (978-1-63555-047-4)

Holding Their Place by Kelly A. Wacker. Together Dr. Helen Connery and ambulance driver Julia March, discover that goodness, love, and passion can be found in the most unlikely and even dangerous places during WWI. (978-1-63555-338-3)

Landing Zone by Erin Dutton. Can a career veteran finally discover a love stronger than even her pride? (978-1-63555-199-0)

Love at Last Call by M. Ullrich. Is balancing business, friendship, and love more than any willing woman can handle? (978-1-63555-197-6)

Pleasure Cruise by Yolanda Wallace. Spencer Collins and Amy Donovan have few things in common, but a Caribbean cruise offers both women an unexpected chance to face one of their greatest fears: falling in love. (978-1-63555-219-5)

Running Off Radar by MB Austin. Maji's plans to win Rose back are interrupted when work intrudes and duty calls her to help a SEAL team stop a Russian mobster from harvesting gold from the bottom of Sitka Sound. (978-1-63555-152-5)

Shadow of the Phoenix by Rebecca Harwell. In the final battle for the fate of Storm's Quarry, even Nadya's and Shay's powers may not be enough. (978-1-63555-181-5)

Take a Chance by D. Jackson Leigh. There's hardly a woman within fifty miles of Pine Cone that veterinarian Trip Beaumont can't charm, except for the irritating new cop, Jamie Grant, who keeps leaving parking tickets on her truck. (978-1-63555-118-1)

The Outcasts by Alexa Black. Spacebus driver Sue Jones is running from her past. When she crash-lands on a faraway world, the Outcast Kara might be her chance for redemption. (978-1-63555-242-3)

Alias by Cari Hunter. A car crash leaves a woman with no memory and no identity. Together with Detective Bronwen Pryce, she fights to uncover a truth that might just kill them both. (978-1-63555-221-8)

Death in Time by Robyn Nyx. Working in the past is hell on your future. (978-1-63555-053-5)

Hers to Protect by Nicole Disney. High school sweethearts Kaia and Adrienne will have to see past their differences and survive the vengeance of a brutal gang if they want to be together. (978-1-63555-229-4)

Of Echoes Born by 'Nathan Burgoine. A collection of queer fantasy short stories set in Canada from Lambda Literary Award finalist 'Nathan Burgoine. (978-1-63555-096-2)

Perfect Little Worlds by Clifford Mae Henderson. Lucy can't hold the secret any longer. Twenty-six years ago, her sister did the unthinkable. (978-1-63555-164-8)

Room Service by Fiona Riley. Interior designer Olivia likes stability, but when work brings footloose Savannah into her world and into a new city every month, Olivia must decide if what makes her comfortable is what makes her happy. (978-1-63555-120-4)

Sparks Like Ours by Melissa Brayden. Professional surfers Gia Malone and Elle Britton can't deny their chemistry on and off the beach. But only one can win... (978-1-63555-016-0)

Take My Hand by Missouri Vaun. River Hemsworth arrives in Georgia intent on escaping quickly, but when she crashes her Mercedes into the Clip 'n Curl, sexy Clay Cahill ends up rescuing more than her car. (978-1-63555-104-4)

The Last Time I Saw Her by Kathleen Knowles. Lane Hudson only has twelve days to win back Alison's heart. That is if she can gather the courage to try. (978-1-63555-067-2)

Wayworn Lovers by Gun Brooke. Will agoraphobic composer Giselle Bonnaire and Tierney Edwards, a wandering soul who can't remain in one place for long, trust in the passionate love destiny hands them? (978-1-62639-995-2)

Breakthrough by Kris Bryant. Falling for a sexy ranger is one thing, but is the possibility of love worth giving up the career Kennedy Wells has always dreamed of? (978-1-63555-179-2)

Certain Requirements by Elinor Zimmerman. Phoenix has always kept her love of kinky submission strictly behind the bedroom door and inside the bounds of romantic relationships, until she meets Kris Andersen. (978-1-63555-195-2)

Dark Euphoria by Ronica Black. When a high-profile case drops in Detective Maria Diaz's lap, she forges ahead only to discover this case, and her main suspect, aren't like any other. (978-1-63555-141-9)

Fore Play by Julie Cannon. Executive Leigh Marshall falls hard for Peyton Broader, her golf pro…and an ex-con. Will she risk sabotaging her career for love? (978-1-63555-102-0)

Love Came Calling by CA Popovich. Can a romantic looking for a long-term, committed relationship and a jaded cynic too busy for love conquer life's struggles and find their way to what matters most? (978-1-63555-205-8)

Outside the Law by Carsen Taite. Former sweethearts Tanner Cohen and Sydney Braswell must work together on a federal task force to see justice served, but will they choose to embrace their second chance at love? (978-1-63555-039-9)

The Princess Deception by Nell Stark. When journalist Missy Duke realizes Prince Sebastian is really his twin sister Viola in disguise, she plays along, but when sparks flare between them, will the double deception doom their fairy-tale romance? (978-1-62639-979-2)

The Smell of Rain by Cameron MacElvee. Reyha Arslan, a wise and elegant woman with a tragic past, shows Chrys that there's still beauty to embrace and reason to hope despite the world's cruelty. (978-1-63555-166-2)

The Talebearer by Sheri Lewis Wohl. Liz's visions show her the faces of the lost and the killers who took their lives. As one by one, the murdered are found, a stranger works to stop Liz before the serial killer is brought to justice. (978-1-635550-126-6)

White Wings Weeping by Lesley Davis. The world is full of discord and hatred, but how much of it is just human nature when an evil with sinister intent is invading people's hearts? (978-1-63555-191-4)